THE DARK

Catriona King

Copyright © 2021 by Catriona King

ISBN: 9798585260797

Photography: Image by adike
Artwork: Jonathan Temples:
creative@jonathantemples.co.uk

Editors: Andrew Angel and Maureen Vincent-Northam

Formatting: Rebecca Emin

Hamilton-Crean Publishing Ltd. 2021

For My Mother

About the Author

Catriona King is a medical doctor and trained as a police Forensic Medical Examiner in London, where she worked for some years. She returned to live in Belfast in 2006.

She has written since childhood and has been published in many formats: non-fiction, journalistic and fiction.

'The Dark' is book twenty-four in The Craig Crime Series.

Each book can also be read as a standalone or in any order.
Details of the main characters and locations are listed at the end of each book.

The Craig Crime Series So Far

The Property
Crossing The Line
The Depths
The Good Woman
Legacy
The Dark

The twenty-fifth novel in the series will be released in 2021.

The audiobook of the first Craig Crime novel, A Limited Justice, is now available on Amazon ACX.

The author has also released an unrelated science fiction novel set in New York City: The Carbon Trail.

Acknowledgements

My thanks to Northern Ireland and its people for providing the inspiration for my books.

My thanks also to: Andrew Angel and Maureen Vincent-Northam as my editors, Jonathan Temples for his cover design and Rebecca Emin for formatting this work.

I would also like to thank all the police officers I have ever worked with anywhere for their professionalism, wit and compassion.

Catriona King
December 2020

Discover more about the author's work at:
www.catrionakingbooks.com

To engage with the author about her books, email:
Catriona_books@yahoo.co.uk

The author can also be found on Facebook and Twitter:
@CatrionaKing1

Prologue

Under cover of darkness' is a traditional phrase used by writers, to evoke crimes such as murder taking place at night, with shifting black shadows concealing the brutality and helping the culprits to evade arrest.

But with a modern twist a killer could stay far from their victim and use a newer form of darkness as cover; and avoiding capture, should it ever prove necessary, could be as easy as pressing 'escape'.

Chapter One

The Adelphi Playhouse, University Road, Belfast. Sunday, 16th February 2020. 9 p.m.

"Her sister's the murderer. It's obvious."

Lucia Craig pointed ostentatiously at the stage, and as she did so deliberately flaunted her diamond engagement ring at the teenage girl to her left who had been chewing noisily on a toffee for the past five minutes.

Her fiancé Ken Smith smiled to himself, knowing exactly what she was doing and also knowing that only half of her motivation was revenge. They'd *finally* settled on the ring the day before, after months of Lucia hemming and hawing and changing her mind from yellow gold to white gold and finally, to his wallet's great distress, to platinum, and that was before the whole 'simple' diamond versus diamond plus precious stone combo debate that had seen him glazing over and getting elbowed in the side more times than he could count. Now she wanted to display her choice to the whole world, even if it did obscure someone's view of the stage where the nineteen-twenties play 'The Murder of Angel Ryan' was just starting to heat up. Lucia, like her Italian mother Mirella, liked her romantic love announced with a fanfare and lights.

As for her assertion that the eponymous Angel Ryan's sister would be the one who eventually killed her; even though he was the detective in the couple, although OK, only a sergeant so a very junior one compared to her brother Marc, he didn't feel inclined to contradict. Partly for the sake of peace but more so because he wasn't in any position to since he'd stopped watching the melodrama after its opening scene where a butler had bowed in deference to the Lord of the Manor, a gesture that had greatly offended his belief in equal rights.

It was a belief that had developed after years spent in the British Army, seeing deference based more often on

1

rank than ability, and part of what had made him leave after becoming a Captain; well, that and the fact he was sick of being posted halfway across the world at a moment's notice and always having to dress in a noxious shade of green.

Since Ken had switched off from the play he'd been scanning the audience absentmindedly, curious about people in general and in particular whichever group he found himself in. Tonight's looked as if its members hailed mainly from the theatre's hinterland of Belfast's prosperous Malone and Stranmillis Roads and had an average age of seventy. The exceptions were students from the nearby Queen's University, a handful of whom were gathered in the cheap seats at the back. Lucia's teenager was an anomaly in the front stalls and he wondered if her chomping had been as solace for her social isolation and to make her presence felt.

It was in this fugue state that the detective sergeant registered someone collapsing on stage and dismissed it as merely another piece of overblown acting. Until the screams. The first, from an on-stage maid, was piercing, but perhaps to be expected. She had after all supposedly just witnessed Angel Ryan's murder and screaming was part of her job. But when it was followed by an incongruously high-pitched one from the burly six-footer playing the waiter, and a jeans-clad stage manager then raced in from the wings, Ken realised that none of the cries had been scripted and startled Lucia by hurtling towards the stage.

As he ran, he produced his warrant card and barked instructions at the manager, now standing over the recumbent cast member with a stunned look on his face.

"Police! Get the curtain down and don't touch anything."

As the barrier dropped, Ken scanned the face of each person on the stage slowly, not really sure what he was looking for although guilt was somewhere on the list. With none of them wearing a sign that said, 'I did it' he said, "Remain in place until I say differently."

Then he knelt down cautiously beside the body lying on the boards, a young woman that he'd been vaguely aware of on stage earlier, now blue-lipped and staring-eyed and wearing an expression that fell somewhere between horror and surprise. Tuning out the distressed murmuring of the audience that he could no longer see the detective made some urgent phone-calls, then he began running through the drill that he'd been taught to perform in the face of a sudden death.

****

The Craigs' New House. Stranmillis Road. 10 p.m.

Marc Craig was having quite a fruitful Sunday. True, it wasn't in his usual crime solving, villain busting way, but it was no less satisfying for that. For once he was performing an activity that most of the population would have considered normal; he was painting his infant son Luca's bedroom at their new house blue and Katy, his wife of almost two years, was applying fluffy white cloud stencils to each wall after it dried. It was the first room in their new and still uninhabitable home, an old Victorian schoolhouse, that they had tackled and they wouldn't be able to move in for several more months, so the decorating was largely symbolic but it made them both feel better to have tried.

With only one wall left to do Katy called out, "Wine time" and phoned for a takeaway, getting no argument from her spouse. Short of someone committing murder Craig was there for the night.

Although to say he was off-duty would be overplaying it; one of the drawbacks of being a Chief Superintendent was that should either of the sections that he headed, Murder or Intelligence, start getting antsy, he would have to drop his paintbrush and run.

But Katy Stevens was nothing if not an optimist. Luca was with his grandparents overnight, they had her iPod playing blues, a rug, wine and a takeaway, and the night was young. Craig was just on the verge of telling his wife how beautiful her eyes were when his mobile rang suddenly and blew any notion of romance to hell.

His, "WHAT?" was unnecessarily brusque and he knew it, and the fact it turned out to be his best friend John Winter calling and not work made him feel even guiltier for the sharpness of his tone, John being a gentle soul. But not *so* guilty that the, *"What do you want?"* that followed didn't carry a subtext of 'bugger off'.

Northern Ireland's Head Pathologist smirked to himself, knowing exactly what he'd just interrupted. Craig could normally be phoned any time, including when he was in the shower, and he would be brisk but pleasant, but woe betide the person who interrupted his now all too infrequent alone times with his wife.

He pictured the scene: Luca with his grandparents, wine, soft music, perhaps even candles, and DCS Latin Lover winding up to give the balcony scene of his life.

Trying hard to keep his tone smirk-free the medic hurried to explain why he'd called.

"Sorry, Marc, but blame your sister."

Craig thought he'd misheard for a moment, then the worst possible explanation for the pathologist phoning flashed through his mind and his eyes widened in horror, immediately making his wife's do the same. The words that followed were yelled.

"LUCIA'S DEAD?!"

John recoiled in shock.

"*What?* No! Where the hell did you get that from?"

"You're a pathologist, that's where! And you just called telling me to blame my sister!"

The pathologist didn't know whether to be astounded or affronted. Yes, all his patients were corpses, but even *he* had a better bedside manner than that.

"Do you really think I'd say 'blame' your sister if she was dead? My God, man, what do you take me for?"

Whatever Craig took him for John Winter would never find out, because, having listened to the conversation long enough to work out which wires her husband had got crossed, Katy extricated the mobile from his whitening hand and after a brief, "Hi, John, how's life?" and, "what's happening?" exchange she ended the call sweetly and calmly handed the phone back to Craig, ignoring his now hanging jaw.

"Mystery solved. An actor collapsed and died on stage during a play that Lucia and Ken were watching, and when Ken checked the body he thought something might be off. John clearly agrees."

She topped up the wine glasses as she went on.

"As Ken was already there he took preliminary statements which he'll drop down to you tomorrow, and Liam went to the lab to take a quick look at the body."

DCI Liam Cullen was Craig's deputy and a good one.

Craig sprang to his feet readying to leave but she waved him to sit back down.

"Liam said there was no need for you to go because he's already handled it. He'll brief you in the morning."

Her reward was the frown that she'd expected.

"So why call me at all then?"

"Because you would have kicked up like hell tomorrow if they hadn't informed you."

"I would not!"

"You would and you know it, Marc, because you're a control freak. I am too where my patients are concerned."

She was a consultant physician at the local St Mary's Healthcare Trust, working part-time since their son's birth.

She held out his glass with a glint in her eye. "Your wine, DCS Control Freak."

It was a taunt that she knew her husband would just *have* to respond to, and one guaranteed to ensure that no more painting got done for the rest of the night.

Chapter Two

The Murder Squad. Belfast's Coordinated Crime Unit Building (The CCU). Monday, 8.30 a.m.

"Good morning, good morning, everyone. Lovely day."

Liam Cullen glanced over from the desk that he was lounging at, his feet propped up on it and his chair tilted backwards at an angle of forty-five degrees, and gave his boss a knowing look.

"Good weekend, boss?"

Craig perched beside his deputy's size thirteens and gave them a cheerful nudge to the floor.

"Yes, thanks. We got Luca's bedroom painted at the new house."

The sceptical look he received in return said he'd done more than that, but Craig was too gentlemanly and his right-hand-man too keen to avoid an earful for anything else to be said.

"Right then, what's this about a suspicious death at the Adelphi, Liam? John said you'd caught it, so thanks for that."

The DCI smiled and sat up straight. "Bit of a weird one actually, boss. This lady actor, you can't call them actresses any more apparently, it's supposed to be sexist or something, anyway this woman actor was sitting on a chair saying her lines and just collapsed."

"Was she supposed to collapse in the play?"

"Aye well, she was as it happens, but later. That was the plot. She was playing some character called Angela Ryan who gets murdered, and the rest of the play was about who did it. Some kind of sleuth thing. Like one of those Agatha Christie ones."

"Except this death wasn't an act."

Liam gave an emphatic nod. "*Exactly*. She just croaked right there on stage. Anyway, Ken got there, saw she was dead and did the immediate needful with ambulance, statements, forensics and whatnot. We might have to retake the statements later for details, but

6

it was a good help last night. Meant that I got home at midnight instead of two."

The husky tones of Craig's PA, Nicky Morris, cut across the conversation.

"Hang on a wee minute, Liam."

"What for?"

When she began searching for something in her desk Craig braced himself for what he knew was coming next.

"I'm just looking for my violin to play a sad song about you having to work on a Sunday night."

"Oh, ha bloody ha. Very funny." He glanced at Craig just in time to catch the tail end of his smirk. "You *knew* that was coming and you didn't warn me. Right, that's going in my retribution book."

Nicky laughed sceptically. "Get away with you. You don't have any such thing."

Liam adopted a 'Don't be so sure about that' expression as Craig waved him on with his report.

"Then what happened, Liam?"

"Oh aye, the body. Well, Ken said the ambulance man was sharp and said it looked like a suspicious death right away, so they took her to the Path Lab and the Doc called me in."

Craig crossed to the whiteboard and lifted a marker.

"Give me a summary."

"Well, there were no cuts, bruises or bullet holes on the body on first viewing. The Doc took bloods right away hoping they'd show something useful and he's doing the PM around now. But when he couldn't find an obvious cause of death I thought poison, so I got uniforms to lock down the theatre and the CSIs are there again now. In full hazmat gear just in case, although no-one else in the cast or audience was affected."

Craig nodded. "Very thorough."

"Grace is in charge."

"Good. If there's anything there she'll find it."

Grace Adeyemi was the lead CSI in Northern Ireland's Forensic Service, having joined the team from Glasgow two years before, and was exceptionally good at her job.

Just then the squad-room's double entrance doors swung inwards and a group of six people sauntered in. Seeing Craig was already there their paces quickened and they branched off, heading for their respective desks. As a tanned man almost as tall as Liam tried to slip past Craig unnoticed, he blocked his way with an outstretched arm.

"Morning, Aidan. Don't bother sitting." He scanned the office until he found the second person he wanted. "Nor you, Ryan. I want the pair of you to go to the Adelphi Playhouse and find Grace."

Aidan Hughes was the third of the team's three DCIs and Ryan Hendron was its Detective Sergeant.

"There was a suspicious death on stage last night and we need in-depth statements taken from the cast and crew working on a production called... Nicky, what was it called again?"

"The Murder of Angel Ryan. I'll give them all the details."

Liam guffawed. "I thought it was Angela. But *Angel* Ryan is a gift. It's Andy Angel and Ryan Hendron all rolled into one."

"You're easily amused, Liam. OK, Aidan, check with Grace whether you need hazmat gear before entering the theatre. She'll explain why." He turned back to his secretary. "Nicky, if Ken Smith calls tell him we should be back around twelve."

"No, I'll tell him to check before coming. You *never* stick to any schedule that you say you will."

Liam clambered to his feet eagerly, knowing that a road trip was on the cards. "The Labs then?"

"Yep."

As Craig turned for the exit he stopped and gazed around the squad-room. He had a strange sensation that someone was missing, but both of the team's analysts, Davy Walsh and Ash Rahman, were there, as was Mary Li their detective constable and Andy Angel his second DCI

That only left...

8

"Where's Annette, Liam?"

Annette Eakin was the squad's extremely effective Inspector, hopefully to be a Chief Inspector if he could persuade her to take the board.

"Court on the McCausland case. And it's that old duffer Osmond on the bench so she'll likely be there all day."

The case was a home invasion murder that they'd caught the June before, yet the court proceedings on it had only just begun. Northern Ireland's legal system was so backed up Craig was surprised most defendants didn't die of old age before justice was done.

"Right, I'd forgotten. OK, let's go. You know where we are if you need us, Nicky."

Her response, if there was one, fell on the closed doors of the lift to the building's basement carpark, and fifteen minutes of Liam's hair-raising driving later they'd arrived at Northern Ireland's Pathology and Forensic Labs on Belfast's Saintfield Road, to find John Winter in Dissection Room One staring down at their possible murder victim.

Craig got straight to the point.

"Is she definitely for us, John?"

The pathologist answered without looking up from his young patient's immobile face.

"Good morning, John. Lovely to see you, John. How was your weekend, John?"

Craig rolled his eyes. "We only spoke last night! But if it'll make you feel better, I'll go out and come in again as if I haven't seen you in years."

The response was a sigh and, "I'm going to insist on only working with women in future. They're far less sarcastic."

"Don't let Mary hear you say that. She'll think you're being sexist."

The team's constable carried her feminist principles through in everything, which was commendable but sometimes made her argumentative and a challenge to work with.

9

The pathologist turned to face them. "In answer to your first question, Marc, yes, I think this young woman *is* for you. But I've no intention of discussing her demise where she can hear me."

It was their cue to move to his office and for Craig to make coffee while his friend changed; ten minutes later they were sipping contentedly at their drinks and the medic's mood had improved.

"Right... well, there are no signs of violence on the body, past or immediately preceding her death, and I can find no pathology that would have led to her sudden collapse. No stroke, heart attack or any other physiological cause. Overall, she was an apparently healthy woman of twenty-seven. Five-foot-six, light brown hair, green eyes, and pale Caucasian skin with no scars."

Suddenly something occurred to Craig. "What's her name? And have her next-of-kin been contacted?"

The pathologist shot him a reproving look. "I was wondering how long it would take you to ask. Her name was Julianne Hodges and she was twenty-seven as I said. Married with a two-year-old son. I contacted her husband and he insisted on coming to identify the body last night. And it was *dreadful,* thank neither of you for asking."

The detectives looked suitably ashamed for a moment until Liam deemed that he'd suffered for long enough, given he'd been up till all hours, and asked the question that Craig had planned to ask next.

"What's her tox-screen say, Doc?"

"It's probably too soon for a result unless Des was here all night. But I suppose we could ask."

Des was Doctor Desmond Marsham, Northern Ireland's Head of Forensic Science. He ran the top two floors of the building and like John was internationally respected in his field.

Craig lifted his coffee mug. "Better bring your drinks with you. Grace is at the scene."

Grace having introduced civilisation to Marsham's

forensic labs with decent tea, coffee and biscuits and even the correct china pots from which to pour the drinks. In her absence Craig knew Des would regress to his habit of foisting used teabags and lumps of decade-old freeze-dried coffee on them, and the caffeine addicted detective drew the line right there.

John was about to do as advised when his desk phone rang and he answered it. "Yes, Marcie."

Marcie Devlin was a resting professional actor who was working temporarily as the labs' PA, and although so far her temporary status had extended to two years everyone knew that she would quit the moment she got her big break. Selfishly John, who revelled in her deep, smooth, drama school tones, hoped that it didn't happen until he was safely retired.

"The mortuary van has just driven in, Doctor Winter. Another sudden death."

"OK, have the body taken to Dissection Room Two and call Doctor Augustus to examine them, then contact their GP for their medical history. I'm going up to Forensics about Julianne Hodges, but I'll be back down fairly soon."

Her sharp gasp was heard by all of them, as were her next words.

"*Julianne Hodges! The actress from The Roaring Heart?*"

It was a popular soap that had run on local television for years.

Liam was on the verge of complaining that he'd been told not to say actress when Craig signalled to take the phone.

"Hello, Marcie, it's Marc Craig here. Did you know Ms Hodges?"

"Yes. Well, only casually. But all the artists and creatives in Belfast tend to know each other. It's a small pool."

"I'm sorry for your loss then, but we may need to ask you some questions about her at some point."

"But if *you're* involved you must think she was

murdered! Who would want to kill Julianne? She was a harmless little soul."

Clearly someone had thought otherwise, although Craig didn't think it was the time to point that out so he passed the phone back to her boss who went straight into bedside mode.

"I'll pop down and see you on my way back from forensics, Marcie. Try not to get too upset."

The men were at the third-floor forensic labs before any of them spoke again. Craig went first, talking as they headed for Des' office.

"Harmless little souls rarely get killed except in random impulse attacks and this doesn't feel like one, so we'll need to know everything about Ms Hodges' life, Liam."

The DCI nodded. "Did she have secrets, what were they, and were they the sort that could get her topped?"

"Exactly."

John cut in eagerly. "You mean because if she turns out to have been as squeaky clean as Marcie believes she was, then this *might* have been random."

The thought made Craig's heart sink. An entirely random victim was the worst thing in the world for a murder detective, especially when no-one had witnessed the act just the result. Without a motive for a murder or the act being witnessed the search for the perpetrator could be long and ultimately fruitless, unless the killer had left something handy behind like DNA and happened to be in the police database for other crimes.

The thought prompted him to look at the pathologist.

"Did you find anything on the body, John? Prints, DNA, hairs that weren't hers?"

"You mean all those routine things that I look for in *any* unexplained death, and have done thousands of times?" The medic's eye-roll was Oscar winning. "Give me some credit for knowing my job, Marc, and yes, there were *lots* of those items at the scene, but not on Ms Hodges' body or costume. They're to be expected during a play so you'll have to rule them out as belonging to other actors or theatre staff."

Craig stopped in his tracks. "Not on her costume? Nothing?"

"No. Why?"

The response was another question.

"Where's her costume now?"

"Des has it."

"OK, good." He turned to his deputy. "Liam, call Aidan and tell him we need to know about Ms Hodges' day. He'll need to interview the husband to find out exactly where she was before she went to the theatre then he'll need to speak to everyone who saw her there up to her moment of death. And we'll need Grace to gather hair samples, prints and swabs from everyone listed."

"We'll need warrants for those, boss, and you just know some of the luvvies will lawyer up."

"So be it. I'll call Judge Standish after we finish here, but give Aidan a bell now, please. Tell him he can have Andy and Mary if he needs extra hands."

As Liam ambled off to do that Craig nodded his friend on towards Des Marsham's office, and when the scientist eventually answered the door on the third knock they were startled by what greeted them inside.

The small office was untidier than Craig could ever recall seeing it, with over half-a-dozen large cardboard boxes stacked in one corner and a similar pile of smaller ones in another, leaving them with hardly anywhere to stand. To top it off, the usual detritus of glass tubes and flasks that always littered Des's high desk was buried by a mound of folders perched precariously on top.

"Hello, Marc. Long time no see."

Craig nodded hello to the robustly built forensic expert but didn't try to hide his astonishment at the state of his room.

"My God, Des! How do you work in here?"

The scientist glanced around him surprised, as if he hadn't even noticed the mess, and responded with a loud laugh.

"This lot? Yes, I suppose it is a bit cramped, but it's

all in a good cause."

He turned to John, the man he thought would best appreciate his excitement.

"I've been asked to take part in a project run by Massachusetts Institute of Technology, on forensic techniques in twenty-first century policing! It's a real honour, I can tell you, and I get a trip to America at the end to present it. But, yes, they do send you a clatter of equipment to set up."

Rewarded by a broad grin of approval from the pathologist, the forensic lead turned back to Craig.

"It'll all be moved upstairs tomorrow but for now I suppose we'd probably better step outside."

Just as they did Liam re-joined the group and a sharp nod at Craig said that his requests were a go.

When they'd decamped to Grace's desk Des stroked his near-Dumbledore proportioned beard slowly, in a way that he liked to believe said 'genius at work'.

"You're here about the Hodges' woman's samples, yes?"

John nodded. "But if you don't have them yet we can call later-"

He was cut off by a shake of his colleague's head.

"I have something, but the details will take a day or so. Her stomach contents were vegetable soup and white bread. Only partially digested, so eaten two to three hours before death I'd say."

Liam volunteered something that he'd just learnt.

"The play started at eight-thirty and she died at nine so if she ate around six that makes sense."

Craig nodded. "She ate before the performance because it would have been too late by the end."

Des nodded.

"Probably. So, there were none of the usual poisons we test for in the stomach contents, but there *was* a trace of something unusual there, and a *lot* more of it in her blood."

Craig's hopes rose. Could they be about to solve this case quickly?

"What was it?"

"Cotinine."

Liam asked before anyone else could. "What's that when it's at home?"

"An alkaloid. Most often a metabolite of Nicotine. You all know what a metabolite is, I take it?"

Craig smiled. "I wouldn't take anything for granted with us so you'd better explain."

"OK. It's basically what's produced when a substance breaks down inside the body. Take ethanol for instance, a basic alcohol. That's made of carbon, hydrogen and oxygen and produces various combinations of those, like say water, which is H_2O, before being removed from the body by the liver. Similarly, when Nicotine breaks down one of the things it produces is Cotinine."

Liam patted his, not as well-padded as it once was but still substantial, abdomen and guffawed.

"Not *my* liver, mate. I'm hoarding every drop of alcohol I've ever drunk till I retire and then I'm telling my body to release it all."

The image of the deputy as a human beer barrel with a tap in his liver and a pint glass held beneath it made everyone laugh.

"I don't think it works like that, Liam, but nice thought." Craig turned back to their host. "Carry on, Des."

The forensic expert dragged his gaze reluctantly from Liam's torso and shook his head.

"That image is going to haunt me forever now. Right, Cotinine is a by-product of Nicotine, which before anyone mentions cigarettes-"

John cut in. "She didn't look like a smoker. Pink lungs, no stains on her fingers, hair or teeth, and she hardly had a wrinkle."

The forensic scientist sniffed.

"As I was about to say, the quantity of Cotinine I found in your patient's blood indicates *far* more Nicotine than even a hundred-a-day smoker would have in their system. One cigarette gives around one milligram of

Nicotine but cigarettes are usually spread out over the day. Here we're talking about Nicotine levels of *five hundred* milligrams. That's five hundred cigs *at once,* and it only takes sixty to kill someone who weighs one hundred and fifty pounds."

"She was nowhere near that weight."

Liam asked the important question.

"Where did it come from if not cigs?"

"There are a few possibilities. Did she live on a farm? Nicotine was used in pesticides in the UK until oh-nine when they were banned, but we know there are still stores of the stuff around-"

Craig cut in. "Locally?"

Des shrugged. "Maybe. Possibly some old cans in a garage or farm shed. They might have been hoarded, or even re-imported from places like China that still use them. Our standards in a lot of things are thought to err on the side of caution-"

John interjected. "Or at least they did before we decided to Brexit, now God knows *what* we'll get. It could be the wild west here in a year's time."

Liam shook his head firmly. "Nope. We'll have a united Ireland by then."

The deputy's Irishness ran through him like stripes in a stick of rock.

But although Craig agreed with some of his team members' political opinions and respected them all, he *did* ask that they were kept to themselves at work, so on his glance Liam's mouth clamped shut and all eyes returned to Des.

"So, what you're saying, Des, is that a Nicotine-containing pesticide could have caused her death?"

"Pesticide's only one possible source. Nicotine is also found in e-cigarette fluid, Nicotine patches and so on. All I can say for now is that Cotinine was present in her blood in extremely high levels with traces in her stomach contents, and it's the only abnormality that I've detected so far."

John checked something. "Just a *trace* in her stomach

contents?"

"Glad you were listening."

"That's not high enough for the Nicotine to have been in her food. So, the only way it could have reached her stomach is by leakage *into* it from the blood vessels in the wall."

"That could work." He considered for a moment then nodded. "Yes, that could definitely explain my findings. And by that logic we'd probably find traces of Cotinine in every organ of her body with a blood supply if we looked."

John was already planning the biopsies he would take.

"Anyway, I'll let you know if I find more potential sources of Nicotine."

But Craig wasn't leaving the topic that quickly.

"The level you found, Des. It would take five hundred cigarettes to produce it?"

The scientist gave a small smile. "Smoked in under an hour, which is impossible. Even Aidan couldn't have managed that..."

The DCI had been a heavy smoker till he'd given up two years before.

"...or Nicotine patches over every inch of her body might have managed it, I suppose, but even then they're geared for slow release so they wouldn't have killed without her showing some symptoms first." The scientist looked thoughtful for a moment. "I suppose *injecting* vaping liquid is a possibility but then John would have found needle marks-"

The medic jumped in quickly. "Which I didn't, and I examined her head to toe. She didn't even have a mole never mind puncture marks. I'm scrupulous in searching for them - we've had too many addicts injecting in unlikely places."

Craig left them to debate the point, raking a hand repeatedly through his dark hair in thought while his deputy used the time to slide open Grace's desk drawer, where to his delight he found a packet of open custard creams and popped one in his mouth.

He closed the drawer again hastily when his boss sat forward to speak.

"OK... so... at the moment all we have is a report of Julianne Hodges collapsing and dying suddenly. John, what are the symptoms of gradual Nicotine poisoning?"

"Nausea, unsteadiness, vomiting and confusion all come before collapse."

"Liam, any reports of that behaviour from our victim before she died?"

"Not that I heard, but I'll get Aidan to check the statements."

"OK, for now let's assume there weren't. Would the symptoms you're describing *only* happen if the poisoning happened gradually, John?"

The pathologist considered for a moment before nodding. "Yes. Nicotine's effects can accumulate and it's usually kids who've been sneaking sips of their parents' vaping fluid over time who present with poisoning. The symptoms I've described often alert doctors in time to treat them before the fatal level is reached."

"What if someone was given a large hit all at once?"

"It would have to be a lethal dose as Des just described, but in that case there *could* be an immediate spike in blood pressure and death from a stroke or heart attack."

"Presenting as collapse and instant death? The woman was dead when Ken reached the stage."

The medic's agreement was grudging but it came all the same.

"I didn't *find* signs of either a stroke or heart attack on post-mortem, but I'll concede that a massive dose of Nicotine *might* have killed her and left nothing obvious behind. But how did it enter her body? We know it wasn't injected or given orally because-"

Craig cut across him. "Did she eat or drink anything as part of the scene?"

Des dashed his hopes with a shake of the head. "She had a drink but it tested clean, and we already know it wasn't absorbed through her stomach, Marc."

John picked up his thread. "Ken said last night that it was a few minutes into the second scene when she collapsed-"

"Was she in the first scene?"

"No, I don't believe so. But-"

He stopped abruptly mid-sentence and Craig's eyes lit up in hope.

"Tell us."

"It's almost impossible-"

"Clearly not, so tell us, John."

The pathologist turned to his colleague. "Transdermal? As with Nicotine patches but a more toxic. *Really?*"

The intellectual thrill of it made Des grin, inappropriately given they were discussing a woman's death. But it wasn't only the intellectual thrill; both he and Liam were transported to the world of James Bond, where spies killed each other in seconds with lethal microdots.

"It's... well, I was going to say, it's impossible, Marc, but it obviously isn't given what happened in England."

In Salisbury in South West England two years before, Novichok, a banned nerve agent absorbed through the skin, had poisoned several people and caused one death.

Craig brought them back down to earth. "Transdermal is an effective avenue for medication?"

John nodded.

"Very, for the right drugs, and Nicotine's one of them. If a large enough bolus of Nicotine had been administered through skin contact, but administered all at once instead of by slow release, it *could* have killed her instantly. No prior symptoms would have meant no time for detection and treatment." The pathologist frowned. "Someone really wanted this woman dead."

"And planned it brilliantly." Craig turned to his deputy. "It must have come from something on stage, Liam. When did they tape it off?"

"Last night, boss, and no-one but the CSIs have been

19

near it since."

Craig turned to Des next.

"Will those hazmat suits protect them from Nicotine, Des?"

Shocked at the thought of his staff being poisoned the scientist stammered his reply. "Well...y...yes...I mean, I think so."

"Check, and call Grace and tell her to keep people away from the stage until we know what Hodges touched. Let's just pray no-one has already handled it, and you'd better watch yourself with her clothes."

While the forensic expert did as requested Liam notified his counterpart at the theatre and Craig rang Ken, setting his phone on speaker.

"Hi, Ken. I can't chat. I just need to know did you touch anything on or around the victim last night?"

The DS was curious why he was asking but didn't let it show. "Only her neck for a pulse."

"What was the neckline of her dress like?"

"Lowish. Lucia said she was dressed as a flapper."

"And you definitely didn't touch its fabric, or anything she'd handled?"

"No. I was tempted to close her eyes in respect because they were wide open, but I thought I'd better not, just in case."

"Good. What did you do next?"

"Once I'd marked all the actors' on-stage positions at the time of death, I sent them backstage and told them not to touch anything. Then I called for an ambulance. When the paramedics arrived, one put a stethoscope on her upper chest and listened for a heartbeat, then he covered her with a sheet and two of them lifted her on to a trolley. They were met at St Mary's Emergency Department by a doctor who certified death and re-directed the ambulance immediately to the labs."

Damn. He'd thought the body had gone straight to John.

"Can you get the paramedics' and doctor's names and call me back with them?"

"Sure. Just-"

But Craig had already cut the call.

"I could have told you about the ED doctor, Marc. Death can't be certified by a paramedic."

"Too late. OK, did *you* touch her clothes, John?"

"Only with gloves on, and my technician the same when she cut them off and sent them up here. It's standard safety procedure."

"Good. Right, Des, would Nicotine leave a stain or mark on fabric?"

"Not necessarily. It's a colourless liquid."

John nodded in agreement. "I saw nothing obvious on her clothing, but that fits because if they'd been visibly stained she wouldn't have gone on stage wearing them."

"Any skin rashes?"

"None or I would have suspected something chemical."

"But we *could* still be looking at skin absorption even without a rash?"

The pathologist removed his black wire glasses and wiped them, something he often did when he needed time to think. When he'd donned them again he answered the question with confidence.

"Yes. A contact rash mightn't have had time to form if she was dosed *just* before death. But whatever she touched must have carried an *extremely* high concentration of Nicotine to kill her so quickly."

"How about if it was spread over her whole body?"

"The dress? Yes, that could have worked. By the way, I overheard what Ken just said about her eyes being open. That goes to the suddenness of her death. She was completely unaware of what hit her thankfully."

It was a comforting but chilling thought and made each of them wonder about the moment they would say goodbye to the world. In Craig's case the wondering only took seconds, him being fatalistic about death and fully expecting to meet it at the end of a gun.

He returned briskly to his point.

"If Des tests everything she wore and handled, one of

those should hopefully point the way to where the Nicotine went in."

Just then the scientist came off his call, looking relieved. "Everyone's OK at the theatre, and I'm heading down there now with some Nicotine test kits to check the props. I've already got her dress running but I'll test anything remaining like her shoes when I get back."

"Her hair, cosmetics and nail varnish too, please, Des. Just to rule everything out." Craig paused for a moment to check that he hadn't missed anything, then he rose and turned for the door. "Call us if you get anything, John."

"It'll be this afternoon at the earliest. We've just had another body brought in."

"Fine. Des, we can give you a lift to the theatre if you're ready. We'll wait outside John's lab." He turned to his deputy as they walked towards the lift. "Once we've dropped him off, you and I need to find out why someone hated Julianne Hodges enough to end her life."

Chapter Three

The Laganside Courts. Oxford Street, Belfast. 11 a.m.

Annette had seen her most tedious movie ever the night before; the choice made by her partner Mike Augustus. Black and white, Romanian with English subtitles, it had been two interminable hours of a woman's existential angst about the futility of existence and the detective could honestly say she would rather have watched paint dry.

In her whole life it was the most bored Annette could ever remember being, and only Mike's smile and warmth beside her had persuaded her to stay put on the settee; most bored that was until that morning, when she'd wasted *another* two hours sitting on a hard court bench waiting to be called to give evidence, only to finally be told by an usher a minute before that not only wouldn't they need her today but probably not for the next week.

She was just about to scream, partly for the pleasure of shocking the wigged barristers striding purposefully past her through the high-ceilinged hall, when she spotted someone familiar and instead decided to follow him and see what was up.

She caught up with Andy Angel as he was lurking outside the Judges' chambers on the courts' second floor and decided to brighten her day by creeping up behind him and giving him a fright.

The DCI allowed her to get within shoulder tapping distance before turning around so quickly that Annette yelped.

"Don't do that! You gave me a scare!"

"As opposed to the scare you intended to give me?"

She conceded his point with a chuckle. "When did you spot me?"

"Downstairs, but I thought I'd let you amuse yourself."

"Smartass. What are you doing here anyway?"

The DCI handed her a sheaf of papers and after a moment's rifling through it the penny dropped.

"We have a new case?"

"Yep. An actress died on stage at the Adelphi Playhouse last night."

"And the chief doesn't think it was natural causes?"

"Nope. The warrants are for DNA. Some of the 'artistes' are kicking up about giving us swabs. Anyway, why aren't you in court?"

She rolled her brown eyes and sighed. "They didn't get to me, so I've to come back tomorrow and wait again."

"Well, if you're finished for today you can come back to the theatre with me. Aidan and Ryan are there already, but there's a lot to do."

Just then the oak door they'd been standing in front of opened, and a small, thin woman nearing seventy reached her hand out for the warrants.

"You would like Judge Standish to sign these?"

"Yes, please. They're for DNA samples in a murder case."

At the mention of murder, a man called out from the room. "Bring them in, Hazel. You know I like murders."

A moment later the detectives were standing across from Judge Eugene Standish, a snowy-haired, sixty-something grandfather. He was a favourite of Craig's and a huge fan of the Murder Squad, and insisted on hearing every detail of the Hodges' murder, seeming quite put out that there'd been no blood involved.

Andy supposed Judges must have their preference for cases just as coppers chose which squads to join, and if you *had* to sit through hours of boring and sometimes perjured testimony at least murder prosecutions probably provided a thrill.

When he explained that they'd only just started the investigation and blood *might* appear at some point Standish perked up markedly.

"So, there may be more deaths, then? Not that I would wish it on anyone you understand, and God knows decent actors are a precious commodity so we can't

24

afford to lose any more of *them,* but your squad's cases *do* always seem to involve multiple victims."

His 'Don't they?' was silent but hopeful but he attempted to mitigate any perceived ghoulishness by adding, "I mean, it's rare that your killers stop at just one, isn't it?"

The detectives exchanged a surprised glance. They hadn't noticed it before but Standish was right, their cases *did* usually involve more than one victim!

The question was, was it just coincidence, or did Craig, as Head of the whole Murder Section, pass on the cases likely to involve only a single victim such as stabbings, muggings and domestic killings to his other murder teams, but deliberately reserve the twisty ones for himself as a challenge? And if he did, how could he possibly *know* which cases would turn out to have multiple victims from the start?

As the questions filled his mind the DCI smiled at the man in front of him, who reminded everyone of Kris Kringle's Father Christmas because of his twinkly smile and benevolent air. Except for criminals when their jury had returned a guilty verdict. Andy had never got over the shock of seeing Standish morph into a modern-day Hanging Judge Jeffreys when he'd sentenced one of their suspects in an earlier murder case. If the jurist could have ordered the man's beheading on the steps of the court, he was quite sure he would have done.

None of these thoughts were voiced of course and instead, as the detective took the signed warrants gratefully, he decided to leave Eugene Standish with a mysterious quip.

"You know, I think you're right, My Lord. All our cases *do* seem to involve multiple victims. Personally, I think DCS Craig has a sixth sense about serial killings even when there's no obvious sign of cases turning out that way. That might explain why we always end up with them."

The judge lurched forward at his large desk; his eyes bright with excitement.

"*A sixth sense? Really?* Ask the DCS to drop by, please. I'd like to discuss that with him. And tell him to bring the funny big cop as well."

He'd captured Liam in three words.

Suddenly Standish's pale blue eyes narrowed and their twinkle took on a mischievous slant.

"Otherwise I *might* just start to think DCS Craig is deliberately killing a few victims himself, just to make up the numbers."

Annette made a note to tell the boss to get down there PDQ.

****

The CCU. 11 a.m.

Davy Walsh was in a good mood and determined that no-one was going to ruin it. Five years after deciding to tie the knot, he and his girlfriend Maggie, the News Editor of The Belfast Chronicle, had *finally* managed to choose a venue for their wedding, well, handfasting actually, both of them having druidic tendencies. Although as neither had told their parents that, disinclined to listen to the flak they would get if they did, even at the age of thirty, they knew they would need a vicar and priest at the ceremony as well.

But after visiting Iceland, Greenland, and every druid site in Great Britain they'd finally settled on holding the ceremony on Scattery Island, off County Clare on Ireland's Wild Atlantic Coast, which had an ancient monastic history and where some of the earliest known Irish script Ogham was still visible on stones.

The date was the next thing they would have to agree on, but twenty-twenty sometime would do for now. One big personal decision a month was enough for the analyst, whose giant brain was far more comfortable dealing with code and bytes.

Davy's zen was disturbed by his ex-university classmate and now right-hand man come junior analyst

Ash Rahman giving a loud whoop. It caught the attention of Nicky as well and made her commit the cardinal sin of typo, so she was distinctly un-zen in her response.

"*Please* stop making that noise, Ash! I asked you twice last week and now you're doing it again!"

The earringed analyst gave her the faux apologetic look that his boss had seen a hundred times when he'd overstepped the mark. It usually fooled people enough to get him a pass but the PA was savvier than that.

"And don't flash those goo-goo eyes at me thinking it'll get you off. I'm from the mean streets of east Belfast." She paused for a moment to stare at him, taking in his billowing shirt and leather trousers and shaking her head. "And *you* wouldn't last five minutes there dressed like Captain Hook!"

As she returned to her work muttering, "Pirate," curiosity about the whoop got the better of Davy and he crossed to his junior's desk, whispering so as not to disturb the secretary again.

"What w...was the noise for?"

He had a mild stammer on 's' and 'w' that only came out when he was feeling shy or tired. Today's was courtesy of the latter, from his weekend researching wedding sites.

Ash motioned him to pull up a chair and pointed to his computer screen, where lines of code were appearing as his fingers danced across the keys.

"Look what happens when I type this code combo."

He typed the short sequence and his computer screen flickered, blacking out completely for a second before appearing again.

"That's happened every time I've typed that specific sequence this morning."

Davy's response was to race back to his own desk and type the sequence there. When the same thing happened, the pair began moving around the empty desks belonging to the team's detectives, waking each computer and having the same event repeat.

Finally, Davy took the bull by the horns and walked

over to Alice, the squad's deputy PA, then to Nicky her boss, who after some persuading both agreed to carry out the quick test and got an identical response.

"Can you check Liam's and the chief's computers for me, Nick?"

The mother of one eased herself grudgingly from her comfortable chair to do so, and two minutes later the analysts had confirmed that every computer in the squad-room was suffering the same glitch.

Davy beckoned his junior. "OK, w...we need to check all the other murder teams' computers."

Nicky pushed back from her PC in alarm, as if it was a bomb about to detonate.

"What does it mean? Should we shut down the whole system and call IT?"

"NO!" came from both men at once and Davy shook his head vehemently, flinging his long, dark hair across his face and reminding him he'd forgotten its customary ponytail that morning.

Seeing her surprise he added, "I mean, not yet, Nicky, but I'd suggest no-one types anything more until we know what this glitch is. You and Alice should back up all your files on detachable hard drives and have some tea."

With that both analysts disappeared off the floor, to reappear thirty minutes later shaking their heads.

"There's nothing wrong with any of the other teams' computers or smart-pads. OK, Nicky, I'll get IT to check the rest of the building and Ash and I w...will do a deep scan of everything here. We can do it far faster than they can."

She made a face. "I think I should tell the chief."

"Yep. It's probably time."

If what they thought was happening with their computers actually was, then Craig really needed to know.

****

The Adelphi Playhouse. University Road.

It was ages since Craig had been to the theatre, something he realised as soon as the car pulled up outside the Adelphi and he saw the posters on its façade heralding new performances. Not that he recognised a single one of the plays' titles, but perhaps that was to be expected? The only constant in life apart from death and taxes was change.

He shook his head in a way Liam recognised himself doing when one of his kids mentioned something written or discovered years after his own youth. It was the sense of your own life suddenly becoming the past.

Change was progress, Craig supposed, but what of the classics? Did *everything* from the past have to be discarded? He corrected himself immediately; unless it was a dispute commemoration it seemed, and Northern Ireland seemed to have a *never-ending* stream of those.

Liam put their thoughts into words.

"I wish they'd put on the old plays more."

Craig smiled at his telepathy. "Yep. I used to love this theatre because it always put on Shakespeare and Miller." He gestured wearily at the posters. "I know new playwrights need to have their work performed, but surely a balance could be struck?"

Des piped up from the back seat. "Like one in five plays, maybe?"

"That sounds fair, or maybe we're just getting old?"

The three men exited the car chuckling and walked into the Playhouse's foyer, where they saw the familiar lanky shape of Aidan Hughes lounging against a pillar. A pillar that appeared to be made of rock hewn straight from a cliff. Craig was about to comment on the décor being as modern as the plays but he swallowed his words; he'd already hit his grumpy old man quota for the day.

At the sight of his team mates Aidan propelled himself to the vertical to avoid the inevitable 'having a nice sleep then?' slagging from Liam, while Des excused himself and headed backstage to work.

"Morning, Guv. Fresh from the morgue, are we, Liam?"

The comment drew a wry smile from Craig, knowing it was part-rivalry, part-joke. Liam's pallor had earned him the nickname of Ghost from one of his snouts years before, and the mortuary humour was a play on the name. The jibes between his DCIs were more entertaining than malicious, or should he say between two of his DCIs; Andy, or Arty as Liam had nicknamed him because of his talent for painting, refused to jockey for position, his aesthetic mind usually on higher things.

Liam rose to the bait. "Yes, *we* are. Why?"

"'Cos the Doc's just phoned saying he needs you back again. Don't ask me why. Maybe he's found a bed for you, Ghost."

Craig intervened before his deputy could retort. "Enough banter. Update us, Aidan. Where have you got to with everything?"

"Best to go backstage first, Guv. It'll give you a better idea of the scene."

A minute later the trio was inside the smaller of the playhouse's two theatres, which Craig was happy to see had retained its original art deco black lacquered walls with ornate gold inlays and had a quartet of opera boxes overlooking the stage. He drank in the space eagerly, picturing himself and Katy in evening dress drinking champagne while watching one of acting's greats strut the boards. There would be a backstage tour as well of course. He'd always wanted to see what went on behind the velvet curtain but had never had the opportunity. Although Camille, a beauty he'd been heavily involved with in London years before, had been a professional actor, she'd always refused to show him, saying that it would spoil the magic. He allowed himself a moment to remember her and the last time they'd been together, then was stung with guilt about his wife and stamped on the memory hard.

Craig's detectives noticed his interest in his surroundings, but just as Liam was preparing a rib him about being a 'luvvie' Aidan distracted them both with something more interesting, pointing to the pulleys and weights dotted backstage as if he'd invented them.

"Those move the curtains, that one opens a trapdoor for panto, and that one there opens a wee flap in the floor that lets smoke appear. It's all mechanics, but I suppose the acting makes it art."

Craig didn't hear the last few words because his gaze was focused ahead. He walked tentatively on to the stage as if he expected it to collapse beneath him, and was pleased to find that it was as robust as logic should have told him it was.

"Show us exactly where it happened, Aidan."

The DCI pointed centre stage. "It was at the start of the second scene of act one, so about thirty minutes into the play. When the curtain went up our Vic was already on stage. The place was set out as an old nineteen-twenties speakeasy and she was sitting at a table pretending to drink-"

Liam interrupted. "That area's been tested by forensics?"

"Chair, table, her glass, the waiter's tray, everything. The backstage crew are pretty pissed at us - all their props are covered in fingerprint dust."

Craig nodded. "And every item from our victim's costume has reached the lab? Shoes, jewellery, bag?"

"Grace sent everything personally."

Craig glanced around him. "Where is Grace?"

Just then a small jump-suited figure appeared at the back of the stage.

"Hi, Grace. Des came with us, have you spoken to him yet?"

Her brown eyes sparked with interest. "Yes indeed, and he told me what you'd discussed. Fascinating. I'd already dusted everything for prints and gathered whatever DNA was present, but we'll go over everything again for Nicotine. Our suits *are* protective."

Craig nodded. "Still. Be careful. If we're talking about skin absorption there could be high doses on any surface

Ms Hodges touched."

She looked unconvinced. "I doubt it was on just any surface or the other actors would be dead too. I think we're looking at something very specific to her. Shoes, bag, dress and so on."

He smiled at her polite rejection of his amateur forensics. Grace was always polite even when she was telling people off, as she often did with Liam over his swearing. Although she was only in her thirties there was something quaintly old-fashioned about her, as if she belonged in a gentler time.

As she returned to the backstage darkness Craig re-joined his men, just in time to see his deputy throw his arms wide and shout, "Friends, Romans, countrymen" to the empty auditorium. Shakespeare's Julius Caesar was clearly on the curriculum of every school.

"Thank you, Laurence Olivier, but let's get back to work. Finish what you were saying, Aidan."

"OK, well Hodges was seated at the table supposedly sipping on a cocktail the waiter had brought her, and he was standing near the back of the stage still holding his tray. Then Hodges' lady's maid entered from there." He gestured towards the direction Grace had just disappeared. "A minute later Hodges hit the floor and the maid shrieked. There was no-one close when it happened. Apparently, the waiter screamed too, and so did the stage manager who rushed on. Ken registered something was wrong, raced down to the stage and the rest you know."

"Julianne Hodges' character was supposed to die later?"

Liam jumped in. "That's right. She was playing the main character Angel Ryan, like in the title."

Aidan picked up his thread.

"She wasn't supposed to die till the second act when her sister shoots her with one of those small derringers that women carried in their handbags. I saw it backstage. Good replica."

Craig nodded, his mind dismissing anything

irrelevant as soon as it arose.

"So, Ken locked down the scene and took preliminary statements."

"Yep. Everyone on stage and backstage, and the first two rows of the audience as well. He got the stage manager to collect the names and addresses of everyone else in the audience too, in case we needed to speak to them."

Good move. It was likely their killer had wanted to watch their work play out, so they may well have been present.

The thought brought Craig up short. He scanned the auditorium hurriedly then startled the others by suddenly jumping into the orchestra pit, surprised at how big a drop it turned out to be and pleased that he managed to stay on his feet.

After searching the pit and not finding what he was looking for, he climbed out again and strode up the theatre's right-hand aisle.

Aidan watched him, bemused. "What are you looking for, Guv?"

"Whatever I can find, but especially those."

He pointed to a small security camera above his head and the finding made Liam bark out, "Get the floor plans for the whole playhouse, Hughesy. We need details of the security layout," before joining Craig's search on the opposite aisle.

"Don't forget they may have an official camera too that they use to film performances, Aidan. It's common practice now. Even the National Theatre does it."

Liam motioned his subordinate to move. "You heard the boss. Chop chop."

But before Aidan had even started walking Craig realised there was a better way of doing things and shook his head.

"So, you *don't* want the plans now, Guv?"

"No, I do, but I need to call Davy while you're getting them." He nodded his deputy to keep searching. "I'll be with you in a minute, Liam."

33

A moment later he was connected to his senior analyst, who was on a hunt of his own.

"Yes, chief. What can I do for you?"

"You sound out of breath, Davy. Has Nicky got you jogging around the office?"

"She w...wishes. I'm under a desk, so just give me a minute to stand up."

Certain that he would find out later why his lead analyst was under a desk instead of seated at one the detective went on as if he hadn't heard.

"I need either you or Ash down at the Adelphi ASAP."

On any other day Davy would have jumped at the thought of an outing, relishing the break from his screen-bound life, but right now it interfered with his hunt.

"Why?" Realising he might have sounded cheeky the younger man added hastily. "Just in case we need to bring anything."

"We're at the Adelphi, and I need you to check if there are any cameras or feeds beyond the obvious ones. Front of house, in both theatres and backstage."

The penny dropped. "You think the perp w...watched remotely?"

"Is it possible?"

"Absolutely. OK, I'll come down myself. How long will the others be there?"

Before Craig could respond, Annette and Andy appeared brandishing papers. He acknowledged their arrival with a nod and turned back to his call.

"There'll be people here for the next few hours so just find Aidan when you arrive. He'll have the building's floorplans."

He cut the call, leaving Davy to explain to his deputy that he was going to have to continue whatever they were up to alone and knowing that Ash was more than capable, and crossed to where the new entrants and Liam were installing themselves in some of the theatre's comfortable red velvet seats. Annette greeted him first.

"Hello, sir. Judge Standish requests the company of yourself and Liam when you get a mo. I think he's

34

looking for entertainment and you're it."

Craig raised an eyebrow but parked the obvious question in favour of one about the papers in Andy's hand.

"Warrants?"

"Yep. We can take DNA from all the actors and backstage staff."

"Good. Get those to Grace, please. She's backstage with Des. But touch nothing unless they say it's safe."

As the DCI's mouth opened to ask why, Craig shook his head.

"I'll be briefing later so I'll tell everybody then."

The alternative being to go through the whole, "'She might have been killed by Nicotine," astonished look and, "What?"' routine several times, and he didn't have the energy for it.

As Andy left in search of the CSI Craig turned back to his inspector.

"Annette, I'd like you and Mary to interview the victim's husband. Nicky has his details."

She gazed at him beseechingly. "Can't I take Ryan instead? I mean, he's here already and it would save me having to go back to the ranch."

It earned her a sympathetic look but a firm no.

"Nice try, but Mary it is. Look, I know Mary can be challenging, but she'll never become a good detective if she doesn't get out there and gain experience dealing with people, so I've decided to rotate her between all of you from now on and get her out on the street. If you take her today Aidan will take her tomorrow."

There was a noisy objection from the stage where Aidan had just reappeared with the plans. "I will like hell!"

Craig's voice hardened. "You will and you'll smile about it, Chief Inspector. Think of it as good practice."

Liam's muttered, "For what? Purgatory?" earned him a dirty look.

Craig scanned the whole group reprovingly.

"This is an order, everyone. You've dealt with drunk,

violent perps for years so you can deal with one young detective, no matter how argumentative she can be."

Annette grumbled noisily. "Well, all I can say is I hope that you and Liam will be taking her too."

Eyeing his deputy sternly Craig nodded. "We will, but not at the start of an investigation when things are urgent. Right, off you go, Annette, and let me know what the husband has to say as soon as you can, please."

She stomped off heavily despite his "please".

"You honestly like the husband for this, boss?"

Craig fell into a seat and raked his hair for a moment before answering.

"Honestly? The answer is I don't know yet, Liam. He wasn't on stage, but this killing didn't require the perp to be present, and what better alibi for your wife's murder than that you were miles away watching your kid?"

"Especially if he was able to watch her die from his laptop at home. OK, I can see it now."

"We'll see. I'm obviously not convinced or I would have taken his interview myself." He switched up the mood by rubbing his hands together briskly. "OK, Davy should be here soon so let's leave the remote viewing possibilities for him to sort out and head backstage." As they approached the stage stairs he called out, "Aidan, how many of the actors and staff are here?"

"A handful of both. They wandered in for rehearsal about an hour ago. The show's cancelled tonight but it's habit, I suppose."

"OK, check who *isn't* present and get them here now. I want all their statements and for Grace to have all the samples she needs by this afternoon."

"I'll get Ryan on it. He's in the Green Room."

"And let me have the names of the ones who aren't here yet. Avoidance could be a clue. Also, what about the statements Ken took last night? It might be quicker to check what's missing from those than start everything afresh."

"He was going to drop them into the office, wasn't he?"

Liam nodded.

"OK, let me think about those. Fresh ones *might* actually be a better idea. We could check them against Ken's afterwards and find anyone who changed their story. What about the floorplans?"

Aidan waved them in the air.

"Spread them out on the stage and we'll be there in a second."

Craig turned to his deputy. "Let's cast an eye over the security arrangements then Davy can take over. Is there anything else we should be doing?"

Liam nodded. "I'll ask ASU to pull the street cams around here from last night. Just in case something jumps out."

The ASU or Aerial Support Unit had access to every publicly owned street, traffic and static CCTV camera in Northern Ireland, and an agreement with most private security firms to supply theirs on request. It had helped the squad in cases before.

"Good thinking." Craig started to climb the stairs. "Floorplans first then we find Andy. I want to know exactly what he's committed us to with the Judge."

****

The Labs.

It wasn't often that John Winter was unsure of himself, well, not in his professional life anyway; in his personal life he seemed to exist in a permanent state of turmoil, *never* knowing what to do for the best.

A dispassionate observer, one not concerned for the pathologist's feelings but simply the truth, might have pointed the finger for most of that uncertainty at his wife, Natalie Ingrams, a surgeon with whom John had lived in marital not-so-bliss for five years. Natalie was a woman who if someone described her as a fireball would be downplaying her combustibility and whose temperament could better be described, using examples from myth, as being Hel the Goddess of Death when she was bad and Freya The Goddess of Love when she decided to be nice, which had been less and less frequently since John had moved out of the marital home.

The reason the pathologist had left was that he'd also been a father for two years, and to stop Natalie ruining their daughter Kit's childhood with her ridiculous perfectionist ideals he'd voted with his feet, taking the toddler with him. But even though his marriage had been fraught with challenges from the get-go he could never regret it when he looked at his child, who held his heart completely in the palm of her small pink hand and sent him to work every day with an incongruous, given his job, skip in his step.

That skip held sway at the moment because he and Natalie were living apart, 'working' on their marriage from a distance. That distance being the mile between Craig's old bachelor pad in Stranmillis where he and Kit were currently living and the decidedly more luxurious marital home on Annadale Embankment where Natalie was still ensconced while he tried to persuade her that therapy, single, joint and perhaps even family, was a necessity before reuniting, if that *ever* happened.

So, at the moment uncertainty was a permanent feature of the medic's private life yet it had never until now seriously troubled him at work, but as he gazed down at the new body on his dissection table then across at his puzzled looking deputy, he was no longer so sure.

Was what he was finding, or rather *not* finding, in their second patient in twenty-four hours, an element in how the woman in front of them had died or just his own inability to admit there *was* no detectable cause of death? An idea that every scientific bone in him resisted.

In his defence, and to persuade himself this wasn't merely ego and arrogance, something that no-one but John had ever accused him of, there *was* another factor in play and it was his main reason for summoning Craig again.

Maria O'Rourke, the woman lying on his table with her black curly hair swept back from her unlined face, had something unexpected in common with their first patient that day.

****

Ballyhackamore. East Belfast.

The interview of Julianne Hodges' husband proved unremarkable, if by unremarkable you meant a young man sobbing his way through every question and answer and upsetting his two-year-old son by shooting him mournful looks. Occasionally, when Morgan Hodges' tears threatened to drown him, Annette was forced to pause her questioning, and in those moments she set down her small tape-recorder and grasped his large hands in her own, really wishing that she could behave as the nurse she'd been for thirteen years before joining the police force, do as her instincts dictated and hug him hard as well.

Back then her sole concern would have been for a broken man's pain, but now that compassion was always tempered by the possibility that the man in front of her might have murdered his wife. Almost forty percent of women murdered were killed by their partners and Hodges could just be giving the performance he thought was expected of an innocent, although if so it was a damn good act.

The inspector did learn *something* interesting during the interview however; that their recalcitrant constable, who'd spent the whole drive there delivering a monologue on feminism and informing Annette that she'd been an unwitting victim of the patriarchy all her life; *like tell me something I don't know, kid!,* was absolutely brilliant with children.

Mary had gravitated towards Hodges' son the moment they'd entered the house, and without removing the child from his father's anxious gaze for a second had enabled her interview by engaging the boy in brick building and crayon scribbling, even joining in that most toddler of pursuits, racing small cars against each other and providing a quiet 'vroom, vroom' soundtrack to great effect.

It was a side of the DC that Annette doubted any of her team mates had seen and she wasn't quite sure what she should do with the knowledge, finally deciding not to tell anyone in the office but to indulge her own curiosity on it when they returned to the car.

They had barely left Hodges' street when she started.

"You were very good with that little boy, Mary. Thank you. It allowed me to ask what we needed to know."

She received the expected 'back off' grunt from the constable in response, but Annette had broken scarier people than Mary so she ploughed on.

"Have you ever worked with small children?"

She watched out of the side of her eye as the constable's fine-featured face contorted, and defiance, secretiveness and a hint of pride vied for space.

Finally, "In a nursery during Uni holidays" squeezed out.

If Mary had thought that would bring an end to the questioning, she was wrong. She had just provided Annette with a stepping stone.

"So, you have small kids in your family then. Otherwise why not choose an easier summer job? Sales, or working in a coffee shop maybe?"

The answer was out before the constable could stop it. "Cousins. Lots."

Then her mouth clamped shut so hard Annette wondered whether she'd bitten through her lip. But she'd got what she needed. Proof that no matter how difficult Mary was at work, some parallel universe existed where she behaved like a human being.

It was knowledge to build on in the future but not to use for teasing or jokes, although she had no intention of telling *Mary* that. It did no harm to keep people on edge sometimes, and she decided to do just that by asking the constable to call Craig and put the call on hands-free.

He answered the call quickly with, "Hello, Mary, what can I do for you?" and was surprised to hear his inspector's voice come back.

"Hello, sir, we've just left Morgan Hodges and I don't think he's our man. He's in absolute bits about his wife. They'd only been married four years and were childhood sweethearts."

As Mary shot her an evil look, knowing exactly why she made her use *her* phone, Craig gave a sceptical grunt.

"It's a nice story, Annette."

"I know, but..."

Knowing she didn't possess his sceptical gene he changed topic. "What does he do for a living?"

"He's a solicitor. He and his wife had a light meal together just before she left for the theatre and he drove her there. The rest of the day she'd spent at home with their son. I specifically asked about his computing experience and it seems pretty basic, just whatever word processing and so on he might need for work. But I guess he could be lying about that, so I'll ask Davy to look into his background."

"Wait till after we've briefed. There'll be a lot of names for background searches so we can make a list then."

He considered for a moment before speaking again, pointing Liam towards a miraculously free parking space outside Laganside Courts as he did.

"Where are you now, Annette?"

"On the way back to the office, sir."

"Divert to the Adelphi and give them a hand taking statements, please. There are quite a few still to take, so you'll still be there after lunch."

He'd decided against using Ken's statements as a foundation, opting to incorporate them later instead.

"On our way."

As he ended his call and climbed out of the car, Craig started scanning the area for somewhere to eat that might not be full of lawyers, finally conceding that it was a lost cause. Lawyers of all types were as prevalent around the Courts as gulls were around the river itself.

Liam knew what his searching signified and rubbed his hands together in glee.

"Munch time! Good man."

"Soon. I'm just looking for somewhere decent."

"Ach, that's wild nice of you, boss, but a greasy spoon will do for me."

It earned him a snort, a nod towards a brasserie on Oxford Street and then a view of Craig's back as he entered the courthouse to invite Eugene Standish to join them for lunch.

Chapter Four

The Labs.

It wasn't often that Marcie was flummoxed, she being a woman who prided herself on always being two steps ahead of any female competition, and by necessity as the sister of many brothers three steps ahead of the male. But today flummoxed was the only word that could really have described her, and there were two reasons.

One, she'd met Julianne Hodges several times on the tight-knit professional acting circuits in Ireland, north and south, and a more 'inoffensive being', as her mum used to say, she would have been hard put to name. Quiet, shy, and backward about coming forward, not qualities that often advanced an actor's career, the young mother had played mainly face in the crowd parts, maids, and even on occasion had helped the stage hands when she'd had no lines to speak, so *how* Julianne had ended up as the lead in The Murder of Angel Ryan, albeit scheduled to die well before the play's end, beat Marcie.

Except that in a way it didn't; Julianne had always been the prettiest face in their classes, so in other ways it surprised her that she hadn't been placed stage-front by some lecherous director years before.

The PA gasped suddenly; *perhaps that had something to do with her death? Maybe some sad old lech of an impresario had done it?* Or perhaps not; but either way she made the decision to tell the Murder Squad detectives of her suspicions when they next appeared.

The second thing flummoxing Marcie was written in the pathology lab's 'book', a heavy, leather-bound, and in these days of computers slightly anachronistic, volume in which John Winter insisted the details of each of the mortuary's clients be handwritten as soon as they were known.

Sometimes there were gaps that persisted for years; those of the impossible to identify, un-mourned, or lost

43

too far from home to ever be named. At other times, such as during The Troubles, when identifying the destroyed remains of bomb victims had proved a particularly heavy challenge, whole pages had remained empty for a week.

But today it wasn't a gap of *any* size that was puzzling the PA. On the contrary every client was named, addressed, and even aged, and it was the last point that was bothering her.

She read the final two entries aloud to herself.

"Julianne Hodges, aged twenty-seven. Maria O'Rourke, aged twenty-seven. I mean, what are the odds?"

She was right. What *were* the odds of two women arriving at the mortuary within twenty-four hours of each other being exactly the same age?

Those were Mike Augustus' words, almost verbatim, as he and John waited for their baked potatoes in a café down the road, and they would be Liam Cullen's exact words later that afternoon.

****

The CCU. 2 p.m.

"Sorry I took so long at the theatre. More to see there than I thought."

Davy threw his lanky frame into a chair and kept talking to the desk his junior was hunkered under.

"Did you find anything? Ash?"

The junior analyst's head popped up a few seconds later and its owner propped himself against a chair.

"No. Well, no and yes. I can tell you what I've ruled out. This isn't system or building wide."

His boss arched an eyebrow, puzzled. "Did you check the routers?"

"That's my first port of call after I grab some food." The junior analyst frowned; the expression looking incongruous on his normally grinning face. "But whether it's the routers or not we could have bigger problems."

44

"You mean if someone's targeted our squad's computers in particular."

"Yep. We might have to find somewhere else to work until this is all sorted out."

Davy puffed out his cheeks before speaking again. "The chief w...won't like that. He loves his river view."

Craig's office had floor to ceiling windows over the Lagan and he'd often said watching the water as it flowed out to Belfast Lough helped him think.

Ash shrugged; scenery was lost on him unless it was the backdrop to a fashion spread.

"More than he'll worry about some hacker viewing his investigations? I doubt it. Anyway, let's make sure of what we're dealing with first, then you can break the news to him."

Davy's eyes widened in alarm. *"Me? Why me?"*

His leanly muscled junior bounced to his feet, his gold hoop earring glinting under the strip lights as he did.

"Because rank has its privileges, that's why. And *you*, my old mate, are the boss. Right, I'm off for lunch."

He grabbed his smart-pad and headed for the exit with said boss in pursuit, objecting noisily. When they were in the lift on the way to the ground floor Ash decided that a change of topic was required.

"What did you find at the Adelphi?"

Even though he knew the question was a diversion Davy took the bait excitedly.

"Man, you should *see* some of the rig they have backstage. Cutting edge s...sound and light effects operated by wi-fi. I thought it would just be a pile of old ropes and pulleys."

It brought a frown from his deputy that he explained once they'd exited on to Pilot Street, heading for their local bar The James in search of a decent sandwich.

"You do realise wi-fi means it's open to the world."

He was surprised when Davy shrugged.

"Yep, just like every computer in the Adelphi's offices and reception. There are also three hackable CCTV cameras sweeping each theatre auditorium and the foyer, *plus* static cameras that anyone with half a brain could have piggybacked to w...watch our victim die. I'm *really* not looking forward to telling the chief."

"You've downloaded everything from them?"

The senior analyst patted his jacket. "All on my smartpad. I'll check it as soon we get back."

Ash pushed open the bar's door, still talking. "Don't sync it to the office computers in case there *is* someone hacking us. You don't want them wiping their footprint from the Adelphi."

The warning brought a tight smile. "Do you think I'm thick?"

"Just testing. Anyway, I've rigged up a standalone encrypted network and transferred all my files to it."

"Nice." Davy ordered his takeaway sandwich absentmindedly and propped himself against the nearest wall to wait, thinking for a moment before he spoke again. "We *could* run the whole office like that."

"You mean isolate *everything* from the police network?"

"Why not? I'll look at setting up an encrypted LAN while you're checking the routers. As long as everyone stays off the police network and doesn't use wi-fi we should be able to keep any nosy parkers out."

A LAN is a local area network that interconnects computers within a limited area, such as an office.

"It's worth a go." Ash took their two overstuffed baguettes from the server and grabbed a soft drink. "But right now, I'm starving, so pay the man, will you? I'm broke."

Davy rolled his eyes, lifted a can of drink for himself and passed the cash across, knowing that he would never get paid back. Years at university with his junior had taught him two things; never to let Ash near your wallet *or* your girl.

****

Oxford Street, Belfast.

"OK, that's old Standish stocked up with murder stories and tales of daring-do for a month or two, so what next, boss?"

Craig chuckled as he recalled the judge's enthusiasm when Liam had talked about some of their goriest cases and pointed straight ahead.

"Home, James."

Dialling the office on the car-phone, he connected almost immediately with his PA.

"Nicky, how are we fixed for a briefing?"

"You mean apart from having no tech and no-one but the computer boys being here?"

Computer Boys made him chuckle; it sounded like a boy-band and made him picture the analysts playing guitars and fighting off fans.

"OK, put the big one on."

Davy was half-a-foot taller than his deputy.

"I will, but Doctor Winter said he'd like to see you again as well."

"Grand."

He set the call on speaker and a moment later Davy's cheerful, "Hi, chief, what can I do you for?" came down the line.

"You could tell me why none of my computers are working for a start."

A minute of geek-speak later Craig's head started to hurt.

"Hold on a second, Davy. So, in English, you and Ash think someone could be trying to access our records?"

"And current investigation. Yes. We can't be s...sure because Ash hasn't discovered how yet, but we're the only squad in the building affected by the screen flickering and it isn't the system so he's gone down to check the routers. If *they're* OK then we can't rule out hacking and we'll have to establish a closed network. But it'll limit your s...searches big time, chief."

Craig was still on why someone might want to hack

47

their investigations at all. All their cases were either closed or on their way to court.

Except for their new one...

He asked another question.

"What did you find at the Adelphi, Davy?"

"Far too many access routes to the outside world, that's what. Computers all over the building on wi-fi, and a wi-fi special effects console backstage, plus s...several sets of CCTV cameras and two fixed ones inside the theatres. It would have been child's play to hack in and watch our victim's death. I've downloaded everything to sort through and Ash and I have taken our smart-pads off the system, so I'll text the others and tell them not to sync their phones and pads till I say."

Although Liam had inserted the key in his car's ignition he hadn't yet started driving, sensing their destination might be about to change. As he listened to the conversation something occurred to him and he waved a hand in front of Craig's face to interrupt.

It brought an irritated, "What?" from the detective that would have earned him a tut if his deputy hadn't been so keen to speak.

"Have you swept the office for bugs or cameras that shouldn't be there, son?"

Craig was taken aback. The idea hadn't even occurred to him! The immediate gasp from his analyst said he wasn't the only one.

"Hot damn, that's good, Liam!"

"Cheers, lad. But it means we can't even hold a briefing at the ranch until it's been swept."

Craig agreed. "You and Ash get on with checking all that and the computer stuff, Davy, and call me when you have an update. Everyone else has plenty to get on with at the scene."

"Do you want Nicky again?"

Craig considered for a moment and decided not. "Just tell her we'll hold a briefing somewhere tomorrow morning and that Liam and I are heading back to the lab and the Adelphi."

He ended the call and immediately fell deep into thought. When he looked up again, they were halfway up the Ormeau Road on the way back to the way to see John.

"That was a great catch on the cameras and bugs, Liam. What made you think of it?"

The DCI shrugged and pulled into the right-hand lane, ignoring the beeps of a driver he cut off in the process.

"Seemed logical, although you're such a grumpy sod you're lucky I bothered saying it."

Craig chuckled, knowing that he was right.

"Sorry. Go on."

"Well, it seems to me that if someone's trying to get into our computers it must be to find stuff out, and the other ways to do that are watching us and listening."

The words made Craig think of something so he made another call, this time connecting with Alice.

"Alice, tell Davy to cover the computer cameras, cut their mikes and call round everyone to do the same with their phones and pads, as well as disconnecting them from wi-fi and Bluetooth. He'll know why. Thanks."

Before the PA could say a word, he was gone.

"Aye, I was going to suggest all that next, boss. As well as disabling *that*."

The DCI pointed to the car's dashcam which Craig swiftly turned off, along with the GPS and tracker fitted to every car they used. But before he could call to tell the rest of the team to disable theirs Liam spoke again.

"But it mightn't solve the problem, boss. Hackers are like bloody termites so what if the boy clears the system and it gets infiltrated again?"

The Boy had been his nickname for Davy for years and persisted despite the analyst reaching his fourth decade.

"Because you *know* there's only one person likely to be interested in the Hodges' case and that's her killer, so they won't stop at one try."

Craig nodded in agreement.

"No, they won't, but it does tell us something about them. They're extremely computer literate, so much so that it might be their job."

"And they're probably young too, to be that good on the machines."

Craig smiled at the quaint term and shook his head.

"You're generalising, Liam. Older people can be good on computers as well."

"Can be, but the odds still point to young. And male."

"For God's sake don't let Mary hear you say that! Her degree was in computing."

The deputy shook his head defiantly. "I don't give a rat's ass. A young female Vic and a computer literate scrote points to a young, male killer."

Craig smiled. As profiles went it wasn't a bad first cut, and he said as much after he'd called everyone about their car-tech and they'd pulled up outside the lab.

They were halfway down the corridor to John's office when a Stevie Nicks lookalike suddenly leapt out in front of them, making Liam stagger back dramatically with his hand clutched to his chest.

"God, Marcie, you nearly gave me a heart attack!"

As she rolled her eyes Craig eyed the height disparity between the five-foot-three secretary and his six-six deputy.

"She's hardly a threat, Liam."

"Ah now, you never can tell, boss. Some of those spy ninjas pack a hefty clout."

The ninja sighed. "You're a big drama queen, Liam, and that's coming from the biggest."

Amusing though the interlude was Craig had work to do.

"Was this just a random attack, Marcie, or did you have something to tell us?"

Two minutes later they knew everything that the secretary did about Julianne Hodges *and* why John had summoned them for the second time that day.

"Another twenty-seven-year-old? You're sure?"

She nodded hard, throwing her long hair across her face in a windswept way that made Liam's secretly romantic heart almost burst from his chest.

"Positive. I had to contact their next-of-kins about the identifications and both women turned twenty-seven in the past year."

Craig wrinkled his brow in a way his deputy knew signified the birth of an idea.

"Right, good. Thanks for the information, Marcie. Particularly the inside track on Ms Hodges. If you think of anything else give one of us a call." He gestured at his deputy. "Or better still, blitz attack Liam again. It was worth our visit just for that."

With a mysterious smile the pocket ninja disappeared, leaving the men to enter John's domain. They found the pathologist dusting the artefacts from one of the many mahogany and glass cabinets that lined the walls of his outer office. He acknowledged their entrance without turning, instead waving hello with what appeared to be a pair of pliers.

"Fixing something, John?"

"No. Why?"

As the medic turned to face them Craig gestured at the implement in his hand.

"Oh, this? No, it's a medieval tongue clamp."

John collected antique medical equipment and torture implements, although which was which was sometimes hard to tell.

He motioned Liam to open his mouth so he could demonstrate, an honour the detective declined.

"Party pooper. I was only going to show you. Anyway, they used this clamp to hold up the tongue as they swiped it off with a knife."

As his deputy mimicked vomiting Craig shook his head in mock despair. "Sometimes I worry about you, John, I really do."

The medic shrugged and replaced the device in its case, motioning the men into his office and busying himself making some drinks. After a full minute of no-one saying a word Craig thought he'd better ask why they were there again.

"You said you'd like to see us? Is it about the second

dead woman being the same age as Julianne Hodges?"

John halted mid-pour. "How did you know that? Have you got a suspect?"

Craig shook his head. "We're not *that* good. Marcie told us."

Liam's eyes misted over at the name, something he would never admit if challenged and *certainly* not in front of his wife.

"Ah, of course. She must have noticed it in the book. She's very sharp, Marcie. Yes, well, it's highly unusual to have two young women, never mind of identical age, brought here within a day."

"What's the cause of death for the second one?"

"That's actually why I called you. She-" Suddenly he abandoned his drink and stood up. "Actually, I think we should take a look."

A minute later they standing beside a young dead woman for the second time that day, and disturbingly this one's petite size made her look even younger than her age.

"She's a kid, boss."

"Not chronologically, but yes, she does look very young. Who is she, John?"

"Maria O'Rourke. Twenty-seven, single, and a junior doctor just starting her radiology training."

Craig sighed heavily. "More wasted talent. How did she die?"

The response was the pathologist drawing the sheet down slightly, to reveal a hole in the upper left side of the woman's chest.

"She had a pacemaker and it's completely fried. It may have malfunctioned and killed her."

Liam's frown matched Craig's own.

"Does that happen often, Doc?"

"Practically never. It's an exclusion diagnosis at best."

"Meaning you can't find anything else that might have done it?"

"Worse than that. I can't find *any* cause of death at all."

Liam's frown turned quizzical. "If it *was* the pacemaker that killed her how would that have worked? The battery packing up or something?"

The pathologist shook his head. "Very unlikely. Pacemaker batteries last an average of ten years and hers was new last summer."

"OK, so give us your best guess then, Doc."

The medic covered his patient and ushered them back to his office before speaking again.

"OK, so a pacemaker does what its name suggests. It sets a regular pace for the heart to beat at."

"And why did someone so young need one, John?"

"Many reasons, but in this particular case she had an inherited cardiomyopathy, a disease that had weakened her heart muscle. She would have died by twenty without the pacer."

"So it was keeping her alive. I'm assuming she had regular check-ups to make sure it was working correctly."

"Yes, and hers was. It was checked just last month at St Mary's."

"We'll need the who and when on that, Doc."

The medic indicated a file on his desk.

"I don't think there was any fault there. This was an acute malfunction. She was in a radiology room this morning reading X-ray films when she died. Alone, which is why she wasn't resuscitated. I got a print out of her pacemaker in the final minutes before death-"

Craig cut him off swiftly. "From where?"

"Oh, sorry, I forgot to say that the pacemaker's action was uploaded constantly to the manufacturer's labs by wi-fi so they could do random checks on it." He saw Liam opening his mouth and nodded. "Yes, I've got those details for you as well."

"Thanks for that, John, but surely if there was wi-fi the device could have been hacked."

The pathologist rolled his eyes. "You've been reading too many thrillers, Marc. Yes, in theory that *could* happen, but it's carefully guarded against and the device should automatically have corrected any arrythmias that were caused. That was part of its function."

Liam shook his head firmly. "*Should* doesn't mean that it did, Doc. I saw a TV show once where hackers made a pacemaker give its owner an electric shock that killed him."

John gave an exasperated sigh. "I'm sure Davy can check for signs of hacking, but do you *really* think I didn't look for signs of electrocution, Liam? An electric shock big enough to stop a heart would show up in the body in other ways, and there weren't any. Look, let me finish explaining then we can discuss everything."

He opened a file on his computer and turned the screen towards them. "OK, this is the ECG printout for Maria O'Rourke's last five minutes. Time of death was eight-twenty this morning and she was found fifteen minutes later."

Craig gestured at the screen. "Translate please."

"It's the perfectly normal ECG of a heart beating at seventy beats per minute. That was obviously the rate her doctors had set it to run. There were no abnormal rhythms and no corrections needed. Completely normal until there." He pointed to the end of the trace.

"There's nothing there but a straight line, Doc."

"It's called asystole and it means the heart had stopped. But the important thing was the lack of warning. There wasn't a single abnormal or dropped beat beforehand. This was a *completely* unheralded sudden death. Her pacemaker just failed, suddenly and absolutely."

Craig thought for a moment before speaking again.

"And definitely no electric shock?"

"None."

"How then?"

As the medic considered the question he rubbed his chin, wondering in passing why he never had stubble, not even when, as happened every weekend now, he didn't shave for two days. His father had been the same, he could never grow a beard or moustache. Genetics was a funny old thing.

Seeing his friend's mind wandering Craig reached across the desk and gave him a nudge, making the pathologist jump as if he'd just woken and blurt out, "A MASSIVE POWER SURGE!"

The smile on the detectives' faces told John that he'd just shouted, so he gathered his dignity hastily and continued in his normal voice.

"Yes, a power surge, that's the only way I can see this happening. There are some things that people with pacemakers are advised to avoid, such as strong electric and radio fields."

"But you said she wasn't electrocuted, Doc."

"She wasn't in the traditional sense, but she didn't need to touch a bare wire for a strong electrical or other field nearby to affect her. That *could* make sense because there are no visible marks on her body." He gazed into space thoughtfully. "I wonder if there are signs of disruption at cellular level..."

Craig could see they were in danger of losing him to science and rose to shake things up. Also he always thought better on his feet.

"OK, three questions, John. Has the X-ray reading-room been sealed off?"

"Yes. The whole Radiology Department has. I requested it." The medic took a scribbled note from his pocket and passed it across. "Here are the details you've already asked for plus the location of the room."

"Thanks. OK, second question, is there anything interesting on Ms O'Rourke's own X-rays?"

"Nothing. We X-rayed her whole skeleton and everything was fine. Maria O'Rourke was a perfectly healthy twenty-seven-year-old who could have lived for decades with a pacemaker."

Craig examined the answer for gaps and satisfied there weren't any he moved on.

"I take it all the usual tox-screens are being run?"

"Of course, but there's nothing yet."

"Right. Final question."

"That's four not three, boss."

Craig ignored the quip.

"How long after death did the body arrive here?"

"About an hour after she was discovered, so just after nine-thirty. You were actually here when she came in. By the time she was found it was already too late to resuscitate her but they still tried, probably because she was so young."

"OK..." Craig rubbed his own chin, stubbly only a few hours after shaving, before speaking again. "Humour me and add another test to your list, John."

"For?"

"Magnetism. If there are any such tests. Although I suppose there must be a-"

No-one got to hear what he'd been about to say because he was cut off by his astonished friend.

"Magnetism? Why on earth?" John's jaw dropped along with the penny. *"You think an EMP killed her?"*

"Could it have?"

The pathologist frowned as he thought things through. "Well... if it had been of sufficient size and close enough, I suppose... yes. Strong magnetic fields *are* another thing pacemaker users are told to avoid. But where could it have come from, and-"

Liam interrupted.

"Hold on, Doc. What's an EMP?"

Craig got his answer in first. "An electromagnetic pulse. It emits a-"

But the DCI only heard magnet. *"You're saying magnets can kill people?* I bought our Rory a set for Christmas!"

Rory was the DCI's six-year-old son, and such a clone of his father in looks and temperament that Craig had thought it impossible short of being grown in a lab.

The question made John smile, recalling his own boyhood experiments with the toys.

"Not that size of magnet, Liam. But perhaps a bigger one."

Craig returned to his theory. "You think an EMP *could*

kill a human being then, John?"

"Put it this way, a large one can damage trees, buildings and aircraft so I don't think it would do any good, especially if someone had a pacemaker. My knowledge on them is patchy, so my guess is it would depend on the size and proximity of the pulse, but I'll need to look into it."

The pathologist waved Craig to sit down again, his eyes full of glee despite the sad situation.

"My God, you *really* think someone messed with an electromagnetic pulse, Marc? That's like something from a movie."

"So is Nicotine poisoning."

The detective sat forward eagerly; his best friend's excitement infectious.

"But *would* one have killed her or just cancelled her pacemaker? That could have reverted her heart in its original weak state, so perhaps *that* killed her?"

John pulled a face. "Even with the cardiomyopathy I'd have expected her to have survived a few hours. Easily long enough to have a new pacer inserted. Her heart actually didn't look too bad on PM; I was surprised." He sighed heavily. "But perhaps she was just unlucky and it *did* fail. In any case, I'll need to examine the organ in more detail before I can say. As far as EMPs go, Davy could probably find us answers in the literature, and Des should be able to help with the magnetism checks. He's bound to have some sort of magnetic field reader lying about upstairs."

"He'll need to check her body and the room where she died, just in case there's still a trace."

"The CSIs can do that later."

The pair were suddenly startled by Liam bringing his hefty fist down on the desk. His original query on magnets still hadn't been answered to his satisfaction and he'd reached the pissed-off point.

"Would you two *please* speak English!"

The words made John chuckle.

"Sorry, Liam, we do get a bit carried away. Basically,

Marc took your electrocution idea and added magnets, making an EMP A large one can knock out electrics, computers and anything else like that nearby, including possibly Maria O'Rourke's pacemaker, and Des might be able to measure if it left any magnetism behind."

"Why didn't he just say that then?" He turned to his boss. "Why didn't you just say that in the first place?" He rolled his small eyes. "I bet you two were hell together when you were kids."

The memory of himself and John contesting every point fiercely at school made Craig smile wryly, then he returned to the topic in hand.

"You said she was in a Radiology Department, John. At St Mary's?"

"Yes. It's just beside the Emergency Department at the back of the hospital. The departments are usually built side-by-side for handiness."

Liam cut in. "What kind of machine could have produced that EMPY thing? And how could it have been carried it into a hospital with nobody seeing? It must've been pretty small."

Craig's eyes widened. "Or there already. Does St Mary's Radiology Department have an MRI machine, John?"

"Three. They're standard equipment in all imaging suites." Realisation dawned. "And the room she was working in was right in the centre of one! Inside the imaging suite of the Radiology Department." The pathologist shook his head. "Damn, that's clever. Someone waited till she was alone and surrounded by giant magnets then threw out the pulse."

"Possibly three pulses at once, which could be why she died." Craig turned back to his deputy. "We'll need the schedule for the imaging suite's use during the time Maria O'Rourke was there, Liam. And a few hours either side to be sure."

"Can do, but..."

"Go on."

"Well, if someone was trying to mess with the MRIs

58

then there can't have been patients there at the time or they'd have been noticed."

John nodded in agreement.

"No patients might have meant no staff around either, which could explain why she wasn't found and resuscitated right away. There's a CT scanner in the suite as well, but it was early morning so it mightn't have been in use either."

Liam warmed to his theme.

"Maybe our man's clever or it was just sheer luck that no-one else was around, but clever would be my guess. He timed things down to the minute."

Craig smiled admiringly. Liam's concrete thinking always came up trumps.

"And another thing, you two Big Brains. How far do those EMPY things travel? How come no electrics were knocked out elsewhere in Radiology, if they weren't?"

John gave a sceptical snort. "Think bigger than Radiology. How come it didn't knock out the whole hospital? EMPs can travel quite a distance from what I've read about them."

Craig stood up again. "All questions that we'll need answers to if we're to find our killer. John, can you chase Des on the magnetism checks? And we'll need a definitive cause of death as soon as you can manage it. Right, Liam, we need to go."

The medic gave a wide grin.

"What's that for?"

"*You* just said killer, which means it's officially a murder."

"Of course it is. Our second in twelve hours."

****

St Mary's Hospital Radiology Department.

Some of the answers to their questions would have to wait until the analysts were around, but when the detectives reached the film reading-room where Maria

O'Rourke had spent her final hour it practically narrated the events that had taken place.

Liam had torn down the police tape at the RD's entrance dramatically, making a nearby CSI roll their eyes and Craig hurriedly knot it back together behind them to keep passing nosy parkers out, then they'd entered a vast maze of X-ray rooms and what looked suspiciously like operating theatres but they discovered later were used for diagnostics. Right in the centre of the department they found a set of heavy doors bearing the badge 'Imaging Suite' and pushed them back to reveal a doughnut of one CT Scanning and three MRI rooms, with a smaller film reading-room at their heart accessed through one of the larger MRIs.

The detectives entered the small, white room and gazed around them. The space was sparsely furnished with a workbench that ran around three walls, moulded plastic chairs dotted at intervals beneath it and banks of X-ray light-boxes above.

Craig had seen the contraptions before, although usually only single versions in E.D.s. Every time he'd broken a bone as a hyperactive child some exhausted looking junior doctor had thrust an X-ray of his battered limb against just such a box, one-handed like some medical gunslinger. After gazing as its light outlined his splintered skeletal part, five at the last count, they'd then sent him with his resigned parent, usually his father, his mother Mirella having remained at home to beseech the saints for a more placid child, to have plaster slapped on him for another few months.

The fractures had been painful at the time but they were fond memories of youthful dynamism now.

Liam guessed what his boss was thinking and decided to compare stripes.

"How many?"

"Five."

The DCI puffed up visibly. "Seven for me. Comes from growing up on a farm." He swept an arm around the room. "It looks like your theory was right, boss. We're smack in the middle of three MRIs and a CT scanner."

"Mmm…"

Craig walked across to the light-boxes and flicked each one on in turn. When no lights beamed out, he gave a small smile. But more evidence was needed that the room's electrics were kaput.

"Try the ceiling lights, Liam."

The DCI obliged and found the same.

"Right, so the electrics in this room are fried. Let's check the others."

Before they could, a tall woman in a white coat appeared from the connecting MRI room, the coat gripped so tightly around her it was as if she expected a tornado to appear and rip it off. It turned out her manner was tight as well.

She gestured sharply behind her at what Craig knew was the crime scene tape across the entrance.

"What's the meaning of that? I had to climb over it!"

As 'Police' was clearly written on the banner Liam was tempted to ask whether she could read, but thankfully his more polite boss got in first.

"This is a crime scene, Madam."

His good manners only served to infuriate her further.

"Do I *look* like a Madam? I'm Doctor Elise Montgomery, the Head of Radiology! And *you* are holding up our work."

Liam was gutted that she hadn't paused after her question. Her indignation had made it such an open goal.

On Craig's signal they both held up their warrant cards. If it was titles that the woman held dear then they had some of their own.

"I'm Detective Chief Superintendent Craig and this is Detective Chief Inspector Cullen. This whole department is a crime scene until further notice so I'm afraid you shouldn't be here, and you won't be readmitted until our evidence gathering is complete."

When a jump-suited Grace appeared a second later looking fit to be tied it became clear some junior CSI had slipped up and let the radiologist pass.

Madam Montgomery was *not* amused by Craig's words.

"You can't close down my department! And what do you mean crime? Doctor O'Rourke's death was sad but there was no-one else involved."

The detective struggled to keep his sigh small.

"We can't discuss an open investigation, Doctor Montgomery, but I can assure you that we'll do our best to be out of here in an hour." Three of Grace's fingers shooting up made him modify his promise hastily. "I mean three. Three hours and we'll be out of your hair. Now, I'm sorry, but you really must leave. Liam, could you show the doctor out, please."

The filthy look the DCI shot him was elaborated on when he returned.

"God, that's a one. She's asking the names of all the CSIs and Grace is telling them not to answer." His scowl changed quickly to a grin. "I bet your missus is just like that at work. Blasting everyone. Consultants are all the same."

The image of Katy blasting people, unlikely though it was, made Craig smile. He'd never even heard her raise her voice never mind shout at anyone, although if Luca turned out to be the teenager that *he'd* been she might well start.

He rubbed his hands together briskly to focus and scanned the small reading-room again. "OK, is there anything else in here that might help us? Before we move next door."

"Ach, you know there is, boss. Those."

He followed his deputy's pointing finger to some ceiling mounted security cameras and smiled. "Just testing."

"And I passed with flying colours."

"Nice of you to award your own score, but you're right. Hospital CCTV is wired in centrally, so get Davy to check the tapes for the whole suite, please. So... our killer may have had eyes on Maria O'Rourke as she worked, and possibly on the rest of the suite too. That means they could easily have picked a time when the place was empty to set off their EMP, or as you said it might just have been luck. Anyway, the electromagnetic pulse or pulses hit, the electrics in here blew, and Maria O'Rourke died."

Without warning Craig raced out the door, his deputy catching up in a few long strides.

"We need to check the E.D.'s electrics."

As they were about to leave the imaging suite they encountered Grace again, now no longer arguing with the consultant but fingerprinting a console that operated one of the MRIs.

"Grace, do you know if the electrics are working in the rest of Radiology?"

"No. The lights and equipment are out in the whole department. I checked when we arrived and called a hospital tech to confirm."

Which hadn't stopped Elise Montgomery blaming *them* for her department's inactivity.

"He also said that the MRIs were damaged."

"Do you know the extent? Is it just the electrics or are they completely fried?"

Her reply was a sniff and a glance towards the exit.

"That consultant went to get someone special to check them. But I'm not allowing them in until we've finished our work."

"Quite right. OK, if you're still here when they work out the damage can you let me know, please?"

He glanced at the MRI room's walls.

"Also, any idea what material those walls are made of? Could you check their properties, please, especially as regards providing a barrier for any magnetism generated by the machines."

A raised eyebrow said the CSI would want to know why at some point, but she nodded and returned to her work.

They exited the department into the hospital's main corridor but as Craig turned in the direction of the E.D. his deputy gave a noisy cough that stopped him in his tracks.

"You want to talk about things, don't you?"

Liam chuckled. "You make me sound like I'm in therapy! I want a minute's catch-up, that's all."

Craig leant against the nearest wall and folded his arms.

"Fire ahead."

"OK, so if the EMPY came from one or all of those MRI machines and fried the electrics and the girl, our perp obviously did it remotely-"

Craig raised a hand to cut him off.

"Not obviously, but likely. Until we view the tapes there's still a chance that he was actually *at* one of the MRI consoles."

The DCI continued in a sceptical tone. "OK, likely then. But you know I'm right. Anyway, if he *wasn't* here then Grace is doing a lot of fingerprinting for no gain."

"Until we're certain what we're dealing with, it still has to be done. You know that."

Liam's scepticism was joined by a shrug. "Fair enough. But I take it we're still assuming, *assuming* mind you, because we've no *proof* how the actress was even killed yet, that these two deaths were caused by the same man? And remotely? And our only reason for thinking that is because our Vics are the same age and sex?"

"Yes, basically. So far anyway." Craig propelled himself off the wall. "Any more questions?"

The DCI considered for a moment then walked off towards the E.D.

"I take it that's a no then."

His deputy's response was to turn right beneath a large sign that said, 'Emergency Department' where the immediate glare of neon lights told them that the EMP, if that had indeed been their murder weapon, hadn't reached this far with any strength.

Craig walked up to the reception desk and flashed his ID at a thin youth seated behind it.

"I'm DCS Craig. Odd question I know, but can you tell

me if you've had any problems with your electricity today?"

The young man's startled look said that the question had sounded just as strange as Craig had thought, but his follow-up shout of, "SECURITY!" was completely unexpected, as was the haste with which a burly uniformed guard hurtled towards them.

The detective raised his hands in peace and held up his warrant card again. "We're police. Here on a case."

The six-o'clock shadowed guard rounded on the youth immediately. "What the heck are you playing at, Darren? I nearly grabbed a cop!"

The receptionist's startled look was joined by a red flush. "He was asking me weird questions, Dad, and it's only my first day, and..."

The guard's weary sigh told Craig all he needed to know.

"Part-time job?"

"Aye, he's saving for Uni."

Liam was about to say something about universities letting in any old eejit nowadays, but Craig anticipated the quip and shot him a warning glance, listening as the man went on.

"I thought if I got him a wee job with me, he couldn't get into trouble, but..." the security man sighed again. "Sorry about that, Officer. Let me find someone who can help you."

With a glare at his offspring he disappeared into a side-room, reappearing a moment later with an elderly woman in a tweed dress.

"I'm Edna Ross, the chief receptionist. How may I assist you?"

Exhausted by the earlier exchange Craig left this one to his deputy and used the time to smile reassuringly at the youth.

The answers to their questions came thick and fast. No, there'd been no electrical problems or power outages that she knew of, and she could check with the clinical staff but no-one had *reported* issues with any medical machinery to her. Although she had noticed a little problem with her patient booking computer earlier that day.

"Can you remember what time?"

She gave a neat nod. "I can. Twenty-past-eight this morning. I made a note for the technical staff."

The exact time of Maria O'Rourke's death.

Craig's ears pricked up.

"Tell us exactly what happened, please."

The manager thought for a moment before saying,

"Well, my board went a little doolally, with lights flashing that shouldn't have been and what not, and my computer screen showed static for a moment. It's never done that before. But it was very brief so I didn't think much of it, although now you come to mention it one of the nurses said the same happened on her computer too."

That was all Craig needed to know so he wrapped things up.

"Thank you, Ms Ross. If there's anything more we'll be in touch."

As he led the way to the exit, Craig noticed the youthful receptionist was still being glared at by his dad and intervened, "Don't worry, he's doing a good job." He gestured at his deputy. "I mean, *I'd* have called security on him too."

He was halfway out of the department when Liam caught up.

"You just said I looked like a thug!"

"I was joking, and anyway, you've said worse about *me* in your time. Anyway, forget all that. They've just given us confirmation of what we thought."

"That the electrics were fine so the pulse didn't reach that far."

"Yes, but also that our killer must have accessed Radiology's systems via the hospital's computer network. That's why *their* booking computer had a glitch. But don't ask me for details because I've exhausted my tech knowledge. We really need to speak to Davy and Ash."

"We need a bloody briefing, *that's* what we need, boss. Two murders in and we haven't even met as a team."

Craig knew that he was right, but until the squad-room was secure there could be no briefings there. And if their killer was in the system that ruled out other police buildings as well.

Liam read his thoughts and carried them further. "And it can't be at anyone's house, because there'll be computers there too that this bugger could hack."

Suddenly it dawned on Craig where they *could* go and be safe.

"OK, call round everyone and tell them to get to my new place on Stranmillis Road now. Office staff too. If anyone moans tell them they'll enjoy the outing."

They mightn't enjoy sitting on packing cases quite as much.

Chapter Five

Crumlin, County Antrim.

'Beat that!'

Noel Robinson, aka STARLORD100, stared at his computer screen for a moment then typed, *'Easy. But it'll have to be tomorrow. I need to get to work.'*

The expected retort from ROCKET789 appeared in a flash.

'Downtrodden by The Man. You're a pathetic work slave.'

Biting his tongue and wishing he could punch his taunter through the ethernet, Robinson responded as calmly as he could. Walk quietly and carry a big stick was an approach that had always worked for his father, and something that the scars on his back never let him forget. He'd hated his old man for them but the approach had stuck; he would bide his time and wait for his revenge.

'The wages pay for my tech fix. I'll beat you tomorrow. You'll see.'

With that Robinson signed off, and linking his hands behind his neck for a moment he closed his eyes and planned what he would do to his adversary if they ever met. A large bloodied stick featured prominently in the fantasy and after playing out a battle where his competitor ended up dead his anger cooled.

He would never actually do it unfortunately, find and kill ROCKET789 in real life that was. He *could*, he was gifted enough in cyberspace to locate him, and he knew that he could kill and get away with it because he'd done it once before; when his father, still mouthy despite his seventy years but much frailer, had pushed him just. that. inch. too. far.

But he would never kill again, for a couple of reasons: things might get messy and he needed his real life nice and neat as cover for what he was really involved in; also, to his surprise, he hadn't actually enjoyed killing, much preferring to live vicariously through others' misdeeds.

Ruminations over, Noel Robinson shut down his central screen, leaving the rest of his computers idling and blinking as they continued their work while he was out. It was his private pleasure to keep watching the world; you never knew what you might see. Most people were careless and *unbelievably* trusting, never thinking of all the eyes out there in the darkness searching for the slightest weakness they could exploit.

Wondering what juicy morsel he would find on his return, he dragged himself away from his faithful companions and grabbed his jacket from the hook behind the door. It was time to visit so-called reality, although he spent less and less time there now; just enough to earn a crust and convince people that he was normal, whatever the hell *that* was. The world felt increasingly unreal to him now with its politics and wars and mess.

His preferred habitat was cyberspace: increasingly firmly in his grip as he grew in skill, easily muted and neat.

Until now. Now he was deep in something so messy that soon there would be no way to save himself but to disappear for good.

****

The Craigs' New House. The Stranmillis Road. 4 p.m.

It took a good twenty minutes for everyone to find dust-free surfaces to sit on and Liam to arrive with the food from Doorsteps, a Belfast eatery famed for such generous servings that once the squad members had clapped eyes on the selection of sandwiches Nicky had ordered not even Mary felt inclined to complain about where they were.

Craig gave everyone ten more minutes to eat, comment politely on the house's potential and how great it would look when it was finished, *if ever,* and listen to

Andy enthuse about having a painting party once the last rooms were plastered; then he started, referring everyone to their smart-pads.

"Right. Check again that everything's disconnected from Bluetooth and wi-fi and your phones are off, not just on silent. Davy's already explained what's happening to some people but he'll do so again now in case anyone missed out."

He used the moment of tech-speak that followed to finish his coffee, then signalled to speak again.

"OK, so we're here because there's a risk that the squad-room is being hacked. Davy, did you do the bug sweep?"

"Yep, and nothing, but I think that's because the hacker was already getting everything they needed through the computers' cameras and mikes."

Andy shook his gelled head smugly. "I never have my computer's microphone on in case I say something that I shouldn't."

Ash smirked. "Sorry, but it *was* on. They all were - I checked. But that tells us our hacker must've switched them on deliberately. Remotely because there were no signs of anyone on the last month's office CCTV. Trust me, I waded through it all..."

He shuddered to indicate the horror of such banal work and went on, "Ditto all your computer cameras. The only people not being watched that way were Mary and us, because *we'd* all had the sense to stick a plaster over our lens."

As the analyst scanned the group disapprovingly with what he liked to call his 'laser stare' Liam blanched so suddenly that everyone immediately knew he'd done something in front of his computer's camera that he shouldn't have, and the thought of what it might have been earned him disgusted tuts from the PAs.

Craig rolled his eyes and moved things along.

"Don't be surprised at anything that happens tech-wise on this case. But that plaster trick sounds worth copying. Davy, can you disable all the mikes and cameras for a week?"

"I can, but it'll be a waste of time if we stay on the Net, chief, because they'll just hack back in and reactivate them. I'm setting up a local area network so we can communicate safely."

Mary cut in. "Encrypt it too, and we'll need a bespoke vault as well, to keep the case files away from prying eyes. I've built one before so I can help." To save herself the inevitable questions she added, "A vault's basically like the Cloud, but I'll make a private one just for us."

Craig nodded. "Whatever you think is needed. Ash, did you find anything amiss with the router?"

The analyst shook his shiny black hair. "Nope. They definitely got in through one of our computers, chief, but as long as everyone stays off wi-fi and Bluetooth we should be good."

Liam nodded wisely, eager to look as if he understood all the intricacies.

"At home too. They could be watching you through your TVs."

Annette gawped at him. "*No way*. Is that true, Ash?"

"It is with some televisions, so good catch, Liam. We're pretty much going analogue for a week because if this hacker has anything to do with our new murders, they'll keep trying to break into our system to see if we're on their trail."

Craig nodded in agreement. "Let's assume that's their interest unless we hear someone's appealing an old case. It fits with what we know. Have the squad-room swept every morning from now on, Davy, and I'm sorry but if anyone needs to do internet searches they'll have to go to headquarters. Or if you're nice to Marcie she might do them for you at the lab. She knew Julianne Hodges so she wants her murder solved."

He rubbed his hands together to signal they were moving from the invisible to the real world.

"Right. Reports. Liam, bring everyone up to date on the Nicotine, please."

It took longer than expected between the incredulous

questions from people who hadn't heard the theory to Liam stumbling repeatedly over Cotinine, which became 'continence' far too often for it to have been accidental every time.

By the time his deputy had finished Craig had decided not to take questions on the science but to ask Des to attend a future briefing to take that particular flak, so he moved on with what even he thought was indecent haste.

"Right, thanks, Liam. Aidan, you were at the Adelphi."

The lanky DCI moved himself from his reclining position between two packing crates, one placed against a wall whose plaster was a distant memory, and the other several feet away supporting his skinny legs. It was prime real estate in a room full of painting tables and booby traps, like roller trays and a precariously perched sanding machine that looked like it might run amok at any moment and turn the session into a horror movie, and Aidan was reluctant to relinquish it by rising to speak.

Craig's narrowing gaze said that he'd better; recumbent wasn't a presenting pose.

With a, 'No-one touches my crates' glare, the Belfast born and bred DCI clambered to his feet and kept his report brief.

"Thanks to the help from everyone here, all statements were re-taken, all DNA swabs were sent, and all props and surfaces were dusted and CSI-ed. The Vic's costume and any props that only she handled are at the lab so there should be something back on those ASAP. The end."

With that he lined up his crates again and resumed his earlier Cleopatra pose.

Craig raised an eyebrow at the performance but said nothing, turning back to his analysts instead.

"The Adelphi's CCTV?"

Lost without a large screen to project his photos and diagrams on to Davy held his seat.

"OK, so there are three moving cameras plus a static one inside each of the two auditoriums. The moving ones overlap, each sweeping through one-eighty degrees-"

He was interrupted by a loud tut from Liam that made Craig sigh.

"*What?*"

"Well, I mean, for God's sake, boss."

"For God's sake what?"

"Theatres watching the people who are watching their plays! What's that about?"

It hadn't occurred to Craig before, but actually he was right.

"That's a good point. Why *would* a theatre have so many internal cameras? I mean people are hardly going to steal the seats."

Ryan shrugged. "To catch them eating perhaps?"

Annette shook her head. "The Adelphi sells sweets in the foyer, so they must know people might have a little munch while they're watching a play."

It wasn't the etiquette for attending events that had been drummed into Craig by his professional pianist mother, but things had clearly changed. Whether it was for the better or not wasn't a debate for right now.

Ash roused himself from his smart-pad to enlighten them.

"They aren't checking to see if someone's eating, they're looking for people filming performances. Theatres are always on the look-out for that nowadays. People flog videos of plays or post them online. Same with comedy shows and gigs. And if audiences could watch everything at home without paying then theatres would go bust."

Craig nodded.

"That makes sense. OK, so now we know why the cameras are there what did you find, Davy?"

"I'm still looking."

"Tell me the Adelphi kept the tapes."

"They're digital cameras but yes, I've got the files from last night's show and I've watched the scene where Julianne Hodges died from all angles, but all it shows is her s...sitting at the table having a drink served to her by the waiter. Then he went and stood near the back of the stage and after that the other character entered."

"The lady's maid who screamed later. When exactly did she enter?"

"About a minute after the drink was poured."

"So...as if she'd been putting their coats in the cloakroom or something. And Des said the drink was tested."

Aidan nodded. "Yep, and it was clear, Guv. I don't actually think she drank much anyway."

"OK. What happened next, Davy?"

"Julianne Hodges collapsed, the maid and waiter screamed and the stage manager ran on. Then there's the whole bit where Ken ran down to the stage and started organising everyone."

Liam nodded approvingly. "Good man. Civvies like to be organised."

Craig chuckled. "I'll tell your wife you said that. Aidan, were there any differences between Ken's statements and yours?"

"Nope, just details that needed tightened."

"OK. Liam, I'd still like you to see Ken and walk him through things again. He might remember something new."

"I'll sort it after this."

"Good. So, there can't be much left for you to check on the footage, Davy."

It earned him a pitying glance.

"Signals, chief. We need to check if someone piggybacked on the camera's digital stream from outside the theatre. To watch."

Andy nodded knowingly. "Voyeurism. We've seen it before. Weirdoes who like watching police investigations up close."

Craig shook his head. "More likely our killer watching their victim die."

"But if they were close-by why not just sit in the audience, chief?"

"I think *someone* was close, but whether it was our

killer or a helper only time will tell. Also, watching is only for that moment, Andy, whereas filming the event means you can watch it again and again."

Liam shook his head. "I think the boy means the CCTV was an *integral* part of the crime."

The 'boy' smiled.

"That's my hunch, but I don't know *what* part yet. Someone might have piggybacked on the CCTV to film it but, importantly, *also* to watch her death as it played out, and I think that bit has some specific significance. But it'll take me time to work out what, chief, and w...we've been a bit busy trying to find out if the office was being hacked."

Craig conceded with a nod. "Fair enough. As soon as you can though. Anything else?"

"Only that there was nothing on the static camera at the back of the theatre that they use for official photography, or on any of the Adelphi's computers. If we do pick up an external signal, I'd say it'll show a targeted attack on the CCTV. Someone wanted a ringside seat to Mrs Hodges' death."

Annette said, "Ghoul," and shuddered, then she gazed curiously at her boss. "But *why* was she killed, sir?"

"To be confirmed. You met her husband, so tell everyone your impressions."

"Morgan Hodges, a twenty-eight-year-old solicitor at a big firm in Belfast. They'd known each other since school, been married for four years and had a two-year-old son. He seemed distraught about his wife's death-"

Liam cut in. "And you believed him?"

"I did."

He snorted sceptically and nodded her on.

"He said Julianne hadn't any enemies that he knew of and he couldn't think of any reason why she'd been killed. From the cosy house and the photos dotted around they just seemed like your average nice young couple. Not well off but happy. I haven't got their background info yet because of the computer issues, but hopefully tomorr-."

Craig cut in. "When he said he couldn't think why someone might have killed his wife, did you dig further?"

He already knew that the answer would be no. Asking someone newly bereaved to think of reasons why their partner had been murdered was rarely a fruitful pursuit, especially if, as it sounded on this occasion, they'd been genuinely loved.

"Not today, sir."

He ignored the chastisement in her tone.

"I'll call him tomorrow after he's had a chance to sort through things. He said his in-laws might take the boy while he arranges the funeral."

"Tomorrow then, but don't leave it any longer than that, please, Annette."

He understood the sentiment that had made her reluctant to force the issue, but they'd had two murders in quick succession so any clues as to why their victims had been selected *had* to be urgently explored.

"No-one gets killed in such an elaborate way unless there was something about them that made the killer want to."

The rationalisation had sounded better inside his head, something he realised when she gawped at him.

"You're saying she was to blame for her own death?!"

Liam responded before his boss could, in a dry tone.

"Now, did he *mention* blame, lassie? It could've just been that our perp didn't like her acting, or her eye colour, or the fact she had a happy life. You *know* that unless it's a random attack people always get killed because of something that someone wanted from them or didn't like about them, and who knows *what* warps these bastards? Thirty years on the job and I still can't work out what turns someone bad."

She glanced at Craig sheepishly. "Sorry, sir. It was just..."

"Hard to see a child so upset. I understand."

He actually *did* understand since Luca had been born. Before that he'd never *liked* seeing a child cry and would have tried not to cause it, but he'd viewed it as something

76

that all kids just did. Now their screams scythed through him like a physical pain, and he could only guess at how a mother might feel.

"OK, speak to Mister Hodges again tomorrow, Annette. The only other personal information we have on his wife is what Marcie told us. She knew her through the local acting scene. Liam, report on that, please. I need more coffee."

He'd spotted a spare one in the carryout tray, and Katy had had the foresight to bring a kettle down to the house at the weekend so thankfully he could heat it up.

When he returned to the group, he found Liam entertaining everyone with an impression of Marcie flitting across a stage and was almost loath to interrupt him.

But he did.

"Right. So, Julianne Hodges was our *first* murder victim."

The emphasis surprised everyone except his deputy and PA.

"But we were called back to the lab to discuss another young woman brought in today. A Doctor Maria O'Rourke. Liam?"

"Aye well, the main reason was her age. Yet another twenty-seven-year-old female sudden death, so she had to have a PM."

Craig joined in.

"Maria O'Rourke was a junior doctor just starting to train as a radiologist at St Mary's Trust, and when she died she was alone at the Radiology Department in what's called a reading-room."

Annette nodded. "That's where they look at X-ray films and write reports on them."

"Exactly. We checked it and it's a small room with light-boxes all around the walls, a bench that runs beneath them and a few chairs. Only one door because access is through an MRI room."

Liam nodded. "And it sits right in the middle of three MRIs and a CT scanner."

"Where in St Mary's is the department, sir?"

"Ground floor at the back, beside the E.D."

The ex-nurse nodded. "They routinely site radiology there, because emergency patients need so many tests done."

"Handy." He saw Andy's finger raised. "Question, Andy?"

"So, the only reason Doctor Winter wanted to discuss this girl with you was her age, chief?"

"And gender. It's a rare occurrence for two people of identical age and gender to die so close together, especially in entirely separate incidents. But Ms O'Rourke's cause of death had something to do with it as well. Essentially, John couldn't find one." He corrected himself. "Well, he could, but it was more because of what wasn't there than what was."

The response was a series of puzzled looks.

Liam grimaced. "Even I'm confused by that and I was there."

"See if you can do better then."

"I will. OK, the O'Rourke girl had a pacemaker."

Aidan roused himself from his apparent slumber. "She was young to have one of those."

"Some heart defect she was born with. Anyway, she had one and it's fried and the Doc can't find anything else that might have killed her, so he thinks it might be something to do with that-"

Ryan interrupted, curious. "Electrocution?"

"No, it definitely wasn't that. The Doc said there'd have been other signs."

The analysts glanced at each other and said in unison. "A programme on the pacemaker was hacked?"

Craig decided to re-join the conversation.

"We're pretty sure not, but I'd still like you to rule it out. John said that the pacemaker stopped working suddenly and her heart with it, although it shouldn't have necessarily. Her heart was weak but it might have coped long enough for the pacemaker to have been replaced. It-"

78

Suddenly he stopped, turning to his deputy.

"The killer *knew* her heart was weak! He knew *her*."

Liam added a flourish. "And he was *banking* on the pacemaker failing. Damn. But it was still playing the odds, boss."

"A gambler? Interesting thought, but let's wait to see what John finds before we go down that track."

Liam brightened up slightly as he realised what else it meant. Craig was already there.

"If he knew Maria O'Rourke then her contacts could help narrow our suspect pool, especially if we find crossovers with Julianne Hodges' contacts too."

He parked the matter to pick up later and returned to his original point.

"John also said that the ECG printout around her time of death showed no abnormalities right up to the moment her heart stopped-"

Ash cut in.

"Where did he get hold of it?"

"The pacemaker's manufacturers. They do constant monitoring on their devices. Anyway, it showed nothing abnormal until the moment of death when it simply stopped."

Andy was frowning in thought. "But in anyone else with a pacemaker, even if it *had* failed, their heart might just have returned to their original pre-pacemaker rhythm and they'd have stayed alive?"

"I imagine so."

Andy's frown persisted. "Excuse the word, but her ECG was absolutely *dead*?"

"Yes. A straight line. John said it was called asystole. What's your point, Andy?"

"So, whatever stopped the *pacemaker* killed *her*?"

Craig was getting exasperated; they'd already been over this.

"Yes. She died without her functioning pacemaker, most likely because her heart was too weak to pick up the work."

Aidan cut across the exchange.

"I think what he's saying is, couldn't the two things have happened in parallel rather than in sequence, Guv? Yes, whatever stopped her pacer stopped her heart at the same time but it did each thing *separately*. I mean, otherwise you'd have thought her heart would have at least given a few beats after the pacer stopped working, wouldn't you? Yet the ECG showed no activity at all."

He turned to Annette, their resident source of medical advice. "Shouldn't it have shown even a blip or two?"

She nodded. "I worked on a cardiac unit for a while, and it's very unusual for there to be absolutely *nothing* on an ECG if a pacemaker stops working, sir. Even if the heart has failed it would at least *try* to beat and that should show up either as an arrythmia, or if the heart is really damaged some form of erratic electrical activity, a bit like static on a malfunctioning TV. It would only be when *that* stopped that you'd get straight line asystole."

As Andy nodded furiously and said, "That's what I meant. Something might've wrecked the pacemaker and heart separately but at the same time," Liam rushed to put the kibosh on the theory.

"Except that the Doc said her condition was very serious, so serious she would have died young if she hadn't had the pacemaker in."

Craig was pleased that he'd been listening so attentively but he was growing less sure that Andy was wrong.

"But John also said the heart didn't look bad, Liam, and it seemed to puzzle him."

The end result of the discussion was that an EMP had both killed the girl *and* fried her pacemaker, but more than that they couldn't say yet, so it was time to move on.

"Andy, tell John your thoughts and see what he makes of them. Also, speak to the pacemaker's manufacturer and whoever at St Mary's did Ms O'Rourke's regular check-ups and run the idea past them. Liam has their details."

The DCI asked one last question. "What was the Doc's conclusion on cause of death?"

"To be decided."

Annette sat forward on her low and rather uncomfortable box seat, which in a previous life had held an electric drill.

"So why is this a murder then, sir? No definitive cause of death and she was alone when she died, unless you think someone entered and deliberately damaged her pacemaker? Have you checked the CCTV?"

"When Liam and I visited the scene..."

Out of the corner of his eye he saw Davy smiling, saying that he was already two steps ahead.

"...we discovered that all the electrics were out in the Radiology Department, although fine in the E.D. next door, but the E.D. *did* report a slight disturbance with their computers at the exact moment of Maria O'Rourke's death. Davy, can you check whether Radiology's electrics just malfunctioned or whether there's permanent damage to any equipment, and-"

Suddenly Ash gasped, *"No way!"* and turned to his counterpart, who was now grinning like a child with a new toy. "It can't be. I mean I've seen them in the movies, but I've never heard of a real one outside a nuclear explosion!"

Davy sat forward eagerly. "Yes, but think about it. You've the perfect s...source, the MRI rooms would've been shielded so nowhere outside the Radiology Department would've been affected, and the sheer amount of energy would have killed her pacemaker stone dead."

Seeing the rest of his team was confused Craig interrupted.

"I wasn't going to discuss this yet but what this pair are getting excited about is something called an electromagnetic pulse, or an EMP Davy, outline what that is, please."

"It's a short burst of electromagnetic energy, either natural or man-made, that can create a radiated, electric, or magnetic field or a conducted electric current, depending on the source."

"Could an MRI machine generate such a wave?"

"No question. But one thing puzzles me, chief. MRIs have safety cut-off mechanisms to stop this kind of thing happening. It should have shut itself down before it ever reached that stage."

"I imagine someone who could make one work remotely could easily bypass its safety protocols."

"Maybe, but I'll need to check. W…Was there just one machine?"

Liam rolled his eyes. "Wake up, son. He said there were three MRIs and a CT scanner surrounding the room the girl was in."

The analyst ignored the jibe and considered for a moment before speaking again.

"Then they mightn't have needed to bypass the safeties at all, chief, just arrange to run all three MRIs on top whack at once. The electromagnetic fields generated might have been enough. But we'll need to check."

Craig nodded. "OK. Go to the hospital and take a look at them, and the reading-room CCTV too. I'm hoping it's centrally wired so still working. Check the E.D. computers while you're there as well. And research the effect of magnetism on the human body. I need to know if it only kills people with electrical implants and all of its possible effects on the girl's heart."

"Heartblock?"

Craig glanced at the team's medic, but Annette's mouth was firmly shut.

"Who said that?"

Ryan raised a finger. "Heartblock, chief."

"What's that?"

"The heart has its own internal electric conducting system composed of nodes and branches running through the heart. They carry electrical signals outwards to make every part of the heart beats in unison, otherwise it could just be a wobbly mess. If the system isn't working you can get what's called heartblock. There are different sorts. Maybe as well as the EMP ruining her external pacemaker it killed her *internal* one stone dead too."

"That could fit with Andy's theory. How do you know all this?"

"I started medical school but dropped out after second year and joined up instead. I hated all the studying but I do remember that bit. There might be nothing to see on dissection so Doctor Winter may need to run some other tests."

Craig nodded admiringly. This was why he loved having a team. Anything he didn't know himself, and there was plenty, one of the others almost certainly would.

Andy interjected. "I think *you* should discuss both our theories with the Doc, Ryan, and let me know what he says."

"Good, that's settled. OK, you all know what you have to do so let's move on."

Craig was confident they would have the definitive cause of Maria O'Rourke's death very soon.

"OK, other reasons why we're linking these two women is that both their deaths were unexpected, sudden, and there's the potential that technology was involved, either actively in the killings, passively in watching them, or both. But we also need to examine any differences between our victims and not miss something basic. One victim was married, one single; one was a mother and the other wasn't; one was most likely poisoned, the other died from damage to her heart; one was an actor and the other a doctor."

Ryan made a face. "More differences than similarities, chief."

Craig couldn't disagree, but, "And yet my gut says they're linked, Ryan, and linked by us as well. In the same short time that these two women were murdered our office suffered an attempted hacking. That makes this personal."

Annette was still on the similarities between their cases. "Could the remoteness of the killer be a link too? Both murders perpetrated remotely and viewed remotely as well."

Aidan was less convinced. "But the methods are so different. One chemical and one techy. Is that *really* likely to be the same man?"

Craig shrugged. "This is only day one, so I'm not ruling anything out yet. Your remote point is interesting, Annette. We're generating a lot of leads, so now we need to follow them up."

He glanced at his traditional, leather-strapped watch to check the time and drew pitying looks from the analysts.

"How come you still wear a watch, chief? At least get yourself a tech one."

"I have quite enough technology around me thanks, and besides, blue screens radiate EMF and my brain's already fried with you lot. OK. Next steps. Davy, go back to the office and set up whatever's necessary for everyone to come in tomorrow morning and work securely. Andy, Ash and Annette, get down to the hospital and check out everything we've just discussed. Aidan and Mary, go and see Maria O' Rourke's family and get whatever you can from them. We need to find any crossovers between our victims that exist."

He motioned to his deputy. "We're heading back to the lab. I've a few more questions. Ryan, come with us and you can discuss Heartblock with John to your heart's content."

When everyone but the two secretaries immediately rushed for the door, Craig summoned them all back.

"Oh no, you don't. You're not leaving this place a mess and getting me blamed for it-"

A snort from Aidan said it hadn't exactly been the Ritz when they'd arrived.

Craig ignored him and went on.

"- *or* dumping Nicky and Alice with the tidy-up as if they were your mums. There are binbags in the kitchen and a plastic bin outside where everything goes. Slam the door behind you as you leave." He bowed to the secretaries. "Ladies, you just sit there and supervise the work."

Smirking all the way to the car, Liam's, "You'll be hell when you've got teenagers" echoed just what Craig had been thinking himself.

****

The Labs. The Third Floor Forensic Offices.

An hour later they were gathered in Des Marsham's domain again and hearing from Grace that the inner workings of the Trust's three extremely expensive MRI machines were now nothing but melted metal. Her impersonation of Elise Montgomery when she'd seen the first one was a sight to behold, contorting her face like a bulldog chewing a wasp and barking out the words, "Someone. Will. Pay. For. This." in a stentorian tone that would have roused Rip Van Winkle from his sleep.

"You've found your new party piece, Grace. OK, so that tells us we were right on the magnetism-"

She interrupted quickly. "We measured the residual field in the department and it still was high hours after the event."

Des nodded. "And there's still one around Maria O'Rourke's body."

Craig leant forward and rested his chin in his hand.

"Interesting. So was Davy correct, Grace? He said the MRIs' safeties wouldn't need to be overridden if they'd used all three machines at once."

"The safeties *were* off, so your perpetrator may not have needed to override them, but they did all the same."

"They weren't taking any chances. OK, Ash will work out how they managed it. What were the MRI rooms' walls made of?"

"There were three layers but the important one is what's called the radio-frequency or RF shield, essentially a Faraday Cage. It's designed to block electromagnetic radiation getting in or out of MRI rooms, and lots of different metals can be used. This one was copper. The walls of each MRI room were single-shielded and then the whole Radiology Department was double-shielded, which explains how even though it didn't stop the EMP killing the woman and blowing the department's electrics it *did* manage to block it from the rest of the hospital, including the Emergency Department next door."

John glanced up from his coffee. "Just as well or the ED's equipment would've been fried as well."

Des nodded. "But how exactly did the EMP kill her? I haven't had time to research them yet."

"Ash is planning some, so chat to him and save yourself some work." Craig turned back to his best friend. "Did Ryan tell you about his and Andy's theory, John? And where's he gone by the way?"

"Back to your office. I did invite him up for some of Grace's coffee but he said he had too much work to do to hang around."

Liam pulled a 'That's us told off' face but Craig just laughed.

"Did your discussion bear fruit?"

"Damage caused directly to her heart by the magnetic field *might* have caused the asystole, or it's just possible that if the pacemaker was magnetised suddenly, because it connected directly with her heart, *it* could have caused what he described."

"So, the pacemaker died and she died, at the same time and from the same cause but not necessarily from a direct link. It's a technical difference that makes no difference to our case. And this could have happened without leaving physical signs on her heart, John?"

"To the naked eye, absolutely. Then..."

"Goodnight Vienna?"

"Elegantly put, Liam. It was clever of Ryan to think of heartblock."

Craig nodded. "He did medicine for two years but didn't enjoy the studying, so he joined us."

The pathologist's eyes widened in interest. "Did he now? I must chat to him about that."

"Just don't try to persuade him back. He's a good

86

officer."

He wasn't joking; there was such a shortage of doctors in Northern Ireland he wouldn't put it past John to poach one of his.

He changed the subject by turning to Des. "Anything more on how the Nicotine got into Julianne Hodges' body?"

The forensic lead stroked his beard slowly as he prepared to answer, irritating Liam so much that he gave him a shove.

"What did you do that for?"

"That stroking's downright disturbing. Get yourself a pet if you need to, but stop it while I'm around. Anyway, go on, Grizzly Adams, answer the man's question."

With a reproving squint, Des did.

"Most likely the dress. Everything else she wore or handled was clean, and nobody else at the theatre got sick. I've a sample of the fabric cooking now." He glanced at the clock. "Actually, it should be ready."

Without prompting, Grace rose and beetled off down the lab. She reappeared a minute later nodding.

"Strongly positive for Nicotine. The material must have been soaked in it."

"Excellent. Let's run the whole dress overnight. That should give us levels by the morning."

The confirmation set Craig's brain buzzing. How had the Nicotine got into the fabric, and why hadn't anyone else who'd handled it got sick?

John answered the second question before either hit the air.

"Theatre dressers wear gloves to avoid snagging delicate costumes. I saw it in a documentary. What was the dress made of, Grace?"

"Silk gauze. Very fine."

"There you go then. It would have been kept covered to protect it until just before the performance and whoever the dresser was would have worn gloves. The question is how did the Nicotine get into the fabric in the first place? Who washes the costumes?"

Craig had the answer. "They're dry-cleaned after a set number of performances. I remember Camille telling me. Only small items like gloves are ever washed." He shook his head as the cleverness of their murderer became clear to him. "The killer must have interfered with the dry-cleaning process. Ingenious."

He turned to his deputy. "Liam, call the Adelphi now and tell the dresser we'll need to interview them, and ask when that particular dress was last dry-cleaned and where. We'll need to check the shop for Nicotine to ensure no-one else gets sick."

"And arrest whoever runs it, boss." As Liam said the words his forehead wrinkled in doubt. "But would our perp really use a *public* dry-cleaners?" Before Craig could reply the deputy had turned back to John. "Can you find out if there've been other reports of Nicotine poisoning, Doc?"

"I can. While you call the theatre, I'll call the poisons bureau. Back in five."

He was true to his word and Liam re-joined them soon after.

"You first, John."

"No reports of anyone turning up at any UK or Irish hospital with even slight Nicotine poisoning in the past six months."

"Liam?"

"The dress was dry-cleaned at the end of last week and Sunday was the play's first night. Some sort of preview performance for punters but also critics and press. The laundry they used is on the Ormeau Road so we'll pass it on the way back to the office, boss. We could nip in."

Craig rose to his feet. "Let's do that now then. Des, let Davy know what percentage of the dress was contaminated as soon as you have it, please. We'll keep you informed on everything else. Let's just hope there are no more dead twenty-seven-year-olds this week."

As soon as he said it, he knew there would be. Kills in such quick succession meant they didn't just have a serial killer on their hands but one who was on a spree, and spree killers wanted every possible thrill that they could get in the shortest time. The complex murder methods and their squad-room hacking said their killer's thrill seeking probably extended to enjoying seeing *them* confused. It felt like some addictive computer game and no-one stopped playing one of those after only a day.

The problem was, which *type* of spree killer were they dealing with? The sort who would keep racking up the kills until they stopped them, or someone who was focused only on a specific victim type and would stop when that pool was exhausted? Two twenty-seven-year-old women suggested the latter, but their perp couldn't possibly kill everyone in the region who fitted that bill so was there another factor in their choice of victim beyond their age? If there was, uncovering it could help identify the next victim and save their life.

A timely, "Earth to Craig" from his deputy made the detective return to the here and now. His speculations would have to wait; right now they had a laundry to inspect.

Explaining why exactly the inspection was necessary to John Rogan, the owner of Bright Day Dry Cleaners, proved a challenge, but thankfully the bemused elderly man didn't add to their woes by requesting a warrant for the search, and even obligingly checked his records for which machine had been used to clean Julianne Hodges' silk dress the week before.

As expected, there was nothing to see on the equipment, so all they could do was shut the place and call Grace down with her Nicotine tests.

While Craig did that his deputy asked the basics.

"How's the machine operated? Do you push a button or something?"

Rogan pointed to a computer console that neither detective had expected to see in such a small mom and pop business.

"We input the length of time and the type of dry-cleaning fluid required, depending on the fabric and whether there are any stubborn marks on the item, then the computer selects a canister of fluid and does the rest."

Including spraying Nicotine all over a dress.

"Was anything else cleaned in the same batch?"

"Yes. I always keep a list, just in case." The business owner sighed wearily. "People sue over the tiniest things nowadays."

Craig ended his call and joined the conversation.

"We'll need that list, please."

Nicky wouldn't thank him for the calls she would have to make to the other items' owners, but if it stopped another death.

When the list appeared, Liam asked another question. "How many of the pieces still have to be picked-up?"

"Most of them I expect. We state seven days before cleaning can be collected unless it's our twenty-four-hour service, just to give ourselves leeway. I'll check which items are still here."

Craig jumped in hastily. "Don't open their plastic covers, it mightn't be safe. Our forensic team will need to test them first."

Five minutes later Nicky's contact list had shrunk to two names, and Craig decided to just phone them then and there, relieved when he discovered that both their garments remained untouched. After negotiating the items immediate return citing a chemical fault the detectives left, Rogan calling to confirm the items' receipt just as they entered Pilot Street.

Craig motioned his deputy to park in front of the CCU.

"That's the damage limited, Liam, but there's one thing that we haven't really addressed."

The DCI nodded. "Aye, motive. Why *these* two women, and why now?"

"Exactly. I'm hoping the interviews and history will throw some light on that, but if there's nothing there-"

"If there's nothing there we could be stuffed unless he kills again. It depends how well our perp's covered his cyber ass."

The words made Craig chuckle.

90

"Say that to Davy and Ash tomorrow. It might give them a laugh. Right, I'm going upstairs to see how far they've got, but you go on home. We'll start afresh at eight-thirty."

Liam glanced at his watch. "*Five-forty!* I haven't been home this early in years. Danni will think I'm feeling guilty about something, or else she'll start expecting it every day and then I'll get an earful when I don't."

The upshot was *both* of them heading for the tenth floor.

Chapter Six

Tuesday. 7 a.m.

It had been a long night-shift but Noel Robinson had smiled right through it. Smiled at his obnoxious colleagues, smiled at the lady in the staff canteen who always short-served him compared to the better looking men on either side, smiled at the people who'd walked up to his desk to complain, ostensibly about the behaviour of a stranger but in reality about life in general with that person merely becoming the focus of their thwarted ambitions, disappointment, or general disgruntlement about the endless drudgery of existence.

He'd smiled at all of them for years, building up the reputation of being 'Smiler Robinson' that had started on his first day on the job. A chuckle cracked his slightly lopsided face, not hideous but with its acne-pocked irregularity one that only a parent could love, if his could have been bothered. Its unattractiveness had spelt death to any kind of social life or romance, although it softened slightly when he smiled, so he always had, a lot.

Back then he'd smiled out of genuine enthusiasm and schoolboy innocence and later from an optimistic belief that people couldn't *really* be as bad as they seemed. Except that they were, all of them, clients *and* colleagues: dishonest, unfaithful, petty, drunken and violent; the animal kingdom's finest masquerading as mankind.

Since then he'd smiled to retain his sanity, rarely listening to what was said to him and instead just singing a song inside his head. Any song would do, this week it was an old Elvis number, just as long as it had enough melody and beat to drown out the other voices that he heard. And not just from the people *actually* speaking to him nowadays, no, *they'd* been joined a few years back by another voice inside his head.

He'd ignored it at first, its moaning, angry, sometimes cruel words far less pleasant than his music, but now it grew louder by the day. Discontent, furious, pointing out

92

all the ways that his life wasn't what it should be, and all because of humanity and their perceptions of how he deserved to be ranked.

Rarely the one who got promotions no matter how hard he worked, never the one who'd got picked for teams since school, and *never ever* the one who got the girl even though he tried so bloody hard to be nice to them; flowers, dinners, gifts, none of it seemed to work.

He'd watched how other, handsomer men were dismissive, rude, and even subjected women to physical abuse, yet still they returned to them, almost begging to be hurt.

It had taught him the way of the world and now the cyber-world as well, and brought him to the precipice he'd first stood on and then stepped over. Now there was no way but down.

****

The CCU. Tuesday, 8.30 a.m.

"How's it going, Davy?"

Craig had half-mouthed the greeting, hoping their stalker's ability to manipulate computer microphones didn't extend to rendering them hypersensitive to sound.

In return he got a thumbs-up from his head analyst and a glance at the pirate to his left, who after typing for a few more seconds flashed a white grin.

"All sorted, chief."

Craig looked sceptical. He didn't believe in miracles, or at least not ones that happened so fast.

"LAN *and* vault?"

"Yep. Everything's set up."

As belt and braces Davy turned to the woman whose idea the vault had been and after scrolling through different screens for a moment Mary nodded, sending her bell of green-tipped black hair into a swing.

"All secure."

Craig, always more comfortable with things that were

visible, remained unconvinced.

"Which means, Davy?"

"That as long as everyone stays off the internet w...we can work here securely. Also, this floor is secure for audio and visual. I'll do a sweep for bugs twice a day anyway, but as long as no-one sends anything outside or opens emails, even internal police ones, we can't be hijacked again. I've just sent a message to everyone saying that."

"Smart-pads and phones too?"

The analyst nodded.

"Texts, calls, instant messages and emails are all safe as long as people limit them to the closed group I've set up to cover us and the labs. I'm hoping we can trace the hack to its source soon, but really it'll only be safe to surf the Net once you've caught our perp, chief."

Heaving a sigh of relief Craig perched on the nearest desk.

"No more packing cases. Excellent. Right, tell me what you know so far."

"We think the hacker got into our system using a Trojan horse virus, that's malware that misleads users as to its true intent. It probably got it through an email attachment or link somebody clicked on. My guess is it was disguised to look relevant to work so I'll start searching there."

"When did they send it?"

The computer experts shrugged in unison, and Ash expanded what it meant.

"Maybe a few days ago, or it could've been in our system for a while lying low and they just decided to activate it a few days back. But we've got some clues to chase on that. The whole police system is given an in-depth virus scan fortnightly, and I set up another one to run just on *our* computers every Thursday overnight."

Nicky called across from her desk. "Why Thursdays?"

It brought another shrug.

"Because Thursday's the new Friday? Anyway, I set it to run overnight because it slows the computers down a bit, and when I checked on Friday morning it was clear."

94

"Would it definitely have detected this Trojan?"

The question earned Craig a derisive, "DOH! Even my quickest scans detect everything active, chief. If an active virus had been here last Thursday it would have been quarantined and I'd have seen it on Friday when I got in."

Craig nodded. "So that tells us we were hacked sometime after that."

To his surprise the analyst didn't say, "Yes".

"Umm... there's a chance an *inactive* virus could've been here for longer, although the police fortnightly sweep would've picked that up. It's pretty tight."

Craig's eyebrows almost hit his hair.

"We could've had a virus in our computers for a fortnight?"

"Chill, chief, it couldn't have done anything to our computers until it was activated, and it definitely wasn't before Friday morning. Look, the good news is I'm running another scan now so we should be able to actually see our Trojan soon."

Craig came off the boil.

"OK. And then?"

"And then we," he indicated Davy, "start looking for clues where it came from."

Mary was voice of doom. "Which we may never find. Computer viruses can do lots of different things. Erase data, twist it, encrypt it, freeze a system to hold the user hostage until they pay up, which for somewhere like a bank could cost millions. Many of the more advanced ones have built-in destruct mechanisms which means they'll erase themselves and their data trails if we try to examine them, so we'll really have to be careful or we could lose clues."

Craig looked at his head analyst.

"Can we stop that happening?"

Davy chewed his lower lip thoughtfully for a moment before answering.

"It depends on the virus. We may have to bring in a geek."

Craig tried not to smile. "A bigger one than you pair?"

The analyst didn't take offence, instead staring wistfully into space. "We're talking someone who spends their whole life on computer security. Those guys have some serious skills."

"You sound as if you'd like to be one."

"In another life I would have. Anyway, if we need that then one of our ex-classmates would fit the bill, but let's see what the virus is first. Different types are popular with hacker groups in different countries, so that could give us clues to our man. And if not, we can always look on the Dark Net."

Working on the Dark Net or Web always made Craig uncomfortable, never enjoying staring into the abyss in case, Nietzschean, it stared back. But he trusted his team.

He changed the topic.

"Where's everyone else this morning?"

"Interviewing mostly. And Annette got called back to court. She didn't get to testify yesterday."

"Right. I'd forgotten about that. OK, I'll be in my office. Nicky, send Liam in when he arrives, please."

He needed time to think, time which was in short supply nowadays between the new house, Luca, and the stream of grandparents that seemed to follow him wherever he went. He'd never realised a baby came with its own entourage.

He stood in his favourite position by the window and gazed out at the river, considering what they had on their case so far.

Their victims were women of twenty-seven with no other obvious similarities, both killed in different, unusual and completely hands-off ways. Someone had also tried to monitor their investigation by hacking the squad-room, someone whom it seemed fair to assume was highly computer literate.

One word seemed to fit both activities: remote. Hacking allowed remote surveillance and the killings had been remote, so it felt significant to the character of their crime. But how?

Craig turned the word over in his mind, but hard as

he tried nothing came forward so he moved on.

Murder was based on one thing; gain. Gaining money, power, freedom from oppression, sexual gratification, thrills, vengeance, and probably a million other things, so which one applied here? Neither of their victims had been wealthy or powerful, neither appeared to have oppressed anyone, and whatever sexual gratification or thrill their perpetrator might have obtained from killing them hadn't been hands-on, although that *didn't* rule one out.

Power and hate were sexy to some people so vengeance of some form seemed likely, but he wasn't prepared to narrow things yet so he kept thinking.

Neither killing had involved hands-on violence, rape or bodily contact of any kind. That *could* point to a female killer, whereas the hacking might *just* point to a male. It took him no further forward on their perpetrator's sex so he shifted to method. Both methods of killing had been clever, Nicotine poisoning and an EMP, so they had an intelligent killer, which wasn't good news for their chances of catching them.

In fact, the methods been *so* clever that there'd been no guarantee they would have uncovered them at all. So...had the perp wanted their methods revealed or not? But if not, then what a waste of ingenuity. If the causes of death were to remain hidden what had been the point of all that effort? Why not just use a sniper rifle to shoot their prey? It would still have been remote.

Or had their killer banked on *his* squad, with its high clearance rate for even unusual murders, identifying the methods? Had he wanted them to take the cases? If so, was this some kind of challenge? Was his team now part of a game? It might explain why the squad-room had been bugged; a killer sizing up their adversary. Not to mention that it might help them stay one step ahead and avoid get caught.

Craig sighed heavily. He was tying himself in knots trying to understand their killer's motivation, but what else motivates a psychopath but their own needs?

Perhaps remembering that was worth all his thinking, even if it did make his head ache.

He was just rubbing his temples to ease the pain when his office door flew open and Liam's bulk filled the small room.

"Morning, boss. What's happening?"

Craig took a seat and waved his deputy to another.

"Davy and Ash have secured the system and should have information on the virus soon, Annette's in court, Mary's doing something on her computer, and the others are off interviewing trying to make some sense of our deaths."

The DCI lounged back in his chair and was just about to throw his feet up onto the desk when he remembered he wasn't in his own room and crossed his legs instead.

"Good luck with that, 'cos I don't think there's sense to be made. I was thinking about it last night. Killer's usually get caught because they get careless or predictable, yes?"

Craig decided to play his game. "Yes."

"And we get clues from patterns or things that they accidentally leave behind. DNA, prints and whatnot."

"Agreed."

"So, if I was a perp, I would keep my Vics random and never get within six feet of them. That way I could go on killing for years."

Not what Craig wanted to hear, but strangely not enough to make his heart sink.

"You're right. These murders are clever and remote, and so far the only commonality between the women seems to be their age."

The DCI went to accept the praise but his boss had already moved on.

"But... we haven't gathered all the information about them yet, so they may not be as random as they first appear, and even though our perp may not have touched them physically to leave prints or DNA, they *have* touched both the crimes and this office electronically and I think there's something important there. Plus, I think the pace of the killings, two in twelve hours, means they *might* be working to some sort of deadline. This is a spree, and if it isn't over yet we may be able to get ahead of our perp."

"Aye, well, I suppose you could be ri-"

Liam's grudging acceptance was interrupted by a polite knock on the door and Craig saw his lead analyst's outline through its rippled glass.

"Come in, Davy."

As the IT expert entered Liam gave the chair beside him a hard kick that sent it flying into his legs. Accepting the gracious offer, Davy sat down.

"You have something for us, son?"

"A confirmation and something else that might be nothing."

"Fire ahead then."

Producing his smart-pad from his jeans Davy set it on the desk facing Craig.

"OK, the Adelphi's cameras. The hacker got in by piggybacking on the wi-fi of the special effects console backstage then spread out to the cameras. As far as I can find they didn't bother with the rest of the place, just the auditorium Julianne Hodges was performing in. I haven't traced the signal back to its s...source yet, but it was pretty strong so I'd say they weren't far away. Outside the building and maybe up to two streets. It'll take me time to find out exactly where they were, and even then it might not be the s...signal's true origin because they could've bounced it through relays. But I'll keep digging."

Craig smiled admiringly. "Good work. At least now we're sure someone was watching her death. We definitely have a voyeur."

It fitted the remote nature of the killing and gave him a sudden inspiration about seeking outside help.

He turned to his deputy.

"Liam, you were going to check the street cameras around the Adelphi, weren't you?"

The sudden widening of his eyes said he'd forgotten.

99

"Aye, aye, I'm on it."

Meaning he would be as soon as their meeting ended so Craig let it pass.

"What was the other thing you came in about, Davy?"

"Ash hasn't isolated the virus yet but w...we do know the date it was introduced."

"Introduced into the police system originally or activated?"

"The first one."

"OK, and?"

"It was the day after the last force-wide scan. So, on Saturday the eighth."

The information made Craig frown.

"The very next day? That's a bit of a coincidence."

"Or else it isn't because they knew what date the main scan was on."

Liam hated people discussing things he didn't know about and said as much, so the analyst brought him up to speed. As he finished Craig rested back in his chair and linked his hands behind his head, staring at the other men challengingly.

"OK, so you're a hacker who wants to plant a virus in a well-guarded system, what do you do?"

Davy sat forward enthusiastically. "Look for weak spots for access."

"There aren't any."

"There *always* are if you look hard enough." The analyst's eyes widened as he suddenly got Craig's point. "Like just after the last scan has completed and the next one isn't due for a fortnight."

Liam shook his head "But you just said Ash does weekly scans between the big ones so he had less time than that."

"Not if he left the virus inactive, Liam."

"It's still tight, chief. The last thing you want is to activate a virus only to have it detected and quarantined. You want it to have time to do its w...work."

Craig picked up the thought. "OK, so they planted the virus on the eighth and activated it sometime after Ash checked his scan last Friday, the fourteenth, which tells us three things. They must have known about Ash's scan to leave the activation of the virus until after it, so how?"

"Easy to detect Ash's scan once they were in the police system, chief."

"Fair enough. Also, they activated the virus *days before* the first killing on Sunday, so they were probably hoping to watch us right from the start, *but,* they must also have known that Ash's next scan this coming Thursday would've picked up their virus and *ended* their viewing of us. That tells me their murder spree will happen this week."

He frowned. "They'd probably hoped to watch us all week, except Ash spotted the hack yesterday and shut them down."

Liam pulled a face. "Pity about that, boss. We could have been feeding them all sorts of false info."

"I hadn't thought of that, but they might still have learnt things that we didn't want them to as well, Liam, so the safest option was always to end it. You look like you have a point to make, Davy."

"Yep. How did they know?"

"Know what?"

"The date of the big system scan. They obviously did, so how?"

The detectives stared at each other for so long that he waved a hand to break their gaze.

"What are you two thinking?"

Craig shook his head noncommittedly. "I'm not sure yet."

He was, and so was his deputy, but neither was ready to say.

"It might help to know exactly when the virus became active, Davy."

The analyst nodded and was just rising to leave when Liam waved him down again.

"Aren't we missing something here, boss?"

"That the hacker didn't *just* want to know about our investigation but wanted to make us part of their sick game too?"

He was surprised when his deputy said, "Aye, but not that. Why are we assuming the hacker is also our killer, boss? We could be looking at a partnership."

Davy nodded. "Ash said that too. He said *if* the hacker had anything to do with the murders. Mind you, he was talking about our office hacker not the hacking linked with our crimes."

"The same person could be hacking everything, Davy, and Liam's right, there could be more than one person involved here. But tempting though it might be to assume a clean division of labour, one hacking and the other doing the killing, it might be a job-share."

He added 'partnership' to his list of things to explore.

Liam hadn't finished.

"Also, couldn't they have been watching us for an even nastier reason, boss?"

"Which is?"

The DCI swallowed hard, reluctant to voice his thought because of the shit it might bring on all their heads. He did it anyway.

"Because we have a twenty-seven-year-old woman on our team that they might fancy making victim number three."

Craig's jaw dropped, Davy's too, and he followed up by hurtling out to the main office to stare so hard at Mary that she stuck out her tongue. When he re-entered the room its owner was rubbing his neck hard and swearing.

"Damn, damn, damn. How could I have missed it?"

Liam took him off the hook. "To be fair, I did too, boss. It was Danni who suggested it."

"You told her the details of our case?!"

The DCI rolled his eyes. "Ach, now, I'm going to pretend I didn't hear that, you numpty. I've better things to do than bring my bloody work home. No, we were watching the news last night and a bit about the Hodges girl came on, not saying she was murdered but just that a twenty-seven-year-old woman had died on stage. Anyway, Danni said, just chatting like, 'Isn't Mary that age soon?'"

Davy answered the question before Craig asked it.

"She was twenty-seven last month. Don't you remember contributing to her cake and gift, chief?"

"I do now. And as we already have two victims that age Liam's absolutely right, it *does* raise a concern, and one that I know attempting to deal with it is going to cause everyone grief."

Guessing what was coming next Liam shook his head hard.

"No way, boss. Actually, no *bloody* way. Don't even *think* about asking me to tell her. I've seen enough explosions in my life."

Liam had been a copper in Belfast all the way through The Troubles and had seen several bombs explode so it wasn't hyperbole, but such comments, which might horrify people in the rest of the world if uttered as casually, were often heard scattered through Northern Irish speech, with parents even telling their teenagers to tidy their bedrooms because, 'It looks like a bomb's gone off in here'. A coping strategy for a traumatised people perhaps?

But while explode might have been a dramatic description of Mary's anticipated reaction, everyone in the room knew that any offer to protect her would be unwelcome and might even be regarded as a patriarchal infringement of her rights. But while the offer would doubtless have to be phrased carefully, Craig had already decided it would be happening whether she liked it or not.

Davy decided that siding with the boss was the best way of ensuring *he* didn't get asked to tell the constable, so he shot Liam a look intended to make him feel guilty.

"Well, it *was* you who mentioned it, Liam, and you *could* think of it as being her knight in shining armour."

How little he knew his adversary. If guilting had *ever* worked on Liam Cullen its expiry date had been breached several decades before during his church-going youth, so the tactic got the disdain it deserved.

"I've been guilted by the Jesuits, son, so you're not even skimming the surface."

When his deputy folded his arms emphatically Craig knew it was time to admit defeat.

"OK, Davy, leave this with me."

As the analyst exited Craig smiled, conceding that the only person who should tell one of his team they might be under armed guard was him, although preferably when Annette was back from court so she could help him with Mary's inevitable rant. His argument for that contingency not being cowardice was that the women had worked together the day before, but it still felt weak so he moved things quickly along.

"Have you spoken to Ken yet?"

"No, I was planning for this morning."

"OK, do that now."

"You're staying here, boss?"

"For now. I'll meet you at the lab later, but right now I need to make some calls."

"Watch the phones, remember."

"I'm aware. Tell Nicky we'll be briefing at five, all things being equal. Now, off you go."

Alone with his thoughts again Craig ranked his things to do in order of urgency. Arrange an armed officer and a safe house for Mary - but that would have to be done from headquarters; the last thing they needed was their hacker somehow getting wind of where she would be staying. Any new information that emerged from the day's interviews he could deal with later, so that just left contacting Katy, but not in a social way. A moment later they were connected and he got what he needed: the number of a medical expert who might be able to help with their case.

When Craig left the squad-room twenty minutes later he had three places to visit: headquarters, Queen's University and the lab. A whispered instruction to Nicky that Mary wasn't to leave the floor even for food brought a flash of inspiration from the PA and damage to his wallet. She was going to pre-empt any possible objections from the constable by ordering lunch for the whole squad.

****

The Medical Biology Centre, Queen's University. Lisburn Road. 11 a.m.

As a general rule Craig avoided doctors, apart from the one he was married to and John. He couldn't quite put his finger on why, except perhaps that even the ones who weren't arrogant assholes seemed to look at everyone they met in an uncomfortably invasive way. Even at parties when Katy introduced them he felt they were examining him, their touch during a handshake searching for fever or tremors, their gaze as he walked towards them estimating his height, weight and gait. And when they were actually face-to-face making small talk, well *that* felt like he was being psychoanalysed through whatever he said.

It had given him a particular aversion to psychiatrists, which was why what he was just about to do went against his better judgment. But if they *were* dealing with a spree killer then speed was of the essence, so he would take any expert assistance he could get, which in this case was Doctor Jock Armstrong, Head of Psychiatry for Queen's Medical School.

As he waited outside the consultant's neatly labelled office Craig had three thoughts: the first, that at least this time he wouldn't have to approach a medic from a distance and have his walk analysed; the second, why were psychiatrist's chairs so comfortable, even in their waiting rooms? He thought he might already know the answer to that one- it was clearly to relax their waiting victims, sorry patients, and lull them into a semi-comatose state in which they would spill their guts. His third thought was trivial and he knew it; had the medic been named Jock at birth or was it a nickname? It was hard to picture a doting mother taking one look at her

105

new-born and saying proudly, "He looks like a Jock." Jock Armstrong sounded like the bearded captain of a Scottish rugby team, a lead mountaineer or a heavy-set man who slapped people on the back, not a baby.

Neither did he look anything like the man that emerged from the office one minute later. This Jock Armstrong looked... it took Craig a moment to put his finger on it but he got it; *this* Jock looked French. Average height, slim and expensively dressed and coiffed, the psychiatrist had olive skin, slicked back dark hair and a neat to the point of geometric precision goatee beard and moustache. The man wouldn't have looked out of place hosting a salon at the court of Louis the Fourteenth.

Thankfully the time it took Craig to process his assessment was only the same as it took for Armstrong to extend a hand and say, in an unmistakeably Edinburgh accent, "Chief Superintendent Craig. Happy to meet you. Katy said you were never late."

Craig couldn't imagine his wife *ever* saying that about him but perhaps it was the sort of information that doctors thought important to convey. 'Never late' meaning professional; a man who wouldn't waste Armstrong's valuable time.

Either way he was still focused on the psychiatrist's French looks and Scottish accent and wondering whether he had come through the Jacobite line, but somehow managed not to ask.

"Thank you for seeing me, Doctor Armstrong."

He was waved into a very orderly office and shown to a chair, not quite as plush as the ones outside he noted so the psychiatric consultations obviously took place elsewhere. Armstrong offered coffee, then leaning forward at his desk got immediately to the business in hand.

"Katy didn't say why you wanted to see me, simply that you thought I might be able to help you with a case?"

Craig set aside his cup and countered the leaning by resting back in his chair, not sure whether he quite liked a man who used his wife's name so freely but suppressing his urge to take a swing because he needed his help.

"It's possible that you could, Doctor Armstrong, but if you accept the task then you'll be bound by confidentiality not to discuss the case and you may be called to give expert testimony in court. If that doesn't seem too onerous and you agree, then I'm afraid I'll have to ask you to sign to that effect."

There was silence for a moment while Armstrong scrutinised him, thinking something or nothing, and if something whether it was mundane or deep the detective couldn't tell. The stand-off, if it wasn't only one in his mind, ended with the psychiatrist nodding briskly and reaching for his pen to sign the form that Craig had brought.

"I've consulted for the police before. Not here, in Scotland. I'm happy to put you in touch with the officer I worked with there, if you wish."

"Perhaps later. First I'd like to lay out what we're looking at with this case."

It took a good five minutes to lay out what they knew about their victims, so far very little, how they'd been killed, patchy but slightly more, and the office hacking which may or may not have been linked with their deaths, then Craig sat back and waited for his counterpart to speak, hoping that Armstrong's next words were golden, although also that the medic struggled slightly for certainty in them like any normal human being.

The psychiatrist didn't respond immediately, instead tapping his goatee several times and refreshing their coffees, then he moved across to a bookcase that Craig hadn't noticed and returned with a very modern looking textbook titled 'Cyberpaths'. He set it on the desk and sat back, folding his arms.

"Cyberpaths are psychopaths who use the cyberworld and technology as their murder weapons. The cleverer and more remote the method the better."

Their two murders certainly fitted that description.

"But this is just my first assessment so I'd be grateful if you didn't take it as gospel."

"I understand. The case is evolving so I'm sure your view on it will as well."

"Fair enough. Well, with that understood I'd say your deputy might have been right when he suggested there was more than one person at work here. I'll tell you why specifically in a moment, but in general in any partnership one member is the primary or dominant and the second takes a more passive role." He tapped the book lightly. "The advance of the internet has brought a whole new dimension to criminality, which is why the police and international agencies consider cybercrime such a threat. In the past, killers, thieves and even terrorists had no option but to get hands-on to commit their crimes, but now many crimes can be committed remotely and in fact it's really only crimes of impulse, such as random acts of violence and theft, and contact crimes such as rape that *couldn't* be committed online nowadays-"

Craig cut in. "Yes, they *could* be, but the majority still aren't because of a lack of technical skill, equipment or intelligence in the perpetrator, and perhaps also a lack of inclination. Criminals often commit crimes for the thrill of it and that thrill is diluted when the victim isn't there in front of them so they get to see and feel their fear."

The medic gave such a precise smile that Craig wondered whether he'd practiced it in the mirror.

"Just so. The majority of crimes *are* still face-to-face, which has the advantage of leaving evidence behind, whereas the only evidence of a cybercrime is in the ethernet."

"Our analysts are working on that and they're very good."

"Excellent. But back to the sort of person who commits a cybercrime, and I would take this to apply to both if it's a partnership. In general, and this is *very* general because we're early in the crime cycle-"

Craig's heart sank and he cut in.

"Because of the scanning dates I'd wondered if the spree mightn't end this week."

Armstrong looked unpersuaded.

"It might, but people like this enjoy what they do so I believe they're likely to continue killing. They may have expected their virus at your office being detected and intended inserting another after that. So, although more information will emerge as you go along, so far I'd say you're looking at a socially isolated male. Killers like these thrive in the dark and there's nowhere darker than the internet. He'll be intelligent but not high up in his real-world career."

"You're positive he'll have a job?"

"Yes, because he needs to indulge his real interest which is technology, and to do that costs money. Technology alters every day and he'll want to keep up with all the new developments. It will be a matter of pride with him. So, he'll have a job but he won't be prepared to put in too many hours because that would take him away from his computers. He might even work for himself."

Craig nodded. This was someone who did the minimum and took the money. He sometimes wished he could be that way; it might lower his heart attack risk.

"Age?"

"A little older than the women, I'd say, but not by much."

"Can you explain why?"

"Because this man is socially awkward or even inadequate, so younger women will be less intimidating to him that those of his own age. But not too much younger because he knew these women somehow and it's always easier to know someone if you socialise in the same circles. That's most often decided by age."

It confirmed Craig's gut feeling that they were going to find a link between Julianne Hodges and Maria O'Rourke but raised another question.

"He knew them in real life or just in the cyberworld?"

It gave the psychiatrist pause for thought.

"I hadn't considered…"

It felt good to have the man off-balance, even though Craig knew it was a childish thrill.

After a moment Armstrong spoke again.

"I'll need to think about that. He *could* just have met them online, although I think it's unlikely. It's hard to develop an obsession with just a picture. More likely he's met them in real life somewhere."

"And if he only met them online then could he be any age and just have *posed* as someone near the victims' age?"

Armstrong shook his head. "No, my age estimate still stands because of his social awkwardness. There is a *small* possibility that he's older and has never really socialised, but older men tend to go for even younger women than this and ones who aren't professionals. Also, tech skills like your killer's are still on balance the premise of the fairly young."

"So, we have a late twenties or early thirties man, with an average job in which he doesn't stand out. Employed or self-employed but with a steady wage."

Armstrong nodded enthusiastically. "Yes, and that last part's very important. He needs job security. The last thing he wants is to get sacked and not be able to afford his toys. So, I would say if he's his own boss he's moderately successful, or-"

The next words came from both men at once. "Public sector!"

Craig ran with it. "He works in the public sector because it's steady, guaranteed employment with less threat of getting sacked. Also, there are more public sector jobs in Northern Ireland than private."

Armstrong smiled. "So now we have a youngish man, either in a routine public sector job where he treads water or working for himself. Socially awkward, but not hugely so or they couldn't hold down work. Possibly just shy, especially with women. I'd also say he's physically unattractive, because even if someone *is* shy, if they're physically attractive they'll be flirted with and won't remain quite as isolated or shy for long."

Craig nodded in agreement before moving on. "Right, so our man or men spend all their spare time online?"

"I'd say so, to be this good at it."

Just then something occurred to the detective and he scribbled himself a note: *tech and game suppliers*.

"Will he be a gamer?"

Armstrong equivocated for a moment. "He could be..." his certainty grew, "yes, yes he is. But I wouldn't say he'd go to competition level because that might mean appearing in real life and this man's *much* happier in the shadows. He may game online and I'd say he's definitely a member of some tech chat-rooms. That may be how he met his partner in crime."

Craig stopped him there. "You seem very sure that he has a partner. Can you explain why?"

The psychiatrist tapped the book again.

"Because he's killing remotely and people like that are essentially cowards, too cowardly to do something like this on their own, even at arm's length. These aren't brave people in the way you might be."

The words reassured Craig, which struck him as odd since he'd been unaware that he'd needed to be. But men who were competing never emphasised their rival's skills as Armstrong just had, although what they were competing about and why it should matter to him the detective had no idea.

Then it dawned on him; he was jealous! Not of Armstrong the man but that he'd known Katy before him. Of course, that didn't mean the psychiatrist had ever asked her out, did it? Maybe he should ask?

He didn't get time to follow the thought through because Armstrong went on.

"These men don't fight in real life, so don't look for any criminal record of violence. They kill fictional characters in games online and watch films with battles to compensate for their own lack of courage. But it allows them to *feel* brave and raises their adrenaline and dopamine levels until they become convinced that anything is possible. And if this *is* a partnership, although the primary will choose the victims, they'll urge each other on."

He paused to sip his coffee and went on.

"In online games this pair might compete against each other for higher and higher scores, but bring that into real life and they'll work together. And however they found each other I think you're now looking at a Folie à deux."

"A delusion shared by two. Which in psychiatric terms means?"

"A shared psychosis or delusional disorder transmitted from one individual to another. Classic examples are Fred and Rose West and Myra Hindley and Ian Brady. They fed off each other and it made each worse. Add in the cyber element and all constraints of physicality and geography are removed, making the possibilities for killing endless."

Two psychopaths whose weapon of choice was technology feeding off each other. It made Craig long for an old-fashioned thug with a gun.

Craig ordered his thoughts before speaking again.

"So, if the choice of victim is being made by the dominant, *they* must have seen the victims in person to choose them. They live locally."

The psychiatrist nodded slowly. "That makes sense. Both may even live locally, although I can't be sure. I'm not certain of this next bit either, but if the primary partner names the list of victims the two of them *may* compete to invent deviant ways to kill them. Perhaps the secondary is even allowed to make a list at times, which means there could be past victims out there. And another thought, although both partners will be around the same age, they may not both be male. Women have just as vicious urges as men, it's just that a smaller percentage act upon them. That inaction is sometimes due to them lacking the physical strength to wield a weapon, strangle and so on, but in remote killings those inhibiting factors no longer apply."

If he'd expected Craig to be shocked, he wasn't. They

dealt with female murderers before.

The medic leant forward on his desk. "But overall, I think you've got a dominant male selecting the victims who either runs their own moderately successful business or works in the public sector, and a similar more passive male or female partner that they met online. Both skilled in technology and socially awkward and both with similar sadistic impulses, although the secondary might never actually kill. Voyeuristic too. There's a definite hint of the snuff movie about these killings..."

Armstrong had confirmed they were on the right track.

"...also, I wouldn't limit your hunts for similar deaths to the UK or Ireland. Even if they both live here the internet frees them geographically. And I'd say the more kills they have the more confident they'll get and the harder to catch."

Which is why it was time for the detective get off his ass, but not until he'd asked something that had occurred to him a minute before.

"Could one or both of our perps be Incels?"

The question took Armstrong aback, but he rallied quickly.

"Yes, in the sense that they're probably involuntarily celibate which is where that label comes from. Their targeting of women supports that. But not all Incels are violent by any means. Many are just lonely and like belonging to groups where they can vent their unhappiness. Which isn't to say they can't be harmful and make some worse."

"And groups like 4Chan and 8Chan?"

Armstrong puffed out his cheeks before responding.

"They're interesting. 4Chan is basically an imageboard used by lots of groups, and yes, it's attracted radicals. 8Chan too. It's like all the online fora. Some people will be criminal, some not, some mentally ill and some not. There's a lot of hate speech against women and descriptions of the violence online, as well as right-wing propaganda. I presume you're thinking of which cyber chat-rooms to explore?"

"Those and whichever other corners of the dark web these people lurk in."

Armstrong fell silent for so long that Craig realised he'd exhausted his knowledge on the subject, so he rose and extended a hand. The psychiatrist had given him plenty to get on with and he knew what he had to do next. After thanking the medic and saying he might be back to see him, he sent Davy a long, acronym heavy list of sites to explore and headed for the labs.

****

The Consulting Room of Doctor Amanda Beresford. 12 p.m.

John had lost track of how long they'd been sitting in silence because he couldn't look at his watch without being rude, but the therapist opposite had spent a considerable amount of time recapping where they'd got to the fortnight before.

Her summary had sounded remarkably like the one she'd given then as well *and* the one before that, and so on since Christmas and it was all making him despair. If no progress was being made in their marriage therapy then what was the bloody point of continuing? Natalie just sat through every session in tight-lipped silence; attending physically to comply with the court mandate so she could see Kit but not actually engaging at all.

His thoughts must have been written on his face, or else Amanda Beresford was telepathic, because without warning she lifted a red pen from her desk, held it in the air and said, "Enough."

The word hung there for a moment without explanation until she set an official looking document in front of her and placed the pen on a line at its base, one clearly designated for a signature.

In John's experience signatures written in red ink

114

were never a good thing so he intervened quickly before something irreversible transpired.

"Stop!"

Beresford lifted her dark eyes languidly to his, their gaze urging him to say more.

When his words came, they were uninspired.

"Don't write it. I mean, whatever you were about to write, please don't."

"Tell me why not."

He knew the challenge wasn't aimed at him but responded all the same.

"Because I think that's a form for the courts to say Natalie's failed to engage with therapy, and if it is then you're about to stop her seeing Kit."

His wife's tight lips unclamped instantly and an indignant, *"You wouldn't dare!"* shot out, making him want to groan. Natalie had never learned that when someone holds your future in their hands politeness is the minimum standard advised.

He rushed to translate her words.

"What she means is, *please* don't. Let's discuss things first."

The indignation was turned on him. "That's not what I meant at all! Please don't, *please* don't. Pretty please. When on earth have you ever heard me say anything like that, John? Kit is *my* child, and no therapist's going to tell me I can't see her, so that red pen can go-"

The pathologist surprised himself with the force of his, "BE QUIET!" and the add-on, "for *once* in your life, Natalie, just have some bloody sense!"

Unlike anyone else in the room, the surgeon seemed genuinely shocked by the words.

"What do you mean have sense? I have *plenty* of sense. I have an IQ of one-seventy and the equivalent of five degrees!"

Her husband was unimpressed.

"As does everyone else in this room, so just do as I ask, *please.*"

He left her to contemplate how commonplace her

intellect actually was and turned back to the therapist.

"Doctor Beresford, I realise that engagement in these sessions is a requirement for Natalie's access to our daughter, and I know what she's done since Christmas couldn't *possibly* be described in that way..."

He ignored his wife's eyebrows shooting up.

"...but please don't give up on us yet. *Please*. Kit needs her mother."

The therapist said nothing, forcing him to fill yet more silence himself.

"Natalie pushes for Kit to be perfect, which is wrong, but perhaps if we could get to the bottom of why she does it-"

Ms Perfect barged in again.

"Why is it wrong to want Kit to be the best she can possibly be? And what do you *mean* 'get to the bottom of why I do it'? That sounds like you think there's something wrong with *me*!"

Beresford's response was to turn her gaze on the surgeon and arch an eyebrow. Her message a clear, 'And *you* think there isn't?'

Natalie responded as if she'd actually heard the words. "No, I don't! But if you disagree and you're so smart, then tell me what it is!"

John opened his mouth to speak but closed it again at a shake of the therapist's head, leaving the floor entirely to his wife, whose small face was turning a striking shade of red.

"I know what you think. *You* think it's because I was adopted, don't you? So, I always thought I had to be perfect in case they sent me back. Well, that's rubbish. I just wanted to be perfect because I wanted to, that's all! And it was *nothing* to do with what the kids at school said!"

John struggled not to show his shock. He'd never heard anything about children teasing her, and for her pain to be so evident decades later he could guess at how cruel the taunts must have been. He wished the little creeps were in front of him now so he could tell them a few home truths.

When he saw his wife's eyes brighten with tears he turned pleadingly to Amanda Beresford, praying she would tell him what to do for the best. He wanted to take Natalie's hand and comfort her but she might pull away, and he was afraid to say a word in case it was the wrong one.

But painful as it clearly was, it felt like they'd made some sort of breakthrough. If Natalie had lived in fear of rejection by her adoptive parents and being perfect had been her way of mitigating that risk, could she in some strange way feel that by teaching Kit to be perfect she was protecting her from future pain?

He knew Natalie's parents and they were lovely so he was positive rejecting her had never even entered their minds, so surely there was some way to demonstrate that her fears hadn't actually been based in reality and therefore there was no need to teach Kit coping techniques?

As he pondered the problem the silence in the room deepened, broken only by an occasional sniff from his wife. Amanda Beresford stared at each of them at length until eventually she gave a nod.

"Good. Now we know why you behave towards your daughter in the way you do, Doctor Ingrams, we can work on breaking those patterns."

John sat forward, indicating the still-hovering red pen. "So, that means you *won't* sign a negative report for the court?"

The therapist glanced at the document in front of her and smiled.

"You mean this?"

"Yes. Well, I mean, signing something in red is never good news, is it?"

"Not even my new dog licence?"

The pathologist's jaw dropped in astonishment. She'd called their bluff to break the stalemate and it had worked. In the previous five minutes Natalie had said more about what made her tick than she had since they'd met seven years before.

Unfortunately, the revelation left her feeling vulnerable, so the rest of the session consisted of Natalie giving Beresford hell about her 'unprofessional' red pen ploy and *him* hell about being such a soft touch.

Considering that two weeks earlier she'd called him a bastard in a solicitor's letter he would take any progress he could get.

****

The Labs. 12.30 p.m.

Craig was bursting to share the psychiatrist's theories, so as soon as he saw his deputy in the pathology carpark everything that Jock Armstrong had hypothesised came blurting out, stunning Liam into silence for a moment then prompting a, "Bloody hell!"

"Yep. It was quite a session. I'll tell you more later, but Armstrong was very good."

As they made their way to John's office the DCI asked a question that stopped Craig in his tracks.

"What did he say about Mary? How long should we keep her under guard?"

"Damn! I knew there was something I'd forgotten to ask!" He raked his hair for a moment before going on. "OK... so... if any common themes emerge between our two victims we'll check to see if they fit Mary. That should tell us how much danger she's in. Or rather Annette will check. I can't imagine Mary allowing the rest of us to dig around in her private life."

"And if they don't fit?"

"Ask me if that happens, but my fear is they will. By the way, did you get anything new from Ken or Lucia?"

"Nope. Lucia wasn't there obviously but Ken did say she wanted to be updated on any progress with *her* case."

Craig chuckled, picturing his younger sister saying the words. She'd been demanding since she was a toddler so it wasn't a huge surprise.

When the detectives reached John's office they found it empty, so they diverted to Marcie's office and found her scrolling through theatre sites in search of work.

"You're not leaving us are you, Marcie?"

"Not until I get my big break, no. I just want to keep my hand in with some piece work. A TV advert would be nice. They pay well."

Craig chuckled. "I can just picture you appearing during breaks in the evening news. I'd buy the product."

Liam grinned in a way that bordered on lascivious, or as his granny would have said 'bold'.

"Me too. I'd have a dozen of whatever."

"Considering the advert I'm looking at is for nappies, I can't wait to see that."

Craig didn't hide his smirk. "She got you there. Right, Marcie, we'll leave you to it as soon as you tell us where John is."

"With his wife."

The sniff she added after the words said that her opinion of Natalie wasn't very high.

Both men knew there was only one place John went with his wife nowadays, despite an extremely expensive romantic break over Christmas that he'd hoped would put their Humpty Dumpty of a marriage back together again; the therapist that the couple had been attending on and off since twenty-eighteen.

It had always amazed Craig that anyone could talk about their problems to a stranger, and even more that said stranger didn't get bored to tears, but then we're all made for different things in this world as his mother was fond of saying, usually in a martyred tone while highlighting her disappointment that neither of her children had followed her into the classical music world.

Despite his thoughts Craig merely responded, "Right then. Des it is" and headed for the lift, leaving Liam to detach himself reluctantly from the dainty actress' orbit, something he moaned about all the way to the third floor.

Liam, for all that he was a physical mountain of a man, was attracted to, no *fascinated by* petite women, as well as pretty much all female ornamentation. It explained his wife being five-foot-two, his gazes of admiration at Nicky's elegant hands, which even though she worked them to death every day typing up reports were things of beauty framed with long, perfectly varnished nails, and his adoration of the miniscule Marcie, the epitome of womanhood according to the DCI.

Craig could see the attraction but they all lacked one thing; Katy's perfect pale-blonde curls. Her below-shoulder mass of hair was a pre-Raphaelite masterpiece just waiting to be painted, and someday soon, when he'd found an artist that could do her justice, that was exactly what he intended to arrange.

But for the moment both policemen would have to relinquish their romantic fantasies and face the reality of the forensics. They emerged from the lift to be greeted by a Grace who seemed barely able to contain herself, not a sight they often saw.

She pulled them behind her with virtual ropes into Des' office and blurted out, "Tell them!" in a sergeant major way that her boss had grown so familiar with it now barely caused him to blink. It was hard to take offence when your NCO was wearing a flowery dress and a fluffy pink cardigan with matching beads shining in their earlobes.

Des ushered them out of his office again and on to chairs, then announced that they'd been *exactly* right in their hypotheses on both victims and took each in turn.

"OK. Julianne Hodges. We *thought* she'd been killed using Nicotine because of the Cotinine in her blood, but now we have forensic proof as well-"

Grace cut in. "From two sources."

"Yes, two. First, the dress itself. We sampled it in ten different places and each sample contained a lethal dose of Nicotine."

Craig signalled to interrupt. "So, you're saying if *any* of those areas had touched her skin she would have died?"

"Yes, but possibly more slowly than she did. But as she was touched by several lethal doses at once she died almost instantly. I phoned the Adelphi's dresser and she said because the frock was so delicate Mrs Hodges had only put it on two minutes before the scene started-"

Liam cut in. "And the dresser's gloves?"

"They saved her life. We tested them and they were covered in Nicotine but it hadn't soaked through to her skin. She was very very lucky."

Craig nodded. Their killer would just have considered her collateral damage.

"OK, so Julianne Hodges put the dress on two minutes before the scene and died. How far into the scene, Liam?"

"Ken said she'd only been on stage a few minutes."

He turned to the scientists. "So let's say five minutes of wearing the dress before the Nicotine killed her. Does that timing work?"

Des deferred to his CSI.

"Yes, because there was a petticoat sewn into the dress beneath the main fabric. Silk is clingy, so it was there to make it sit better and it acted as a thin barrier. Otherwise she would probably have died in two."

Craig tapped his chin for a moment, thinking through the timeline, then he nodded the Head of Forensics on.

"OK, so before the dresser handled the dress it was covered in a plastic wrapper from the dry-cleaners. We tested the inside of that plastic and it was strongly positive for Nicotine and Grace has just checked the dry-cleaning equipment and it was the same."

Liam had a thought. "Here, if the whole batch of clothes was contaminated-"

"It was. All the other items cleaned in that batch were Nicotine positive too."

Liam turned to his boss. "Then how do we know Julianne Hodges was the real target here? Anyone who'd collected their cleaning could have been killed."

Craig had been waiting for the question. "It's a good point, but don't forget we have *two* twenty-seven-year-old victims."

But a need for certainty sent him to his phone, giving his deputy time to cajole Grace into making some hot drinks. When Craig returned to the group he was handed a coffee and sipped it gratefully as he told the others what he'd found out.

"I wondered if Rogan had made a separate arrangement with the Adelphi, knowing how important costumes are for opening nights. He had. It turns out he does all the dry-cleaning for the theatre so he'd arranged for the dress to be collected on Saturday, the day before the play opened. My guess is our killer knew all that so they were confident Julianne would die first. But the fact cops would get involved and might possibly find the other dry-cleaned garments in time to save the rest of Rogan's customers was neither here nor there. Our killer wouldn't have cared if they'd all died."

Liam greeted the information with a snort. "The perps got lucky. If she'd decided to wear a different dress on stage that night their murder would've been well messed up."

Craig shook his head. "Most theatre companies only have one specific costume for each scene, and my sense is these killers don't rely on luck in anything. But time will tell."

Des suddenly registered they were using plurals. "*These?* You think there's more than one killer?"

"To be confirmed, but possibly. OK, so that's Julianne Hodges. What can you tell us about Maria O'Rourke?"

"Just one last thing on Hodges before we move on. The dry-cleaning machine carries six canisters of cleaning fluid on a carousel and the right one for the job is selected through the operator's instructions. At first sight there's no obvious sign of how any canister *could* have been contaminated because they're all sealed, but we tested the one used on the dress and it was loaded with Nicotine. We'll test the rest now as well of course, but Davy should really take a look at the console in case there's something clever going on there that let them select the contaminated canister."

Liam turned to his boss. "A pre-contaminated and planted canister? And old man Rogan hadn't a clue it was there?"

"It looks like it. OK, I'll send Davy down there, Des."

"Don't bother. We have everything here. The business owner says he'll be doing things by hand for a while."

"I don't blame him."

"And before we move on, don't you want to know where the Nicotine came from?"

Craig's eyes widened. "You've traced the source?"

He'd thought it might take months of following illegal chemicals across Europe before they got an answer, but it seemed not.

"No, but I know the sort of fluid that was used. It was vaping fluid."

Liam pulled a face. "The sort people put in those steam pipes that make them look like walking chimneys?"

He hated smoking of any sort and it was on the increasingly long list of things that his children would never be allowed to try.

Craig was surprised. "The same stuff you can buy over the counter, Des?"

"Exactly that, except concentrated many, many times. Someone must have bought litres of the stuff and condensed it down to increase the percentage of Nicotine."

He saw Craig's mouth open to ask another question and shook his head. "Before you ask, I don't have a bloody clue how it got into a canister."

Ignoring Grace's immediately pursed lips at his swearing the scientist carried on. NCOs were far too prudish nowadays.

"There's a chance we may be able to trace its exact origin, but it's a tiny one so don't get your hopes up. It's international law for substances to be tagged with chemical markers, but that's ignored by some countries for substances they deem less dangerous and vaping

123

fluid might fit that bill. Anyway, other than that, Grace's team printed everything inside the dry-cleaner's shop so she can tell you about that."

He nodded the CSI to pick it up again.

"We printed everything and eliminated the staff's prints. It left us with a single clear print on the shop's back door."

"And?"

"It's not on any of the usual databases, and it could just belong to postal or maintenance people or even a casual passer-by, so it might turn out to be nothing."

Liam's knowledge of Belfast's streets made him immediately curious. "Where did the back door lead to?"

"On to Elysée Alley."

Craig was impressed. "That sounds nice."

The DCI shook his head. "Trust me, it isn't. It's a hokey wee dead end. There's no way there was a passer-by around there, or a runner before anyone says it. The print could be something, boss."

"Yet there were none on the console, canisters or equipment, Grace?"

"None but the staff's. Although those are such obvious places the killer probably remembered to wipe them and just forgot the back door."

Craig went to nod, then shook his head firmly instead, surprising everyone.

"The print doesn't belong to our man. Sorry. He won't have gone anywhere near the crime scene, he's too clever. He'll have contaminated the dry-cleaning fluid at its source instead."

"The factory it was packaged in, boss?"

"Exactly. Then the contaminated canister was delivered to Rogan's shop and innocently inserted in the carousel."

His eyes widened as something occurred to him.

"But how could our killer have been certain the right canister would've been uploaded to use on the dress?" He turned to his deputy. "Liam, call John Rogan now and tell him they'll be closed a bit longer. There could be a lot of contaminated canisters amongst his stock."

Grace jumped her feet in alarm. "We only tested the one used on the dress!"

Craig waved her to sit again.

"Which was perfectly logical. But now let's collect every canister in his stock and test them."

Just then Liam finished his call. "Poor sod, I feel sorry for Rogan. He's losing business because of this."

"Better that than killing more customers. OK, let's think this through. Our killer won't have wanted to touch anything. That's too personal for him. So first he manipulated the Nicotine into the factory's chemicals somehow, then he rigged the delivery system so that the contaminated batch or batches were delivered to Rogan's shop and we know the rest."

"He wouldn't have needed to mess with the console if every canister on the carousel was poisoned, boss."

"Good point. OK, so all the tricky hacking to add the Nicotine and divert the shipment probably took place at the factory. So how did he manage it?"

Des shrugged. "Easily, I'd think. He concentrated the Nicotine off-site and replaced one of the cleaning fluid's normal components with it, probably by just relabelling it and diverting the normal stuff. Then it was added to the mix as normal, innocently packed in canisters and shipped to Rogan's shop. If he's as good a hacker as you think it would have been child's play, Marc. Clever bugger."

Liam shot him a warning look. "Careful now or Grace will tell you off."

The CSI gazed at him balefully. "I'm approaching numbness."

"Spend a week with me and you'll be beyond redemption, M'Lady. We might even get you swearing yourself. I managed to wear Annette down."

Craig batted the offer away. "That took years. Just ignore him, Grace, he needs a refresher on good behaviour and I have just the seminar to send him to." Ignoring his deputy's groan he went on. "It sounds like

Davy and Ash need to visit that factory."

"Aye, and all its fluids will have to be tested too."

"More than that, Liam, they may need to shut it down and recall their products. OK, Des, let's move on to Maria O'Rourke. What more can you tell us?"

"Her pacemaker essentially directed the field towards her heart's conducting system, as well as getting fried itself."

"You're certain?"

"Yes. John's found massive cell disruption."

Liam shook his head.

"Killed by giant magnets feels like an awful way to go."

Craig swallowed hard, picturing the young woman's death.

"I suppose we should be grateful no-one else was in the imaging suite to die. Did you get the schedule, Liam?"

"Eventually. The health service is, like Yeats said, dropping slow. The imaging suite's schedule was completely clear between eight and eleven that morning, boss. Seems like more than a coincidence, doesn't it?"

It definitely did; their killer *had* to have arranged it, probably by altering appointments online. But as they knew he wasn't averse to collateral damage he'd probably just wanted to avoid anyone being around to help Maria O'Rourke, rather than caring if they died.

"He arranged or waited for the suite to be deserted before throwing the pulse, and he knew the exact moment because he was watching."

Des arched an eyebrow. "You say that like it's a fact."

"It will be when Davy proves it. There were CCTV cameras in the Radiology Department and in the Adelphi's auditorium too. I think our killer or killers like to watch their victims die, and in the case of Maria O'Rourke it also told them when no-one else was around to help her."

He stared at the floor for a moment, mulling things over. When he decided he'd got as far as possible for now he leapt to his feet, startling everyone in the group but his deputy who'd seen the sequence play out many times before.

"Right. There's a lot to get on with, so we'll leave you to it. Tell John I called if you see him."

He didn't wait for a response, instead heading for the lift with his much more relaxed deputy ambling in his wake.

****

High Street. Belfast City Centre.

The man was getting twitchy. It used to be that he could manage twenty-four hours without logging-on to his gaming sites, then twelve, then eight, and now it only took four for the urge to overwhelm him. It wasn't the games but the company that he missed. It was a world where he was known and understood, a world where people liked him regardless of how much he did or didn't earn *or* what lay in his past.

In a real world of shallow celebrity and almost grotesque wealth, seemingly based less on talent than on Instagram filtering skills, fake people who were good at nothing but narcissism and good *for* nothing at all received the plaudits. But not in Nate World, as the alternative, cyber universe was known to its afficionados.

Dungeons and Dragons had been his entry point as a teenager but he'd graduated quickly to other games and spent hours slaying monsters and rescuing damsels in distress, so often that back then he'd believed real life would be the same. All you had to do to impress a girl was rescue her from some near-death threat; easy. A sword thrust here and kill a dragon there and the prettiest girl in the kingdom could be yours. No, *would* be yours; the princess was *always* so full of gratitude that she fell into the hero's arms.

But he'd learnt fairly soon that only happened in Nate World, not the real one. In real life pretty girls only ever dated handsome jocks, and the geeks and nerds like him were made fun of in changing rooms. Back then no-one had heard of tech millionaires like Bill Gates, Steve Jobs or Elon Musk or known you could make a fortune from a bright idea. *Now* the geeks and nerds were probably crowned King of the Prom.

Timing was everything and he'd been born in the wrong decade. Add in fourth wave feminism and everything was just too difficult now for men, except in Nate World, so that was where he spent every waking hour that he didn't need to work.

He wasn't alone there. There were thousands, millions of men like him and his friend Noel, and their problems were all the same. They were the lost generation, man-children some called them, advanced and yet not advanced in the ways of normal life. Doomed by the world that had bred them to be alone except for each other and the internet. Society had made them and society had made them into a problem, and now society had to pay.

In cyberspace he could talk to like-minded faceless others, and even if he wanted to kill for their applause, so that's what he was doing, and he was good at it.

At the moment he was finding the lure of the next kill almost impossible to resist, but he thought of Noel just recovering from another grinding shift and out of loyalty decided he would limit himself to gaming. Until tonight, when together they would tick another name off his list.

****

The O'Rourke Home. Portaferry, County Down.

Aidan Hughes liked working alone, no, he actually preferred it, picturing himself as some lone Cheroot-chewing gunslinger in the Wild West, or on quieter days the shiny badged sheriff of a one-horse town, moseying down its mud-caked main street in his dusty leather boots and chaps. With his cowboy hat tilted back slightly so he could alternate squinting up at the sun like a Clint Eastwood tribute act with scanning his kingdom for wrongdoers, he would bring order to the wayward streets.

The DCI already had the lean, tanned, world-weary look down pat, but unfortunately his cheroots had long ago been replaced by chewing gum and there was no amount of convincing anyone that hats were sufficiently back in fashion that would get one past Liam without it being flipped off.

Aidan couldn't even indulge in his lone star act nowadays, as he acknowledged with a baleful glance at the quiet sergeant by his side. Still, it could have been worse, he should have been paired with Mary again but she was staying in the office for some reason. It wasn't that he disliked the constable so much as he just never knew what to say to her, and he didn't think that was just the age gap. His young cousin was only twenty and they *always* had a laugh.

The DCI shrugged pragmatically, knowing that he shouldn't really complain. He'd struck lucky with the easy-going Ryan and as they parked up outside Maria O'Rourke's family home he plastered on a smile.

"OK, Ryan. They were at the morgue last night when Mary and I dropped by, so let's not mention that. It'll only remind them of seeing their daughter dead and there's nothing to gain. As far as they're concerned this is our first contact, OK?"

Normally the sergeant would have said yes, him having a placid nature, except the facts dictated that he couldn't this time.

"Sorry, Guv. No can do. You left your card, remember? Mary mentioned you put it through the letter box as you were leaving."

Damn. He was right.

Aidan thought fast and regrouped with a satisfied smirk.

"If they ask I'll say a uniform left it, not me. OK." He opened the car door. "Anyway, let's get to it. They'll have noticed we're here by now and I don't want to prolong their agony."

129

He meant it, because at his core Aidan Thomas Hughes was a decent man, although selfishly he was also hungry and food beckoned when they were done. But his decency more often than not outweighed his needs nowadays and he put that down to being happier in his private life. He'd started 'seeing' a DCI called Deidre Murray, dating sounded too prom-date juvenile for a fortyish DCI, and so far it was nice, nice being as enthused as Aidan had allowed himself to get about anything in life since his fiancée had died of cancer years before.

But nice was good, and his contentment was seeping into his work life, so instead of leaving his sergeant scrambling to catch up as he'd have done in the past the DCI actually waited before knocking the door of the neat townhouse. It was answered almost immediately, saying that he'd been right; the family had noticed them arriving and something about their demeanour had clearly said they should answer the knock.

Aidan wondered fleetingly when he'd changed from being a gangly student in ripped jeans that policemen had viewed as a potential prisoner most Friday nights to someone with an appearance of authority, and whether it was his walk or suit that gave his job away. The analysis would have to wait as the front door swung back and a small, swollen-eyed woman appeared in front of him. Her eyes shouted grief but her unlined face, jeans and T-shirt said she couldn't possibly have been Maria O'Rourke's mum. But she was; Áine O'Rourke, forty-five, was the mother of their twenty-seven-year-old victim and it made the DCI feel every day of his years.

Ryan thankfully wasn't so preoccupied with anno domini and remembered to produce his ID. When they'd both handed theirs over for inspection the woman ushered them into a warm sitting room at the back of the house where a toddler sized version of her was piling bricks into a tower.

"Suzie, go and find Daddy. He was in the kitchen."

A moment later they were joined by a man whose grey

hair and worn expression made Aidan feel more comfortable, and when the little girl had been ushered to her bedroom to play the detective got to the reason they were there.

"Mister and Mrs O'Rourke, we're here about your daughter Maria."

It brought a tight sob from the man that made him pause for a moment before continuing.

"I'm DCI Aidan Hughes and this is Detective Sergeant Ryan Hendron, and we're really very sorry for your loss."

He never used to utter such kindnesses before-Deidre but now he did. Would before and after meeting her become a marker of his maturity? And would it be shortened to something catchier like B-D and A-D one day when they told stories to their kids? The thought pulled Aidan up short. *Kids?* When did *that* happen?

It was only Ryan's presence of mind that prevented the DCI asking the question out loud, as, spotting his boss' brain blip, the sergeant stepped smoothly in.

"We're from the Murder Squad in Belfast, Mister and Mrs O'Rourke."

The words brought such a loud gasp from Áine O'Rourke that Aidan returned to earth, just in time to hear Gerry O'Rourke put his wife's outcry into words.

"Murder? But Maria was alone at work, and the doctor at the hospital said that her pacemaker had failed."

Aidan shook his head slowly. "Sadly, we think things are more complicated. We won't know exactly what happened until our investigation is complete, so I'm afraid I need to ask you some quite detailed questions about your daughter. Is that all right?"

Questions that would show whether she'd had more in common with Julianne Hodges than just her gender and age.

The married couple looked at each other, the messages of years transmitted in a flash; *What do you think? No, what do you think? Well, we really need to know what happened to Maria, and if the police can*

131

help...

How many years of coupledom did it take such telepathy to develop? It was a question for another time.

"Ask whatever you need to, Chief Inspector. We need to find out why we've lost our elder daughter."

"Thank you, Mister O'Rourke."

It was polite but Aidan also meant it. If they didn't have help from their victims' families then there might be another death. A feeling that there was likely to be one in any case instantly swept over him; each murder case had a momentum and this one felt as if it had quite a way to run.

****

The CCU. 1.30 p.m.

Liam's insistence that despite having eaten three of Grace's biscuits his stomach thought his throat had been cut, translation - it was time for lunch, saw them not arrive back at the office until one-thirty. They were greeted by two stressed-out analysts and a frustrated Mary being body-blocked by Alice, a nimble ballroom dancer, as she tried to leave the floor.

Seeing the new entrants had left the doors open Mary took her chance and bolted, only to be stopped by Liam this time.

"Here now, Missy, where are you going?"

"Not that it's any of your business..."

A quick glance from Craig said to let her cheekiness pass.

"... but I'd like to go to the loo, if that's OK with you?"

The DCI considered the request with a solemnity he normally saved for life-changing events like buying a new house and shook his head.

"Not without a companion. Alice, are you free?"

In perfect mimicry of a catchphrase from the seventies, the "I'm free" that came singing back made everyone but Mary laugh.

Her next question, "Why am I being treated like a prisoner?" told Craig his constable was completely unaware that she was under house arrest and his hope that some kind soul might *just* have let it slip in his absence to save him earache had been in vain.

Instead he was forced to beckon her into his office, and when Liam tried to slope off into his own to beckon him too, although with a much more violent jerk of the fist.

Once seated behind his desk Craig gazed up at the reddening face of his most junior officer, who'd pointedly ignored his invitation to sit, then turned to his deputy.

"Chief Inspector, tell Mary why we don't want her wandering off."

With a look that promised dire retribution later, the second in as many days, Liam summarised.

"Twenty-seven-year-old women are dying. You could be next."

The constable gawped at him and slid mutely on to a chair.

Her silence didn't last for long.

"That's ridiculous!"

She turned to Craig and repeated the words, with not a 'sir' to be heard.

"In fact, it's... it's worse than ridiculous. It's just stupid, idiotic, and dim!"

Craig arched an eyebrow. Being called dim wasn't on his bucket list.

"I know you're upset, but watch your tone, Constable Li."

Liam winced, knowing that in Mary-World mentioning emotion was tantamount to accusing her of behaving 'like a girl'.

"Upset? *UPSET? I'm not upset, I'm furious!* Without consulting me, yet obviously telling others, you seek to limit my freedom! For what? Some nonsense that I might be killed because of my age!"

Liam interjected helpfully. "You're female too."

"And my gender."

133

"And the hacking."

"And..." She turned to face him. "What?"

"This office was hacked, and probably the Adelphi, the X-ray reading-room, and maybe a dry-cleaners and factory as well."

She turned back to Craig, confused, but recovered quickly and was preparing for another onslaught when he raised his palm in a recognised signal that he'd reached his bullshit limit and to only cross that Rubicon if you dared.

The constable deescalated fast, but her glare persisted as Craig spoke.

"There have been two unnatural deaths of twenty-seven-year-old women since Sunday, and to date we have nothing to link those women other than that they died in unusual ways. We now believe both were carried out remotely using technology and we also believe the killer or killers may have watched the deaths."

As Mary opened her mouth to speak again, he closed it with a shake of his head and went on.

"This office was, in that same time period, hacked. We can speculate that it was someone just trying to find out about our cases generally, but as it began at the same time as these murders it seems safe to assume that the two are somehow linked. It was also drawn to my attention, and no I won't say by whom, that you fit our victim profile. As such we need to remove any chance of you being next, however slim that possibility might be."

A grunt from his deputy said that at this point Liam wasn't sure if he cared what happened to the constable or not. Craig was tempted to agree, but he had a duty of care to his team members no matter how much they resisted it and he led with that when he spoke again.

"As one of my officers I have a duty of care for you. Therefore, and I had intended to tell you this on my return..."

The glance he got from his deputy said, "*You big liar! You were going to wait till Annette was back and get her to do it!*" but he ignored it and carried on.

"...but here we are. So, Constable Li, from now until this case is resolved you will be under twenty-four-hour armed guard at an unknown location-"

That was too much for Mary and her next words were a screech.

"I can't even come here? I'll go bonkers with boredom!"

Craig back-tracked swiftly.

"You can come to work if it helps, but you'll stay in the office under Annette's supervision and she'll be with you everywhere you go within working hours. An officer from the Armed Response Unit will take over at night and there will be others in the street as well."

"The ARU? That seems like overkill."

"It isn't."

"Huh. Well, why can't I stay at home?"

"Because our killers may already have that address."

"But all my *stuff*..."

The last word turned into a whine but Craig didn't relent.

"Annette will take you home to gather whatever you need, then you'll be staying in a hotel under guard."

Liam had been counting how long it would take before the 'S' word reared its ugly head and he'd just hit twelve when Mary blew, springing to her feet to give her indignation weight.

"This is sexism! I'm reporting the whole lot of you to my union rep, and The Equality Commission, and the Human Rights people, and..."

When she'd run out of steam Craig gave a heavy sigh.

"Sit down, Constable Li."

Only when she had, did he go on.

"There's *nothing* sexist about this. Had the victims been thirty-year-old males Davy and Ash would be in lock-down, forty-something males and most of us would be, but they weren't. On this squad only you fit the victim profile. Now, I'm sorry if you feel this is an injustice," he wasn't really but it sounded good, "and please feel free to consult all of those organisations, but this is what it is."

Mary crossed her arms defiantly. "What if I refuse?"

The possibility hadn't even occurred to him and it showed, so Liam leapt to the rescue.

"We'd have to consult Chief Constable Flanagan, and he would decide if it was a disciplinary offence."

It was inspired and Craig held the bluff.

The thought of a black mark on her file made the DC retreat slightly and her next words were framed more as questions than demands.

"I can go home and collect my things? And it'll only be for a few days?"

Craig's, "Yes" was punctuated by his deputy's sarcastic, "We'll catch the perp faster than Speedy Gonzales, just for you."

Whatever Mary was really thinking as she left the small office, she did so in a calmer manner than she'd entered so Craig waited just long enough for her to disappear before he allowed himself a sigh of relief.

"Disciplinary? That was brilliant, Liam."

The DCI feigned surprise. "You mean you *don't* think Flanagan would've backed us up on that?"

"My ass. There's no way he'd have penalised Mary if she'd refused, although he might have asked her to see a therapist and sign a waiver, and insurance would have been an issue."

"Aye well, the bluff worked. So, what's the next problem?"

Craig chuckled. "Telling Annette."

****

The Labs. 2 p.m.

John had returned from his therapy session with a worse headache than the one he'd got in twenty-sixteen when he and Craig had competed in drinking each other under the table and he'd discovered the meaning of a hollow leg. Determined not to be beaten, although God knows why, he'd matched the former Jock drink for drink until the bitter end, his last memory being a wad of chewing gum stuck to the underside of a bar table and a bouncer's exasperated, "Right, mate, you've had enough. Get out."

Then nothing, until he'd woken the next day on the sagging sofa in Craig's flat, one he now sat on every night, and managed to dash for the bathroom just in time to avoid throwing up all over it. It had taken him three days to feel right again and the headache had chewed at his skull for another two. Today's session with Natalie had generated the same pain in a single hour.

As the medic scrabbled around in his desk drawers for a painkiller his office door flew back. He'd just groaned the "Ca" of "Catch it" when Des failed to and the door hit the wall with a thud he felt in every corner of his brain.

Seeing his friend's pain the scientist mumbled a cursory, "Sorry" then asked, "is that fresh coffee?" helping himself to a mug before thudding again, this time into a chair.

John stared at him balefully, his eyes half-closed to cut out the light.

"To what do I owe this honour? You hardly ever come down here."

The appearance of a memory stick from the scientist's pocket gave him his answer, but as Des threw it across the desk to him he fumbled the catch.

"You'd make a terrible Gaelic player, John."

"I'm devastated."

He retrieved the stick but did nothing with it, motioning the forensic expert to explain instead.

"That holds everything we've found on our two deaths. I just thought you'd like an update. Marc and Liam were here while you were out so they've already had one."

"Later."

The word, uttered in a croak and still with half-closed eyes, made Des lean forward to scrutinise his colleague.

"Have you been on a bender? And if so, why didn't you invite me?"

It earned him a pained look. "Therapy session, but the

137

hangover's the same."

John was just about to add that he needed to rest when the door thudded open again, making him groan.

"Doesn't anyone knock in this place? Or know how to open a door *normally*?"

The sight of Marcie, someone who normally cheered him up, did nothing to improve his mood. Much as he liked her, the PA always brought work for him to do. He wondered if the sight of Nicky sometimes made Craig want to hide but decided such cowardice would be deemed undignified by an ex-Jock.

If Marcie could see his heart sinking, she completely ignored it, exclaiming brightly, "I didn't expect you both to be here."

"Hmm... what can we do for you, Marcie?"

Please just be here to tell me you'd like to leave early.

No such luck, although John was a lot better off than his next guest.

"We've another body coming in, Doctor Winter. Estimated time of one hour. She died this morning but it took the hospital a while to get organised."

The medic raised an eyebrow. "She died in hospital? Staff member or patient?"

"Patient."

"Why didn't their pathologists take her then?"

He didn't wait for an answer, already knowing what the answer would be. The death was suspicious in some way.

"Fine. I'll see if Mike can do the PM."

He was mildly curious why she'd felt the need to announce the arrival in advance when she never normally did, but his head was too sore to ask.

Marcie told him anyway.

"You'll want to see this one yourself. It's another twenty-seven-year-old."

Craig was about to have an even worse day than him.

Chapter Seven

The CCU. 5.20 p.m.

Craig was halfway through briefing when his need for fresh coffee became too strong to ignore and he called a five-minute break, trying to ignore the still-huffy gaze of his 'imprisoned' constable and the pained stare of his inspector as best he could. He understood both their feelings but empathised far more with the second, trying to imagine listening to hours of Mary raging against 'The machine', of which in this case he was the incarnation, without wanting to shoot her, and deciding that ten hours of non-stop crying from his son would feel like bliss in comparison. Annette deserved a gift of some sort for agreeing to take on the task of babysitter, which he'd had no power to compel her to do, and an even bigger one for doing it with only a few pointed sniffs and "You owe me" jibes.

Otherwise the briefing gone smoothly. The analysts had been told about their road trip, which they'd welcomed with such dizzying speed that it made him resolve to let them out of the office more, and in return they'd confirmed that the hacker had *definitely* accessed the Adelphi's cameras from outside by piggybacking the backstage console with their signal and pinning down its source was already underway. Their killer had watched Julianne Hodges' demise as it had happened and probably recorded it to share with others, making a snuff movie that would bring the Vice Squad in on their hunt.

The analysts had offered *that* tasty morsel in return for their visit to the labs and dry-cleaners, but when Craig had mentioned the factory junket, they'd almost tripped over themselves in their eagerness to give him more. Namely that Des had called to confirm the Nicotine solution *had* been chemically tagged so they were already working on tracing its origin, although the caveat was always that it could dead end with some vendor on the Dark Web.

At that point Davy had felt the need to earn his title of Head Analyst and explain in great detail the effect of electromagnetism on their second victim's body, specifically John's finding of destruction at a cellular level.

"Doctor Winter said it looked like nothing he'd ever s...seen before."

They now had definitive causes and mechanisms of death for both their victims and Craig built on the information when the session resumed, standing at the front of the squad-room and tapping the whiteboard on 'CCTV'.

"Davy, you got a signal on the Adelphi's cameras, anything on the X-ray reading-room's yet?"

His response was to give his junior a 'take it away' nod, so Ash did, playing with his earring as he spoke and making Craig feel nauseous. He'd couldn't stand piercings and had made Katy promise never to get any until he was dead. She'd had no any intention of getting one anyway, having *way* too much respect for disease transmission, but she didn't tell her husband that of course and instead extracted a quid pro quo that *he* would never let himself get fat.

Averting his eyes from the offending earlobe Craig listened as the flamboyant IT expert ran through what he'd found, eventually cutting through his tech-speak to boil it down to, "So you found an external signal at the hospital too?"

"Yep. And a virus."

Ash moved to the screen beside Nicky's desk and showed a slide that held three lines of code.

"OK. We've finally located the viruses, three so far. The first is from *our* computer system, which probably got in by someone opening a link they shouldn't have, or maybe just clicking on an email that had been made to look official. Hackers call it spear phishing and lots of people take the bait."

He scanned the team's faces for signs of guilt, until finally Ryan caved in and nodded.

"I got what I thought was an email from records but when I opened it, it was blank."

Crag nodded. "Easily done. Hackers can mimic pretty much any sender now."

"Yeh, no worries. We caught it before anything about this case had been entered on the system. Just as well we were on the ball."

Craig knew he wanted praise and was just about to give it when Liam yawned noisily and patted his mouth.

"Yeh, yeh, you're brilliant. Give the kid a balloon."

Davy jumped to his friend's defence. *"You're* a balloon!"

It earned him a laugh that left Liam wishing he'd never started. But once in the deputy was all in, and Craig saw him winding up for a retort.

He cut it off quickly, earning a scowl.

"Yes, well done you two. Anything more on our virus, Ash?"

"Well, the date it was inserted shows the hacker was familiar with the police cyberscanning schedule, and probably my interim scan too. Mine only covers our computers, so although I know *they* were safe until at least Friday I can't rule out the hacker accessing a camera in here last week."

He glanced meaningfully at the now-disabled CCTV camera on the ceiling above his desk.

Aidan's interest was piqued.

"You're saying our hacker's a cop?"

It was exactly what Craig and Liam had thought when Davy had discussed the scans, but the analyst shook his head.

"It's way too soon to say cop. There are analysts, cybersecurity teams and administrators closer to the police scan than any cop, *and* more likely to be tech savvy. But it's likely that *some* sort of police employee was involved so," he turned to Craig, "this could be s...sensitive, chief."

The detective nodded briskly, "So we keep it in the squad for now. You mentioned three viruses, Ash?"

The analyst returned to his slide.

"OK, so virus one was ours, and there were also viruses in the theatre and MRI consoles."

"The same sort?"

"Only in that all three were Trojans. Their functions were all different. The one here allowed the hacker to control our computers and read everything on them, as well as switch on our mikes and cameras. The Adelphi's virus made its CCTV cameras vulnerable to piggybacking from an external signal, and the MRI virus did the same for the cameras in Radiology, *plus* it allowed the three MRIs' safeties to be disabled so the hacker could push them to run high."

"They sound sophisticated."

"The hacker was, but the virus functions themselves are pretty straightforward-"

Davy cut in. "Although neither of us has seen these particular viruses before."

Liam thought it was time to reassert himself. "Would you recognise them? I mean there must be millions of the wee buggers."

"There are, but most hackers stick to a few viruses they like and between us we've collected most of the common ones-"

The DCI's shaking head cut him off. "Now that's just plain sad, son. You need to get out more. Tell him he's sad, boss."

Davy continued as if he hadn't spoken, "-but these are completely new."

His junior joined in enthusiastically. "Which means they were probably bought on the Dark Web, the D.W. is what most people call it. Viruses are bought and sold there all the time, the nastier the better. Some of them could steal a bank's reserves in seconds if they got into their systems."

Craig nodded. "Which is presumably why commercial cybersecurity teams get the big bucks. When you get to the factory you'll probably find a fourth virus that allowed Nicotine to be added to the cleaning mix, and then diverted the contaminated canisters to our local dry-cleaner."

That's if Grace found contamination in all the canisters which he was betting that she would.

Confirming that Ash had finished his slide Craig moved briskly back to the centre of the room.

"Right. So, you're on the cameras and viruses. What can you do on the Dark Web? Use chat-rooms again?"

They'd been useful in a case linked with Galway months before.

Davy nodded his junior to answer.

"That mainly worked in the Galway case because the perps *wanted* us to know what they were up to, chief. Because they were killing for a cause. But I doubt if this git will advertise his existence. I *could* go on the D.W. posing as a buyer interested in new viruses and see if a seller bites, and I could also boast about these amazing new viruses I've found in some chat-rooms and see if someone approaches me there. Game-rooms too, and I'll speak to our Cybercrime team."

"Good. But speak to Cybercrime *before* you go wandering on the dark side, please. There may be investigations of theirs they don't want you to cross. If you're lucky they may have something on these viruses already."

Craig turned back to the real world. "OK, normal policing. Tell me anything new about our two victims."

It was Aidan's cue to sit forward and assume his usual reporting posture; dangling his long arms between his knees. That and his permanent russet tan made Liam think of an orangutan.

"OK, so we went to see Maria O'Rourke's parents and raised the prospect of murder-"

Craig interrupted. "They didn't know?"

"Nope. And it was a shock, I can tell you."

Craig tutted in annoyance. "I thought John might have mentioned it when they ID-ed the body."

"Aye, well, after they got past the shock they were mostly puzzled because they'd thought their daughter had died from pacemaker failure, but they were keen to help. They didn't have much of use though. Maria was the older of two daughters, they have two boys as well, and according to them she'd never been any trouble. Wanted to be a doctor since she was knee-high apparently and had just studied hard for years."

"Boyfriends?"

"None apparently."

Annette pulled a face. "At twenty-seven? None that they knew about more like."

The DCI nodded. "I agree. They seemed to think she was a paragon of virtue. Studied hard, didn't drink, smoke, do drugs or date."

Liam gave a wistful sigh. "Exactly what I want for Erin."

Annette suppressed her immediate urge to snort. She'd met Liam's eight-year-old daughter many times and precocious wasn't a strong enough word for her. Ferociously bright and as cute as a button he would be lucky if she wasn't running rings around him before she hit her teens.

Craig moved on quickly in case someone else was less diplomatic.

"Maria may have been everything her parents believe or not, but it's clear that *they* didn't know if she wasn't. So, suggestions please."

Annette volunteered, "Her friends will know more about her. School or student friends, and people she was close to at work."

"Good. OK, Annette, as hospitals were your world, you and Mary visit her work. Aidan, go to her old school and university and see if there's anything useful there. Davy, run the usual checks on her and the family. Include anything like drug fines, DUIs and so on."

Liam objected noisily, still keen for there to be some untainted role models for his daughter in the world.

"Isn't that victim shaming, boss? Like, let's see if she'd done something bad enough to make someone kill her?"

It earned him a tut and a sigh.

"You know better than that, Liam. We *always* need to know everything there is to know about our victims, to see where, if anywhere, they might have met their killers. We'll be doing the same with Julianne Hodges, but I'll come back to her in a moment. Everyone got all that about Maria O'Rourke?"

A series of nods said yes.

"OK, Julianne Hodges. Annette, you and Mary were looking deeper into the husband, so what's your feeling on him now?"

"His background checks were squeaky clean, but when I called to go back and see him he was out arranging the funeral."

"OK. Mary, what did you think when you met him?"

"A nice bereaved man with a small child. He seemed genuinely broken up about her death."

"And yet, some nice people still murder their spouses. So, in addition to doing all the same checks for both women let's look into Morgan Hodges' business and finances, and check close relatives in both cases. Andy, I'd like you to lead on that with Ryan, and Davy, you and Ash run the checks. I want everything there is on these women, especially any links between them. Even the smallest thing could connect to their deaths."

Liam was frowning thoughtfully, an expression that his boss had learned not to ignore.

"You have something, Liam?"

The deputy looked uncertain for a moment then he shrugged and started to speak.

"So, this hacking could be done from anywhere in the world, right?"

The question was clearly meant for the analysts so Ash obliged with a nod.

"OK, but...these are *local* women dying. Why? If the hackers could be anywhere."

Craig knew they were about to get into what he and Jock Armstrong had covered and the follow-on thoughts that had kept him awake the night before, so he scribbled 'Remote' on the whiteboard as his deputy went on.

"So... I said to the boss before that there could be more than one person involved here. Maybe one far away and one more local."

And then it came. The thought that had kept Craig awake.

"But what if it's really a group?"

Ash cut in excitedly. "A hacker group?"

Liam shrugged. "Some online bunch of clowns anyway."

Craig could tell that a lengthy discussion was about to start, so before it did he outlined his visit to Jock Armstrong, ending with Incels and the Chan boards.

Liam had heard some but not all of it before and had a question.

"How do we know that right now this isn't happening somewhere else in the world too? Twenty-seven-year-old women being offed in strange ways, I mean."

Craig nodded. "We don't, so we need to find out. Davy can you run a check with the other agencies? FBI, Interpol and the rest."

"Ash has the contacts there, but yes."

"But don't just use twenty-seven-year-old women as the key, look for any groups of two or more killings with identical features, no matter who the victims are."

He ignored the eyes widening all around him and nodded his deputy to continue.

"OK, so... let's say there's this group of geeky creeps," he grinned at the analysts, "no offence, geeks."

Davy smiled. "None taken."

"So, they're sitting in their wee dark rooms tapping away and they come up with this plan to kill, but you can only kill what you see, can't you, boss?"

"You have to see something to choose to kill it might be a better description. But I know where you're heading with this, Liam, and although that's the most likely scenario it doesn't mean that one of our killers, if there is more than one, *had* to see the women in person."

He wanted them investigating with open minds.

"They could have just seen them on social media, but

even if it was a local sighting it could have been in passing on the street. Stalkers often don't speak to their victims. That reminds me, Davy, check for stalker reports on both women and dig through their social media profiles, please."

"Already on my list, chief."

Of course they were, because he was good at his job; it made Craig wonder whether he was just conducting an orchestra and should just step back completely on one case to see how his virtuosos performed alone. *And* if he was missed.

Liam was unpersuaded by the argument and noisy about it.

"Aye, it's true they don't *have* to be local, boss, but the odds are at least one of these pervs saw our Vics in the flesh at some point. Met them more likely, otherwise why kill them?"

"I did say that was the most likely scenario."

But agreeing with Liam never stopped him when he was on a roll.

"I mean, you have to hate or lust after something to kill it, unless you're a complete psycho who just gets off on snuffing people at random, and if that was the case there'd be a lot more unsolved cases. And also, these women were both the same age. What's the odds of being *that* accurate on social media? Everyone I know on social media shaves ten years off their age. Or did they go through the electoral roll and select them?" He answered his own question with a shake of the head. "No, I think one of these humps knew at least one of our Vics, probably both of them, and *that's* why they chose them to kill."

Folding his arms with a flourish the DCI sat back.

"I hope you're right, Liam, I really do, because at least that way we'll stand a chance of catching them. If these murders were hatched and executed completely in the ether then we might not. But I have to be honest, there's very little about them that *couldn't* have been done that way."

He tapped the 'Remote' he'd written on the board.

"Our victims could have been selected remotely from social media and the ways in which they were killed were remote as was the hacking of our office. And that might only have occurred because we were the closest murder squad to the scenes and so likely to take these cases."

Or not.

Craig decided that he was depressing everyone by playing Devil's Advocate so he smiled and drew himself up straight.

"But I agree with Liam. We have to work this case as if our victims *weren't* chosen at random because most people do kill for a reason, however flimsy that reason may seem to us. And if there *was* a perceived reason then it came from somewhere in our victims' pasts, and that means legwork, so get on with it."

With that he nodded Liam to come into his office and closed the door.

"This is all starting to fit Armstrong's profile, Liam. A pair of killers working to select victims and killing them remotely, one more dominant than the other who makes the picks and may live locally. He called them cyberpaths; voyeurs and sadistic killers, but highly computer literate and bright. If it is a pair he suggested a joint psychopathy. He also agreed when I suggested they might be Incels, involuntary celibates."

"I wouldn't doubt it, slimeballs like that. No sane woman would touch them. Didn't he also say they could move on somewhere else once they'd finished here, and there was no time frame for it?"

Craig slumped in his chair. "Yes. But he could be wrong."

"You sound like you want to prove something to him. Get under your skin, did he, boss?"

The observation made Craig chuckle. "Well spotted. He was a bit too perfect for my liking, and..."

The way the word tailed off told Liam all he needed to know.

"You don't like the fact he knew the wife first, do you?"

Craig's indignation jolted him upright. "He *didn't* date her!"

"I didn't say date, I said *know*, and I didn't mean in the biblical sense."

That would've been more than his life was worth.

"Just as well." Craig climbed off his high horse slowly. "OK...well...yes, maybe...I admit I didn't like him calling her Katy. It was too damned familiar." It sounded childish and he knew it, so he scrambled for something more serious to add, failing abysmally with, "And he had a goatee. I can't stand those."

Liam tried not to laugh then gave up, his guffaw audible outside the room.

"You jealous bugger! Catch a grip of yourself, man. Next you'll be saying he breathed too noisily!"

"He did." Craig joined his deputy in laughing. "But, although it pains me to admit it, his profile *was* pretty accurate."

"I guessed we were dealing with a partnership first."

"Yes, but he said one of them might be a woman."

The DCI raised an eyebrow, which given they were as straight as pencils was always a feat, then dismissed the point with a shrug. "I doubt that. But maybe they'll prove me wrong and kill an all-male list next. Mary would probably like that. I reckon you'd be top of *hers*."

"I can hardly wait."

Craig raked his hair slowly and prayed for inspiration.

"We *really* need to find something to link these women, Liam."

Just then he remembered the note he'd scribbled at Armstrong's and after a quick search found it and read aloud.

"Tech and game suppliers." He looked at his deputy. "We're going to visit some local tech and game shops."

"Because?"

"Because if our dominant killer *is* local and as tech savvy as we suspect he's bound to frequent one. Nip out and ask Davy to give you the names of the big ones locally, and get him to compile a list of the relevant magazines as well so we can check their local mailing lists."

The DCI thought Craig's brain had sprung a leak but did as he was asked, leaving his boss thinking deep thoughts until his PA entered the room. Nicky's expression said she wasn't the bearer of good news.

"Doctor Winter says can you call him urgently."

"That doesn't sound good."

"It isn't. He says there's been another death."

Craig raced past her to the door. "Call him back and tell him we're coming down, Nicky."

Liam caught him up by the lift.

"What's the rush? I've got the shops and we've plenty of time to get there. Davy said they stay open till nine."

Craig jabbed the lift button twice, the second time so hard his deputy knew something more serious was up.

"Calm down, boss. We'll get there."

The response came with another jab. "We're not going to the shops. There's been another death."

****

The Labs.

"Twenty-seven?"

As those were the first words out of Craig's mouth when he pushed open John Winter's office door its occupant was slightly taken aback. It took the medic a moment to work out just where they were in the discourse the detectives had clearly started on the way there.

Liam nodded in sympathy, having been consigned to silence on the journey by whatever conversation his boss was holding inside his head.

Craig saw the confusion and elaborated.

"Please tell me we don't have another twenty-seven-year-old female victim, John."

The medic sighed and waved the policemen to sit, not moving to make their usual drinks because they wouldn't be in the room for long.

"I can't. I'm sorry, Marc." He lifted the folder he'd set to one side just a moment before, opening it at the summary. "Felicia Barker, twenty-seven in October, died at ten o'clock this morning on Rochester Ward St Mary's Hospital."

Craig opened his mouth to say something but the pathologist forged on.

"She was a brittle diabetic."

When Liam raised a finger, he paused to allow the obvious question.

"Brittle?"

"It means poorly controlled. Either her diabetes treatment regimen was inadequate or she wasn't sticking to her diet. Either way the control of her blood sugars was poor, which is why she was on a medical ward."

He set down the file, staring at Craig in an invitation to speak.

"How did she die, John?"

Even as he asked it Craig knew technology had been involved. He was right and this time it was at quite a simple level compared to their first two deaths.

"She was getting controlled doses of insulin through a pump and it dispensed a massive overdose. She was admitted to hospital last week and they had a tough job settling her blood sugars at first, but they managed it at the weekend and were just keeping her on the same dose of insulin for a couple more days before they allowed her home."

"How long had she been diabetic?"

"Since she was seven. The notes say she'd been erratic with her insulin injections since she started handling them herself at puberty. It's not uncommon with teens with medical issues. They sometimes resent being different from their peers and lash out. Anyway, she'd been seeing a psychiatrist for depression for six months but there was no suggestion of suicidal thoughts, I checked, and in any case the insulin pump was sealed. There was no way she could have altered the dose herself."

Craig nodded wearily, suddenly feeling every minute of his lack of sleep.

"The pump was connected to her in her room, but the dose instructions were sent via wi-fi from elsewhere, am I right?"

John nodded. "From the nurses' station on the main ward. But there's no suggestion of foul play there, Marc. Although I guess that's up to you to determine."

Liam interrupted the exchange. "Have the CSIs been down yet?"

"Grace has a team there now. An eagle-eyed junior doctor noticed Ms Barker's age and remembered hearing about your squad investigating Maria O'Rourke's death – apparently he knew her - so he sealed off the room and equipment immediately and asked for an urgent PM."

"You did it, Doc?"

"No, Mike. But when we saw her blood sugars we tested her insulin level and found a massive overdose. She would have gone into hypoglycaemic shock very quickly."

Craig dragged a hand wearily down his face. One Nicotine poisoning, one electromagnetic pulse, and now murder by insulin. All without laying a finger on the women. Damn, this guy was good.

"OK. Give Andy a call, please, Liam. Tell him to get down to..."

"Rochester Ward. Third floor, east wing."

"...and check the lay-out. And ask Davy to see if a virus entered the system. Also, the CCTV outside and inside the dead woman's room, if there is any. But say that can wait till tomorrow. The analysts have got enough to do today"

As Liam left the room to make the call, Craig turned back to his friend.

"Anything else in that file, John? Like her job."

To his surprise the medic shook his head.

"She didn't work. She qualified as a maths teacher but was on long-term sick leave because her diabetes was so uncontrolled."

Which *could* have meant her spending more time on social media. Or did the fact that two of their victims had died at St Mary's point to something there? He was reaching for anything that might bring logic to the choice of victims and finding it hard to get a foothold beyond their gender and age.

The pathologist rose and headed for the door. "I presume you'd like to see your victim?"

'If I must' popped into Craig's head but not out of his mouth. Dead people might be the reason he had a job but that didn't make them his favourite things.

"Lead the way."

They caught up with Liam by the vending machine and waited for him to end his call before entering the freezing cold dissection room together, Craig in the fugue state that usually accompanied his visits to the newly murdered.

It was an oddly detached yet intensely frustrated feeling of a life lost unnecessarily, the majority so recently that the dead looked not quite dead yet, just pale and sleeping and as if with a good shake and a spot of defib they would sit up and ask for tea and toast. It always angered him, the sense that if he'd *just* got there in time, *just* got there before the grim reaper in whatever human form he had manifested, then that person might have been dozing in their own comfortable bed instead of lying immobile on one made of steel.

Recognising the mood John nudged his friend's elbow to return him to the land of the living and drew the sheet covering their latest victim down to her collar bones, revealing an elegantly long-necked woman with red hair who looked older than her years even at rest, perhaps a sign of having been chronically unwell.

What was glaringly obvious was that for all their age similarities their three victims had looked nothing alike; Julianne Hodges' hair had been a wispy light brown, Maria O'Rourke's jet-black and curly, Felicia Barker's red. The three women had also been different heights and weights. It felt like another failure to the man grasping for any commonality that he could find.

Liam put Craig's thoughts into words. "One redhead, one brown hair and one black."

John knew the game and joined in. "Not to mention different builds, jobs and religions, plus Julianne Hodges grew up in France and only came here as a teenager. Her mum's French."

Craig's dull tone reflected his mood.

"In other words, our victims still have nothing in common but their sex and age."

John led the way back to the corridor where Liam felt less decorum was required and gave his boss a slap on the back.

"Nil desperandum, boss. The lads will find something they all share. Have faith."

Craig did, but it didn't prevent him suffering the odd dip.

Dip over, he nodded.

"Do we need to see Des, John? I mean she definitely died from insulin overdose and it definitely got in through the pump?"

"And there was nothing strange in her stomach contents and no other injection sites or toxins, so I'll just ask Des to call you with whatever he gets from the CSIs."

Nodding the detective turned towards the exit. He didn't speak again until the car had pulled out onto the Saintfield Road.

"Go right, Liam. One of the tech shops is in the Forestside Shopping Centre, so we might as well visit it while we're near."

Ten minutes later they were in a neon-lit shop full of cables, games consoles that cost eye-watering amounts of money, and screens displaying various animated acts of violence and mayhem, and Liam was staring down balefully at a young man whose badge declared he was called Sammy and whose greasy hair and stubble said that he probably hadn't bathed in a week.

He stared for a whole thirty seconds before the youth

realised that the thing blocking his light was human and Craig watched in amusement as Liam's height registered, then as Sammy's narrowed, screen-squinting eyes widened at the sight of his ID.

"I'm DCI Cullen and this here is DCS Craig, son."

Liam's booming bass had an unexpected effect on the teenager and his thin body jerked instantly into straight-backed rigidity, telling Craig that he'd had reserve or full-time army experience which meant that a decent show of authority should extract whatever info he had.

As the boy wilted under the glare of Major Cullen, Craig displayed his own authority by barking for a list of all the latest tech and games then getting to the thorny subject of buyers.

"Do you have a note of who bought any of these?"

Sammy was still chin up, head back so he motioned, 'At ease' and watched the grubby youth resume his earlier slouch.

"Can't tell you that."

The words brought another glare from the Major and a sigh of disappointment from his commanding officer.

"Please don't say confidentiality. You're not a doctor or a priest."

The youth's face folded into a stubborn sulk.

"It's because of some finance law. We can't give details without a-"

"Warrant. OK then, warrant it is. Chief Inspector Cullen, who's nearest the courthouse?"

"The lassies."

"Tell them we'll need information warrants for every tech and game shop in Belfast and the magazine lists." He turned back to the youth. "Will that do?"

"I suppose."

A sideways glance from Liam and he jerked upright again.

"I suppose, *sir!"*

The response was parroted verbatim, making Craig fight off a smirk.

"Very good, Sammy. Someone will be here within the

hour with a warrant for that information, so get your list of the latest products and their buyers ready. If it isn't, I'll have my officers search the whole shop and it will take you a week to tidy up."

They heard the young man muttering and rummaging as they headed for the door and to Craig's joy his deputy turned back just long enough to shout, "ATTEN -SHUN!" and treat them to the sight of Sammy springing up from behind his reception desk so fast that he cracked his head on the wood.

It almost compensated Craig for what he knew was coming; another sleepless night spent searching for clues to help crack their case.

****

The CCU. Wednesday, 8.30 a.m.

Davy was slightly luckier with his inspiration. In fact, it had woken him in the middle of the night and made him fall out of the single bed he was still forced to sleep in at the home he shared with his mother and grandmother. Well, when he said forced what he actually meant was compelled, not by the women in question but by his own sense of guilt, born of years of attending a strict Catholic school.

Which hadn't actually been as bad as it might sound to some people. It had given him a more than solid, in fact a superheated, education that he valued and a robust sense of right and wrong that try as he might, and *boy* had he tried when he was a teenager, was so deeply ingrained in him that he couldn't deviate from it now if his life depended on it. His sister Emmie had benefited similarly which was why she now lectured at a prestigious London university, but anyway, the upshot of all that teaching and moralising meant that although he and Maggie had been sleeping together for years it only ever happened at her apartment, which meant he only needed a single bed at home affording two women that

156

he respected deeply the belief that he was still a good little boy. It was a small sacrifice and if it made them happy then it made him happy, except when he had one of his 'eureka' dreams then it almost always resulted in him falling out of bed on to the floor.

But the inspiration had been worth the sore arm he'd got in the process and had brought him into the office at seven-thirty to check something, so that by the time a bleary looking Craig arrived an hour later Davy had something that he knew would make him smile.

As the detective read the smart-pad thrust at him, it did. He scanned its screen swiftly and returned it to his analyst.

"You're sure about this, Davy?"

Stupid question, but then it *was* before his second coffee of the day and it usually took three before he could think clearly.

"Yep. I know Liam w...wondered if our peeper could have been nearby from the start, but the radio signal that highjacked the CCTV could have been relayed from anywhere in the world. Except it turns out that it wasn't, it was *boosted*, which means whoever was sending it had to be close. I mean inside the building or one street along close."

He perched on the nearest desk before going on.

"I doubt we'll get anything on the O'Rourke cameras *during* the actual murder, because the EMP blew the room's electrics and the room had no natural light, but I'm sure the weirdo was watching right up to the second he flipped the switch and there's a recorder on that system because it's a hospital, so we *might* get something just beforehand. With the Adelphi death we should definitely get something-"

Craig cut in. "And the insulin murder?"

The analyst's brown eyes widened. "What insulin murd..."

The word tailed off as he realised there'd been a third death.

Craig nodded him to come into his office, where he

made them both drinks.

"I'll cover the detail when everyone gets in, but a third woman, same age, was killed at St Mary's Medical Unit yesterday when her insulin pump overloaded. It was run via wi-fi from the nurses' station so I'm pretty sure it's our perp. But that will give you more hacks to check."

The analyst tried not to look excited given that another person had died.

"Also, when are you and Ash heading to the dry-cleaners and factory?"

"Right after you update. But I actually think Ash should go alone now, 'cos I really need to pursue these signals."

"Whatever you think best. But just returning to what you said about the signal's origin being close. Could that have meant inside-the-hospital close in the case of Maria O'Rourke?"

"Possibly, although the Radiology Department's near the hospital's back door so the carpark could've worked as well. For this latest case on the medical unit I'll need to check exactly where that is. If it's at the core of the hospital then the signal might've been sent from inside."

"I remember visiting Katy at the unit once and I'm pretty sure it *is* near the centre of the building."

"Then we might be lucky, chief. If they were inside the hospital when they sent the signal, they might have been caught on internal CCTV. But the Adelphi's still our best bet. The auditorium's outer w...wall is on Fountainville Avenue, which has street and traffic cams. So, if we're *really* lucky we might see the perp."

"You've a lot of work ahead."

Craig fell so deep into thought for a moment that he forgot the analyst was there until he coughed.

"Sorry, Davy, I was just chasing something. Liam and I visited some of the tech stores yesterday but only one would give us anything on their customers without a warrant."

The analyst chuckled. "Anyone would think they were doctors."

"Exactly, which led me to another thought that I'll tell you about in a moment. But you'll have the magazine mailing lists today too, won't you, so give those and the list of shops to Mary to start working on overlaps. We need the name of anyone buying the newest tech or games locally in the past six months and any local subscribers to the magazines. Ask her to pass the full lists on to the agencies as well. We're looking for names, occupations and any criminal records at this stage, and photographs if there are any, to help your CCTV search. That brings me back to my earlier thought. I wonder if our man has a psychiatric history."

The IT expert nudged his untouched coffee away surreptitiously as he formulated his response. He'd become a vegetarian two years before and felt better for it; now it was time to try giving up another chemical and caffeine was the drug of choice. He could have gone for alcohol, but Friday nights wouldn't be Friday nights without a nice bottle of wine.

"Even with names it's going to be hard to get any doctor to admit that, chief."

"Impossible I'd say, but I could hedge around it and watch their response."

"And I've drawn a blank on stalking charges, s...sorry."

Craig sighed at the slamming of another door.

"Don't worry, it was always a long shot. Our man's too clever to be that obvious. Everything hinges on finding those names..."

When Craig tuned out and started staring past him into space Davy took it as his cue to leave, and as he emerged from the office he met Liam and Nicky bantering their way on to the floor. The sound brought Craig out for just long enough to greet his PA and beckon his deputy inside, where he reiterated what he'd just said to Davy, ending with, "What do you think?"

Liam's reply was typically blunt. "I think you haven't a snowball's chance in hell of getting a doctor to talk, shortlist or not."

"Thanks for that vote of confidence."

"Aye, well I know you're married to one of them and all, and you can probably get *her* to tell you anything, but no amount of your Latin Lover charm will persuade some psychiatrist who wants to keep their medical licence. Doctors won't even confirm someone's their patient never mind tell you what's wrong with them. They're as bad as priests."

"Or as good, depending on whether you're the one spilling your guts. And trust me, Katy tells me *nothing* that she doesn't already want me to know."

"So, what's the point of thinking about trick cyclists at all?"

Craig chuckled at the slang term for psychiatrists. He hadn't heard it since John was at medical school.

"Because I'll know if they're hiding something by watching their faces as I read out each name."

Liam's chuckle came from deep within his chest.

"And you're *seriously* going to do this with every psychiatrist in the six counties?"

"If necessary. How many can there be who only see adults?"

"Too damn many. There has to be a way of narrowing it down."

"There might be once we get some likely names from Mary. We could check which GPs they're registered with, and *they* either refer patients to specialists near where they live or where they work."

Liam was still only slightly persuaded, the words 'clutching' and 'straws' writ large in his mind.

"I *suppose* I can see that. But even if we're damn lucky and all those things fall into place, we'll still only get a suspect not proof. It sounds like a lot of work for nothing, boss."

Changing direction again, Craig leapt to his feet. "OK, let's go. I need a catch-up to see what new info we've got."

Ten minutes later it was clear what the answer was; not a lot. At first sight all the beat-pounding the day before seemed to have produced was negatives.

Annette reported first.

"Maria O'Rourke was well liked at work and there's nothing bad lurking in her background. No cautions or arrests for anything and just one outstanding parking ticket. She didn't even cheat on exams."

Aidan, who'd been yawning after a late drinking session with friends, something he'd had very few of for years before dating Deidre and was having to get used to again, nodded.

"We met a few of her friends from university and they all confirmed the parents' story. She was a straight arrow. No drugs, cigs, the odd glass of wine at a party and not even many of those. She was a studier and pretty quiet."

Craig wasn't giving up yet. "Men?"

"No boyfriends at school and no-one serious since."

"Any chance one of the less serious ones fixated on her?"

"I asked, and nope."

Ash concurred, not bothering to shift from his usual semi-recumbent position to repeat what Davy had said, "There were no stalker reports on either woman."

Craig was getting exasperated. "Social media? *Anything?*"

A sudden narrowing of his junior analyst's eyes made him hope.

"Well... there was a little thing, and it *might* mean nothing."

"But?"

"But her FaceChat and Swatter accounts were set to private. I mean, the highest level of security on both. Which struck me as kind of unusual for a young woman. I mean, my friends post selfies all day long and they want the whole world to see them."

Annette shook her head despairingly. "Don't they have anything better to do?"

He shrugged. "We're the most photographed generation ever."

Liam quipped, "But not because you're better looking.

161

I blame smart-phones and that reality TV shite. Bunch of idiots up their own-"

Craig cut him off before the very polite Alice imploded. *Exploding* would have been too rude.

"Thank you, Liam, I think we all get the idea. So, you believe Maria O'Rourke's social media lockdown is relevant, Ash?"

"I think I'd like to dig further."

"Dig away, but after your road-trip. What about Julianne Hodges' social media?"

"She didn't have any accounts, so my guess is she got enough public exposure on the stage."

"Or she had some and shut them down for some reason?"

The analyst scribbled himself a note to check.

"OK, everyone keep going on Maria O'Rourke. Take it back further, to school friends, ask her teachers about her, you know the drill. Right, the Hodges. Andy, you and Ryan were looking at them. Anything?"

The DCI felt almost ashamed to say how little he had and wished that he could have gone first.

"Not much, chief. Sorry. She was a young mum and happily married according to everyone we asked. Her drama-school friends confirmed she'd met her husband at secondary school and never been unfaithful, and even though she was very pretty she'd never really got bothered at parties because she'd been wearing an engagement ring for years. Nothing criminal for her or her family. She smoked a few cigarettes occasionally and had the odd glass of wine, but she was pretty serious about her work. We've got the name of her school, Brushford Academy, so we'll be visiting there next."

No-one noticed Mary blanching except her boss.

The words galvanised Aidan. *"Brushford Academy? Near Holywood? One of Maria O'Rourke's friends said she went there too."*

Finally, their victims had something in common. Craig wanted to cheer but instead he made a rewind motion.

"So, you're both sure your victims attended that school?"

He knew of the school because it was close to where he'd been raised but had never been through its doors.

The DCIs nodded.

"When?"

Staggered "Two-thousand-and-four to two-thousand-and-eleven" s came back. Their first two victims had attended the same school at the same time.

"OK, if you haven't already done it get their class schedules. I want to know what classes they shared if any, and-"

Liam signalled to interrupt.

"There's something obvious we need to ask first, boss. Was the school mixed sex?"

It wasn't as strange a question as it might have sounded in other western countries because the majority of Northern Ireland's secondary schools were single sex. People seemed to prefer their children not only separated on the grounds of religion, only seven percent of all schools being named as integrated, but completely avoiding the opposite sex until it was impossible not to at university or work.

The point hadn't occurred to Craig because he'd attended a mixed-sex grammar, but Liam hadn't *officially* spoken to a girl except his sisters until he was eighteen, which could explain a lot.

"Well spotted, Liam. Is it mixed sex? And back then?"

Andy replied. "Boys have been admitted there for twenty years. You're thinking our killer may have been amongst them?"

"I'm not sure, but it's a thread so let's pull it. OK, anything else on the victims?"

When there was silence he turned to his analysts. "Right, what have you got that's new?"

Much of it was work in progress but Ash did have one useful point.

"The agencies did a search of murders of twenty-seven-year-old women and there was nothing. Not in the

States, GB, Europe or further east."

Craig was about to move on when he spoke again.

"But there *was* a similar spate of murders of nineteen-year-old women in France, and a handful of twenty-year-old men in London and *seven* sixty-two-year-old men in Italy, all in the past three years."

Craig's mind started racing.

They weren't dealing with a pair of killers; they were dealing with a group. Or were they? Was this Folie à deux simply moving beyond killing potential love objects to killing any person in their life who had done them wrong? Even older men as surrogates for their fathers? And *could* the young men who were killed indicate, as Armstrong had hypothesised, that the second member of their partnership was a woman?

A nudge from his deputy brought Craig back to earth.

"Sorry about that, everyone. I was just thinking about something else Doctor Armstrong said to me about the killer."

As he outlined more of Jock Armstrong's thoughts Annette couldn't conceal her scepticism.

"I know we've seen lots of female murderers, sir, but really?"

"That was my initial thought as well, Annette, more because of the level of tech obsession here than any higher level of virtue in women."

Seeing Mary's nostrils flair Liam intervened with what he thought was a definite save.

"Although on average, women *are* a bit nicer than we are, lads. Let's be honest. Or not as inclined to kill people at least."

Craig shot him a grateful look and joined in, "And Mary of course is an IT expert, but *on average* there aren't as many women obsessed with this stuff, or as likely to kill as men. That's just a fact."

The noisy sniff and, "I can think of plenty of reasons to kill" that came from the constable made him move swiftly on.

"OK, Ash, that's very interesting but I'm not sure what

164

it means yet, so let's focus on what we have. Unfortunately, what we have now is a third victim. Liam, cover that, please."

He seized the opening to get a fresh coffee and when he returned his deputy was finishing up with, "So, we obviously need to check her school now, but rule out all the other stuff too."

Craig took over smoothly. "Andy, you and Ryan take Felicia Barker. Aidan and Annette, go down to that school and find what's written down and what isn't, especially info on any teenagers who had links or crushes on our victims or any trouble surrounding them. Andy, as soon as you know which school Ms Barker attended phone it through to Annette."

Mary cut in. "Am I not going with Annette?"

"No, I have another job for you, but first, I noticed you were very quiet during the school discussion, Mary. Did you attend Brushford by any chance?"

The shifting of position and gaze averting that followed said yes and confirmed that they'd been right to put her under guard.

"OK, when?"

"Just for two years. Oh-seven and eight. Then my parents moved me to a school with a better science department."

He turned back to the group. "This confirms that one of the reasons for our office hack may have been to access Mary, and that means she's at risk. Most of you won't have known this, but because Mary's the same age as our other victims she's been under guard since yesterday. With the school link that will now tighten."

"Other victims? I'm not dead yet!"

"Sorry, slip of the tongue. The point is we've had three deaths in supposedly safe locations and I'm not having a fourth. Mary, I want you to tell Annette everything you can think of about your two years at the academy before she and Aidan leave. Get it down on paper."

He turned to his analysts. "OK, there's a lot of work on the IT side still to do. Davy, you have those lists for

Mary to work on, so she'll stay in the office and do that, and..." he turned to his PA, "On no account is Constable Li to leave this office unaccompanied at any time, Nicky."

Her smirk said she was going to enjoy playing the jailer.

"Ash, you'll be going to the dry-cleaners and factory alone because Davy has other work to do. He'll explain. But have you done anything on the Dark Web yet?"

The analyst grinned, displaying his spectacular teeth. "Yeh, I'm chatting about these new viruses I've discovered, but I'm trying to be subtle because I don't want to scare people off. I've also posted a buyer's notice on a handful of sale boards on the D.W., so let's see if anything comes back on that."

"Good. I take it those can run themselves for a few hours?"

"Sure. I'll pick up any replies when I get back from the factory."

Craig stared hard at the computer expert for a moment, trying to form a difficult sentence and really, really wishing that Ash could just read his mind.

Liam already had, and had no qualms about saying what needed to be said.

"He's working up to tell you to dress more official when you go out on visits, son. Like, wear a jacket, a tie and a pair of trousers that aren't leather. You're wearing half a cow for God's sake, and there isn't a ranch in the land! Generally, just remember you're representing the squad and don't act the lig. And bring your official ID with you otherwise no-one will believe you're for real. OK?"

The analyst was so dumbfounded that all he could do was nod, while Davy was still wincing at the thought of the dead cow.

Craig smiled and rose to his feet.

"OK, this is going to be a busy day so get to it. We'll reconvene at five."

He beckoned his deputy into his office, waiting for the door to be closed before bursting out laughing.

"Half a cow? Brilliant. Listen, thanks for doing that, Liam. I hate having to tell people how to dress, especially civilians."

The DCI fell into a chair. "No problem. Always happy to oblige when you need someone insulting." He looked thoughtful for a moment. "So, Mary... it looks like we were right. That really pisses me off, you know."

"That this bastard's targeting one of our own, you mean."

"Yeh, that and the fact he tried to do it right under our noses, the cheeky git." He sat forward briskly. "Right, *they're* all busy so what about us?"

"We find out if John's come up with anything new on Barker then it's off to the scene of the crime."

But that would have to wait, because suddenly Craig's office door flew open to reveal his sister and his desk phone rang; clearly Nicky calling to warn that Lucia was on her way.

To say he was surprised to see her was an understatement.

"What are *you* doing here?"

In response she plopped down on a chair, tossed back her long tawny curls and shot Liam a megawatt smile.

"Hi, Liam, how's the family?"

"Great, thanks." He gazed pointedly at her ring finger. "Nice rock."

"Oh, this old thing?"

She waved her left hand in the air, trying to catch the light and almost blinding them because of the diamond's size.

Craig rolled his eyes at the display and returned to the reason for her visit.

"Look, it's lovely to see you, Luce, but this is my work so why are you here?"

She sniffed haughtily and rested her hand flat on the desk, continuing the jewellery exhibition.

"I'm here to find out what's happening with my case, of course. I dropped round to see Katy earlier but she wouldn't tell me, so now I'm here. How's the investigation progressing? That woman *did* die in front of me you know, Marc, so I must say I'm more than a bit shocked that you haven't interviewed me."

Craig knew he shouldn't have been even slightly surprised by what his sister had just said, well aware of her need for drama. It seemed to grow stronger with each year, to the point where he wondered whether one day she was going to fulfil the adage 'All women turn into their mothers' and morph into Mirella. He really hoped not; two of them on earth at once could make for a *very* noisy old age.

But Lucia wasn't at that point quite yet so he reckoned he could handle her, in the same way he had when she'd invited herself into his teenage bedroom when she was tiny. He walked around the desk, stared down hard at her until she began to feel awkward, then pointed a very straight arm at the door, which Liam had obligingly opened in anticipation.

"Out."

The technique brought the same jutted-out lower lip and crossed arms that it had brought all those years before.

"No."

"Go home, Lucia, or to work or wherever. Anywhere as long as it's not here. I'm busy, and I can't discuss confidential case details anyway and you know it."

Outnumbered, she rose to her feet and stomped to the door, then turned back with the defiance she'd always possessed and said, "I'll tell Ken" as if it was supposed to scare him, which it didn't, unlike the, "I'll tell Daddy" that she'd employed decades before.

Then, with a hair toss that would have done a supermodel proud she flounced off the floor and headed for the stairs, leaving Craig laughing in astonishment.

"It worked! It never worked that well when we were kids."

"Aye well, she *knows* she's in the wrong now, that's why. But good job anyway, boss. Very macho. Right, that was entertaining and all, but isn't it time to go?"

168

As they marched past Nicky, acknowledging her apology for an intruder slipping past her, more than one member of Craig's team was stifling a laugh.

Chapter Eight

It wasn't often that Ash got out; of the office that was. As far as his home was concerned he was hardly ever in, to the dismay of his prim accountant mother and his aunt and grandmother who shared a basement apartment in the family's four-storeyed Victorian terrace on Belfast's Antrim Road. His restaurateur father made his disapproval of his youngest child's party lifestyle clear too. His own mantra was 'work, family, work' and although he was secretly proud and frequently boasted about his computer genius son to anyone who would listen, he *did* worry that Ash would never find a nice girl, settle down and produce more members of the Rahman family line.

Ash however had other plans for his future, which mostly consisted of buying clothes, socialising, mainly at Queen's Old Staff Common Room using the card he'd nicked from Davy or somewhere on Belfast's thriving wine bar and club scene, meeting girls who his religious Hindu parents would *definitely* disapprove of and having an outrageously good time.

When, no make that *if* he ever settled down, his future wife would hopefully be a bossy, pierced, genius atheist who dressed as flamboyantly as him and made her living as a musician or running a nightclub so he had a legitimate excuse to hang about in one until he popped his clogs at eighty-five. As soon as he met her he was moving out of the family home, but for now he had the best food in Belfast on tap and work to use as an excuse for staying out when he had 'other business' at night.

The upshot was that the analyst got out plenty between the hours of seven p.m. and a.m. but not often in between, and it showed. As soon as he walked through the wide glass doors of Bright Day Dry Cleaners and his gaze lit on a kneeling jump-suited CSI, his tentative amble became a definite strut and he experienced a strange desire to high-five everyone that he passed.

He managed to stop strutting when he reached the

staffer, introducing himself to the top of her hooded head and requesting to see the console from which the Nicotine tainted fluid that had caused Julianne Hodges' demise had been dispensed.

The scientist looked up at him curiously, as if she wasn't quite sure what he was. He wasn't a cop, that much was obvious from his tie, which looked like it was strangling him and was so old-fashioned that she guessed he'd nicked it from his dad, and his too-large grey suit, also about two decades out of date and probably belonging to the same man. She was right; the only suit of his own that Ash possessed was a powder-blue obscenity that his mum had made him wear at his sister's wedding a decade before.

When he toughed out her silent critique with a 'So what?' look, the CSI smiled and introduced herself.

"I'm Sorcha."

The name made her seem very young, as did her voice, and immediately set the computer expert wondering what she would look like in her normal clothes.

The brisk, "Who are *you*?" that followed brought him crashing back to earth.

"I'm Ash Rahman, senior analyst on the Murder Squad."

The 'senior' was out before he could stop himself but he knew that she would never check.

"I'm here to look at the dry-cleaning equipment and console, to check if it was hacked."

He'd been on his way to the lab to check it when Grace had called to say that they'd sent it back.

The CSI's interest was piqued.

"How do you do that then?"

"Virus scans. We're looking for a Trojan that let the hacker load the contaminated fluid."

"We were wondering how that happened. With six canisters in the carousel how did they get the right one to the dress?"

"You're assuming only one was contaminated."

He already knew that they'd *all* been because Grace

171

had finished testing them and told him that too, but he wanted the conversation to continue so he acted mysterious anyway. The ploy fell flat and the CSI pointed a small, gloved finger towards the back of what was a surprisingly long shop, with washing machines lining its side walls and notices advertising service washes for ten pounds. The analyst made a mental note of the information; it might be useful when he eventually left home. He was optimistic he would have more to do with his leisure time than fluff and dry.

"The console's down there by the computer. We brought it back from the lab earlier. You might want these," she passed him a pair of gloves, "it's filthy with print dust."

With that she gave him another smile; wider and warmer than the first, and he couldn't be certain but he thought it *might* have been accompanied by a flirtatious gaze. Marking that for future follow-up Ash moved as assertively as possible towards the equipment and got to testing, and ten minutes later a new virus appeared on his scan. Another Trojan, but more unusual than the others. Their hacker was cutting edge and that wasn't good; much as he enjoyed a challenge, he preferred his homicidal adversaries to be as thick as two short planks.

Knowing that he needed to get to the factory and it was a train ride away the analyst postponed a deeper interrogation of the console, wiping its software and saving the virus on a USB before turning back to his new friend.

"You'll need to tell the owner to reload all his dry-cleaning programmes. I found a virus so I had to wipe everything just in case. It won't take him long. And tell him to set up a LAN here or someone could infiltrate his network again."

She smiled again and this time it was definitely flirtatious. "I'm sure he'll know what all that means, but if not I'll get him to call you. Do you have a card?"

He didn't, an omission that he would have to raise with Davy, but he had a pen and paper so he went old school, knowing now that even if the business owner didn't call him, Sorcha *definitely* would.

****

The Labs. 11 a.m.

While his junior analyst was advancing his love life Craig and his deputy were at the labs yet again, leading John to quip that they should probably just move in.

"Actually, that's not a bad idea, John, but the other way around. If the CCU had a few more floors your whole building could decamp there."

The pathologist rolled his eyes. "Yes, and I'm sure the corpses rolling up at all hours would *really* please the other squads."

It earned him a chuckle from Liam. "Boy, you're getting sarky these days, Doc. Been taking lessons from the wife?"

Craig winced, knowing that Natalie was a sore spot, but to his surprise John just considered the words for a moment and gave a nod.

"You're right, although bitter is probably a better word for it than sarcastic. Anyway, I won't depress you with my personal life other than to say psychologists and psychiatrists should just be honest about what they are. Surgeons who slice open your mind."

He shook his head to erase the memory of the day before's therapy session and got to the reason the detectives were there.

"You want to know if there's anything more on Felicia Barker, and there isn't. Not on the forensic side either, and I know that because Des and I have just talked. The only prints on the insulin pump belonged to the doctor who checked it yesterday morning, and there were none on the wi-fi console that shouldn't have been there. I suggest you ask Davy to do his thing on that."

"Is it still at the hospital?"

"No, here. Marcie has it."

"OK. We'll collect it on the way out." Craig ticked the device off his mental list and moved to his next point. "Have Ms Barker's relatives been here?"

"No. They ID-ed her at the hospital after death, but I did call them after the PM."

"I'll need a copy of your notes."

"Fine. Give me a second to phone Marcie. She can bring everything in."

As he ended the call, he asked a question. "Are you still searching for commonalities between the women?"

Liam responded.

"We have one for the first two Vics. They went to the same school. Brushford Academy."

The medic frowned. "But they're too old for-"

"For school to matter now, Doc? Maybe not. Some pimply wee scrote could have been holding a grudge for years."

Just then the secretary entered with the notes and a forensic bag containing the console. She brought a warning for Craig as well.

"Doctor Marsham says if your people ruin his evidence with their hacking, then he'll hack you too."

"Charming. But tell him not to worry. We'll get everything back to him in one piece. He might need it for court." He sighed heavily. "That's if we ever find a killer to take there."

"You honestly doubt it, boss?"

An arched eyebrow said that Craig just might.

"Even if one of our perps *has* some local historical reason to kill there's no guarantee that they're still living locally. We could identify someone who comes from Cullybackey and still not be able to convict because they're hacking us from South America." He gave a disgusted tut. "This is why I hate cybercrime. These bastards could be sitting in a dark room anywhere in the world."

Liam nodded glumly. "I hate it too, but because they're cowards. Give me a perp who has the balls to fire a gun or chuck a knife at me, not all this push-button stuff."

"Armstrong said they were cowards too."

John was feeling left out so he added, "I much prefer a good old-fashioned stabbing or shooting any day."

Marcie interrupted the testosterone fest in a bored voice. "Yes, well, if you gentlemen have quite finished, I'll be off."

Liam clambered to his feet, eager to follow her out.

"It's time for us to go too, boss. Arty's at St Mary's and he should have the Barker girl's school by now."

Craig nodded. "Thanks, John. I'll call you later to discuss your psychiatric trauma."

The medic wasn't sure whether he was joking or not.

****

Rochester Ward. St Mary's Healthcare Trust. 12 p.m.

Twenty minutes later they were standing at Felicia Barker's taped-off crime scene and its lack of remarkability was making Craig sad; just a small, hospital side-room with an empty bed and locker, a secured window, and no entry or exit other than through its single door. He wondered how many deaths the room had seen since its build and hoped that the others had at least been natural.

They moved on to the nurses' station, now minus its console, which the sister accompanying them was less than pleased about.

"When will I get my equipment back, Chief Superintendent? That other detective gave me some flannel about analysts and it isn't good enough."

Andy had been nowhere to be found when they'd arrived and now Craig knew why.

"Soon, I promise, Sister. Our analysts just need to run some tests on it and-"

He stopped abruptly, wondering whether he was talking rubbish. *Could* Davy detect a Trojan from the

175

console alone, or would he need the desk computer as well? He decided that any attempt to seize the equipment now might start a riot and made a note to send Ash down to examine it when he returned from his trip.

Smiling their way off the ward the detectives stopped in the corridor outside to talk.

"What now, boss?"

"We find Andy and hope he knows where Ms Barker went to school."

They located the invisible DCI on the road to Holywood and he filled them in. Felicia Barker had been yet another Brushford old girl!

"You informed Aidan?"

"Yep. He and Annette are there now gathering everything they need, so Ryan and I thought we'd go help with the interviews."

Liam was sceptical.

"Interview who? Our Vics left the school a decade ago."

"There could still be teachers there who remember them, so while Annette and Aidan check the old class schedules, we can interview them. It'll speed everything up."

Craig agreed.

"OK, anything else useful on Ms Barker?"

"Only that her parents were adamant she was too unwell to socialise and ruled out any disgruntled boyfriends being her killer. I think the school's our strongest lead, chief."

"I agree. OK, we'll see you back at the ranch later."

As he ended the call Craig realised it was lunchtime and wondered why Liam wasn't complaining. The explanation came when they returned to his car and the DCI opened the glovebox, showering Craig with energy bars.

"When did you start eating these?"

"Last week. Danni discovered them and they're not half bad. The usual ones taste like cardboard but these have raisins and stuff."

As Craig read the labels it became clear 'stuff' meant caramel, syrup and butter, the sweet-toothed Liam's idea of heaven and his of hell. If they'd read caffeine, red wine and olives he'd have been in like Flynn.

"Right, so you don't need lunch. Stop at a garage so I can buy a sandwich then."

The words earned him an indignant look.

"Wash your mouth out! I *always* need lunch. These are just to tide me over between meals."

Without another word he headed for the Cathedral Quarter in search of somewhere to eat.

Chapter Nine

As Ash was exploring the factory that had produced the lethal dry-cleaning fluid, Davy was at the police Traffic Section, Mary's workplace for years before she'd joined the squad.

Try as he might, and he really had, he hadn't been able to stop her old boss, Inspector Gabe Ronson, bothering him repeatedly as he'd checked the tapes for cars driving past or around the theatre and hospital at the times of their three victims' deaths.

It had been an impossible task even without the interruptions, with the sections of tape the analyst had asked to view run so quickly that they were blurred, either because the junior officer assisting him was so used to images that he really *could* tell a car's make and model at that speed, or because the short-sightedness that Davy denied even having was at fault.

The only thing to do was save the clips to a memory stick to view at his leisure back at the ranch, and Davy had just finished uploading them and was readying to leave when Ronson stepped into his path yet again.

"You should have put your viewing request to me in writing instead of just turning up, Mister Walsh."

"I'm sorry, sir. It's an urgent situation."

The response was a brusque, "Huh! *Everything's* urgent with your squad. You lot at the CCU think you're *so* important, you and that Flash Harry Craig, but without *our* constant vigilance you'd be nowhere. I could easily be running one of those squads, they asked me to many times, but I prefer to stay here. *We* solve your cases for you. Without our footage to show you'd lose in court."

He was probably right on that, but Davy also knew a man whose ambitions had been thwarted when he saw one. As the analyst wasn't someone whose self-esteem depended on always winning, he took the path of least resistance and nodded, watching the puffed-up Ronson, who'd obviously been longing for a fight, deflate like a balloon that had been unsealed.

Before his air dissipated fully, the uniformed inspector asked, plaintively Davy thought, "Does Mary miss us? She should never have left our happy band and I'm sure she's regretting it now."

The junior officer who'd assisted Davy gazed at him pleadingly to say yes; if he pointed out that in fact everyone in the place looked miserable, Ronson might make their lives an even worse hell.

He needn't have worried; the analyst was a kind man so he smiled reassuringly and offered to ask Mary to give them a call, then he fled from the Twilight Zone to the literal semi-twilight of the ASU viewing room and after a normal discussion and some map scrutiny there left its commander, Theo Sheridan, with the dates and times of their murders and a request to download any relevant camera footage for him to view.

With an estimated wait time of an hour Davy was just about to go in search of a snack when he had a call from Craig.

"Hi Davy, where are you?"

"Outside the ASU, chief. It'll take them an hour to download all the footage I need so I was just about to get something to eat."

"OK, good. We are too so we'll come and pick you up."

Liam's groan as he changed course said he wasn't impressed by the delay to his meal.

"I'll need you at the hospital afterwards, Davy. We have the wi-fi console from Felicia Barker's ward but you should check the desk computer too. I was going to send Ash but you'll be quicker. Just a warning. If you try to remove anything the ward sister's likely to skin you alive."

The analyst chuckled. "Fine."

"Where's Ash now?"

"At the factory. He did Bright Day first."

"And the corridor and ward CCTV for Barker?"

"I can pick that up when I'm there."

Just then he saw the car pull up and they headed for lunch.

Brushford Academy. Outside Holywood Town, County Down.

The route to the school had led Aidan and Annette through the centre of Holywood, the town of Craig's birth and no doubt the setting for many of his adolescent misdemeanours. Annette had busied herself admiring the mixture of quaint shops and coffee houses that lined its main street, one of which may well have fostered Craig's caffeine addiction when he'd returned from school in Belfast too early to do homework and desperate for somewhere to hang out. She pictured her boss in his school uniform, blazer off no doubt and tie definitely askew, trying to look cool over an espresso as he watched the local girls walk by.

It was an amusing if overly-long imagining, given that the main street was so narrow that with cars parked on either side of it their progress had been stop, start, inch forward and stop again all the way to its end.

When they'd eventually arrived at Brushford Academy it had announced itself with a discreet nameplate on an impressive stone wall; a long driveway through a wooded copse hid the school building entirely from the road. Once there a placard proclaimed that it provided 'Excellent, integrated education for eight hundred and thirteen pupils aged eleven to eighteen.'

It prompted Aidan to say exactly what Annette felt.

"Oh, great. Eight hundred gobby tweenies and adolescents pointing and whispering as we walk past. I think it's time for the Fear of God Scowl, Annette."

Even she, the mother of one future tweenie and two former *extremely* gobby adolescents and now opinionated beyond all reason university students, had to agree. She hated walking past groups of teenagers. Her youth as a plump and at best homely in the looks department girl had made her the victim of many mimicked earthquakes when she'd passed the boys in her home town and she still felt the pain.

Some strategic shifting of their guns to the front so that the ensuing bulges were unmissable and they were ready, and just about to stride across the playground in the hunt for the headteacher's office when they saw a familiar Volkswagen Golf approaching up the drive.

Andy waved cheerfully out the window at them.

"We thought you might fancy some help with the interviews."

For once Aidan didn't object to having another cockerel in the henhouse. Andy might be theoretically higher in the DCI pecking order than him, well, in fact there was nothing theoretical about it, but he didn't wear it ostentatiously.

The arty DCI's next words removed any lingering doubts.

"This is your show, Aidan. Just point us at who you want interviewed."

"Grand. We're parked over there. We'll wait for you."

"Fine. And cheer up, you two. At least we won't be interviewing kids."

A quick flash of their Glocks' prominent new positions made Andy smirk and drive off to park.

The new arrivals' appearance cheered Annette up considerably. Four of them marching in with bulging jackets should tame *any* teenager with a glance.

As it happened their 'Magnificent Seven' entrance was overkill, the school building's bright, high-ceilinged corridors silent, and empty of all but the occasional, clearly naughty, child standing outside a classroom door. All that was to be heard as they made their way towards the cheerfully named headteacher Daisy Brontë's office was the chanting of French verbs and a strangely haunting song emanating from what was clearly a music room.

By the time they arrived at what was in fact a suite of offices their guns and striding just felt embarrassing and Annette made up her mind to adjust her gun's position the first chance she got, unless she encountered a mouthy teenager who made a crack about her appearance of course, then all bets were off.

The first person the detectives met in the suite was a woman who just had to be Brontë. Middle-aged, slightly overweight, with grey hair cropped tightly against her head and a pair of overly large spectacles dangling from a chain around her neck.

Aidan took the lead and showed his ID.

"Good afternoon, Ms Brontë. I phoned earlier. DCIs Hughes and Angel, Inspector Eakin and Sergeant Hendron from Belfast."

The woman stared at him in silence and then at the others in turn, before turning on her heel and disappearing through an inner door. When she emerged again a full minute later Aidan was ready for a fight. He hadn't expected the red carpet to be rolled out, but a quick, "Yes, Chief Inspector, I've been expecting you" would have been nice.

It came a moment later when the dour woman, who turned out to be a secretary, was followed from the inner room by her boss, the actual Ms Brontë. As soon as she saw her Annette wanted to giggle. She didn't of course, because, you know, *Glock carrier,* but when she noticed Andy smiling it gave her permission to do the same.

Daisy Brontë, or 'Miss' as the pupils insisted on calling her even though it was outmoded, looked like every children's television presenter who'd ever existed rolled into one. She had a mass of thick, wildly curly, auburn hair that almost hid her small face, a button nose, a bright wide smile that showed her gums, and she couldn't have been more than thirty-five, and Annette guessed she must have looked exactly the same at birth for her parents to have named her Daisy. The name fitted her like a glove, as did her trendy green boiler suit and high-heeled boots.

Andy's thoughts were much more lascivious and he countered what he knew was their inappropriateness by wondering about her surname. Could she be related to *those* Brontës? Their father Patrick *had* come from

Rathfriland, only forty miles away.

Suddenly a small pink hand was thrust into Aidan's large one, taking him aback. The action was quickly repeated three times then the Head ushered the detectives into her large but cosy office, took a seat behind her desk and nodded them to pull up chairs, getting straight to business.

"Right now, DCI Hughes. What can I do for you? Agnes said you didn't elaborate on the phone."

Aidan gathered his thoughts quickly, wondering when headteachers had changed so much. His own had been a fiercely taciturn man whose transit down every corridor had parted his pupils as effectively as Moses had the Red Sea.

"Yes, sorry. I didn't give any details because it's quite sensitive, so I'll have to ask you to keep this discussion entirely to yourself."

A gentle nod said the teacher was well used to confidentiality so he continued, and in two minutes had laid out the generalities of their three murders without giving details on the victims or their causes of death. Andy was nodding too, approvingly; he couldn't have summarised better himself. He was also approving of Ms Brontë's curls, which were so enticingly shiny he wanted to stroke them.

Aidan's, "That's as much as I can tell you" brought him back to earth and he watched as the headteacher's forehead wrinkled into a frown.

"So, three twenty-seven-year-old ex-pupils of this school have been murdered."

"Yes, and we may have a fourth at future risk."

"Their gender?"

He considered for a moment, finally deciding she would need to know to find their records.

"Female, all four."

A brisk nod said it would do for the moment and she walked swiftly past them to open the door.

"Agnes, can you bring me the records of the two-thousand-and-four entries please."

"The full roll?"

"No, just the girls please."

Annette realised with a start that Mary had been just eleven then, and it made her wonder if perhaps they didn't expect too much maturity from her and should be more tolerant at times. As she was making a mental note to do just that, Andy leant in to say something to his counterpart.

It prompted another request.

"Our potential victim joined that cohort in two-thousand-and-seven, so perhaps you could pull any new additions for that year as well."

As they waited for the secretary to bring the records, he realised that he'd probably just given away Mary's name, unless more than one girl had joined the class that year.

As it happened three girls had, so confidentiality was, sort of, maintained, and the files of those three plus one hundred others soon landed on Daisy Brontë's desk.

"Right, now obviously everyone here understands the privacy rules so let's stick to generalities where we can."

Seeing Andy had something to say Aidan nodded him on.

"Were there problems with any of the girls during their years here? Not necessarily because of them but involving them. Particularly trouble pertaining to male pupils."

If their victims had been killed out of hatred then there was no time in a man's life quite like adolescence for planting that seed. That's *if* their killer was male of course.

They waited as Brontë sifted her way through the pile of notes, occasionally punctuating the rifling of pages with asides like, "I was here as a student teacher then," and, "I worked mainly with the music classes."

So she was musical. Andy made a mental note.

After what seemed like an age during which Annette wished they could have given the teacher some help without prejudicing her findings, and Ryan wished he'd eaten before they'd come, Daisy Brontë set nine files to one side and opened the office door to give the others back.

She took her seat again and rested a hand on top of the pile, clearly perplexed as to what to do next without breaching confidentiality rules. Aidan put her out of her misery. Julianne Hodges' death had been so public that the papers had released her name, so that one at least they could be open about.

"You'll have seen news reports about a woman called Julianne Hodges, I'm sure."

She gawped at him.

"She was *murdered*?"

An immediate 'Damn' popped into his head as he worried the papers hadn't reported that, but he was reassured quickly by Annette's nod. It *had* been reported as a murder but Brontë had obviously missed it.

"Yes, she was murdered. It was reported in The Chronicle."

Maggie was always first with any scoop, and not because Davy gave her inside information.

Hoping it would jog the teacher's memory Annette volunteered that Julianne Hodges' maiden name had been Harbinson, and Brontë's eyes grew as round as coins.

"*Julianne Harbinson!* She's one of the names I've chosen, and I remember her as well. She was really gifted in music and drama." Her face fell. "Such as sweet girl too. That's very sad."

Aidan seized the opening. "Why did you pick out her file?"

The headteacher pulled a face. "Her file says there was an incident with a boy."

"Can you elaborate?"

She sighed heavily and sat back in her seat. "It seems there was a boy two years ahead who liked her. Julianne was a very pretty girl."

Aidan expanded on 'liked'. "You mean he bothered her?"

"Constantly, according to the records. And not only her." She tapped the stack of notes. "Every girl in this pile complained to the headteacher back then."

He counted quickly.

"All nine of them?"

"What?" She glanced at the pile quickly, realising what she'd said, and removed the files of two of the three girls who'd joined late. "No, sorry, seven. These two girls joined in third year but never complained."

"OK, let's set them to one side at the moment."

It still left seven girls, three of whom were undoubtedly their victims.

"So, seven girls, six who started in two-thousand-and-four and one who started in oh-seven, *all* complained about the same boy?"

"That's what the files say."

"Exactly what did this little prince do?"

She pulled a face. "Well, it seems it started innocently enough with each girl. He waited around in corridors to see them, told them how pretty they were. The usual."

Andy sighed to himself; it hadn't been usual for him - he'd been painfully shy at school.

"Then he started saying crude things to them, talking about sex and so on, so the files say that each of the girls approached their mentor at that point."

"A mentor is?"

"Back then it was a named teacher that each pupil could go to with any problems, but we have a different system now. And it was a different mentor for each girl so there was no chance of them lining up their stories, although they were remarkably similar."

That was more than coincidence; their teenage lech had clearly had a routine.

"And after the boy was reported?"

"He was spoken to by *his* mentor, then when his behaviour didn't stop, by the headmaster."

"Did that sort him out?"

Brontë sighed heavily.

"It appears to have done, except in Julianne's case. It

escalated with her to physical assault. One day after school she was playing tennis and it appears..." She paused, reaching for the file to check her facts and reading aloud. "He waited until her tennis partner had left the girls' changing room and went inside. 'Waiting for me', those are Julianne's words, 'to come out of the shower'.

The teacher closed the file sharply as if she couldn't bear to read on. "Then she reported that he pulled her towel from her and touched her inappropriately. She screamed and thankfully the gym teacher heard her from the sports hall and ran in. In time to prevent something worse happening, thank goodness."

Annette's blood ran cold; both her children had gone to mixed schools. She made up her mind to ask them if anything like that had ever happened there.

Aidan was thinking similar thoughts and vocalised them. "How often does that sort of thing occur?"

Brontë shifted uncomfortably in her seat. "Not often, and it's usually just clumsy attempts at kissing, but I have known it to happen before at mixed schools."

It made up his mind that if he ever had kids they would be locked away with their own sex until they were eighteen, just as he had been. It hadn't done him any harm, although he was honest enough to admit he should probably get an outside opinion on that.

"Right, so Julianne wasn't raped?"

A look of horror crossed her face. "God no! It was stopped before he got that far."

"I need the date, please."

She gave it reluctantly, adding, "He was punished severely. He was expelled and had to study for his A-Levels at a sixth-form college."

Ryan had been listening quietly to the conversation but couldn't hide his dismay.

"Expelled? Is that all?"

The headteacher nodded. "Julianne's parents felt the same as you. They reported it to the police and he was taken to court." She shook her head sadly. "It was very sad. He ended up in prison and was put on the sex offenders' register."

Ryan kept his *'Good. That should make him easy to find'* thought to himself, while Aidan kept his focus on the reason they were there.

"And this same boy harassed all seven of the girls in that pile?"

"Yes."

"I'll need their names, and before you say no, Ms Brontë, I *can* get a warrant if you'd prefer."

She squeezed out, *"I would prefer"* through gritted teeth.

"And for the boy's records?"

"The same."

He turned to Annette. "Take my car and go back and organise those, please."

"The rest of you are staying here?"

"We are."

As the door closed behind her Aidan turned back to the headteacher.

"We'll stick to generalities until the warrants arrive." *Even though you not cooperating will double our bloody work.* "But we'll need the class schedules of all seven girls and the boy, names redacted obviously until we get warrants, plus the names of any teachers still here who taught them and a private space set up where we can interview."

Her expression said, 'Would you like me to iron your shirts as well?', so he softened his approach slightly.

"Look, I realise that you're protective of these children-"

She cut him off sharply, showing a fire that piqued Andy's interest, although he doubted Brontë would be interested in *him* by the time they were done.

"*These children* as you call them were in our care, and I won't stigmatise them even if *you* will."

Aidan continued as if she hadn't spoken.

"- but three women are dead and I'm betting that all three of their names are in your pile. If they are then that means we have to consider the other four women in that pile at risk too, and this boy is a common factor. He *may* have nothing to do with our murders. It could be pure coincidence, or a friend or family member intent of avenging his criminalisation killing on his behalf. But he *could* also be our murderer and as such you'll be obstructing our investigation if you refuse to yield those records once we have warrants." His voice hardened. "That could bring charges for you, Ms Brontë. Do you understand?"

Her startled look said that she did suddenly. "Very well. You'll get the records as soon as you have the warrants, Chief Inspector."

She left the room to get the boy's records and placed the whole lot in her desk drawer, locking it ostentatiously with a key that she produced from a chain around her neck.

"I'll gather their schedules for you now."

"The boy's as well, please."

"It will take me a while."

"We'll go and get some coffee in town." *Since you clearly aren't going to offer us any.* "Call us when you have everything in one place, please, and by that time we should have the warrants."

He stood up, not extending his hand because he was sure it wouldn't be welcomed.

"Thank you for your assistance, Ms Brontë, and please remember that we're not the bad guys. We aren't here to stigmatise anyone. We're just trying to save lives."

The words made her look ashamed, which Andy knew had been exactly their purpose.

He broke the tension with, "We're not as grouchy as we seem, honestly. But this has to happen."

The smile he received in return almost made him float back to his car.

****

Wryson's Chemical Factory. Newtownards, County Down.

Ash loved factories. He had done ever since he'd watched a programme on how chocolates were made when he was a kid, with each step of the process from combining the raw materials, melting, moulding and setting the scrumptious products, and then packing and ferrying them out to shops keeping him riveted to the screen. It had become such an obsession with him that he'd badgered his father to buy him a toy factory at five, and when he was older copies of black and white programmes that showed how everything from parachutes to railway engines were produced. His passion had even made him think of studying engineering. But he'd settled on computing because engineering students were expected to work in the cold and wet and the hard hats that they wore were decidedly uncool.

But his early love of assembly lines and mechanised processes came flooding back as he watched the different dry-cleaning ingredients arriving, being filtered, combined and poured into canisters, before being sent in different directions on conveyor belts and packed in mechanically labelled boxes. All without a single human hand having been involved except to press a switch.

He turned to the young manager beside him excitedly.

"It's *all* computerised?"

Rodney McCann smiled. He loved factories too and would talk about them all day except that he knew it bored people, so it was great to meet a fellow enthusiast.

"Yeh, well apart from loading the boxes on to vans. We could have used machines for that too, but the van drivers do it just as well."

The analyst nodded, then he scanned the factory floor quickly in search of a console, covering his actions with a fake sneeze. There was none visible, and seeing through his ruse McCann pointed overhead to a glass booth.

"If you're looking for our electronic brain it's up there.

I'll show you."

A minute later Ash had come home. The whole factory was being run from a single computer!

"The instructions for each machine are selected from a pre-typed list and fed by wi-fi down to them on the floor."

The computer expert nodded, tuning out the manager's words as he examined the very basic PC. It took him only seconds to decide his next steps.

"You'll need to shut down the production line."

McCann shook his head instantly.

"Not a hope! If we turn it off it'll take an hour to reboot and we've orders to complete."

Ash gave his most tolerant smile.

"What if I could guarantee that wouldn't happen?"

"How?"

"I can put the system into sleep mode."

Seeing the manager's scepticism, he hurried on.

"Trust me. I understand computers." Seeing McCann was still unpersuaded he used his clincher, playing to the man's ego by sweeping a hand across his domain. "Just like you understand all this."

The gesture had the desired effect. There was nothing quite like the 'Master of all you survey' routine to make a man play ball and Ash was totally unashamed of using it.

'Whatever works' was his motto. He should get a tattoo of it someday. Although he did wonder slightly uneasily how many times people had used that same routine on him.

The administrator glanced at his watch then down at the factory floor before speaking again.

"Just for a minute?"

"I promise."

The second McCann called the system halt Ash began to scan and thirty seconds later he'd found exactly what he'd been looking for; a juicy big virus even better than the rest.

The manager greeted his obvious glee with alarm.

"What have you found?"

"The virus that fed a lethal dose of Nicotine into your dry-cleaning mix."

"But how? We don't keep Nicotine on site, and no-one even vapes inside the factory, so where did it come from?"

"They introduced it into your production chain, probably through a bogus supply, then used this computer virus to add it to your mix. I'll need details of all your supply deliveries for the past month. OK?"

McCann nodded silently, clearly in shock at how easily his systems had been corrupted. As he watched Ash loading the supply schedules to his USB more questions hit the air.

"Do you have the exact date it happened? And surely that means there could have been contamination of other batches?" He gave a low moan. "Oh, God, there are fifty canisters produced from a batch of fluid and we'll have to recall every batch we produced. Half of them went over to GB! And is the Nicotine definitely out of our systems now? And the virus? It can't stay here! You have to get it out!"

Ash didn't reply, just moved his chair closer to the computer and kept typing, wondering how to tell McCann that the brief pause he'd just promised him was going to turn into a complete shutdown, to get the factory's systems flushed out and deep cleaned.

He decided to approach the topic laterally.

"I've removed the main virus, which is great, but there's another one to find so just give me a moment. The first one just ordered the mixing in of the Nicotine to the fluid, but there must have been a separate virus that made sure that particular batch of mixture was sent to the right destination."

He kept his eyes on the screen, watching as lines of code flew across it with increasing speed. Suddenly they stopped dead and a 'quarantined malware' sign popped up.

A moment's more downloading and the analyst rose to his feet, knowing that he couldn't avoid telling

McCann his fortune any longer, although he *could* drag it out.

"So...OK... I've got everything now and the time they were planted, so that's a win."

The manager didn't share his enthusiasm. "You're *sure* our computer's clean now? And what does that mean for us?"

"Positive. But just to make you happy." The analyst hit a few more keys and initiated a full virus scan. "That'll take about an hour, sorry, so you should probably go and get some coffee."

As he watched McCann's mouth open to object, Ash had a flash of inspiration. There was no point in him going through the whole decontamination speech and then calling Grace down to help the factory organise it, was there? Not when she could do both at once and save him the grief. He knew that some might call the approach cowardice, but he preferred to think efficient was the word.

"I just need to make a quick call, then I'll catch you up."

The manager was less trusting than he'd hoped, and when Ash descended the steps to the factory floor five minutes later he was waiting at the bottom.

"I've called down a colleague to answer any questions you might have, Mister McCann. She'll be here before the scan has finished."

The analyst continued quickly towards the exit but soon realised that he wasn't alone. He was clearly going to have to talk to the manager, so the question now became, how little could he get away with telling him and how fast?

"Can I help you with something else, Mister McCann?"

To Ash's surprise the question was a tech one.

"How can we stop this ever happening again?"

He was back in his comfort zone.

"Your security programme's fine, and I very much doubt you'll be bothered again in this way. But the truth

193

is if someone like this wants to hijack you or any other company, they'll do it. Even governments and banks who spend millions on shielding get hacked, so just load any security updates that your system offers and pray."

He on the other hand was going back to base to examine his new viruses and see if anyone on the internet was ready to play.

****

Felicia Barker's Hospital Room. St Mary's Trust.

"Why are we back here, boss?"

Craig shot his deputy a sceptical look.

"You have other plans?"

"No, well yeh. I always have *other* plans. But I mean were we just here an hour ago."

In response Craig motioned to the door. "Davy needed a lift and the sooner I get him back to the office the sooner we'll get answers."

Liam conceded the point with a shrug and threw himself into a chair beside the bed.

"It doesn't look like much, does it?"

Not waiting for an answer, he went on.

"Blank walls, vinyl floor, nothing that makes it stand out from millions of others. Not the place I'd like to meet my end, I can tell you."

Craig was about to quip that he'd probably want his name carved on the bedstead when his senior analyst entered and added another voice to the debate.

"I get what you mean, Liam. I want to die somewhere beautiful, like by a lake, w...with all the people I care about around me."

The DCI nodded vigorously. "Now, that's what I mean. Right, I've made up my mind. I'm never going into hospital unless there's a guarantee I'm coming out. Write that down, someone."

Craig rolled his eyes, said, "It's seared on my brain" and shot his computer expert a questioning look.

"Anything?"

The younger man nodded and leant against the wall to elaborate.

"I've checked the console you brought, the desk computer and the insulin pump, and you were right. There was a virus in the console and another in the PC. I've downloaded both so Ash can check them with the others, but our victim was definitely killed by a computer hack."

"Which did what exactly?"

"Increased her insulin units by a factor of ten. It just meant adding a nought to her dose, but it did the trick. I'm hoping that when we line up all the viruses they'll give us something."

Liam didn't hide his scepticism. "Like what?"

"We might get lucky and be able to tie them to the same Dark Web marketplace."

Craig nodded. He'd read a paper on D.W. marketplaces the week before, on an Operation the drugs squads in England were running called DisrupTor, a Tor being a private internet browser that enabled anonymous communication, and was sometimes used by people up to no good. They were hoping the Op would help them disrupt drug dealing in Norfolk that was being run out of London, but whether it worked or not would take six months to tell.

He realised his analyst was still speaking and tuned back in.

"Marketplaces are a lot more efficient than buying and selling through message boards and individual chat-rooms."

"Like the difference between a department store and lots of wee shops on a high street."

The comparison made Davy smile.

"Exactly. There used to be one main market on the Dark Web called Silk Road and most people bought and sold there, but the cops shut it down years back and now there are markets and sellers dotted all over the place..."

Truth be told Liam didn't understand how *anything*

195

on the Web worked, never mind the dark one, but he *did* understand shopping, having a wife whose credit cards remained frozen, literally, in a saucer of ice in the freezer, to stop her impulse buying on QVC.

"...so it'll mean a lot more work finding where these viruses came from," his next words were addressed to Craig, who always wanted answers right away, "and *that's* going to take time."

"You have until yesterday."

Craig changed the subject by indicating a small CCTV camera in a corner of the ceiling.

"What about that?"

"I've downloaded the footage from hospital server of the ward and corridor outside, and now I've got the street and traffic footage from every other scene hopefully things will speed up."

Liam's, "That means you saw Gabe Ronson," was imbued with a mixture of pity and gloom more commonly heard from a vicar at a graveside.

"Yeh, well, let's just say I can see why Mary left Traffic." The analyst smirked at Craig. "He called you Flash Harry and was moaning about how everything was always urgent with the Murder Squad."

Craig chuckled, picturing the St Trinian's character of the same name. "I've been called worse."

"Aye, and it's nothing to what Mary calls him."

A final scan of the room and Craig headed for the door, "Right, we'll drop you back to the office, Davy. Tell Nicky we'll be there within the hour."

"You heading to the lab again, chief?"

"Yes. Why, did you want to come with us?"

"Might as well. Ash is still at the factory and we can't really move on the viruses till he gets back with his, and I'd rather not listen to Mary's moaning till I have to."

"Fine, but she does have reason to moan, Davy, so try to be sympathetic. You wouldn't like being under guard either."

"Wh...What's her excuse the rest of the time?"

He was still waiting for his answer when they reached

Des Marsham's office and the conversation became about the complete absence of useful forensics at Felicia Barker's scene.

"Sorry you had a wasted journey, Marc, but it's nice to see you, Davy."

Before the analyst could reciprocate Liam intervened.

"You never say that to me!"

"I see you every bloody day! In fact, it would be nice *not* to see you occasionally-"

The scientist stopped abruptly, noticing a troubled frown on Craig's face.

"Something you've thought of, Marc?"

The detective shook his head. "A feeling more than a thought."

"Not a good one by the looks of it."

Liam read his mind.

"You're waiting for the next shoe to drop."

Craig's shake turned to a nod. "That's it, yes. This killer's enjoying himself, killing three women in as many days. We need to get ahead of him *now* or we'll have a fourth."

He only knew one way to do that; make a plan.

He turned for the door. "Thanks, Des. Even no evidence is some information, but we need to go."

He was surprised by what came next.

"John said if you ever need us to come to a briefing, we're both free this afternoon. And even if you don't need us, I'd quite like to escape from here. Grace is after me to tidy my office."

"The more the merrier. Nicky will call once we've agreed a time."

Chapter Ten

The CCU. 4 p.m.

Craig moved the briefing forward an hour, which gave everyone just enough time to get back from wherever they were, chase info, tidy their notes and do whatever had to be done, and at four o'clock the squad-room was buzzing with noise. At four-oh-one it was silent apart from the sound of the detective pacing at the front of the room. Eventually he stopped and turned towards his team.

"Three women are dead and Mary is under guard to prevent her becoming the fourth. All our victims attended the same school but all led different adult lives. They also had-"

He looked to his analysts for any information and Davy obliged.

"Zero contact with each other that we can find, not even on s...social media."

"Put that on the board. So, let's look at the school. Aidan, take that, please."

The lanky detective ran quickly through the events at Brushford and stopped when he reached the list of seven girls. Or rather he *was* stopped by Liam's horrified, "*Seven?* Bloody hell!"

"Yup. We already know four of the names, and one of the other three died of natural causes last year-"

Mary interrupted in a shocked voice. "Which one?"

"Brid Smyth. From leukaemia."

She dropped her eyes to the floor.

"Brid sang in the choir. She was nice."

Craig understood her sorrow. There were people he'd known at school whose deaths would make him feel the same way.

"I'm sure she was. Go on, Aidan."

"So that just leaves two potential victims, plus Mary of course."

The words brought the constable's head shooting up

again, and drew a groan from Annette that Craig understood but ignored.

"We called the other two, Olivia Kenzie and Romaine Martin, and explained the situation, Guv. They agreed to have squad-cars posted outside their homes."

"They'll need a visit too, Aidan."

"Agreed for the morning."

Andy, who had been doodling a face that looked remarkably like Daisy Brontë's, raised a finger to say something.

"And we only got halfway through the interviews, so Ryan and I are going back to the school to finish those."

The sergeant added a post script. "We'll need to go to the boy's sixth-form college too."

Craig looked at him quizzically and turned back to Aidan for information.

"What boy?"

"Sorry, I was just coming to him."

The DCI moved to the screen by Nicky's desk and nodded her to display his first slide.

"OK, so there was a boy called James MacArthur at the school who harassed all seven girls. The six who started together in oh-four and Mary who joined in oh-seven."

All eyes turned to the constable but a sharp signal from Craig brought them back to the front.

"What ages were they when it happened?"

"The boy was two years ahead, so sixteen/seventeen and fourteen/fifteen mainly when it happened, although the harassment was staggered. He'd bother one girl and get knocked back, then try the next and so on."

"Give us the generalities, please."

He had no intention of asking his constable to detail her experience in particular.

"Well, he started with following them, hanging around and talking about trivia, but when that didn't get the feedback he wanted, he moved on to leering and saying things that were increasingly crude. With Julianne Hodges it escalated and he followed her into the

199

girls' showers, pulled off her towel and touched her."

Craig's eyes widened. "Sexual assault! Was it reported?"

"Yes, and he was expelled. He had to take his A-Levels at the sixth-form college Ryan just mentioned. Julianne's parents also reported him to the police and he was charged and sentenced to a year at Wharf House."

Wharf House was Northern Ireland's only prison for women and males under eighteen and it occupied a picturesque setting high on the North Antrim coast. The place was widely regarded as a soft touch, and Liam's sneer of, "The Holiday Camp" echoed what many others were thinking and prompted Aidan to add some slightly tougher love.

"Plus, he was put on the sex offenders' register."

Ryan sighed heavily. "That would've hammered his future."

Annette was less sympathetic. "He deserved it, the little pervert."

Craig looked at her questioning. "I agree he deserved to be sentenced, Annette, but to end up on that list so young?"

Aidan joined the justice debate on his side. "And he came from a pretty crap family, Annette. The father disappeared when he was three and his mum took to drink. The kids were in and out of foster care most of their lives. But, anyway, the registration was only for five years as long as he kept his hands to himself."

"And did he?"

"Nope. He groped a girl on a train a year into it and ended up doing more time, this stretch was at Magilligan. He got out in twenty-twelve and there's been nothing since."

Liam gave a cynical grunt. "Nothing he's been caught for you mean."

Craig couldn't disagree. "OK, where is he now, Aidan?"

The DCI screwed up his face, displaying far too many wrinkles for his age courtesy of years sunbathing at his parents' holiday home in Spain, and swopped to his next slide, which held some facts about James MacArthur.

"That's a bit of a problem, Guv. MacArthur's listed on the register as living in Larne, but the last time anyone checked was a year ago and he'd disappeared. A neighbour said he'd been evicted by the landlord for rent arrears. I'm chasing where his mail is being sent, but he didn't arrange forwarding so the post office said it'll take a couple of days to follow the trail. He could be living rough for all we know."

Ash shook his head. "If he's our hacker then where would he keep his tech, chief? He must be living somewhere."

"That's a very good point. Check local internet providers for a subscription under his name or similar, Ash. His criminal file should have any known aliases. Try pay-as-you-go suppliers too." He turned back to his DCI "Aidan, get his last photo aged up and check the usual passports, driving licenses and so on. You know the routine. Get it out to all stations as well. I want this guy found."

After chewing over his options for a moment, Craig turned tentatively towards his constable. He didn't want to make Mary a victim in her teammates' eyes but at the same time she *was* the only person there who knew James MacArthur.

She saw his mouth opening and shook her head.

"I won't discuss what he did to us."

'Us' felt far less personal than 'me'.

"And I wouldn't ask you to, but I do want you to tell us whatever you know about the boy that James MacArthur was."

He watched her go to refuse and then shrug as she changed her mind.

"I didn't know him as well as the others because I was only at the Academy for two years, but I did take two classes with him. Maths and IT."

She frowned grumpily, as if even thinking about the youth annoyed her.

201

"At first he just seemed like a typical nerd. He was tall for his age and really skinny. I remember the bones in his wrists sticking out. He wore thick-rimmed glasses that had broken at some point so there was a band-aid over the bridge. I remember they were too big for him so he used to keep pushing them up his nose. He carried his books around in a plastic bag instead of a backpack like everyone else, so some of the other boys gave him grief about that, and I remember him having a black eye a couple of times, but I don't know whether he got it at school or home."

Annette immediately felt guilt for her earlier comments. Perhaps the boy's problems really *had* come from a harsh home life.

"Was he bright?"

"He was actually. Especially at computing. But that just made some of the sporty boys pick on him even more so he tended to hang around the girls."

"He probably thought they would be kinder."

"He was right, until he started standing too close and saying rude things. I didn't know many of the girls in my year because I wasn't there long, but I do remember Julianne. I didn't recognise her name as our victim because she was Julianne Harbinson back then, but she was very sweet and James *definitely* bothered her the most. I know she tried her best to be kind to him so I'm not sure what went wrong. I knew that there'd been trouble of some sort but I didn't know the details until just now because the teachers kept it very quiet, but looking back I'm not that surprised. There was something 'off' about James even back then."

Craig risked a pointed question. "Do you know if he actually asked any of the girls out?"

A faint blush crept across her cheeks. "Yes. He asked me and I said no, and I heard later that a lot of other girls had turned him down as well. Some tried to be nice about it but he was pretty persistent, so I remember Maria O'Rourke and Romaine Martin being harsh."

Craig nodded. MacArthur's dysfunctional childhood

and school bullying experiences had turned him towards the girls, where he'd thought he would get some comfort. Except not in the way his teenage hormones clearly desired.

"Thank you, Mary." He turned back to the group. "Right, we have two aims now: protecting our potential victims and finding James MacArthur."

His deputy didn't look convinced.

"You disagree, Liam?"

"I agree on both, but something about this MacArthur feels off. Like we haven't quite got him yet."

"Explain."

The DCI prepared for his grand exposition by slinging his feet up on the desk in front of him and linking his hands behind his neck.

"OK, so we've been working on the basis that our perp, or perps let's not forget, is an IT whiz, and OK, MacArthur might fit that. But tech costs money and he was evicted for not paying his rent, so where's he getting his dosh? He must have a job. That means we can use his tax and national insurance to find-"

As Davy was scribbling the words down Craig cut in.

"Unless he's doing cash-in-hand work. Working for himself and not declaring it."

"Aye well, there's always that." After a slight pause the DCI added, "But most people have a bank account, so that could help find him as well."

John spoke up from the back.

"Unless he's using an alias like someone said."

"He might be, Doc, except you need ID to open a bank account, so *if* he changed his name it must've been long enough ago to at least build up some utility bills." He turned to the analyst at his side. "Got all that, son?"

A dry, "Yes, Dad" came back.

"Cheeky pup. Anyway, *if* MacArthur's buying tech he'll need somewhere to store and use it, so I agree with Ash about him having an address. It'll have to be somewhere secure enough to house expensive things, so as well looking for internet suppliers I'd check for home insurance. If he loves his stuff, he probably insures it. But that's not my only niggle here, boss. Didn't that psychiatrist say he'd have a secure job with a steady income? Maybe even public sector?"

Craig interrupted. "Or that he'd work for himself and be doing quite well."

"That makes more sense to me, boss, because to work in the public sector he'd have needed an Access NI check."

Access NI checks were pre-employment checks used to assess an applicant's criminal history at one of three different levels depending on what was required of a particular job.

"And he'd *never* have passed one of those being a sex offender. In fact, that would limit his job prospects no matter how liberal the employer." He turned back to Davy. "Check for social care benefits too. See what's up with his family as well. Is he crashing with them? It might sound unlikely if they bashed him as a kid, but there's nowt as strange as folk. But aye, if he isn't on the dole then he's probably running his own business."

Craig couldn't fault anything his deputy had said.

"I know that's a lot of searches, Davy, but Mary can pitch in. Anything else, Liam?"

"Aye, there is. Remember what MacArthur likes, boss. He likes *women*. At close quarters. So, what job would pay him cash and get him close to girls?"

"Bouncer, club or bar work-"

John cut in.

"Driving a taxi would pay better *and* he'd get to be alone with them."

"Nice one, Doc. But not with one of the big firms because they do criminal checks. This guy's a solo operator. A roamer."

Craig groaned. So-called roaming cabs trawled the streets for passengers even though they were unlicensed, and there were always enough stupid people pouring out of clubs and pubs at three a.m. to make it worth their while. People who thought ten minutes was too long to wait for a registered taxi and so instead risked life and limb in cars that were rarely maintained or insured and with drivers who might have criminal records as long as their arms, including for sexual assault.

"OK, Liam, give Jack Harris a call on that."

Jack Harris was the desk sergeant at High Street Station and the most experienced of his rank in Belfast. He and Liam had trained and worked together during The Troubles and he helped the squad out on cases where he could.

"He can pass the info to all stations and the official taxi firms. One of them may have been approached by MacArthur looking for a job. Also, Annette, check for any reports of women being harassed in taxis over the past six months. There might be something there."

Andy was unconvinced. "But Mary said MacArthur was clever, chief."

"Go on."

"Clever enough to arrange arm's length killings and not leave a clue. So, is he *really* going to risk everything for a quick, sorry to be blunt, grope in a taxi that would see him arrested, ID-ed and chucked back in jail?"

Craig considered the point. "Criminal sexual behaviour *can* defy logic, Andy, but let's follow your point through. If I were MacArthur and knew my urges could get me into trouble, I would *avoid* any job that brought me into contact with women-"

His deputy gave a derisive snort. "*You* might, boss, but he's a perv who'd look for chances to explore them."

"Let me finish, Liam. I was going to say, I would avoid them if I had a *bigger* plan."

Andy nodded smugly. "Exactly. Like serial murder. He wouldn't risk all that for a grope."

Liam frowned in thought. "So, we're looking for a cash business that brings him *no* contact with women? OK... They probably exist, but the income could be erratic and he'd have to be doing pretty damn well at it to pay for all his tech. I'm really starting to believe in this invisible partner, boss, and that *he* has the steady job."

"Agreed, but let's stick with who we have first and that's James MacArthur. Everyone, any suggestions on cash-in-hand jobs where contact with women is limited should go to Davy, but for now let's move on. John and Des, could you report now, then we'll take Ash and Davy on the viruses and CCTV and Mary on the shops and magazines."

As he knew what the scientists were going to say Craig went to refresh his coffee, and twenty minutes later the scientists had updated their pathology and forensic findings and the analysts had revealed that several different viruses with varying functions had been found between the squad-room, dry-cleaners, factory, Adelphi theatre and St Mary's Trust.

Ash was particularly excited by the intricacy of Julianne Hodges' murder.

"The skill it took to get concentrated Nicotine into that factory, make sure it was added to the normal dry-cleaning mix to generate a batch of contaminated canisters, then ship them to John Rogan's shop-"

Craig cut him off. "So, *all* the canisters on the carousel were contaminated with Nicotine?"

Des answered before the analyst could. "Yes. And we found more in the shop still in boxes."

"How many in total?"

"Twenty plus the six in the carousel."

Craig turned back to his analyst.

"How many canisters are generated from a normal batch of mix at the factory?"

"Fifty." Before Craig could point out the obvious Ash did so himself. "Which means there are twenty-four poisoned canisters still out there from that batch, and who knows how many more from other batches produced from that contaminated machine. We've shut the place down for a deep clean and the factory's recalling its stock urgently."

Something still didn't make sense to the detective.

"But surely Rogan must have had some uncontaminated canisters in stock before the contaminated batch arrived, so how did our killer guarantee only poisoned ones ending up in the carousel?"

Davy had the answer. "Because every other canister in the shop had been nicked the week before."

The fingerprint Grace had found on the back door! But it couldn't have belonged to James MacArthur because his were bound to be in the police system and all the database searches had drawn a blank. Had he hired someone for the burglary? It didn't feel likely.

Craig's thoughts were interrupted by his analyst's next words.

"Rogan didn't think to mention it when you saw him because he'd already claimed them on insurance and phoned the factory for new stock. But thinking about it, maybe that call to the factory w...was intercepted by our perp."

"Or listened in on. The shop needs to be swept for bugs." Craig sighed, picturing how things had played out. "Rogan called the factory with the perps listening and they arranged for a batch of fluid to be contaminated and sent out to him. OK. Those other poisoned canisters need to be found before people start dropping."

Liam shook his head. "They're long gone, boss. For all we know the killers shipped them to themselves for future use."

And that could be anywhere in the world. Craig suddenly felt exhausted.

"OK. Let's have a five-minute break. I need to think."

It took ten alone in his office for him to gather his thoughts, but when he returned to the group it was with a certainty that their way forward lay with Ash's work on the Dark Web.

After he'd set out his thinking, Andy asked a question. "Why does he make the murders so difficult?"

Liam shrugged. "Because he's a bastard?"

The quip lightened the mood, but didn't shift Andy from his point.

"I'm sure he is, but I'm not asking in a despairing way.

I'm just genuinely curious why he makes everything so convoluted. I know he wants to be remote from the murders when they happen so part of it will be due to that, but couldn't he manage that by hiring someone to kill for him or shooting the women himself with a sniper rifle?"

It was a question Craig had asked himself the day before.

Aidan shrugged. "He may not be a good shot, and introducing an assassin leaves him open to betrayal."

Craig was torn on the point.

"Agreed. But Andy's right, these methods aren't just remote they're very complex, whereas a gunshot isn't. Assassin or not."

John chipped in excitedly. "It's the challenge he's interested in. Can I kill in this, that and the other strange and intricate way?"

Andy still wasn't satisfied. "A challenge definitely, but I think it's even more than that. I suppose what I'm asking is, is our man challenging *himself* to come up with more and more unusual methods, or is *someone else* challenging him? This feels like a game to me, something that he's playing with someone."

Liam nodded. "With his partner. Yes."

Andy shook his head. "I'm not so sure. I think it could be something more."

"Such as?"

Davy smiled to himself, knowing what Andy was about to say and getting excited, even though he knew he shouldn't because the subject was so dark. He forgave himself on the basis that intellectual challenge was only ever evil because human beings were, and not in or of itself.

The team's most creative member didn't disappoint.

"I think this is a bigger game."

He saw Craig about to interrupt and held up a hand.

"Humour me a minute, chief. What if this is a *wider* game where people volunteer for or accept a challenge? Kill a list of women aged twenty-seven, kill a list of men aged sixty-two, or something equally gruesome. The player agrees to kill X number of people in unusual ways and the others watch online through the CCTV and agree to reward him according to the uniqueness of the murder methods, or maybe even on different aspects of the murders like how long the victims take to die."

Annette felt sick. "You're saying this is for entertainment?"

"Perhaps partly. Then when the list is complete the challenge shifts to another player in the game."

Andy went to say something else but realised he'd exhausted his imagination, so he sat back and waited for the ridicule to start. When it didn't come, he felt more surprised than rewarded.

"Is no-one going to tell me I'm talking bollocks?"

Liam obliged with a few different words. "You're a sick fuck, *that's* what you are."

No-one told him off for swearing because most were still busy staring at Andy, aghast.

Davy and Ash weren't, in fact they were gazing at him admiringly and Craig noticed.

"You two don't look shocked at all."

Davy shrugged. "Nope, and my bet is neither are the Docs at the back."

John confirmed the assertion with a wave. "We think it's a brilliant theory, Marc, and it wouldn't surprise us if it turned out to be true."

Craig smirked and shook his head.

"Nor me, not after some of the killers we've dealt with, so can everyone stop staring at Andy as if he has two heads, please. But brilliant theory or not it's moot at the moment because we can't prove it until we follow our main leads. James MacArthur and the women who are still alive."

Hearing her cue Mary held up a sheet of paper she'd just printed.

"What do you have, Mary?"

"Two lists. One has any local names from the mailing lists of the top tech magazines, and the other is a list of high-end customers from the local shops. So far, they seem to be law abiding nerds but I'll send the shops MacArthur's photo and see what that brings."

"Good." Craig glanced at his watch. "OK, there's still a lot of background research to do, so work until six and go home. We'll pick it up early."

As the group dispersed and the scientists left, he beckoned his three Chief Inspectors into his office.

"That was an interesting theory, Andy. Creative, as I'd expect from you."

"Unfortunately, I can't claim it as original, chief. I saw a movie about something similar. Anyway, proving it will be the challenge, as you said."

"I've had a thought on that."

He motioned them to sit before going on.

"We have the time-frame in which each woman was killed, and hopefully those can be tightened by Davy and Ash."

"So what, boss?"

"So, that's when they were watching the CCTV. *They* being either our killer, our killer and his partner, or if Andy's theory is correct perhaps even a wider spectator group."

"Again, *so*?"

But Andy could see where Craig was heading.

"If there *were* spectators, they might have placed bets on the murders beforehand or perhaps even as they watched. It could have been part of the excitement."

"Exactly."

Suddenly more interested, Liam straightened up in his seat.

"OK, I'll bite, Arty. So, betting via what? Instant bank transfers?"

"No, banks are too open to scrutiny. Bitcoin or something similar would be my bet."

Bitcoin is a crypto or digital currency that was invented in two thousand and eight.

Craig nodded. "E-currency used to be popular on the Dark Web, and Cybercrime can tell us if it's still in vogue.

Someone needs to go up there and see what help they can give us. Andy, this was your idea so do you want to do it?"

To his surprise the DCI shrugged. "I've no problem with you and Liam taking it, chief. Time's a pressure now and I'll be at the school in the morning, so crack on and see what you can find."

The response made Craig smirk. Andy could easily have delegated the school interviews to Ryan and visited Cybercrime himself, so his guess was there was something of far more interest to him at Brushford Academy than mere work.

****

The Cybercrime Division. Eleventh Floor, CCU.

After five minutes in Cybercrime Craig's head started to hurt. He thought of himself as tech capable, but compared to the people there he was as slow as a child just learning to write its name. Not only could they type faster than it was feasible for any human being to move their fingers, but they possessed a vocabulary that told him Davy and Ash must spend their days dumbing down to make themselves understood by his mere mortal detectives. It made him wonder if when the analysts were alone they spoke purely in acronyms like TOR and LAN. Someday schools would probably offer tech as a language as well as a STEM subject, with a whole module devoted to three letter terms.

If it was all making Craig long for plain English it was making his deputy long for the even more leisurely pace of ye olde sort. His whisper saying as much was so loud that everyone on the vast computer floor immediately stopped typing and turned to look at them, prompting an even louder aside.

"They're robots, boss!"

Craig stifled a laugh and waved him into a corner. "Pipe down, will you, we're guests here. You knew they

211

were skilled before we came."

"I didn't know they were flipping Cybermen!"

Just then the person they'd come to see walked on to the floor and Craig smiled in recognition. Sue Jones had done her basic training the same year as him but he'd rarely seen her since their passing out parade.

"Sue! I didn't realise you were the boss here. It's good to see you again." He suddenly remembered they weren't alone. "Liam, this is ... sorry, I don't know your rank, Sue."

"It's DCI but up here they call it Commander."

"Commander Sue Jones," he nodded to his deputy, "this is DCI Liam Cullen."

Her smile widened to a grin. "*You're kidding!* The legend himself." She gripped Liam's hand and shook it enthusiastically. "Welcome. You're famous for breaking rules and getting away with it from sheer cheek." She turned back to Craig. "And the ones you haven't broken I just bet Marc has. He started that in his first week."

Unsure quite how to react, Craig shuffled his feet and made embarrassed noises, whereas his deputy puffed out his chest proudly and made a note to ask more about his 'legendary' reputation another time.

"So, what can I do you for gentlemen?"

As Craig took a minute to outline what they were thinking, Liam watched the red nails of a young analyst fly across her computer. He rarely managed to persuade Danni to wear any but the sight made up his mind that tonight was going to be the night even if he had to beg.

His thoughts were interrupted by Jones saying, "E-currency is a possibility, but only if they're using money and making the transfers contemporaneously."

She nodded towards an office with her name on the door and Craig waited until they were seated inside before speaking again.

"What would they be betting with if not money, Sue?"

The commander clarified what she'd meant. "If they're betting at all it will have a monetary value, but they may not pay their bills using money, either e-currency or real."

"With what then?"

"Barters."

"As in the ancient system used before currency was invented?"

"Yes, essentially. It's the newest trick cyber criminals use to keep us off their tails."

Seeing both men's scepticism she laid things out.

"OK, so I'm Player A and you're Players B and C and we're all betting online on the outcome of... let's say a football game. Right?"

There were nods.

"So, to make my bet I type the number one hundred on my screen-"

Liam cut in. "One hundred whats? Dollars, euros?"

"Either, or pounds, yen and so on. *Whatever* the currency is, it will have been agreed before the game. And because everyone knows what currency they're using they only need to type numbers. The point being that by only writing a *number* there's deniability if the police monitor the transaction. If we're caught, we could just say we were betting one hundred matchsticks, which have negligible monetary value and so would be legal, and it would be impossible to prove otherwise in court. OK?"

Craig was with her so far. "OK, what comes next?"

"Well, when the football game ends a final number representing the amount in the betting pot appears. The winner naturally wants to collect their dues, so this is where it gets interesting and money becomes an issue. Let's say that final number in the pot is five thousand and the group was betting in pounds. If the loser transfers that five thousand pounds to the winner digitally or even using e-currency, then that will leave a solid trail for the cops to follow and land them in jail."

She gestured at the door. "And my team *always* traces money eventually, no matter how many banks or Bitcoin accounts it's bounced between. Criminals are aware of that now, so barters are used instead."

Liam was perplexed, but not by the system. "But why bother with all this subterfuge? I mean gambling's legal, so why go on the Dark Web at all?"

The Commander's face darkened. "Because I'm only using gambling on a football game as an example, but if you're right then *your* perps are gambling on people's deaths. And believe me, we've seen worse than that. Torture, abuse," she shuddered suddenly, "you wouldn't believe some of the things people do online because they think no-one can see them in the dark."

Craig sighed. "Trust me, we would." He sat forward briskly to break the mood. "OK, say so I owe you ten million units, Sue, whatever a unit is, pounds or whatever. What kind of barter would be worth that amount, and how can that barter be moved without your team catching on?"

Back in her comfort zone, Jones smiled excitedly.

"There's a preordained list of barters and their worth, and you can break them down however you like. For example, ten million could be five barters of two million units, fifty of-"

She was cut off by Liam's nod.

"Give us examples of what that means in the real world."

"OK, give me a moment."

She left the room, to return a moment later with three sheets of paper.

"Take one, but I'll need them back before you go. It took us a year to crack this list."

Craig scanned his page quickly and burst out laughing.

"Fifty thousand units is a Mercedes?"

"If the currency was UK pounds, yes. There's a different barter list for dollars, euros and so on."

"There are other cars too, boss, if you fancy a nice people carrier. But keep reading. Twenty million's a Lear jet or a twenty contract kills on your enemies!" Liam guffawed. "I could wipe out the wife's whole tribe."

"Or own a hell of a lot of cars." Craig set his page down

on the desk. "This is how it's usually done now, Sue?"

The commander shook her head. "No. Plenty of people still use e-currency, but they're usually middle grade, stupid, or non-lethal criminals. And the bigger bucks from drug cartels are still done the old-fashioned way. Dispersed by bank transfers to tax-free zones like the Caymans relying on end-to-end confidentiality to cover their backs, which it used to but not so much now. But because the cartels haven't caught the bartering bug yet there've been a lot of drug arrests recently all over the world. If they *do* decide to start using them then our jobs will become a whole lot harder again."

Craig was fascinated by her words.

"Which criminals got into bartering first?"

"People who were up to really dark-"

Liam finished her sentence. "Shit?"

"Exactly. People for whom the stigma of their crime is strongest."

Craig nodded. "So, paedophiles, snuff film producers and the like?"

"You've got it. Financial crime might put you in jail but it doesn't carry that kind of stigma, and drug dealers seem to enjoy their notoriety. But the others you've mentioned and people like *your* perps... they get life sentences or executed in some countries. And even if they escape the death penalty in court, they rarely survive a year in jail without getting shivved by another prisoner, so anonymity is crucial to them and bartering is the way they keep it."

Liam gave an evil grin. "You've gotta love prison justice. Ordinary perps don't like sickos."

"Which makes them desperate to keep ahead of the cops." Craig dragged a hand down his face wearily. "If our killers are smart enough to use bartering, we might never find them, Liam."

Jones gave a small smile. "Never give up, or numquam dare as my Latin teacher used to say. It all depends on how accurate you can be on the time of the transactions and their likely locations."

Craig reached into his pocket for the note Davy had handed him just before they'd come up.

"Our analysts have managed to narrow down the likely times our perps were watching, which is also when any betting would have happened." He handed her the note. "Those are the time frames over the past four days. The first murder happened on Sunday night and the last yesterday morning."

"The deaths were that recent? Good. It will save my team having to dig through archives. OK," She rose again, "hang on here and I'll be back."

True to her word Jones returned a few minutes later, although not with answers.

"I've put one of my best people on it, so they'll check our monitoring across the Dark Web for any possibilities, using those dates and times. Although I have to warn you, they may find nothing. The internet has a lot of hiding places. But if they do, they'll dig deeper to see if it's useful. I can promise you this much, if your perps have left a clear sign of betting or bartering, we'll find it. But do me a favour, Marc."

"Whatever you need."

"Send your analysts up next time. My people would need a translator to talk to civvies like you."

****

Olivia Kenzie's Design Workshop. Ardglass, County Down. Thursday, 8.30 a.m.

Everything was prepped and ready: the virus, their viewers, their real-world alibis. But Noel Robinson had been waiting for an hour and Olivia Kenzie was still nowhere to be seen, and he could feel his jaw tightening with the frustration that he'd felt all of his life at delays.

True, there was nothing special about killing her today; it wasn't the Feast Day of Murderers after all. Just another tedious day in a year of tedious days, but that made his frustration all the worse.

Life was just so fucking boring. Get up, get washed and dressed, drive to a job he hated, take crap from higher-ups or the public, then go home, eat, sleep and repeat. That had been his life for years, punctuated by the only thing that made him truly happy, gaming on the computer array he'd set up at home. That and what it had led to; a whole new world on the Net. At first, he'd just used social media and played popular games, until he'd met some kindred spirits and begun chatting and then he'd descended deeper and deeper into the Dark Web. Now what happened there felt more real to him than anything that took place in the so-called normal world.

The thought made him laugh and he explored his amusement's origin as he scanned the factory carpark waiting for Olivia Kenzie's car to pull in. He found it in The Matrix, a movie about people living in ignorance of their computer-generated reality. Perhaps the internet *was* reality and this world fake, but only he and his online friends knew the truth? And if the women on their killing list hadn't actually been real then he was innocent of any crime; not that he'd killed any of them himself, his role was just to make sure their deaths could be viewed, although no judge would split that hair.

His spiral into lunacy was interrupted by a beep on his smart-pad and a message set to erase seconds after it appeared.

'What's the hold up with the connection? I'm waiting.'
His reply was an angry, *'SHE'S LATE!'*

Soon *too* late to kill that day. He was tasked with keeping their enterprise ahead of the law and if he parked where he was for much longer some concerned citizen might phone the cops, so after ten more minutes waiting Noel Robinson cancelled the show with another message.

'She's a no-show.'

They should have wondered *why* their planned victim was late and investigated. But then criminals' stupidity was what the justice system relied upon, and why the good guys still won more than they lost.

****

The CCU.

By lunchtime and with no sign of another murder Craig began to slowly unclench his jaw. When his mobile rang suddenly, he amazed himself by not jumping for the first time in twenty-four hours.

He recognised the caller's breathing instantly.

"What's the problem, Aidan?"

Knowing that Davy had masked their numbers the DCI wondered if his camera was on, only to have Craig explain before he could ask.

"I recognised how you inhaled. So, what can I do for you?"

Determining not to be such an easy ID in future the detective gave a quick report.

"I've seen the two women and told them they're not to go anywhere till we say so, Guv. They wanted more answers than I was giving, but otherwise they took it well."

"Good. What jobs do they do?"

It could give him an idea of how they might be killed remotely.

"Olivia Kenzie's a fashion designer and manages a small factory workshop in Ardglass."

"So, cutting and electrical equipment to kill her with there."

Aidan was impressed. "I suppose so. I hadn't thought that far. Anyway, the other one, Romaine Martin, is an accountant at a big firm in town, so not much risk on-site."

"There is if there's a lift in the building that could have its brakes overridden."

"Bloody hell, Guv, I wouldn't want to be inside your head."

"It's worse inside our killer's, trust me. Right, you've armed guards outside their homes?"

"Yep. Plain clothes at the front and back of each

house. Mary's being a bit trickier though, Guv. She's fed up staying at the hotel and wants to know if she can go home tonight. Her guards are begging me as well. Apparently, she's been giving them earache."

"Where does she live?"

"A flat up near Queen's. First floor and we can park in the street front and back, so it won't be any harder to guard than a hotel room."

Craig pictured the set-up and did a quick risk assessment.

"OK, yes then, but I want someone posted outside her apartment door as well, and she isn't to leave or have guests. If she doesn't like that, she can lump it. Anything more?"

"Nope. I'm off to practice breathing quieter."

Craig was still chuckling at the thought when a knock came on his door and Davy appeared.

"Do you have a minute, chief?"

He was nodded to a seat.

"How did it go in Cybercrime?"

"They're working on the times you gave me, so once they're ready I'm going to send you up. They're fed up dumbing down for us."

The younger man smirked. "Great. OK, Ash said to tell you Julianne Hodges didn't have any social media accounts. Just never bothered setting them up her husband said."

"Fine. Is that all?"

"Nope. I came in to talk about CCTV."

"Fire away."

"Well, I ran through all the internal CCTV from the hospital and theatre, and as we guessed there was no-one on it who shouldn't have been there. S...Same with the factory and dry-cleaners."

"We know remoteness is important to our killer, so why is that news?"

The analyst pulled a face. "I suppose I still hoped they would slip up, especially as the medical w...ward where Felicia Barker died was in the centre of the hospital and

219

that should've made it harder for someone to piggyback from the street. But their booster must be strong."

The detective leant forward at his desk. "What's the maximum distance that could have worked?"

He prayed Davy wouldn't say ten miles and he didn't. He smiled instead.

"Even the best only boost for half-a-mile, so they must have piggybacked on the hospital CCTV from the grounds."

"Definitely no further?"

"Nope." He woke up the smart-pad that he'd brought and turned it to face Craig. "I drew a half-mile radius on a map and it all falls within the hospital perimeter." His face fell slightly. "The problem is there are a lot of cars around a hospital at any time of day."

Craig was just about to get gloomy when his computer expert brightened up again.

"But then I did the same for all the other scenes so now I've got the circle of coverage for each one, so I really just came in to ask if it's OK if I go back to the ASU to take another look at their cameras? It'll be quicker than waiting for them to report."

"Do whatever's needed to crack this. How's Ash progressing undercover on the Dark Web?"

The analyst laughed. "Now I'm picturing him in a trench coat and fedora."

"Well, don't tell *him* that or his next fashion quirk will be a hat."

He already knew that Davy would, but he was more interested in information than discussing millinery right now.

"So? Does he have anything yet?"

"It's starting to come in. He's monitoring about ten different D.W. chat-rooms and boards."

"Anything more from the in-country agencies?"

"Just the lists of deaths we already have, sorry."

Craig had an idea. "Tell Ash to ask their cybercrime divisions about bartering."

The analyst looked at him quizzically. "What's

bartering? As linked with cybercrime I mean."

"Sue Jones will explain when you go upstairs. And I've just had another thought, Davy. Call Aidan and tell him about the half-mile radius, please, and say I want him to draw similar circles around our potential victims' workplaces and homes, including Mary's. And ask ASU and Traffic to specifically monitor those streets until we say stop."

"Will do."

As he left the room, Craig could hear him muttering, "Bartering. *Bartering?*" under his breath.

****

Brushford Academy. The Interview Room.

Interviewing James MacArthur's old teachers had given Andy earache but little more. Well, unless you counted a vivid memory of being fourteen, which for the DCI had been a decidedly awkward age; less the unfeasibly cool image of a teenager seen in movies and more the unpredictable breaking voice and hair appearing in random patches type. Who *were* those slick movie teens anyway? Because they weren't like anyone that he'd ever known. Although he suspected that Craig might have fitted the mould.

Ryan had had different experiences during his awkward phase, employing his congenital deafness in one ear to his advantage by turning it in the direction of anyone who'd annoyed him, and daring the school bullies or teachers to pick on him knowing fine well that if they had his parents and then the school would have kicked them into touch.

But the detectives had learned little about James MacArthur that they hadn't already known: a bright enough student, bit of a loner with a difficult home background, overly interested in girls and not inclined to take no for an answer, and after he'd assaulted Julianne Harbinson prosecuted and sent to jail. Little but not

221

nothing; it turned out that one of MacArthur's old masters had seen his old pupil in Belfast just two weeks before.

"James was walking down the opposite side of Donegall Place and I called out to him. But he mustn't have heard me because he just kept on walking."

There were a few of Andy's old teachers that would make *him* walk on too, but the sighting could provide a lead so he dug further.

"You're positive it was MacArthur?"

The master gave him a sceptical look. "So, either you think I need glasses or that all children look the same to us."

His sarcasm reminded Andy of a particular teacher he would have paid to exact revenge on, so he took the opportunity to counter with some sharpness of his own.

"Well, all teachers do to kids." Before the master could retort he followed up with, "When was this exactly?"

The man responded grudgingly. "Let me see if I can remember…" After a full ten seconds pause, "It was on the Wednesday of that week" came back.

"That's quite specific."

"Very, I think you mean. And it's correct."

Even Ryan wanted to punch the teacher now.

"I know because the school boiler had burst and we had that day off while it was being repaired."

"Right. So, how did MacArthur look?"

Surprisingly the master's response was tinged with sympathy this time.

"Not great, to be honest. Basically, he was the same lanky boy, although even taller. And he'd filled out a bit. Muscle not fat. In fact, he looked like he went to a gym regularly. But he was unkempt and unshaven, and staring at the ground as he walked. I believe he was muttering to himself as well." He brightened up slightly, as if he'd seen something to prove that his tuition hadn't gone completely to waste. "But he has a job."

"How could you tell?"

"He was wearing some sort of uniform. Not a suit, but

decent black jeans and a nice-looking black hoodie with some kind of badge or logo on the front. The combination was quite smart in its own way. He was too far away for me to read the logo, but it was definitely there."

"Could you sketch it?"

In response the master reached for a pen and produced a dead envelope from his pocket, quickly drawing a sideways oval and scribbling two vertical lines inside.

"I think those might have been letters. No idea which ones."

"Colours?"

"Red outline, white filling, and the letters were black. It stood out against his hoodie."

It was pretty good from a distance.

As Andy considered the information Ryan jumped in.

"Was there anything to suggest he had a trade? Like paint brushes or tools?"

MacArthur could have learned a trade in jail.

"No. I'm sure he wasn't carrying anything because I saw both his hands."

"And his clothes weren't stained with paint or oil?"

"No. They were smart casual. It was his beard and hair that were unkempt."

Trying not to be obvious the sergeant scanned the middle-aged master's neat, side-parted hair and shaved-to-within-an-inch-of-his-life face. What seemed unkempt to him might merely have looked fashionably dishevelled to someone Davy's age.

But MacArthur's outfit *was* interesting.

Andy asked a different question. "I don't suppose you saw where he was going?"

"I did actually. He turned right down High Street. I was going straight ahead so that was the last I saw of him."

Andy thanked the teacher and signalled Ryan to join him outside the classroom they'd been allocated for interviews.

"What does MacArthur's outfit sound like to you, Ryan?"

"Small business maybe?"

"Yes, but most employers expect their employees to shave no matter what the current fashion is, so I'd say the possibility he's running a business himself just went to the top of the list."

"His outfit suggests something modern. Maybe a franchise of some kind?"

"Good call. And probably in Belfast. People usually only wear a uniform near their work." The DCI glanced at his watch. "OK, let's head back to the ranch."

As he walked off Ryan called after him.

"Wrong way, chief. The car's parked back there."

The, "I'm taking the scenic route past the headteacher's office" that floated back didn't require anything more to be said.

****

Craig's Office. 2 p.m.

It was all very well guarding their potential victims and depriving a serial killer of their prey, something that definitely had to be done, but homicidal maniacs were rarely respecters of reason and unlikely to just shrug, "Fair enough" and walk away. Whatever drove them to kill repeatedly was born of obsession and Craig knew that.

Single murders, the majority that weren't committed on impulse, were often based on targeted revenge. Even home invasions normally had a driver of jealousy or greed, with only the people who got in the way disposed of.

But murders like this... Craig shook his head. He wanted to say that they defied logic, except in the mind of a serial killer perhaps not. If this man or any others egging him on to kill *were* cyberpaths as Jock Armstrong had said, then they lived in a different universe governed

224

by different rules.

Craig turned to gaze out at the river, trying to put himself in their killer's place. It wasn't his first trip into a murderer's mind and he never enjoyed it, but it felt necessary now to predict their next step.

He allowed the darkness that lives in all of us to rise to the surface, picturing their three dead victims when they were alive: young, beautiful, vibrant women with years of life ahead of them, lives they were enjoying without *him*. He instantly became an angry, sexed-up teenage boy; again, because he'd already been one decades before. Then he delved deeper, into the mind of a boy who'd been abused at home, bullied by his peers, and rejected by the girls he'd hoped would be his friends, and felt himself grow cold.

Craig went with it, picturing the women as teenage girls, laughing, happy, flirting with other boys but never with him, and felt a burning longing and confusion. He let the feelings wash over him. Why *not* him? *Why didn't they want him?* What was so wrong with *him* that they always chose other boys? He felt his frustration become an urge for action: watching, tracking, stalking the objects of his desire, too awkward to speak normally to them and so always turning the talk to his ultimate goal, sex, but always too fast and too bluntly and seeing their repulsion when he did.

His longing became a furious need and the intent to simply *take* what he wanted. Seven girls who would eventually grow to women, but Julianne Harbinson above all the rest. Watching her and waiting for his moment, and then her screams and her teachers' and parents' fury, and *his* anger and resentment when the penalty he paid for that one mistake impacted on the rest of his life.

As his rage grew into a lust for vengeance Craig felt his fist curl and smash into the window, then as he pictured something or someone getting in his way he lashed out again, this time so hard that a sharp pain shot up his arm. But he *still* had to follow the thoughts.

What if the obstacle in his way was insurmountable? The final names on his list protected by a ring of cops, meaning that even with his remote methods they were immune? And what if his partner or partners were goading and taunting him as a failure, perhaps even changing their bets to gamble on how badly he would fail?

At that moment if Craig could have put his fist through his double-glazed office window he would have done, and that urge told him what their killer was going to do next.

He couldn't walk away and he wouldn't. Instead he would intensify his efforts to reach the last three women, searching obsessively for gaps in their protections until he found them and then killing them one by one.

The implications sent a shiver down the detective's spine.

The opportunities for remote killings were over and soon their killer would realise it. But nothing was going to stop him so next time he would watch a woman breathe her last up close.

****

Outside the room Liam was listening and waiting. He had his own office but rarely spent any time there unless he had a report to write for court, much preferring the camaraderie of the main floor and more importantly the opportunities it brought for annoying people. When he heard Craig stop banging and start pacing, knowing from experience it might go on for a while, he decided that today's lucky target would be Ash.

He *could* have knocked on Craig's door of course, but years of working together had taught him that the combo of banging and pacing rarely made that a good idea, so instead he ambled across to the junior analyst's desk and pulled up a chair, staring at Ash's computer screens as if he could actually understand anything on them and making the occasional ruminating noise.

After the fourth or fifth, "Mmm... yes, I see" the computer expert gave up trying to ignore him and turned round.

"What do you want, Liam?"

The deputy arched an eyebrow.

"Don't you mean, what do you want, *sir?*"

"Nope. Davy's my boss and the chief's his and you look nothing like either of them."

Unable to think of a comeback Liam shunted his elbow off the desk.

"Tell me what you're doing. Now."

Ash toyed with the idea of telling him again that he wasn't in charge of him but decided the earache wouldn't be worth it. He was just about to get his revenge by bamboozling the DCI with geek-speak when Liam said, "In English" and thwarted his fiendish plan.

"Party pooper. OK, well basically, I've two screens running. The left-hand one is where I've boasted about owning the viruses in some chat-rooms and the middle one is where I'm offering the same viruses for sale."

Surprised to find that he'd actually understood him, the DCI grinned.

"Sneaky. So, any takers yet?"

Ash leant in excitedly. "I've two people asking about the viruses, and one's getting into serious detail."

"The sort of detail that suggests they already know about them?"

The analyst nodded emphatically. "Yep. I'm taking it slow because I don't want to scare him off, but if he goes the way I'm hoping he will-"

Liam cut him off. "Why are you saying he? Do you have a name?"

Ash's eyes widened in alarm and he hissed, *"Keep your voice down, will you!"* his follow-on glance at Mary's thankfully empty desk making his meaning clear.

He continued in a whisper.

"I said *he* because I'm being a sexist pig, or that's what Mary would say anyway. I'm just assuming it's a man because most hackers and IT wizards are, but I guess it could be a girl. Anyway," he pulled up a third screen, "this is the payment mock-up where I'll send him if he gets interested in buying. As soon as there's a fund exchange, I'll have his name."

Liam was puzzled. "But why would he buy a virus he already has?"

"To get it off the market. Remember *he* doesn't know I work for the cops."

"Fair enough. But a cash exchange? Why not bartering?"

It was the analyst's turn to be confused, which gave Liam an unreasonable amount of pleasure, but in his defence, it wasn't often he knew more about cyber anything than anybody so he was going to milk it for all it was worth.

That included launching into a lengthy explanation of bartering, which was interrupted first by Craig throwing open his office door and shouting, "LIAM", to Nicky's exaggerated clamping of her hands over her ears and look of disgust, and secondly by Davy's reappearance on the floor.

When Craig saw his deputy was with Ash he strolled across.

"Something exciting?"

"I was just giving the young 'un the benefit of my vast knowledge on bartering."

Davy cut in brightly. "I can do that before I head to the ASU. I've just been up to Cybercrime."

Ignoring his deputy's thwarted expression Craig said, "Good idea. Bring Mary up to date too, please. Liam, join me in my office."

The DCI made his displeasure known by stomping in and hurling himself into a chair so heavily Craig was surprised it kept its legs.

"You've just ruined my chance of teaching a geek something he didn't know, boss, and I was enjoying it too!"

"I'm glad one of you was. Tea?"

The offer was accepted with a mutter and Craig passed him the drink before sitting down.

After a few seconds Liam thawed.

"What was all that banging and pacing about earlier?"

"You heard then."

"That lot up on the space station couldn't have missed the racket you were making. What were you up to?" Just then he noticed Craig's skinned knuckles. "Punching things again, are we? That's not good news."

Craig rubbed them to ease the pain. "It might be. I've just been inside our killer's head and I'm pretty sure our remote killings are over."

Liam took a slurp of his drink and set it down. "Well, what are you looking so worried about then? That means it's all over bar catching him."

Craig shook his head. "Not if he decides to kill his next victims face-to-face."

It earned him a sceptical snort.

"Ach, get away with it, boss. Sure, how can he? He'd have to get past a clatter of cops to reach any of them."

"It only takes one slip, Liam, and there's only so long that we can keep those women on lockdown." He gestured at the door. "If the other two are anything like Mary they're already resenting it and looking for escape hatches. And if they find them so will our killer."

Just then something occurred to him and he raced out of the office, to return a minute later. His deputy knew exactly where he'd been.

"Annette being sent to check up on them again?"

"As soon as Ryan gets back to join her. A daily morale visit won't do any harm and it might keep them focused on their safety."

Something had dawned on Liam during his absence. "Exactly how is this scrote going to spot them escaping? In time to nab them I mean."

Craig saw what he was getting at. Or thought he did.

"There are bound to be local cameras he can piggyback on."

"Right outside their houses? I doubt it. I think we

should check the overlooking houses in case he's set up shop inside one to watch them."

It was clever and Craig agreed, but only in part.

"He won't be *in* the houses. Too many occupants to kill for access, and why bother when it's easier to just set up cameras."

He opened the office door again, just in time to see Ryan and a cheerful looking Andy, who'd managed to get Daisy Brontë's home phone number, enter the squad-room.

He beckoned them in, laid out their latest thoughts and issued orders.

"Ryan, you go with Annette to check on the women and keep them focused on staying home. Andy, take Ash and check the overlooking houses for rigged-up cameras. Ash will know what to look for. Have him check the local street and traffic cameras for piggybacking too while he's there. Aidan's at the ASU so he can give you a steer on where they're located."

As the door closed behind them, he turned back to his deputy to say, "Good catch," but it was Liam's turn to bolt. He returned with Andy again.

"Did you discover anything about MacArthur from the school, Arty?"

The DCI retold the Donegall Place encounter.

"We need to find out where MacArthur's working, boss."

"Andy, ask Mary to run down that logo, and I think you're right about him having his own business, probably in the city centre."

"OK, chief, I'll let you know what we find."

When he was alone with his deputy again Craig ran through some outstanding tasks. "We need to explore Mary's tech lists further and see if Ash has anything useful from the Net."

"He's got someone interested in his viruses and if he decides to buy Ash'll take it from there. That's how we got into our bartering conversation. The one you so rudely interrupted."

"Mea culpa."

There was a pause which the DCI interpreted as contrition but was really just another idea taking shape.

"Liam, ask Aidan to go back over the street footage around our possible future victims' houses for a few days. We may catch a break and see him up a ladder rigging his cameras." He shook his head at what he'd just said. "I *really* need to find a better collective noun for these women than 'possible future Vics'. It doesn't play well."

"How about 'future dead people unless we save them' then? How's that?"

Craig's expletive was heard by everyone on the floor.

Chapter Eleven

The rest of the afternoon was an exercise in drawing together loose ends and watching the Net, camera screens, houses and the clock. Waiting for their killer to make his next move was torment for Craig but the alternative was a fourth body which would have been far worse.

The only concrete new information the squad had acquired by five p.m. was Liam being proved right; their killer *had* rigged up new cameras on the houses surrounding their 'possible future Vics' homes. Tiny, state of the art ones that Mary confirmed could either have been ordered through any of a hundred ads at the back of tech mags or bought at three of the Belfast tech shops on her list.

Tasked with finding which if any of them had actually sold the equipment, the constable had spent an hour on the phone getting bounced around until she'd hit the 'threatening with warrants' stage again, the shops' personnel once more displaying an inflated desire to protect their customers' privacy. The question had to be, why? Did they know something about their intended uses for the cameras?

When the thought that they could have been stalling for time to hide something occurred to her, Craig dispatched his deputy for extended warrants to serve on his way home with back-up from Andy, telling the DCIs to stand over the shopkeepers until the records had been coughed up. Unless the shop owners pissed them off by not cooperating that was, in which case not only could Liam check their sales records but he should order a full hairy-big-men-in-uniform search of their premises and leave them tidying for a month.

The shops might turn out to be dead ends but Liam was glad of something to keep him busy while all the watching and waiting came to fruition, and the thought of kicking in doors always cheered him up.

Meanwhile, after much agonising, Craig and his head

analyst had made the decision to leave their killer's rigged cameras in place.

Yes, it meant that he could still watch his potential victims, but at least they knew where those cameras were and Davy could get on with tracing their source signals. To have removed them would not only have tipped their killer off that they knew what he was up to but he could simply have planted new and probably better concealed ones overnight and started watching again.

By close of play Craig had accepted with a heavy heart that until something fresh came back from their searches or their killer made another move, they were in stalemate, and like his deputy the inertia was driving him mad. By nature he needed constant movement so waiting was the hardest thing that his job asked him to do. But he would watch and wait for a year if it prevented his adversary taking another life.

****

The Aerial Support Unit (ASU). 5.30 p.m.

Aidan was going whatever the tech equivalent was of snow-blind. He'd been slumped in a chair gazing at black and white footage for so long, trying to find just *one* useful image on the fuzzy CCTV from around the three women's homes, that now he was seeing afterimages of cars, pedestrians and buildings on the walls and Theo Sheridan's shirt every time he took a break.

He had also witnessed six petty crimes in passing; mainly red-light runners but also a woman nicking a newspaper as she'd walked past a row of shops, and one particularly egregious incident of someone kicking a homeless person lying in a doorway - that one made him ring the local station and send over the photo file.

By five-thirty the DCI was just about to give up when footage from a security camera on Romaine Martin's street made him press stop hastily and rewind the tape. He expected it to have come from the evening before and

233

was taken aback to see that instead it read two a.m. on Saturday.

He gave the ASU Commander a quizzical look that was answered with a shrug.

"I thought it made sense to start watching just before your first murder. I mean, why wouldn't this bugger have started surveillance on *all* the women at once?"

Aidan chuckled. "I don't suppose you fancy being a detective, do you?"

Sheridan tapped the pips on his shoulder. "Give up these bad boys to start at the bottom again? No thanks. But you've clearly found something useful, so let's see."

He watched as Aidan replayed the clip on quarter time, smiling at the clear outline of a man approaching one of the houses on which they'd found a mounted spy camera and raising his eyebrows as he took a running jump from the pavement onto the flat roof of a standalone garage next door.

"Bloody hell, he's fit! I couldn't do that, could you?"

Being a gym bunny Aidan knew that he could, but to save Sheridan's pride he shook his head and changed the subject by tapping the screen.

"Using this garage roof was smart. It meant no-one inside the actual house would've heard him."

They kept watching and the man, clothed in black from head-to-toe and with his head permanently down, removed something small from his pocket and stretched out an arm to attach it in a smooth movement to the front of the house. He repeated the action twice more and then produced something else from his pocket that was hard to make out.

Sheridan got it first.

"The bastard's brought foliage with him to cover them! That house must already have some on it or it would stand out."

Aidan sat back heavily, shaking his head in disbelief.

"You know what this means."

"That he'd scouted the street beforehand, knew exactly which house to choose and that it had vegetation on it and brought along some that matched. The clever git. You see how he keeps his head down? He probably knows where every security camera is in that street. Your man's been planning this killing spree for a while."

After some more discussion Aidan phoned Craig, breaking the news that he had expected and hearing something unexpected in return.

"We're leaving the cameras in place, Aidan, otherwise it will tip him off. Mary's narrowed their local outlets to three shops on our tech list and Liam and Andy are heading to them with warrants now."

"What about him buying them online, Guv?"

Craig sighed. "We can't rule that out, and it might make more sense with this perp, but if they were careless enough for us to find the link with MacArthur, they might just get careless again. We have to give the shops a try at least. OK, good catch, Aidan. Check the other addresses and send any clips over for Davy to see." He tutted quietly. "It's just a damn pity he managed to conceal his face. Maybe if Davy can do something clever, we'll find it on one of his own cameras."

"I wouldn't hold your breath, Guv. We haven't seen even a flash of white so my guess is he's wearing a mask."

"Typical of our luck. OK, I'll be here for another few hours if you get finished, so send me a copy of anything useful as well."

As he ended the call Craig got an urge to stretch his legs and walked out to the main floor, surprised to find the only people still there were his analysts and Mary. When he checked the clock, he realised why.

"Has everyone else gone home?"

Davy nodded his deputy to answer; he was too busy checking something that he couldn't quite believe.

"Alice and Nicky left ten minutes ago, chief. Annette saw the women then had to collect her daughter from somewhere, so Ryan joined Liam and Andy on the warrants. We stayed here to work."

Mary wasn't being left out. "I did too. Anything rather than go back and see my flat surrounded by cops."

"Fine. Carry on then."

After a quick circuit of the floor and a trip to the kitchen during which he phoned his deputy, Craig could contain his curiosity no longer and made a beeline for Davy's desk, to find him hunched in the same position as five minutes before. When the analyst ignored him completely and kept his eyes locked on his screen, Craig knew something was definitely up.

"Is that the footage from the murder scenes, Davy?"

The only response was a grunt but he decided to push his luck.

"Inside or outside?"

"Out."

More silence followed during which Ash swivelled his chair to watch the exchange, quipping, "That noise you hear is his giant brain working. When you smell smoke, it'll be time to appoint a new pope."

Craig couldn't wait that long so he did something that he hated being done to him. He leant down and put his face directly between the analyst and his computer, biting his lip to avoid uttering the "Beep-Bo" that had become the sound track to living with a one-year-old.

Davy sighed heavily and pushed back his chair.

"You won't wait, will you?"

"Can't more like. I'm not unreasonable, I don't expect answers yet," *although if you happen to have some,* "so if you could just tell me what you're looking for that would be enough."

It wouldn't and they both knew it, but it was one of the lies Craig told himself to defend against the accusations of impatience that had been fired at him all his life.

His head analyst's sceptical expression said that it had failed.

"Does that ever work for you, chief?"

It brought a chuckling, "No, but it was worth a try."

"OK, for your honesty you can pull up a chair. But I'm warning you, I don't have all the answers yet."

By now the others had joined Craig by the desk and

Davy was starting to feel crowded, so he motioned them all to move away and projected a grid of photographs on to the LED screen.

"OK, our three murder scenes had various cameras that our killer could've used to watch his handiwork, but also to perform their basic functions of watching who came and went in the Adelphi and different hospital units. I checked them all out, but as I expected there was nothing to see."

Mary nodded. "Because he'd piggybacked them remotely but never actually been in front of the lens."

"Exactly. The Adelphi and Radiology I knew he could have accessed from the street, but I thought he might've had to go indoors to capture Felicia Barker's images because it's at the centre of the hospital. But no."

Craig was trying not to show his impatience but it leaked out as, *"You told me all this,"* and earned him a hostile, "You lot think it's easy to get tech answers, but we have to eliminate a lot of dross first and that takes time" from his constable.

He ignored her and smiled encouragingly at Davy, who went on, "So... outside the scenes."

He drew a hand down his computer screen.

"This is where things get weird. I checked every camera I could find in a radius of half-a-mile around each scene-"

Ash cut in. "Looking for a repeating car?"

"Initially, but there weren't any. I've been over and over the three scenes for repeat shots of any car, van, motorbike or even a normal bike. Anything that could carry one person close enough to piggyback and watch the murders-"

Craig risked a, "But" and immediately felt six expert eyes on him.

He continued more cautiously. "Surely the equipment needed to piggyback and transmit the images would be too big to carry on a bike?"

Davy struggled not to pat him on the head, knowing that he was probably picturing a giant wireless set with an antenna, like some prop from the movies of his youth.

"Umm no, chief. A smart-phone could do both."

Craig decided to shut up before he *really* showed his age.

"Anyway, so I found no repeating vehicles and that set me scratching my head. What could blend in so easily that I would miss it even if I was staring at it? An emergency or utility vehicle, that's what."

"You mean like electricity vans?"

"Those and gas supplier vans, road cleaners, ambulances, fire engines..."

Craig mouthed, "Police cars" aghast, but no-one noticed and he was grateful that they hadn't; it wasn't a possibility to raise until there was solid evidence.

He raised a hand to halt the analyst.

"What time frame are we talking about here, Davy?"

"The windows in which the murders took place and thirty minutes either side. I looked for everything just mentioned and the only repeating vehicles near the scenes were utility."

"Parked?"

"Sometimes, but other times driving around. They didn't have to be static to hold the signal as long as they stayed in range, chief. Before you ask for more, that's as far as I've got right now."

Craig slumped back in his seat, his mind racing with possibilities. He voiced the only coherent one.

"If the vehicle was moving at the moment of death someone other than our killer must have been driving it, otherwise he couldn't have watched the deaths as they occurred."

"The partner?"

"Perhaps, although I think he would've wanted to watch too."

Mary had a way around it.

"Whoever was piggybacking could've been recording it to watch when they got home." She shook her head immediately, dismissing her own point. "No, they would've needed to keep an eye on the signal's integrity in case they lost the picture, especially if there were others involved like Andy suggested. They must have been parked at the time of the murders, Davy. Anyway, why *not* just park in one place and watch? Why bother moving at all?"

Ash knew that one. "To throw off suspicion. People might call the cops if a stranger's parked in their street for a long time."

"Not if they're an ambulance!"

Useful though debate was, Craig had had enough of it.

"If either the killer or their partner was recording it then why the necessity to stay close at all? They could've just planted the smart-phone nearby where the signal was good, recorded the murder and collected the phone later." He shook his head emphatically. "No. They watched as their work played out. They may have recorded it too, to perv over later, but they definitely watched in real time. The question is, was it the killer piggybacking the signal or their partner?"

He turned to his head analyst. "OK, let's simplify things. Finding out which vehicle that hack came from is your first and only job tomorrow, Davy. Ash and Mary will have to pick up the slack elsewhere. We *need* that vehicle and its reg number, Davy, and preferably a picture of its driver from a street cam. OK?"

The analyst's nod sent Craig back to his office a more hopeful man than he'd left.

****

Tech Wizard Computing. High Street, Belfast City Centre.

Liam gave the corrugated iron shuttering covering the front of the, he thought, rather childishly named Tech Wizard computing store a hard kick. Just to test its lock of course, because if that was broken they could investigate for possible breaking and entering and knock down the shop door on suspicion of a burglar still being inside; packing thousands of pounds worth of nifty computers into his back pack, because of course all burglars were hipsters now.

It was something they couldn't do legitimately otherwise, even with the search warrant tucked in his pocket, because the judge who'd signed it had, a bit unreasonably he'd thought, specified 'open premises in the presence of the proprietor' for their searches, possibly having had past experience of cops rampaging through his own home when he wasn't there and breaking delicate things.

As Liam drew his leg back to administer a second sharp kick to the shutter, he caught Andy's gaze and it wasn't saying go ahead, a brake the DCI applied verbally a second later.

"You can't, Liam. The warrant's very specific."

The deputy's response was to lean back against the shuttering and swear.

"How in God's name are we meant to do our jobs when the legal system's against us?"

Andy rolled his eyes. "You're being dramatic. It's not an unreasonable ask to search a shop when its open, especially when the alternative is breaking things. Look, we did the first two shops OK and we'll do this one tomorrow. Let's face it, with a perp like this he probably bought the cameras on the Net anyway."

"Killjoy. I was in the mood for a bit of door kicking."

"Boo hoo."

As Andy turned back towards the car with Ryan, he saw the deputy's shaking fist out of the corner of his eye and raised his middle finger, an exchange that amused the policemen if not their unseen spectator.

James MacArthur was watching from across the road as the men climbed into Liam's unmarked Ford, in a cold sweat from the moment that he'd clocked them as cops and with his mind racing at what their visit could mean. A police visit was rarely good news and ten minutes earlier or later his shop would have been open and he might be on his way to a station now to be grilled.

240

He thanked his smoothie addiction for saving him and took a gulp of the takeaway one he'd just purchased, then watched his shop for a good twenty minutes longer before finally crossing the street and unlocking the door.

He had to empty the place of anything that could incriminate him before the police came back and that wouldn't leave him much time to do what had to be done before that night's show.

Chapter Twelve

The CCU Staff Canteen. 8 p.m.

It was after seven when Mary finally escaped the squad-room, refusing to leave until Craig had, and then the joys of the staff canteen had seduced her for another hour, if joy was the right word for day-old sandwiches and tea so strong that it looked like Windsor soup.

But the good thing about the CCU was because there was always some squad pulling an all-nighter the canteen maintained a skeleton crew, although as the constable had searched through the tired looking rolls and tray bakes for something that would save her having to cook when she went home, she thought skeleton might apply to her too if she dined there too many nights.

Her dallying was deliberate, the thought of even a familiar 'cell' unattractive. She knew she was being dramatic describing her apartment that way, after all she'd lived there for over a year and it was cosy, but right now it was the way she felt. That and angry.

Angry that some bastard killer was targeting women, because... well, why? Why *was* this psycho targeting them? She bit as hard as she could into the caramel square in her hand, imagining biting off the killer's head.

Was it just because he could or had Craig been right – the killer *was* James MacArthur and his motive was personal? She recalled the sombre, withdrawn teenage boy who'd watched everything and said little and thought that it might be true. But if it wasn't James seeking vengeance then why? What was this creep getting out of ending their lives?

There'd been no direct contact between killer and victims so the usual male-female power display wasn't a factor, and neither was sex apparently because there'd been no rape. No thefts either, which meant money wasn't his motive, so what exactly *was* in the killings for this man? She arrived at hatred and power.

But those could just as easily apply to male victims so

why the hell hadn't their perp killed men? She was fed up having to live her life always on the look-out for danger, and she knew that all her female friends were as well.

Not walking down dark streets alone and assessing every male that passes for risk, taking cars or taxis everywhere, which cost a bloody fortune, and the one that *really* annoyed her, not being able to have a quiet drink alone in a wine bar without some prat taking it as an invitation to sleaze across and bend your ear.

She could feel a feminist anthem bursting to get out, but a quick scan of the canteen, empty apart from an elderly female helper, said there was no point. The constable had heard all her own songs and arguments many times before: rehearsed inside her head or in front of the mirror, aired to her friends and family ad infinitum, and on the podcast that she'd never released and never would while she was on the force; so without a new audience there seemed no point. She somehow doubted the old lady behind the counter would welcome her belting out a chorus of 'I Am Woman' and telling her that she'd been oppressed all her life and should rise up.

Eventually Mary rose herself and made her way to the lift and basement carpark, walking to her car under the watchful gaze of the officer Craig had stationed there, to set off for home and join the six more marking its perimeter. She'd had to fight with him not to have someone inside her car and flat too, and even though she knew her parents would worship him for guarding their baby and she should be grateful, she really wasn't. That would be an admission she *needed* protection, and as a small woman with an overprotective father and uncles she'd heard that mantra all her life. Craig was just the latest member of a patriarchy that she loathed.

If she was being honest that resentment was probably partly what had made her join the police, to kick ass physically in the way she could do it verbally, and yet here she was, an officer of six years being guarded, just because. If she'd had more insight perhaps the constable might have questioned why someone who loathed the patriarchy so much had chosen to work in a giant one, or acknowledge that she was working on changing it from the inside and lobby accordingly. But Mary wasn't big on insight, still being at the rage against the machine stage of life.

But none of it was the carpark officer's fault so she waved goodbye to him pleasantly and drove the ten minutes to her Eglantine Avenue apartment, performing the waving ritual again with the next batch of armed men and relieved to finally close her front door on the one parked outside in the hall.

It was just as well she'd had no plans that week with one of her handful of friends, none of them a boyfriend. As she dropped her bag and coat on the sofa and kicked off her shoes Mary carried the thought through; she really must do something about that someday, get married and have children even, just as soon as she found a man who didn't try to tell her what to do.

As his youngest detective was settling in for the night Craig was across town fending off his mother and sister, who genuinely seemed to believe that because Lucia had witnessed their first murder she deserved to be 'kept in the loop'.

Normally in arguments with the women in his family he, like his placid father, took the line of least resistance - avoidance, but as his mum had been babysitting that day while Katy worked and had cooked dinner for everyone, inviting Lucia and Ken round to join them, there was no escape.

Craig's mother followed him from room to room like a bloodhound, alternating picking invisible bits of fluff off his shirt with telling him that he needed a haircut to a soundtrack of, "Lucia *need* to know, Marco."

Need and want had always had interchangeable meanings to his slightly spoilt baby sister, and unfortunately his parents had pandered to both verbs to a similar degree.

When he hit the balcony, leaving the only place left to go the river, Craig finally turned and stood his ground.

"*No, Mother.* The details of a criminal case are confidential."

As he only ever called her Mum, or Mama if he was speaking Italian, he thought the word conveyed his seriousness. But Mirella completely ignored it so the tactic failed miserably, and as he pressed his legs back against the balcony railings in the final step before diving, Craig could see his father in the living room chuckling and shaking his head.

The combination said 'give up', but when Tom Craig saw his son's jaw locking he recognised that it was time to intervene, so the quiet man marched out on to the small balcony and turned his wife firmly towards him, and with a gaze that still made Mirella melt even after over fifty years of marriage he distracted her long enough for Craig to make good his escape; this time into the bedroom where he could lock the door, ostensibly to get changed.

He was praying for a diversion when his phone rang and Liam brought him up to date on the shops. Two down and one to go.

"You've nothing else for me, Liam? No new murder scenes I need to attend?"

His deputy's guffaw said that he'd sussed what was going on.

"Your mum?"

"And Lucia. They're demanding an update on Julianne Hodges' death. So, I'll ask you again, Chief Inspector Cullen. Do you *need* me for anything? *Anything* that can get me out of here for a couple of hours."

"Sorry, boss. I wish I did, but no."

It was a masterclass in tempting fate, and they would soon be sorry that Craig had.

****

Tech Wizard. 9 p.m.

James MacArthur had pleaded his case for cancelling that night's show but nothing had shifted. Even when he'd mentioned the policemen's visit the others had insisted he proceed, their avarice and desire outweighing any sympathy for him losing his business and having to flee. Some had even upped their stakes for fear it might be his last time.

Regardless of how often he'd told them that although he'd cleared the place of paperwork and wiped the data from every computer, if the cops had got this close who was to say what they already knew, his faceless supporters had been unmoved. Either put on the show as agreed that night or they would cut him and Robinson out of future ventures. He couldn't bear the thought.

Thankfully plans had already been made so all that was left to choose was the participant. MacArthur took out his phone and gazed at the three women he'd been watching, thinking longingly of the preparations he'd made for each of their cyber demises, all at an advanced stage. If the others had just allowed him to postpone, their deaths could have been so beautiful, each one fitting the woman perfectly just as the others had before.

He delved into his photo archive, smiling at the first image that appeared. Julianne, pretty, pretty Julianne, whose face had made others gaze at her wherever she'd gone. What more perfect way for vanity to die than in front of an adoring audience? Watching as her beauty froze and grew as cold as she'd once been to him, not caring how badly she'd ruined his young life.

And intellectual Maria, killed by her high-powered job. He chuckled quietly. Far too intellectual to ever date an average boy like him; well, who was cleverer now? He flicked to the next photograph and experienced a second's remorse when Felicia Barker's face appeared. It didn't last. She might have suffered with her health since her teens but it hadn't given her compassion for others. She'd been the bitchiest rejection of all so she'd deserved

246

whatever she'd got and worse.

As the scrolling led back to his three future victims MacArthur's frustration started to build. A list had been written and lists were only *ever* written so that the items on them could be crossed off. It was symmetrical and satisfying and the thought of not being able to kill all of the women and complete his tally made him seethe. The physical act of erasure gave him a release that he couldn't achieve otherwise, and the knowledge that he would *never* have closure now made his heart thump and his vision mist.

When it cleared ten minutes later, James MacArthur gazed around at the chaos that had once been his shop. Where there had been glass display cases and smooth computers there were now razor-edged shards of glass and fractured screens. He smiled maliciously. It was a fitting full stop to his life in Ireland and made him feel better that the cops would find only mess when they returned the next day. But his relief was only partial and left him wanting more and his mind darkened to thoughts that he had never dared vocalise, not even to himself.

He focused on the words, repeating them over and over in his mind, allowing them to grow from a whisper to an indecipherable roar. Their meaning was clear; he needed to commit a hands-on killing now to compensate for his unfinished list and the idea both petrified and thrilled him.

But first he had to decide which woman, and how could he reach any of them when they were being so closely watched? He switched his phone to video and gazed at the homes of those left on his list. All three lay on quiet, late winter streets, all with unmarked cars carrying armed police at their fronts, sides and rears. Accessing any of them undetected would be challenging, even concealed by the dark, but there was little to choose between their difficulty and none would be truly impossible with Noel's very special help.

But who should be his victim? Olivia Kenzie, Mary Li

or Romaine Martin? All of them teases and bitches who had rejected him, although Kenzie had been nicer about it than the rest so he decided magnanimously to let her live. That left Romaine Martin, whom he hated the most, and Mary Li, who'd always been too wrapped up in exams and 'causes' to pay attention to anyone around her, including him.

He watched the videos for a while longer, assessing his chances of accessing each property and leaving it alive, and came to a decision. After notifying the others to start watching their screens at midnight he made a call to put his back-up in place.

If he only had time for one last victim then his choice had been made.

****

Maggie Clarke's Apartment. 9 p.m.

Across town something was niggling at Davy Walsh and had been all evening, so much so that he'd barely tasted the dinner Maggie had cooked, well, unpacked from a takeaway bag, and was now lying on the settee with his arms wrapped around her, watching a movie but not seeing it at all.

Something far more interesting and elusive was hovering in his mind's eye, but Thor, God of Thunder kept appearing on the TV just when he thought it might come into view, so the analyst adjusted his position slightly so that his fiancée couldn't gaze up at his face, not that she seemed inclined to with a Demi-God on the screen, and closed his eyes waiting for the illusory something to appear.

When it finally did Davy focused hard until the image crystallised and realised to his surprise that it was a police car. *Why was he thinking of cop cars during his time off?* He went with it until not only the car but its location clarified, realising to his shock that it was Claremont Mews, a small street close to the Adelphi that

248

he'd seen on a tape that day. *OK, he'd been staring at tapes all afternoon, but why this particular street?*

Suddenly his eyes widened and with an abrupt, "Oh, shit!" the analyst jumped off the settee so fast that his girlfriend was turfed unceremoniously onto her, thankfully, carpeted floor.

Her shocked, *"What the hell, Davy?"* fell on deaf ears as he grabbed his mobile to phone his junior, who through the gabbling that followed could just make out, "The force's fortnightly scanning schedule. Who else would know it but admin and IT?"

"What?"

"You heard."

Ash hurriedly set down the weights he'd been using to exercise, grateful to have an excuse, and murmured the question back to himself while he went over their work that week. It didn't bring anything new.

"Same answer as before. In theory anyone on the force, but far more likely someone working in security, IT or admin."

"Exactly! *Not* a uniformed Bobby."

"No. I'd say they're the least likely." As the conversation was beginning to look like a long one Ash sat down on the floor and reinforced his response. "Definitely not. Although they would be aware of the scans. We all are."

"What if a Bobby was working with someone particularly skilled in IT?"

The weightlifter's eyebrows rose quizzically. "OK... but how is this new?"

Davy took a deep breath and laid out his thoughts logically.

"On the CCTV outside the scenes, we s...saw cars and vans."

"Yes, and you've eliminated some vehicles from enquiries so far, but not others. So?"

"It came to me while I was watching a movie with Maggie. Who can hide in plain sight?"

"Emergency and utility vehicles. Again, not new. We

discussed this earlier, Davy."

"Yes, but I've just realised there was only one utility vehicle near *all* the crime scenes at the right times. I must have been screen blind before because I didn't register it, but-"

Ash's patience gave out and he cut across his boss' stream of consciousness. "So, what was it?"

"A cop car! An ordinary patrol vehicle."

Davy couldn't see it but his junior's expression said he was decidedly unconvinced.

"You don't know it was the same car, and couldn't it just have been part of the investigation?"

Davy's voice tightened.

"*No, no, no!* Its appearance coincided with the times of the *killings*, not afterwards when the police had been called. It was parked in a mews near the theatre at the time of Julianne Hodges' death. I can see it in my head. I'm heading back to the office to check. Can you meet me there?"

A quick glance at the dumbbells and the answer was a definite yes.

"Twenty minutes. And bring your best game."

Davy cut the call and grinned apologetically at his now indignant girlfriend, whose response was to sniff and then stare pointedly at the more muscled man on the screen. As he grabbed his car keys and made for the door, he wondered whether he should alert Craig to his thoughts now or wait until he had a good reason to ruin his night.

****

The CCU.

Thirty minutes later Davy's suspicion had become fact. At every one of their three murder scenes, in the windows of time during which they'd been committed, a liveried police Skoda had been parked in a street nearby.

He projected the clearest image onto the LED screen

and both analysts peered at it until at last Ash spoke, pushing the Trilby he'd bought that afternoon back from his face. Davy had made the fatal error of telling his junior the trench coat and fedora story, so he'd bought an assortment of hats on his way home.

"It's impossible to tell if it's the same car, Davy. There isn't a single clear shot of the reg number."

His boss nodded wearily. "Or the driver. I know. But it *has* to be the same guy, Ash. The odds are for it."

After some more thought the junior analyst agreed. *And* issued a warning.

"OK, yes. But we need to firm it up before we bother the chief, otherwise what have we got to tell him? We *think* there could be a copper involved in the murders, chief, but we've no idea who?"

As Craig was a man who liked facts there was agreement that wasn't a good idea. Clearly, the analysts had no concept of how willing Craig would have been for *any* excuse to leave his home that night, wild goose chase or not, but because they hadn't, they set to work tightening their case.

"W...We need to check the schedules for patrol car allocations in Belfast on each of the three days. They're in the D directory on the mainframe."

"Fine, you pull those up while I check sign-out sheets against uniformed constables."

"Don't forget sergeants. They take cars out too. Check Belfast coppers first to rule them out."

"They could have driven here from anywhere, Davy, but OK. I'll check solo patrols first. There was no sign of anyone else in the cars you found."

Davy's hands froze above his keyboard. "Unless they killed them." He dismissed the idea as ridiculous right away. "Nope, this guy's focused on specific prey."

The words made Ash chuckle. "You sounded like the chief there, debunking your own theory."

"Better than swearing like Liam, although that'd be fun."

Their laughter got them through the next hour of

frenzied activity as they narrowed the list of officers who'd signed out patrol cars to three and then one. Sadly, too late for the woman that James MacArthur had chosen from his list.

****

Eglantine Avenue. 9 p.m.

Mary had just finished a call with her mother when her mobile rang again, and she was surprised and pleased to see Ryan's name on the screen.

She liked the sergeant; he 'got' her when lots of others didn't, and if she was being honest her life was a bit lonely outside work. Her parents had moved to Belfast from Dublin during her teens and she'd attended three different schools before Uni which hadn't exactly helped with making lifelong friends. The constant moving had made her standoffish and she knew she was hard work, but her granny had always said good people would persevere and get to know her so she was sticking with the approach for now.

She accepted the call and curled up in her favourite chair.

"Hello, Sarge. To what do I owe the honour?"

"I just wanted to check up on you. Do you need anything?"

"No thanks. I'm just going to have an early night. There isn't much chance of partying with all the cops outside."

He chuckled at her dryness. "You could always invite them."

After a minute's more banter Ryan signed off, satisfied that his junior was safe, and Mary decided to stick to her word for once and get ready for bed.

The Victorian terrace she lived in suffered all the creaks and rattles of advancing age, including the clunking and gurgling of ancient plumbing as she showered before changing into the fleecy red pyjamas her mother had bought her for Christmas; if there was any chance the cops might rush her out during the night she was determined to look her best.

The plumbing's chorus repeated as the constable ran the tap to brush her teeth, the combination of it and water running so noisy that it drowned out the arthritic scrape of her living room's sash window being opened, and the whirring of her electric toothbrush covered the creaking back of her wooden bathroom door.

After that a small injection saw to it that things went smoothly, Mary's instant passivity giving James MacArthur a thrill that was entirely unexpected. He'd felt excitement before of course, but only when his victims had been voiceless images on a screen, their death throes playing out in shocked looks, facial contortions and sudden immobility, like over-dramatic silent movie queens.

The others had applauded him choosing Mary for his final show because she was from the police, their biggest opponent, promising an extra bounce to their bets because of it and requesting that her manner of death should hit the force particularly hard.

But her warmth and softness were a shock and made MacArthur long for more time with her than the others would allow him. It promised different, more intimate, adventures with other women to come.

He pushed the thoughts from his head and focused on the task in hand, moving back towards his entry point to descend to the street. With Noel providing cover he'd been able to mitigate the risk of capture and still hold his audience's interest, not killing the girl expediently at home as they'd requested but promising something much more elaborate in a few hours' time.

As he lowered the unconscious constable from the window into the arms of his partner, James MacArthur was already picturing her demise in his mind.

****

Katy Steven's Apartment, Laganside. 10.00 p.m.

Mirella was just renewing her pursuit of her son when a call came through on his mobile, and the name that flashed up on the screen sent an unexpected dart of fear through Craig's chest.

If Liam's name had appeared it would have meant, yes, there was trouble somewhere but he would likely have had it under control already, but Davy phoning... the analyst almost never called at night so whatever was prompting him to now had to be really bad.

Craig's thoughts reflected themselves in his abrupt tone.

"What's wrong?"

Years before such sharpness would have made the analyst retreat and stammer copiously, but age had helped Davy control the latter and experience had taught him that Craig's bark rarely became a bite and to stand his ground, so he started with, "We think a cop's involved, because..." and ended a minute later with, "...Sergeant Noel Robinson. Night Desk Sergeant at Belmont Road Station in East Belfast. And I've matched his prints from the staff database with the one found on the back door of the dry-cleaners, so that makes things pretty sure. He must have forgotten he'd left the print, or reckoned we would never run it against the staff database."

Craig had been holding his breath since, "We" and exhaled in a drawn-out whoosh. The next thing he did was bang his forehead with his hand so hard that his analyst heard the thud.

"I thought of police cars this afternoon, so why the hell didn't we pursue it? No, don't answer that because you didn't miss it, I did. I should have told you my thoughts. It would explain how they got the force's computer scanning schedule." The detective paused for a moment to gather himself, then came back with a plan of attack. "OK, is he on duty tonight?"

"No. He went home at this morning and has two days

254

off. I've got ASU eyes on his local traffic cams but they only go as far as the roundabout three streets before his house in Crumlin. I've messaged the address to you. But as far as we can tell he didn't drive through there any time in the past few hours."

"He's unlikely to be home but I'll send uniforms just in case. What does he drive?"

"An old Saab. That red wine-gum colour."

As a description it was perfect; every kid in Ireland had eaten the sweets.

"I've an alert out on it already, so if he passes any cameras, we'll have him. But he may swop cars."

"Extend the surveillance to a fifty-mile perimeter in case he heads out of town anyway. Also, alert the ports and airports to keep an eye out."

"Already done."

"Mmm..." Craig sucked in air for a moment, thinking. "This guy's the accessory. The one who piggybacked the CCTV signals. His partner's the dominant."

"You mean James MacArthur?"

"Probably, although we've no proof of that yet. OK, call everyone in and I'll be at the office in thirty. I'll get Liam myself."

He was about to hang up when he remembered to say something. "Bloody good catch, Davy, and tell Ash the same. Right, now get on with it."

He cut the call and gave himself a second to breathe before making another. His deputy was just settling down to watch the football highlights and his pissed-off, "Ah, God, boss" was predictable.

"Sorry. Davy's called and it's all hands to the pump."

"I can't drive, I've had a beer."

"I'll collect you."

Once he'd managed to run the noisy obstacle course of his mother and sister that was, and make guilty excuses to his father who passed him his jacket with a pleading look that said, 'Take me with you' on the way past.

255

****

Twenty minutes later the squad's two most senior detectives had checked Noel Robinson's house in Crumlin and found it in darkness, lingering just long enough for some uniforms to arrive and take up post and find the wine-gum Saab parked in a linked garage that Liam had conveniently found open. Craig decided not to ask how he'd gained entry without leaving a mark on its up and over door, already certain his deputy had been a criminal in a past life, and an extremely enthusiastic one.

They headed from there to Belmont Road Station, but not before Craig had made another call, this time to Jack Harris, who knew everyone who was anyone amongst Belfast's cops. His information on Noel Robinson was enlightening in its blandness.

"He's such a boring bugger I doubt he's involved in anything. Work, home, work, home, never comes out for sergeants' drinks, and no relationships that I've ever heard of and he must be around thirty. In fact, about the only thing Robinson *does* seem to do is grin. He's always bloody grinning, God knows what about. Oh, aye and he plays computer games. I hear he buys a truckload of tech."

Craig's gut tightened in the way it always did when something was important, and his next question was squeezed out.

"Any idea where he buys it? Local, internet?"

Jack's curiosity was piqued.

"What's he done then?"

Craig kept it clean. "Driven patrol cars where he shouldn't have."

The sergeant spluttered. "He shouldn't have been driving them at all! Robinson's a desk jockey. So scared of the street he couldn't get off it fast enough. The big wimp."

An interesting titbit, but they didn't have time to explore what it meant.

"His tech, Jack? We're in a bit of a hurry."

"Sorry. Aye, I do know where he buys it, but only because the shop's just across from my station. It's on High Street just past the post office. Wiz something."

Liam's expletive was so loud it drowned out Craig's next words and made Harris chuckle, "That sound means Old Eejit Cullen's missed something."

Even though the car-phone's reception was excellent Liam felt the need to lean forward and shout his response into the set.

"It bloody does not! That Tech Wizard place was shut when we called earlier."

"You messed up so just own it, man."

At another time the argument might have amused Craig but right now it was just a pain in his neck, so he cut them off with a sharp, "You can argue later over a pint. Anything else on Robinson, Jack?"

"Nope. Boring bastard who grins a lot. That's about it, sir."

"OK, thanks. If you see him hold him for questioning, we've uniforms waiting at his house to do the same."

"On what basis?"

Craig sighed heavily. "We think he's involved in three deaths."

Boring people have secrets too.

****

The Countryside Near Newcastle, County Down. 10 p.m.

It was like one of those mornings, very early, very dark winter mornings, when you wake from a shallow sleep that has given you no rest but left the legacy of a headache behind. A half-hangover they used to call them at Uni, with all the dry-mouthed, mucky-gummed, sour taste of a hangover, but none of the memory or pleasure of getting drunk. And there was something else too. An odd, metallic taste. A bright taste, if that makes sense, which along with the rhythmic throbbing of her head made Mary suddenly want to throw up.

Stumbling frantically towards what should have been her bathroom she collided with a hard wall instead, her hands recoiling instantly from the unexpectedly cold surface and then returning to it confused, fingers first jabbing tentatively and then running slowly across it, feeling rough exposed bricks which immediately coloured red in her mind with the narrow tracks between them concrete grey. Then her soft palms pressing hard against them, as if she could push right through with enough force, but expending too much for too long and exhausting her energy so that eventually she slid down the barrier to the floor.

After a long moment, in which the pitch-black space ceased to be her bedroom and the detective considered her predicament, knowing that it was still night - the same night?, and she'd been taken from her apartment just after nine but with no memory of how or by whom, she repeated the tactile exercise with the floor she was sitting on, feeling its smooth but not as cold surface and picturing vinyl, until a splinter informed her abruptly that it was wood.

So, it was night and she was somewhere with brick walls and a wooden floor. The combination spelt one of two things; she was either in someone's home or a trendy office, with the latter seeming less likely due to possible discovery even at night, and she doubted whoever had taken her would want that.

Further exploration told the detective that the space she was in was small and had a single door, with a window opposite whose lack of chill around the edges said it was either unusually well-made or double-glazed. There was a metal latch at one corner that said it might be opened and Mary's heart leapt when she didn't feel a lock; it might provide a way out! But to where?

She pressed an ear against the glass to listen to her surroundings, disappointed to hear not the night-time traffic and voices of Belfast but an occasional quiet birdcall that said most of their kin had settled for the night. She was in the countryside.

The realisation made Mary's hopes of rescue plummet. Ireland, if that's where she even was now, was *mostly* countryside, which meant that anyone searching for her, if they'd even realised she was gone yet, could take so long to find her that she might die.

Suddenly sickening fear overcame the young constable, and love for the family that she would leave behind, something she knew she should have expressed more often, but life was so busy and she'd honestly expected to have more time. She found the wall again and slumped against it, trying her best not to cry and failing, sobbing so hard that her nose began to run and the only hanky available was the hem of the pyjama jacket that she'd donned to wear in bed. Her mum wouldn't be pleased. The thought of her tutting disapproval made Mary laugh unexpectedly, causing the man observing to peer into his screen and watch curiously as his infra-red camera transformed her mouth into a garish maw and made her eyes shine white with tears.

The crying was over in a minute and replaced by focus. One door, one window, and countryside outside which probably meant grass. Easy to run on even in her bare feet, but to get there she first needed to find something to help her escape.

As Mary's eyes adjusted to the darkness, she divided her small prison into three by three grids and scanned each one slowly, searching for the things that she just *knew* had to be there. Their murderers were voyeurs and she was their next movie star, so unless they were planning to move her somewhere else before killing her then there had to be at least one camera in the place.

James MacArthur gazed at the woman the teenage girl he'd known had become and smiled approvingly. She'd been light to carry and pretty even in her sleep, so he was definitely going to enjoy what came next. As Mary's head slumped forward on her chest in apparent slumber, he was relieved that she'd given up fighting the inevitable, it would make things easier, but the teenage girl had grown into a determined, fiery woman, something he would soon find out.

He turned to the back of the observation room where Noel Robinson was seated against a wall.

"Come here and look, Noel."

"You look. You're the one who's going to kill her."

MacArthur's tone hardened and he jerked a thumb at the computer screen.

"Come here and bloody watch her! I need to get some rest before we start the show at midnight."

Robinson shook his head brusquely. "Not yet. We need to talk."

"About what? I'm not changing my mind, Noel. This one will be my masterpiece."

The police sergeant tutted irritably.

"I don't mean about killing her. You'll do that whatever I say. I mean about what we do afterwards. The cops have been at your shop, and it won't take them long to pick up my trail."

MacArthur stared at him surprised. "How could they? There's nothing to link you to any of the girls. I'm the only name they could possibly find."

He was answered by a derisive snort.

"*Are you serious?* We've poked the bear, mate! It was bad enough when you hacked Craig's office to get information on this one, but then the Hodges girl's case lands on his desk and him like a fricking bloodhound keeps it, instead of passing it on to another team like we'd hoped." With a sharp intake of air he gestured at the computer. "*Then* you decide to go out in a blaze of glory by kidnapping his constable! You promised me she would go last-"

MacArthur cut across him angrily. "She *is* last, because we're blown! And you helped me, don't forget! If you hadn't been a cop we could never have covered our asses this long."

"I know, I know. But everything's so rushed this time... and you left me with no bloody choice. All my money's tied up in tonight!"

MacArthur shrugged. "I'd have preferred to do Romaine and Olivia first. I had all the plans made. But time's short and Craig's pissed me off by finding me so fast, so it's goodnight Mary Li."

"Well, now he'll hunt us till we're pensioners so I hope you're happy! And his buddy Cullen, now he's *well* known for being a vindictive fucker. He was legendary for some of his manhunts during The Troubles, and word is he didn't always colour between the lines. I give them another day before they discover I was involved."

Not even that.

MacArthur gave a low whistle and sat back in his chair. "When did you start thinking all this?"

Robinson rubbed his stubble thoughtfully for a moment before he answered.

"I suppose... yeh, after the O'Rourke girl. Once they had street footage from two scenes to compare I got nervous, but I still thought we'd have a couple of weeks to get through everyone. Now I reckon they'll have clocked the squad cars and checked the sign-out log by tomorrow, and after that..."

"Well what do you want to do about it?"

"Leave the country with you tonight. I've got my passport with me. So, what's your plan?"

As MacArthur laid out his flight to London, Eurostar to Paris and then cross-continental trip to Switzerland where he planned to restart his tech business with the night's winnings, he felt a twinge of annoyance. He'd never reckoned on having a companion on the trip, and Robinson wasn't the person he would have chosen if he had. The copper was all right as a means to clear his list and even as a cyber buddy, when everyone was focused on their screens and the inventiveness of the next kill, but in real life he was as boring as fuck. If he insisted on tagging along then he might have to kill him eventually, and as a copper who'd trained with guns that might not be as easy as he hoped.

Robinson's slightly croaky voice cut across his

thoughts.

"OK, let's book my passage now then."

He saw his ally's look of alarm and shook his head.

"Don't worry, Jimmy, I don't like you anymore than you like me, mate. I like watching your shows but I'll do that a *long* way away from you in future. As soon as we're well clear I'll go my own sweet way and we'll only ever meet again on-line."

MacArthur didn't bother concealing his relief and got on with making the arrangements, then before he went for his pre-show rest, he turned back to his screen and pressed record.

He wanted a something extra to watch once the main event was over; how a victim slept when she knew that she was going to die.

****

The CCU. 10.30 p.m.

Craig scanned his team members' exhausted faces, allowed himself a second's sympathy, and then turned to the LED screen again.

"Davy."

The analyst pressed play and a short slideshow told everyone how they'd got to where they were. As it ended Aidan asked the question on several minds.

"There's no doubt a copper's involved?"

Davy was about to say something equivocal to sooth the obviously wounded police egos around him when Craig snapped out a brutal, "No."

He perched on the front desk and went on.

"A squad car at every scene when none were allocated to be there, with the same sergeant signing them out each time. A sergeant who just happens to spend all his cash on tech in one of the three shops that sell our spy cameras locally. Nope. Sergeant Noel Robinson's in this up to his USBs."

It brought a chuckle from the analysts that wasn't quite loud enough to drown out the sound of someone typing. A quick scan and Craig found who it was.

"Are you searching for something, Annette?"

She nodded, typing for a few more seconds then cracking a smile.

"I've found it."

"Tell the rest of us then."

She went one better and projected the computer search onto the screen. The list that appeared was one that Mary had been working on and she gave the constable full credit.

"This is the crossover list of local tech shop customers and magazine subscribers."

One of the names against several magazines and a single shop called Tech Empire was Noel Robinson's.

"Tech Empire. That wasn't one of the shops that sold the spy cameras, Annette."

"All will become clear, sir."

Liam gave a loud tut. "We might have known this earlier if I'd booted in Tech Wizard's door. That's your fault, Arty, for stopping me."

Craig responded before an indignant Andy could.

"That list says Robinson went to Tech *Empire*, Liam."

"And Jack said Tech Wizard."

"And entering on a warrant that didn't allow access to either would get our whole case thrown out of court, so wind your neck in."

Craig crossed to the screen and tapped on Robinson's name. "OK, we know Noel Robinson subscribed to magazines and shopped at Tech Empire. Now we need to connect him with Tech Wizard. We also need to connect MacArthur to Robinson."

Annette raised a finger. "Mary has something on that as well."

"Go on."

"She researched the logo on MacArthur's hoodie and found it was the brand of an old shop called Computer Empire, which became Tech Empire in twenty-twelve-"

Ash nodded. "I remember that place."

"- Mary's notes say it was a big franchise chain at one

point but was broken up four years later because of bankruptcy, and the branch in Belfast's now known as, guess what, Tech Wizard. She checked its records and found a dummy company-"

Liam cut him off with a disgusted grunt. "I hate those things. They're sneaky."

She continued as if he hadn't spoken.

"- with a Jimmy Mac listed as its owner. What are the odds that Jimmy Mac is really James MacArthur and he owns Tech Wizard, sir?"

This time Liam howled. "I *told* you I should've kicked down its bloody door! We might even have found the wee scrote inside!"

Craig had no time for what-ifs. "Well, you didn't, so move on! Ash, tighten that up, please, but it certainly looks as if James MacArthur owns Tech Wizard and Noel Robinson is his loyal customer. So, both are tech experts and both local. But I still think there's a bigger group behind them online."

He paused for a minute to think and Andy seized the gap to make an enquiry.

"Anyone know how Mary is?"

Annette responded first. "I know she was here and in the canteen till around eight, got home around a quarter past and was in for the night. I called the guards to check."

Ryan nodded. "I called her at nine and she was pretty bored and said she was going to bed."

The exchange seeped into Craig thoughts as he crossed to the whiteboard and lifted a marker.

"OK, so MacArthur may know you called at his shop, Liam, and we have to assume he does if any of the other local shopkeepers saw you. Did they?"

"Aye, probably. I'm hard to hide and the street was busy."

"In which case he won't return there. Any home address, Davy?"

"Just that old one he was evicted from. But there's a flat above that shop so he could be living there."

"OK. Liam, go bother a judge and get that warrant upgraded. We're entering the shop and flat tonight."

He scribbled the point on the board and moved on.

"We have Robinson's house under watch with orders to hold him on sight, but as his car's in the garage my guess is he's not coming back."

Davy gawped at him. "When were you going to tell *me*? Half the country's looking for that Saab."

"Sorry, we checked on our way here." It was as much contrition as the analyst was going to get because Craig had already moved on. "Ash, the ports and airports are already locked down but get face recognition up and running at them. Let's catch this pair before they flee the jurisdiction. I want to see their faces when they go to jail."

He turned to his inspector. "Annette, run point on that and get ARU officers to those exits. Liaise with the Garda Síochána as well in case they go south. The more eyes we have on them the better. Davy, supply everyone with the best images you have of both men, please."

After more scribbling he tapped the marker against his chin thoughtfully. Something was niggling at him but it wouldn't come to the front of his mind.

He busied himself with what would instead.

"Aidan, go back to the ASU and review any footage from around Robinson's station and home. What's his last sighting at both, which direction was he heading, and was there anyone with him? Jack Harris said he had no social life but check his parents' address and known associates as well. You know the drill. And as soon as Liam sends you word from the shop, do the same for MacArthur as well. If *he* isn't at home then where did he go today and so on? Let's see if we can pick up their trails because my bet is these two are together now and up to something nasty."

Andy frowned. "Like what, chief? The women are under guard. If that pair have any sense they'll have started running."

And then it came. Craig's niggle stopped niggling and

kicked him in the head so hard that he almost dropped his marker. He thudded down on a desk, his mind racing. The women were under guard, yes, but did that mean they were *safe*? His next words were urgent.

"Andy, go and lay eyes on each of them. Call ahead for the uniforms to recheck every lock and bolt for forced entry, but check on each woman yourself. I don't care who you have to wake."

Liam was sceptical. "You really think these dickheads will try something with cops around?"

"I think it's a compulsion with MacArthur, so he might. And remember, Robinson's a police officer, so if he'd flashed his ID at some constable before Jack got the word out then he could have gained access. Do it now, Andy. They're going to try something, I'm certain of it. One last hurrah before they run."

The DCI was at the exit before Craig finished speaking. He called after him. "Take Ryan with you, and check on Mary first. She's the closest."

As the glass door's swung closed behind them Craig was wracking his brains for what more needed done. Ash got there first.

"I'll hike up my checks on the Net, chief. Just in case there's activity on the viruses or betting."

"Yes. Good. But check the betting first. If they're planning another show there may be indications online already. Get Cybercrime to look for bartering."

He ignored the confused looks from those who didn't know what he meant. There would be a time to explain but now wasn't it.

Realising he'd exhausted the tasks he could think of for now, he turned to his deputy.

"Right. Which judge?"

There was only one possible choice. Eugene Standish, the only person on the bench who wouldn't bite off their heads for calling late at night.

Before they left the squad-room Liam gave Ash a pointed look that said he'd noticed his new headgear, and they *would* be discussing it at another time.

Chapter Thirteen

Near Newcastle. 10.40 p.m.

Mary may have looked to her captors as if she was sleeping but resting was the last thing on her mind. Instead, her analytical brain was whirring with calculations and options for escape. She had to try; if she stayed put, she wouldn't live to see another day.

She'd located the room's sole camera ten minutes earlier, an occasional flicker of blue light around three feet off the floor the only sign that it was there. It had to be high spec because of who their perps were, and night-vision to see her clearly in the dark, and at any other time she would have relished examining the piece of equipment. But right now it was a threat, one that she couldn't eliminate without bringing an even bigger one in its wake.

She focused on the room's two exits instead, calculating the distance of each from her position against the wall and how long it might take her to reach them. Whichever one she went for she would need to be fast; her captor could be watching constantly or have a motion sensor rigged up to alert them if she moved, but either way it wouldn't take long for them to appear.

And if they *weren't* watching... the thought made her shudder because that could only mean they thought there was nowhere to run to if she escaped. They might be right, but that wouldn't stop her trying.

After further thought the detective dismissed the idea of a sensor. What if she shifted in her sleep? They would be checking on her several times an hour. Perhaps they had alarms on the exits? It didn't matter, because by the time *they* went off she could already be gone.

No, they *had* to be watching her, and with no interior window or mirror in the room to peer through the camera was the only way. If she blinded it her abductor would come to check, but if she left it alone and moved very slowly so as not to alert them, she might just have a chance. Mary didn't know it but her escape was being assisted by her captors' absorption in planning their own.

She stared for what seemed like minutes at the door before deciding that it was out as a possibility. With no idea what lay on its other side she could be running into her captor's arms. The thought almost made her vomit but she forced it down hard, remaining as still as she could while she finished formulating her plan.

She had to leave by the window, it was her only chance of success. But how would she do it? Breaking the glass wasn't an option; there was nothing in the room to do it with and the shards would shred her bare feet. The latch was a possibility, and the more she thought about it her only one.

Mary's gaze turned back to the camera. What was its range? And was it trained forward with a wide lens or set to follow her silently around the room?

She decided to test it, inching a foot and then two and three feet to her left and right and watching as the blue light didn't move. She pushed her luck further, to four feet and then to the ends of the wall without seeing a change in the glow. The lens had been set to panoramic view to cover the whole room. Neat.

Assessment made, the constable turned just her eyes to look at the window; it was around five feet to her right and sat at her chest height, so if she managed to reach it without anyone coming to investigate then she could just stand a chance. She inched her way achingly slowly until she'd made it safely to the wall beneath it. One problem down and two more to go: how to open the window and where to go when she did.

The young police officer peered through its glass into the jet-black country night. There wasn't a house or street light glowing anywhere so she would be running blind, but it was better than what awaited her if she stayed put.

Slowly she ran a hand around and beneath the window frame checking for wires and alarms, grinning when she found nothing. Their killers might be good at tech but they were over-confident. Weakness number one.

She slid her right hand upwards and grasped the smooth window latch, praying that someone had oiled it in the recent past, and couldn't believe her luck when the lever shifted smoothly and she felt a cool breeze enter the room. Suddenly something new occurred to her and she glanced at the camera for some sign of temperature detection, sighing in relief when the glimmer stayed blue and no-one entered the room.

Redoubling her efforts Mary opened the window so wide that the night's chill made her gasp, but nothing was going to deter her and with one hand on the handle and another on the sill she levered herself through the opening smoothly and landed on some very welcome grass below, where she took less than a second to orient herself before running like hell.

****

Tech Wizard. High Street.

It had taken Eugene Standish ten minutes to wake from his, to the detectives, oddly early sleep and make sense of what they were saying, but only one to extend their warrant to cover everything they desired. A quarter of an hour later they were standing outside Tech Wizard, and after snapping the metal shutter's lock Craig gave Liam his head.

With a short run and as hard a kick at the shop's front door as his six-foot-six frame could muster, the deputy performed as expected and they were in. Craig gawped at the glass and detritus strewn store that greeted them and, exchanging a glance with his DCI that said MacArthur had clearly had a meltdown and wasn't returning, signalled the uniformed officers he'd borrowed from High Street to begin the search.

In less than a minute a young, bearded constable

proudly indicated his find at the back.

"There's a door, sir. Should I knock it in?"

Craig stifled a smile. The youth was clearly a fan of Liam's mode of entry.

"You could, but did you try knocking?"

The embarrassed P.C. did so quickly, and when there was no reply he got the thumbs up. A swift kick later the flimsy door lay against the wall and a small flight of stairs led them up a storey into what was clearly James MacArthur's home, although judging by the level of tech there it could easily have been an extension of his shop.

Craig divided the small apartment in three and took the main living area himself, digging through empty pizza boxes, unopened letters and piles of memory sticks, searching for anything that might say where the owner had gone. But even a psychopath isn't that careless and if MacArthur's forwarding address *was* there it would take them days to find it. The detective was just calling in CSIs when his deputy reappeared, with no better news.

"There's no sign of a passport, boss, but I called the boy and MacArthur definitely has one. And a credit card, so he's checking for hits on it and any Robinson holds. I've got the geeks checking the land registry as well, just in case one of them owns more property somewhere."

Craig shook his head glumly. "Men this tech savvy will have scrubbed their trails, Liam, but try anyway. Give me a minute to make another call and I'll meet you at the car."

"OK. I checked out the back and MacArthur's car's not here. Ash says he owns a Mini of all things."

It didn't feel right to Craig.

"There's no way they could transport anyone in that, Liam. Call Davy back and ask if there's a van registered to this business."

The answer was yes; a Ford Iveco and they had the reg.

"OK, go look for it, Liam. There's a multi-storey carpark across the street."

While he did that Craig called Aidan, who was ensconced in front of a bank of screens at the ASU with an exhausted Theo Sheridan watching over his shoulder. The commander had been home for the night when his sergeant Ellie had called to say the Murder Squad needed urgent access, and not trusting Aidan near his equipment because he was so impatient he could as easily pull a knob off as turn it, Sheridan had driven the twenty miles back in.

Ellie was easily impressed and likely to let one of the 'big boys' from Murder run amok, or so the commander had thought, but when he'd arrived back at his kingdom he'd been surprised to find a very subdued Aidan sitting bolt upright in front of a screen with his sergeant standing arms-crossed behind him.

As soon as Sheridan relieved her for coffee the Murder DCI began to moan.

"Jeez, Theo, you'd think I was going to break her precious equipment or something the way she looks at me!"

"You broke a switch when you were here before on a case."

The detective rolled his eyes. "A whole switch. Big deal."

The sergeant returned just in time to hear him. "That switch cost fifty pounds and six weeks to requisition!"

As Aidan pulled a face and stared back at his tape, she handed her boss a mug of coffee and sipped her own, making Aidan moan again.

"Where's *my* coffee?"

"If you think you're handling liquid anywhere near our equipment you've another think coming. Anyway, eyes front or you'll miss whatever you're looking for."

Before Aidan could retort his phone rang.

"Yes, Guv."

"We're leaving the shop now, Aidan, and MacArthur was definitely living upstairs. Liam's checking if his van's still around, but if it isn't I'll need you to follow that trail too."

Just then Liam reappeared, nodding.

"Hang on, Aidan." Craig crossed to his deputy. "The van?"

"And the Mini. Both parked across the street. Robinson must have picked his buddy up."

"Damn, that means they've got another vehicle." Craig returned to his call. "Did you hear that, Aidan?"

"Yep. I'll need to try and find if Robinson and MacArthur connected and in what sort of vehicle. It'll take a while, Guv. I've street cams for the front of the shop, but the back's only covered by a security cam at the shop next door."

"*Bugger that*." Craig raked his hair in annoyance. "How long will it take to get hold of the footage?"

Sheridan had been listening and cut in. "We already have it, Marc. Under a voluntary scheme with shopkeepers to reduce crime."

"Excellent, thanks. OK, Aidan, you know the drill. If MacArthur was collected in a vehicle find and follow it, ditto on foot, same for Robinson, and then get the info to Davy and me. Thanks for putting up with him, Theo, and don't let him make a mess of your place. His desk is a bloody shambles."

The line went dead before Aidan could retort and the detectives made their way out of the shop.

"This lot know not to touch anything until the CSIs finish, don't they, Liam?"

"Of course. Jack runs a tight ship."

"In other words, stop teaching your granny how to suck eggs. OK."

Craig moved at a quick stride until they reached the Ford, where he stopped dead and gazed down at the paving stones for a full minute. Liam could almost hear the noises inside his head; loud ticks as tasks got marked off a list, scribbling as more were added, and his own voice shouting to do better.

Then as suddenly as he'd stopped Craig moved again, climbing into the car. He was just about to say, "Back to the ranch" when he had another thought.

272

"Remind me where Andy is."

"Checking on the women."

"OK, he'll call if he has anything, so back to the squad-room."

A U-turn put them in the right direction but it was wasted, because just as the car straightened up Craig's phone rang and a tense Andy came on the line.

"Mary's gone!"

Liam's, *"What do you mean she's gone?"* prompted an exchange that gave Craig time to think, and when he spoke a few seconds later it was with cold logic.

"The guards saw and heard nothing?"

"No. Not even the one outside her apartment door."

"The windows?"

"Living room's open making that the likeliest route."

"Taken?"

It was a waste of a question and he knew it; Mary would hardly go clubbing while she was on a killer's list.

"The signs are there, chief. Tap left running, toothbrush on the floor, window open. But no indications of a struggle where they went out so he must have had her subdued."

That meant either the abductor had threatened her with a weapon or drugged her. Craig shook his head, dismissing the first; even with a weapon held on her Mary would have called out. She'd been drugged, probably in the bathroom.

"Is there a rope or ladder outside?"

Andy sighed, not from annoyance but from guilt. Irrationally he felt he should have protected the constable better even though he hadn't been guarding her.

"Neither. I've been down and there are footsteps in the mud below, so I've called forensics to get casts, but they're definitely man-sized and the trail of mud leads out to the pavement-"

Liam cut across him. "Where more bloody guards were posted! Were they asleep in their fricking cars or what?"

"They say not, but we can argue that another time. The mud gets fainter on the pavement and stops about three houses down beneath a large Beech tree."

It was Craig's turn to sigh. "Deciduous, providing cover all year round. They picked the perfect position to park; hidden and behind our guards. They'd scouted the street beforehand to know about that tree."

"The street light being out didn't help either."

"They probably broke it."

"Yeh, well there're bound to be local cameras, so we should still be able to get views."

"OK, call Aidan at the ASU and tell him *that's* the vehicle we need. Stay there, we're on our way."

It was the signal for another U-turn and non-stop swearing for two miles.

****

Mary had been running for what her lungs said were hours but she knew had been only minutes, a sign of how unfit she'd got since she'd become a detective and taken to a desk. Resolving to remedy the situation when she got out of her current predicament seemed pointless. Of course she would, but right now it was a case of if not when. She was terrified and alone but she was still a logical thinker and could calculate her poor odds as well as any bookie, even if she might prefer to live in ignorant hope.

But poor odds weren't zero odds, and as the detective's breath finally gave out and she sheltered beneath a hedgerow to think she comforted herself with that fact momentarily, before turning her attention to more important things.

It was so dark she could hardly see a foot in front of her, but she trusted her internal clock and it didn't feel like the wee small hours yet. So when? Elevenish? Probably, since she'd decided to go to bed at nine, although so much had happened since it could have been later. But eleven o'clock or midnight, neither was good news. The odds of anyone having discovered she was gone yet were slim. She chided herself instantly; slim odds weren't zero odds either, so there.

OK, so it was elevenish, and grass, hedges and no lights definitely meant the countryside. The glass-clear, star-scattered sky overhead said that it was countryside far from a city's pollution too, which meant no chance of shelter or help unless she found either a building or a road.

On the bright side it wasn't raining, a miracle in Ireland in February. She surprised herself by chuckling, suppressing the sound immediately but still feeling its positive effect inside. OK, so now she was delirious, which wasn't necessarily a bad thing if it helped to get her through.

It was time to think tactically. Yes, it was pitch-dark and there was no help in sight, but hopefully her captor or captors mightn't yet know that she was missing; she couldn't hear any movements of pursuit.

Even so, James MacArthur, if that was who'd taken her, *would* be coming for her soon, alone or with a partner. An image of the sullen teenage boy sprang into her mind and she cursed any kindness that she'd ever shown him; if she'd known back then what he was going to do to her she would have got in the first strike.

Mary shook the pointless thought from her head and tried to focus. From what Davy had said about bartering there were more people than just MacArthur and his mate invested in her kidnapping, and they might have started betting already if her death was to be performance art. They wouldn't want to risk their winnings, so as soon as she was noticed missing the chase would start.

But she would put up a good fight; she had mixed martial arts skills, something her parents practiced and had forced her to learn when they'd heard she was joining the police. Even so, her height and weight were disadvantages and while she could certainly do a man some damage even without a weapon she would soon tap out.

A weapon... the thought galvanised the constable and she edged along the rough hedgerow feeling the earth as she went, until her advance was interrupted by an obstacle that made her stop dead and hold her breath. But only for a second, until she realised its smooth surface didn't indicate a man's shoes as she'd feared but the worn root of a tree. Where there were trees there was refuge if they were tall enough, and if not then perhaps a weapon like a fallen branch.

The young detective scrabbled frantically through the earth at its base but found nothing but leaves. It made her want to cry again but she strangled the urge and kept moving, marking the distance back to the tree in case she needed to climb it fast. It was a good decision because around ten feet further on Mary found what she'd been looking for, a gnarled branch as thick as her arm and heavy enough to do serious damage if it connected with someone's head. Happy as the find made her, she still knew the weapon would mean nothing against a gun. It was a real pity pyjamas didn't come with a built-in holster or she could have brought her own.

She curled beneath the hedge's brambles for a minute to think. But not only to think, to listen; for the familiar sounds of the countryside so that she could hear beyond them. The singing breezes, bird calls and scurrying of small animals that normally went unnoticed by people in a rush were each identified and discarded as she listened harder, for the distant roar of a car and its changes in surface, a plane overhead to provide her position, or that most terrifying of all sounds, steps.

Her eyes were wide open as well as her ears, alert to shifts in light that might say her abductor was approaching. But there were none, not yet anyway; she saw nothing but the shades of black, grey and purple that she slowly realised made up the night. It was the most aware of her surroundings that Mary had ever been and her alertness was finally rewarded, by a soft droning noise that froze her to the spot in fear.

The sound of a machine! Coming through the hedge in front of her. Not close but close enough, and with no shifts in pitch to say that it was moving.

Turning to peer through the hedgerow the detective saw a bright, almost luminescent light and closed her eyes tight for a moment, in case it was her imagination. She'd read about the bright white lights that some people claimed to see, but usually only when they were dying and their brains were being starved of oxygen, or when it was some nutter claiming to be abducted by aliens and there weren't too many of those around. Although some of their politicians...

Her sense of humour in dire straits amazed her and she wished someone else from the squad was there to hear her jokes. But she knew they wouldn't believe it even then and the knowledge made her wish she was a bit more likeable. She knew she wasn't because likable people were less argumentative than her and she didn't want it *that* much. Or at least she didn't think she did.

But ruminating wasn't helping so Mary shook her head to stop it and focused on the light again, calculating its distance and height. Around twenty feet on the other side of the hedge and standing the same amount as high. Definitely not an idling car.

What was it then? The answer came quickly; farm equipment of some sort. She recalled seeing a harvester on a family trip to the country as a child. But did people harvest at night? Perhaps they did. Either way it was literally the only light on her horizon so she couldn't be picky.

But there was a down side to approaching it. At the moment she was hidden but as she got closer the light would put her in full view, and if her captor was close and fast enough, *they* could reach her before *she* reached whoever was operating the machine.

The detective shuddered suddenly as if her body was urging movement, but she ignored it and held her ground, her only concession to the lure of the beacon to edge forward until she was directly parallel to it and speculate whether she could burrow through any existing breach in the hedge. There wasn't one large enough, so just as Craig discovered that his constable was missing, Mary Li started to widen the largest gap that she could find.

****

The CCU.

"That's the ports and airports sorted, Davy. I'm off to Cybercrime for ten."

Davy immediately raised a palm in a halt sign and typed for another moment before turning to his deputy.

"Before you go, Ash. Anything on another vehicle for MacArthur or Robinson, or a second property they own?"

"No to cars for both, so I'd say they probably just nicked one from somewhere, and the property searches are running now."

"What about your chat-rooms and sale boards?"

The junior analyst perched on the nearest desk. "There's been a lot of comeback on the viruses we found, but no-one offering to buy."

"What kind of comeback?"

"One guy asked how I detected them, which was suspicious, so I've searches running on his location."

"You won't get much from that on the D.W. They'll all be using private browsers."

The cyber sleuth tapped his nose. "I have my ways." He hopped off the desk. "Now, if you don't need me for a bit, Cybercrime says there's been a spike in bartering in the past half-hour so I'm off to suss if it's MacArthur's audience gathering."

"For a murder show? They'd need a victim first."

Just then he had a call from Craig that said they already had, and she was one of their own.

Chapter Fourteen

Mary's Apartment. Eglantine Avenue. 11 p.m.

Liam was waiting for the explosion, and he hoped it came soon because if it didn't then he would set off one of his own.

They'd arrived at Mary's small flat five minutes before and since then Craig hadn't said a word, just donned full forensic gear before stalking its three rooms several times with a face like flint. His sequence was always the same: in and out of the cosy, almost frilly bedroom, which seemed, to Liam anyway, nothing like Mary; through the pristine grey and white kitchen-sitting room, which for him *did*; and finally, and always alone, entering her tiny bathroom and staring at its sink and shower as if they would suddenly speak and recount what had happened there hours before.

It was a sequence Liam had watched before on a few cases, and on those rare occasions it had always ended in the same way, with Craig reaming out the undoubtedly careless culprits, in this case the cops parked in Eglantine Avenue, the officer in the hall guilty only of not hearing a probably minor scuffle through two closed doors.

The DCI had wanted to do it himself, go into the garden where the four dozy bastards had been told to wait till the boss completed his walkthrough and rip each of them a new one, but that honour didn't belong to him. So, to say that he was disgusted when after another minute of silence Craig merely dumped his forensic gear and walked straight past them to the car was an understatement. Not only did Liam think they *needed* the bollocking and not to give it was neglectful parenting, but he'd been looking forward to hearing the blast.

With a glare that said Andy had better do the needful when they'd gone, the deputy stomped to the car and climbed into the driving seat, shoving his key hard into the ignition and giving a disgusted tut.

Craig's response was to gaze straight ahead and say, "You'd like me to read them the riot act" in a monotone.

It wasn't a question but his deputy answered anyway.

"Yes, since you ask, I would. Or at least let *me* do it. Those twats completely missed a woman being carried out past them and there's no bloody excuse."

Craig stayed eyes forward. "I agree, but will it help us find Mary?"

"No, but that's not the point!"

"And will it take up valuable time that we could be *using* to find her?"

"Aye, well it would, but it'd be time bloody well spent!"

"In your opinion, not mine. So, let's get moving."

They were halfway to the office when Craig got tired of his deputy's muttering and moaning and spoke again.

"I didn't bollock them because if I'd started, I would never have stopped, Liam. And you know my temper well enough to know that's *never* a good idea. Also, it would have made me feel guilty afterwards and right now I need my mind on other things. But don't worry, they feel like crap right now, and they'll be reported to their C.O.s as soon as I have time, trust me."

Liam seized his chance. "Can I do it?"

"Knock yourself out. It's one less job for me." Craig sat forward slightly, frowning. "OK, Mary was taken, in what vehicle we don't know yet, but with any luck Aidan should find out soon and follow it. Meanwhile..." He dialled his chief analyst. "Give me an update, Davy."

"We've Robinson and MacArthur's mugshots circulated so the ports and airports are locked down, and Ash is upstairs checking something with Cybercrime."

"OK, we'll be there in ten so get him back for then. Is Annette there?"

He transferred the call.

"Hi, sir. How can I help?"

"Have you liaised with the Gardaí yet?"

"Done, and they've agreed to do the same with their ports and airports as the north." Suddenly she noticed the tension in his voice. "Is something up?"

"I've another call coming through so I'll cover it when I arrive."

It was Aidan on the line and he got straight to it. "A grey Ford transit van entered Eglantine Avenue at eight-forty-five from the Lisburn Road and left it at nine-ten by its Malone Road end."

"That could fit."

"That's what I thought. The bad news is it had no rear plates so I'm checking the Malone cams for a front one. Failing that I'll keep eyes on it until it stops, Guv."

"Is that the last location you have?"

"No, I found it again on the upper Malone at nine-twenty, turning onto the A24 twenty minutes later."

"OK, good work, Aidan. Don't lose it. And try to locate it even later if you can."

As he ended the call he saw Liam pulling a face.

"The A24 heads south out of town, boss. They could be well over the border by now."

Craig wasn't unconvinced. "Yes, they *could* be heading south, but they could equally stop nearer home. We won't know for a while."

He dialled another number and it was answered by an out-of-breath Andy.

"Running up Mary's stairs?"

"Nope. I've just finished doing the needful with the idiots."

The police guards hadn't got off as lightly as Liam had feared and he gave a grinning thumbs-up.

"You've just made Liam a happy man. OK, I need you to get to the ASU and give Aidan another pair of eyes. He thinks he has the vehicle. Send Ryan back to the ranch. I'll need him there."

"Done. I'll call if there's anything at all."

****

Near Newcastle.

Time is an odd... what? A logical concept laid out in physics? Something that moves very inconveniently in only one direction and all too often runs out? Or is time something more abstract and romantic? A river, a thing of beauty, offering endless possibilities until decrepitude or death eventually catch up?

Mary shrugged at the direction that her thoughts were taking. Evidently, she had a scientist, a philosopher and a poet living inside her head, so why did she only ever give the first one control? That might be something to address if she ever got home, unless the last two inhabitants were just signs of delirium or the drugs that she'd been fed. Either way, *whatever* time was she wasn't making the best use of hers by sitting under a hedge in the freezing cold and gazing longingly at a light.

She'd gleaned all the information the beacon was going to give her from a distance. White and very bright, so probably halogen generated, and sitting high off the ground, which meant it was probably attached to something. The only new thing she'd learnt since she'd first seen it was that it moved forward very occasionally, the movement always accompanied by a deep rumbling sound. That said it was attached to something heavy that probably needed an operator.

But what if the operator was unfriendly? Or worse, linked with MacArthur in some way? When she dismissed the questions more slowly than usual, she knew the mixture of drugs and cold was beginning taking a toll.

She had no option but to take the risk, did she? Soon she would either freeze or be dead at MacArthur's hand so she needed to shift.

But time is something other than poetic or pressing, it's also relative. Not just as Einstein described it but in the way that people can *perceive* it as running at different speeds because of how they feel. And the time that it had taken Mary to find her hiding place and think through her options was far shorter than she realised; just long enough for her captors to book Noel Robinson's flight and take a break.

Break over, James MacArthur went to take a look at his captive, and seeing too much stillness on his computer screen decided he needed to see the golden goose in the flesh.

And there it was, or rather Mary wasn't, and the clock was started on her pursuit.

****

The CCU. 11.15 p.m.

Craig gathered the handful of his team who were physically present and asked Aidan to join them on the screen, then he ran swiftly through what they knew before turning to the person that he needed to hear from most.

"Ash. Anything from Cybercrime?"

"Yep. There's been a spike of activity on the Dark Web. On its own that could've been anything but they said their bartering exchanges started rising twenty minutes later."

"So, MacArthur or someone posts that he's putting on another show and the punters took twenty minutes to decide whether it was worth betting on and arrange their funds?"

"That's my thought."

"I don't suppose there's a street address attached to any of it?"

The analyst's tight smile said he wasn't holding out hope.

"Sorry, but Cyber *have* narrowed the betting stroke bartering rises down to Spain, The Czech Republic, and one much closer to home..."

Craig held his breath.

"...the area around Newcas-"

Annette cut across him, her anxiety about Mary

making her terse. "Newcastle upon Tyne or our Newcastle?"

"The second. Here in County Down."

Craig turned to his deputy. "It has to be our men, Liam. They're betting on their own game."

The DCI chuckled. "God bless them. Right then, Geeky, can you narrow it any?"

Ash felt a rush of pride. After years on the squad he had finally earned one of Liam's nicknames, and no matter how derogatory they were they were always a sign that he'd accepted you and thought you were OK.

"I'm working on it now and so is Cyber-"

Davy interjected. "I'll jump on too."

Craig nodded in approval. "Aidan and Andy, use that to focus your vehicle search."

"We already figured Newcastle might feature, Guv, so Andy's been following the A24/A2 merge to the town centre."

"Excellent. And?"

Andy's excited voice came from the screen.

"I found it! It was on the outskirts of Newcastle at ten-fifteen, chief, and there are lots of cameras in its centre so we should be able to see where it goes."

Craig's heart sank at the news. Their killers had almost reached the border an hour before, which meant they could be anywhere in the rural Republic by now. He felt an immediate urge to race out the door after them but held himself in check, plastering on his game face. The boss *had* to project calm even when he didn't feel it, and they couldn't afford to miss something important from haste.

"Right, so-"

Liam jumped in. "There's seven miles from the A2 junction to the town centre, boss."

After some typing Davy looked up from his screen impressed. "Six-point-nine to be exact. Boy, you were close."

His deputy knew Northern Ireland like the back of his hand so Craig wasn't surprised.

"Applause later. OK, so seven miles to the centre, but they would only have gone that far if they were heading over the border. They'll need complete privacy for whatever they're planning and that's hard to find in the centre of a town. If not south then my gut says they're in the town's hinterland somewhere. Somewhere rural north, east or west of Newcastle would be my guess."

Annette nodded. "They'll want somewhere remote, especially once they..."

When her sentence ended in a shudder instead of a word Craig moved on quickly before anyone got upset.

"So... somewhere remote and private in the countryside. A farm!"

He leapt to his feet, feeling relief that he could finally put the energy he'd been using to stay still to better use.

"OK, Ryan, make a list of farmers in the area. Take your lead on the best radius around Newcastle from Ash and then plot them on a map, get their phone numbers and the number for the local cops, but don't call anyone until I give you the word."

He turned back to the screen.

"Andy and Aidan, whatever you do *find* that van. We'll be calling you from the road for directions. Annette, you're with Liam and me."

Annette knew Mary best and that might help when they found her.

Craig stared at his two analysts for a moment before speaking, corralling his emotions so they didn't show in his voice. They were a mixture of hope and pride at his team and fear and dread at what might happen if they found Mary too late, but he managed to keep everything but logic from his words.

"Your work is always important in catching killers, but this time it may get us there in time to save the life of one of our team. So, do *whatever* you need to do and do it fast."

Then he was across the floor and hammering on the lift button, barely aware that his deputy and inspector were with him, seeing only the healthy face of his young

constable and the future broken bodies of the men who
had taken her if they found her in any other state.

Chapter Fifteen

Noel Robinson was an unhappy man, but not in the way that normal people think criminals *must* be unhappy, and warped and flawed and weirdoes who've all had bad childhoods because otherwise how could they possibly do the things that they did? No, Robinson was normally quite happy with his many foibles and predilections because he didn't often feel for other people; in fact, he hardly recognised them as mattering other than as victims whose fates he could enjoy.

When his colleagues had sympathised with some of the sad sacks they'd locked up in the cells, and definitely with their victims, he'd been quick to mimic their facial expressions and make the appropriate noises but had rarely understood what they'd felt. He possessed not exactly zero but little sense of others, driven by fulfilling his own needs and one need in particular, voyeurism, but without anyone similar who had understood him, it had been a lonely life.

Which was why he'd been ecstatic when he'd chanced on first one then another group of people like himself on the web. Those groups had opened his mind and expanded his horizons, and for years his knowledge of criminal procedure had helped their members stay one step ahead of getting caught, something that had brought more and more lucrative rewards from his grateful 'friends'.

Life had got even better when one particularly juicy chat with a 'Jimmy Mac' had developed into a local connection, and he could still recall his excitement when he'd first entered Tech Empire as it was then and connected with his hero Jimmy Mac, aka James MacArthur, in the flesh.

MacArthur had actually dared to *do* the things that he'd only ever watched online and their friendship had opened his mind to new possibilities, so when it had come Jimmy's turn to produce a list for the Kill Room, he'd been thrilled to assist in any way he could.

The Kill Room was a cyber realisation of fantasy, a gathering of like minds from across the world who turned their dark urges into reality through technology, supporting and encouraging each other's wildest desires online. He'd been happy to just watch the acts they'd all performed and help Jimmy with his. In fact, Jimmy's list had given him a happiness that he had never known.

Until now.

Now Noel Robinson wasn't happy at all. Hard as it had always been for him to name what he was feeling, he recognised fury, and it was coursing through him.

As they stood in the open doorway of their pleasure room, somewhere that he'd used with sex-workers many times in the past, always more comfortable with physical contact than his partner, the police sergeant was incandescent with rage and it was directed at the man by his side.

They'd eased open the door at first, hoping to check on Mary without wakening her, not through kindness but because they really didn't need to hear her wailing till it was unavoidable. When calling her name several times hadn't brought movement or even a murmur, *he* had taken the initiative and thrown on the light, gawping and then storming straight to the open window before turning back to his companion and, forgetting his normal passivity, yelling at the top of his voice.

"WHERE THE FUCK IS SHE, JIMMY?"

James MacArthur was stunned into immobility but his mind was racing with questions. How long had she been gone? Had she made it to the road on the south side of the fields and waved down a car? What would the others do to them for messing up? And most importantly, how long before the cops arrived?

The only word he uttered was, "Gone," but as Robinson stormed towards him he clenched his fists.

He was stronger than the cop so he would win any fight where there wasn't a gun involved. The policeman knew it too, so he slowed his pace as he neared his partner and shook his head.

"We're fucked, Jimmy. The others will be furious. The banker will seize their money for cancelling and they'll come after us for it."

"She can't have got far. We'll find her."

To his surprise Noel Robinson shook his head. "Not me. I'm out of here, mate."

When his partner immediately showed his displeasure, Robinson tried to soften the blow.

"Look, there are plenty of other women. We could..." he searched for an example that took into account how wedded the man with him was to his special list. "We could move on to one of the other's lists and then, when things have calmed down here, come back and get *all three* of your women, not just this one. It won't take long. Even Craig won't have the budget to guard them for more than a month."

As he said the name, he had simultaneous urges to spit in disgust and strike his companion to the ground; if Mac hadn't targeted Craig's constable, they'd be a damn sight safer now! It showed just how little he knew about the detective. Once Craig took *any* murder case it stayed open until he or another force had ground the killer's face into the dirt.

MacArthur's jaw had tightened at his friend's suggestion and now his fists joined in. Seeing his violent determination Robinson hurriedly changed tack.

"OK, look, the girl hasn't seen our faces, so forget her and let's go back for one of the other two. There'll be time if we postpone for a few hours. That way the bets won't be wasted and we'll keep our stake."

He reckoned it was a fair compromise but he'd forgotten something; while all killers enjoy what they do, *some* become obsessed with it, and James MacArthur was one of those.

MacArthur shook his head emphatically, "No. She's in bare feet, doped and it's freezing, so she won't have got far. We'll find her."

He sent out an alert delaying the show to one a.m. and made for the door, barking at his companion.

"Come or don't come, but make up your bloody mind!"

With that Jimmy Mac grabbed what he needed and strode into the night, not checking or caring whether he was on his own.

****

The A24 to Newcastle.

"Right, we'll hit the A2 in twenty miles."

Craig leant into the car-phone to hear better above the roar of wheels on tarmac, courtesy of Liam driving like a bat out of hell. It was only the fact that they needed directions that had stopped the DCI playing the tune as well.

"It's definitely the same van, Aidan?"

A brief pause while he checked something and the DCI came back with a firm, "Yes. Andy's found a screen shot of the number plate. It's the same one all right."

"What time's on that clip?"

"Ten-thirty."

An hour earlier.

"Where were they?"

"Turning on to a Blackstaff Road, north-east of the town. The problem is that's where the cameras stop, Guv, so we're blind. It's mostly fields, farms and mud-tracks after that."

"It's not all bad news. We were right about the farms, and that the killers were staying north."

Less optimistically, their kidnappers had an hour's lead on them and God only knew what they were using it for.

The thought made Craig suck in air so noisily that both men at the ASU heard it, although only Andy knew how to respond.

"They won't harm her until the show, chief. They'll *have* to stick to the agreed timing because there's money riding on it."

The words conjured such a brutal image that Annette, in the Ford's back seat and only hearing half the conversation, winced. But she knew that the DCI was right. Mary would be safe until the designated show time, whenever that was.

Andy's next words were also right, but this time chastising.

"And Mary won't thank us for seeing her as a damsel in distress, no matter *what* it says in the chivalric code. She's an officer in trouble, that's all, and she'll be embarrassed by any hint we think this happened because she's a woman."

Liam's objection was so fast and noisy that it made Craig jump, and the other men glad that they were twenty miles away. The deputy been concentrating on the road, weaving in and out of lanes at one hundred mph, overtaking and undertaking perilously trying to shave precious minutes off their pursuit. It was dicey work and required focus so he'd left the chat to his boss, but he couldn't let Andy's last comment pass.

"Ach, away and scratch yourself, man! All this PC bullshit really gives me a headache. If she *hadn't* been a woman, she would never have been on MacArthur's list in the first place!"

"Well, I just meant-"

Andy didn't get to finish because a full metal jacket Liam cut him off.

"I mean, I'm all for women's lib and stuff..."

Annette smirked at the old-fashioned terminology.

"And having women in the job has been all good. But for fuck's sake, the girl's five-foot nothing and weighs less than my dinner so of course that has something to do with it! Do you think he'd have been able to carry any of *us* out a window without a sound? Eh? Even drugged? Do you?"

He glanced towards the back seat and added, "Except Annette" only avoiding a clip around the ear because she didn't want to crash.

Craig could feel a fight brewing between his chief

inspectors, and while he would have paid to see that throwdown with Andy's logic pitted against Liam's street smarts now wasn't the time, so he cut his deputy off just as he was inhaling for round two.

"You're both right, and wrong, and you can debate the ins and outs of feminism with Mary to your hearts' content once she's safe, but right now we're going to retrieve a kidnapped officer who'll be embarrassed at being taken, just as *any* of us would, and I want no cracks about female fragility when we do. Do you hear that?"

Two mumbles of "Yes" emerged from the phone, but hearing none from his deputy Craig repeated his question, until eventually he got a grudging grunt that he knew would have to suffice.

After checking they were still going in the right direction he ended the call with instructions to update him on any changes and settled back to think, only to have a taunting, "You agree with me, boss, you know you do" come from the man at his side.

****

The fleece lining of Mary's pyjamas had finally lost its battle with the cold, and the damp, almost frozen earth between her toes had made them numb, but unfortunately not so numb that she couldn't feel them harden and curl with cramp. She'd managed to fend off the worst of the pain by breathing on her hands and rubbing her feet hard with them, but the time between cramps was growing shorter and pretty soon she knew frostbite would set in. Once that happened the option of walking would be gone so she really needed to move.

While she'd been thinking the light had moved twice more, each time after what felt like a different interval although it was only the second that she'd tried to count, using the 'one-one thousand' technique she'd used at school to calculate how long was left till the end of a class when a teacher confiscated her phone, which had happened a lot. What wouldn't she give for a phone right now, with its clock, geo-location, and best of all facility to simply call someone to come and pick her up!

The constable pictured her sleek black smart-phone, placed like every night on her bedside table before she took her shower. Why hadn't she worn a dressing gown into the bathroom and slipped it into the pocket instead? She already knew the answer; she didn't possess a dressing gown despite her mother wanting to buy her one, only caving to the offer of pyjamas when her, "What happens if you ever have to go into hospital, Mary?" common sense had worn her down.

Now she wore a pair every night in the winter, grateful for their added warmth, but if she'd accepted the dressing gown offer too then she wouldn't be so bloody cold and would have her smart-phone with her now.

It was a Utopia that Mary had never expected to long for at twenty-seven, and pointless thinking of it. She didn't have a phone, a gun, a dressing gown, or a hope in hell of anyone rescuing her because they couldn't possibly know where she was, so she needed to get off her ass and help herself while she still could. The thought of ending life as a hedgerow popsicle, or worse getting dragged back to her cell, galvanised the young detective, and with a final scan of her surroundings she grabbed a handful of hedge and pulled herself agonisingly to her feet and through the opening that she'd created to take her towards the light.

Whether it was dark wit or delirium she was sure some shrink would tell her if she ever escaped this mess, but the idea of walking towards a bright light made her giggle. She'd had a mixed Christian/Taoist upbringing and practiced mainly cynicism now so she wasn't sure she believed in an afterlife, but if there *was* one, she really hoped not to see it anytime soon.

The thought preoccupied her until she was through the hedge and found herself on a narrow mud track beside a field with a large iron gate. Opening it wasn't an option because who knew when it had last been oiled, and a loud creak in the quiet of a country night might as well have been a flare to anyone in pursuit. So she climbed it, slowly and painfully, its chilled iron like hot coals against her freezing toes. Eventually she landed in the field where only a sea of tall wheat lay between her and her light.

It was then that Mary noticed the contrast between her pyjamas and her surroundings, something that hadn't mattered in the dark. Their red silk shone so loudly against the yellow-gold of nature that it might as well have shouted 'here I am'. There was only one thing she could do to be less conspicuous, turn them inside out so that the white fleece lining showed, so as quickly as she could manage and shivering so much she was almost vibrating that's exactly what she did. It was an improvement, but not much.

As she drew closer to the beacon the constable realised two things: it was coming from a spotlight on a pole attached to a large machine making rolls from pre-cut vegetation, and the combination was unmanned. The second realisation made her slump to her knees and sob. Despite all her efforts there was still no-one to help her get home.

The shafts of wheat provided more warmth than she'd expected and tiredness and despair made her eyes droop as she considered her next step. Someone would collect the machine in the morning, they were bound to, so if she could just evade capture until then…

****

The CCU. 11.40 p.m.

"Damn, the traffic on the Dark Web is really ramping up!"

Davy moved quickly to his junior's side. "Show me."

Ash's hands flew over his keyboard for a moment and a four-way split-screen appeared.

"OK, these are the sites Cybercrime told me to watch and the betting and bartering has been rising on all of them since about ten-thirty. Plus, the guy who was interested in my viruses said he had to go then. He said he'd contact me tomorrow but he had business tonight."

He tapped the bottom left corner of the screen. "This one's a big site, and it's busy busy."

The information made Davy frown. "Hang on. The chief said the perps would just be showing the event to their group-"

The event; it sounded so much nicer than 'Mary's murder' and cold coming from him, but it was necessary as a distancing tool because if he allowed himself to think about what was *really* about to happen then he would be no damn use at all.

"- so yeh, I can see *them* laying stakes on it, but why all the w...wider betting activity?"

Ash's eyes saucered in realisation. "They must be showing it to a bigger audience! Like a football match."

"What?"

Davy wasn't an aficionado of sport, never mind betting on it.

"With a footie match there'll be some people in the directors' box watching the game up close, and then there'll be people viewing on TV at home or in the pub and placing bets from there."

The comparison was horrifying but useful.

"And the advantage of being in the box?"

"Better view and proximity. Although I doubt proximity applies this time because only the killers are local. But the people in the box might get more options too."

Davy pushed through his revulsion to nod him on.

"Home or pub betting will mainly be on a match's final result and have to stop before kick-off, but the directors' bets could continue. Live betting *during* the match."

"On what?"

"Details. Like, how many penalties will there be, will the ref issue any yellow cards, and maybe even will he raise them with his right or left hand? Little things like that."

The thought of what that might translate to during a woman's murder made Davy feel ill.

"But the wider group only gets to bet on the result?"

Ash pulled a face. "Well, that's the weird thing here. I mean, if the guaranteed result here is that the woman dies then what are they betting on? No bookie's going to pay out on a sure thing, are they?"

His boss considered the available options.

"They could be betting on how long it takes them to die, what method is used to kill them, what their last words are."

"Yeh. Maybe."

"But the directors' box gets far more options than that and all the way through. Nuances that I can't think of right now. Which means that when the bulk of the betting and bartering activity stops, the people still at it be the inner group MacArthur works with. Wherever they are in the w...world."

Such a brilliant deduction would normally have warranted a high-five but no-one was celebrating.

"That'll help us ID these bastards *after* the fact, Ash, but w...we need to do better. I've another question about l betting."

"Fire away."

"How soon before a football match does the betting close?"

"Usually fifteen minutes at a real-life bookie's, but maybe half that online."

It made Davy pray that the betting kept going for hours.

"OK, I'm nipping up to Cyber to explain so they can focus on the wider group that stops betting first. We'll concentrate on the few who keep going as soon as they become obvious. But I want you to focus on that internet signal in the Newcastle region, Ash. I know these bastards will bounce them all over the world trying to fool us but have a go. Before I leave, has anything happened at the ports or airports?"

Ash shook his head. "Nada. But it's still early. If they're going to run it'll be after the show."

He was reckoning without a pissed-off Noel Robinson.

****

Near Newcastle.

Noel Robinson had waited only seconds after his partner had left to pursue Mary to set off himself in the opposite direction. Jimmy Mac was beyond reason now and if he wanted to tank his life then that was up to him, but he had other plans and they definitely didn't include prison. A cop like him wouldn't last a month inside.

He took the van and was on the A24 heading back to Belfast when he realised that they couldn't include returning home either. Mac may have been the instigator of their little adventures: *his* list, *his* ingenious killing methods, and mainly his computer wizardry, but the part that *he* had played by piggybacking the CCTV signals and now helping abduct the girl were too big for him to argue that he'd been led astray. There wasn't a court in the land that wouldn't lock him up.

The realisation shocked the corrupt sergeant so much that he pulled off the road to throw up. *How could he have been so stupid? He'd thrown his job, his house, everything, away for a sensation.* With a dull thud Robinson realised that the sensation he'd sought hadn't been so much the thrill of the women dying as the feeling of acceptance he'd got from being welcomed by the group.

Oddly the thought cheered him up slightly; there would be other Dark Web groups to join and other gamers to play with in the future, although it would mean buying new tech in a new country and for that he needed cash. He had a go-bag of passport, documents and some currency with him, but the girl's escape was such a cock-up it might take more to evade capture now, especially if the cops located Mac and found their flights on his computer. He needed a *lot* more cash and a new way out.

While the now ex-copper searched his phone for the next flight to anywhere and set off in search of as many cash-points as he could find, Ash Rahman saw an alert flash on his screen and smilingly lifted the phone to the detectives at the ASU.

****

When Mary eventually woke again, she was confused. Not so much that she was lying on the ground in her night clothes but about how much time had elapsed since she'd discovered her longed-for saviour was an automaton.

It took her a moment to orient herself but she did. The same depth of darkness and absence of birdsong said that she'd probably only slept for minutes and it made her hopeful that her captors wouldn't yet be close. Until she listened, and no matter how she tried to convince herself that the rustling sound coming from the direction of the hedgerow was the scurrying of a small animal she knew that something far larger was loose.

It could be the farmer coming to retrieve his machine or someone far less welcoming and she couldn't risk showing herself to find out, so the constable burrowed deeper into the dry wheat, curled up in a ball and held her breath, praying hard that whoever or whatever was making the sound didn't approach.

Listening helplessly as the rustling grew louder and became the sound of wheat being thrust aside, her fears grew. Would any farmer treat his crop with such disrespect? Then a moment of optimism when heavy male footsteps passed around ten feet to her left and kept moving ahead, bypassing her on their way to the machinery! It must be a farm worker after all! But she would wait till the engine turned over to be sure.

As the young constable listened for the sound of the ignition, a shadow fell across her and she turned, just in time to feel the sharp prick of a needle for the second time that night. The luck that had opened the window and concealed her until now had just run out.

Chapter Sixteen

The CCU.

"Look! There!"

Ash jabbed a slim finger at his computer screen, something he hated when anyone else did it because of the smudges it left but he forgave himself the transgression because these were tense times. The strain showed in his voice and brought Davy back to his side.

"What?"

"Cash-points, I mean ATMs. Look."

A quick tap and the screen split in two, one side displaying a map marked with three purple dots and the other an image from the camera of an ATM. It was fuzzy but clear enough to make out the user was a man in his twenties or thirties.

"Robinson?"

"Has to be. It's his debit card being used, so unless he gave it-"

Davy cut him off; it was unusual for him but time was short.

"OK, and the dots are ATMs he's used?"

"Yep. All three on the A24 north. The first was just above the junction of the Newcastle and Downpatrick Roads and he's taking the max out each time on different cards, so unless he's planning on a shopping spree at midnight-"

"He's getting ready to run."

Davy sat down at the nearest desk and pressed his forehead against it dramatically, saying, "Think, think, think, think" in quick succession until he evidently followed the instruction and his face reappeared bearing a grin.

"Something's gone wrong with Mary! Has to be."

Ash was torn between asking why he looked so happy about what sounded like bad news and querying his logic. He opted for the second.

"Because?"

"Because Robinson's out gathering cash and your map shows he's heading back to Belfast."

He paused, tapping his chin in the same 'think' rhythm. When he spoke again his words carried an added certainty.

"Which means he's either going home, which is doubtful unless he's so dumb he doesn't realise we'll have sussed him, or he's looking for a way out." He peered at the map again. "But I'm more interested in where he's coming *from*. Pull up all the ATMs between the first one he used on the A24 and the border."

Three more dots appeared.

"OK, now pull up *every* ATM there is on the A24 on the way back to Belfast."

The three Robinson had already used were followed by another four.

"Seven north and three south. Brilliant."

"Again, *because?*"

"Because Robinson used the exact three cashpoints shown here, which means he used the same search technique to find them as you. If he hadn't then he'd have missed at least one driving along trying to spot ATMs in the dark. Or diverted to use a different machine elsewhere."

Just then another of the seven ATMs on the road to Belfast pinged, backing up Davy's theory.

"How much has he withdrawn this time?"

Ash typed quickly before responding, "The max again. A different card."

"How many does he have?"

"Three credit and two debit that I could find."

Davy was about to say, "I wonder why he didn't just use all of them at one stop?" when he realised that a) panic made people do stupid things, and b) it was just as well that Robinson hadn't because he would never have left them such a clear trail.

"OK, he's still got one card he hasn't used, so while we're w...waiting for it to ping, show me the three ATMs between the A24 and the border again."

The earlier three dots reappeared and Davy pointed at the screen excitedly.

"That one! Furthest north from the border. Where is it?"

His junior enlarged the map. "A village called Arera just north of Newcastle. Population three hundred according to this."

"Half-a-horse town. OK, pull up the area between it and the first cash-point Robinson used."

Several acres of rural land appeared.

"Enlarge it. I want to see what's there."

It soon became obvious there was nothing but fields but Davy wasn't deflated.

"Right. I'm off to phone the chief. Get me the name of who owns that land and their phone numbers. They should already be on Ryan's list. Pull up all property and planning sketches too. We need sight every outhouse, cottage and barn in that area."

The analyst found Craig belting down the A2 at ninety miles per hour, Liam only dialling back from the ton when his boss couldn't hear himself think over the noise of the road.

"What have you got, Davy?"

"Robinson's card has been used at four ATMs on the A24 way back to Belfast, withdrawing the max each time. We think he's legging it."

Craig felt a sharp stab of excitement.

"You're sure it's him?"

"One of the ATM cameras showed a man in his twenties or thirties. The image was poor but it's probable. I think the partnership's split up, chief."

"And Robinson's running."

It could be good or bad news for Mary so he stayed calm.

"OK, Annette's got the airports and ports locked down with armed police. Send through your map of cash-points north yet to be used and she can do the same for those." After a brief pause he added, "But that's not the only reason you phoned, is it, Davy?"

He saw Liam's focused scowl begin to thaw. The game was on and they both knew it.

"No. There are another three ATMs s...south of the first one Robinson used but he didn't touch them, so my guess is the most northerly of *those* is just south of where they're holding Mary-"

Liam's deep voice cut across him.

"And the first one he *did* use is just to her north. Stellar work, lad."

Craig chuckled. "Yes, what he said. Tell us more."

As the analyst laid out his next steps on property and planning, Craig had a thought about the ASU. He mentioned it when Davy paused for breath.

"The ASU-"

"Will have aerial maps. Yes, I'd thought of that, chief. Ash is pulling up any farm buildings, and as soon as w...we have outlines I'll get in touch with Aidan."

"Maps are only part of it. The ASU have access to aerial support as well. They share a surveillance helicopter with the local Met Office and it can be in the air in thirty minutes. I'll call the commander now to scramble it and you call Aidan about the maps ASAP. Remind him they'll need their vests. MacArthur's bound to be armed."

The analyst made positive noises but behind them he was wondering whether to tell Craig what else had just appeared on his computer screen. The detective read his mind.

"More?"

When the computer expert exhaled heavily Craig knew it was bad news.

"I've just got back to my desk from working with Ash, chief, and Cyber have sent something through. We asked them to monitor betting activity on the Dark Web, and they've just messaged me to say that the widespread betting's started slowing."

Craig thought he knew what that meant but he wanted it laid out.

"And?"

"We think the widespread betting is a proxy for a Dark Web-wide audience betting on Mary's outcome. A far bigger audience than MacArthur's special group."

Liam was quick off the mark. "If the outcome's always death then where's the bet?"

Davy's response was gloomy. "Betting on her exact time of death and method of killing to mention two."

Craig felt like he'd been kicked in the chest; it was the murder of his youngest team member that those bastards were betting on! He'd like to roast every bloody one of them on a slow spit.

It took effort but he managed not to explode.

"So, you're saying that when this group eventually stops placing bets the show will start."

"Ash said that in football the kick-off is usually around fifteen minutes later, but that's just what *we* think, chief. W...We could be wrong."

"I doubt it."

Craig frowned to himself; why did he feel something was still missing?

It came to him faster than he would have liked.

"And the *special* group MacArthur's pandering to?"

The analyst tasted bile.

"Betting live during the event on every little variable. You can imagine what those might be."

"It wouldn't help so I won't, thanks. OK, what's the wider betting doing now?"

Davy leant towards his screen, as if a closer view would make him more certain of what he said next.

"It hasn't stopped, but it's gone from a thousand people betting to around four hundred now."

Liam shook his head slowly. "Man, there are a lot of sick fuckers out there."

"Spineless cowards hiding in the dark. Once we've got Mary safe, we need to expose as many of the bastards as we can."

The certain prediction of her rescue made everyone feel better and Craig gave his next orders in an upbeat tone.

"Right, Davy. Sort those maps with Aidan, copy the ATM map to Annette, keep an eye on the betting and when the punters drop to fifty let me know. I'll be in touch."

The call was cut and another one made immediately prepping the ASU for take-off, while Annette shifted armed response officers around on the board. Calls made, Liam put the boot down again and the others watched the scenery fly past as they drew closer to their prey.

****

Noel Robinson was on his fifth cashpoint when he wondered what the hell he was doing. Withdrawing his life's savings in the hope they could take him far enough away to evade the punishment that he knew would come anyway, the only question was when. There were very few places in the world where Craig wouldn't find him eventually, or the bastard's long reach through Europol and the in-country agencies wouldn't snatch him up instead.

But he had to defer that day as long as possible, didn't he? It was what criminals did, run, and that's what he was now after all. A criminal. He felt a sharp twinge as he thought the word then wondered why. He'd known that what he was doing was criminal three corpses ago, no, years before that when he'd watched his first snuff movie in the dark. It hadn't really bothered him then because it hadn't seemed real. They were just images, weren't they? He already knew that the answer was no. Every film of a person dying, and they weren't all women, although he'd enjoyed those the most, had captured a real flesh and blood demise.

Still, he'd lied to himself that because *he* wasn't the one killing them, he wasn't a killer, just like Jimmy Mac had done all the killing that week not him, choosing to forget that without people like him watching and helping, snuff movies could and would never be made.

But he'd *needed* the knowledge that he'd belonged somewhere, that there were other people out there with similar kinks to him, and why should he care about the dead women? He'd been rejected by women all his life unless he'd paid for their company and they'd never given a damn about him.

Even so, he might have, *would* have, been content just watching if he hadn't met Mac, he was sure of it. Happy as a voyeur, living vicariously through others fulfilling their needs.

Without Mac he wouldn't have ended up where he was now, sitting in a dark van beside an ATM on the run to God only knew where. He might as well have stayed to help him find the girl and they could have run together. He glanced at his dashboard clock: midnight. The show had been delayed until one o'clock so he still had time to go back.

The thought galvanised him into making a U-turn across the A road, activating his car-phone as he did, and thirty minutes later he'd reserved two new flights for payment at Dublin Airport as a peace offering and he was nearly back at the farm.

****

A Farm Near Newcastle. 12.30 p.m.

At twelve-thirty all the players were in position. Liam's Ford was parked on the boundary of their designated catchment area and the detectives were staring at Craig's smart-phone, where the outlines of three buildings found by Ash were marked in red. All three of them confirmed as purchased by Jimmy Mac's dummy company, proving they were definitely in the right place.

Noel Robinson had made it back to farm and was grovelling to his partner, trying to explain that he hadn't really fled but gone to get cash, and offering him the new flight from Dublin as recompense.

Andy was in constant contact with the team's

analysts, who'd guessed that Robinson had stopped heading north when no ATM had been used for twenty minutes, and had finally located his van heading back the way it had come and turning on to the quiet Tyrella Road near the detectives' staging post, where it went off camera. That prompted Annette to redirect almost all armed officers to them, where Craig ordered them to spread out along the boundary, effectively sealing their killers inside.

Aidan was having a more adventurous time than any of them, flying with a pilot and a paramedic in the helicopter at ten thousand feet and watching as the lights of Belfast were swiftly replaced by dense black country night. Craig had ordered them to stay a mile out in case their rotor blades were heard by their killers, so there they held, ready to perform what might be the most urgent task of the night; getting Mary to a hospital if she was harmed.

Inside the ten-mile perimeter the constable was back in her small prison still unconscious from her second injection, much to James MacArthur's fury. He took it out on his companion.

"Look at her! It's your bloody fault I had to dope her again! If you hadn't disappeared we could have fetched her back here together awake."

Noel Robinson feigned regret, but he was still ambivalent. He'd never got close to a victim before that night, his only job to capture the images and ensure their connection didn't go down as the rest of the D.W. watched. But tonight he'd helped carry a woman down a ladder, driven miles with her, and now he was standing just three feet away, so close that he could hear her breathe, and it made everything feel uncomfortably real.

As his doubts grew, he realised his biggest one now was whether he should ever have returned. *He couldn't do this; he couldn't be this close to killing a woman even though he'd fantasised about it for years. It turned out that fantasy and fact were very different things.*

But he'd seen the array of guns and knives laid out in

the viewing room and knew if he tried to leave again the girl wouldn't be the only person Mac killed.

He diverted his nervous energy into persuasion.

"She mightn't wake for hours, Jimmy. We'll have to postpone again."

MacArthur rounded on him furiously, his blue eyes burning.

"NO! WE DON'T POSTPONE ANY MORE!" His voice quietened to a near whisper even more threatening than his shout. "We proceed on time with whatever method the group votes for."

The police sergeant couldn't hide his shock.

"What do you mean? The girl's on *your* list so *you* choose how she dies."

He wasn't sure why he thought that might be better, or why he even cared, but for the first time he actually did.

His partner-in-crime smiled maliciously.

"Not tonight. This is my first close kill so I've asked for their input. They'll devise the method," the smile widened to reveal his teeth, "or maybe even *methods* if they change their minds partway through. It'll make things go on longer and improve the bets."

Suddenly Robinson recalled that lying amongst the weapons there'd also been a silk scarf. Mac could strangle, stab or shoot the girl, perhaps all three, and there was nothing he could do in case he got killed himself.

A barked order broke his fugue.

"Put her in front of the camera while I work out how to wake her. The wider betting's winding down so it'll soon be time to start."

The policeman felt nauseous. He didn't want to smell which shampoo the girl used on her silky hair or feel her warmth again; the thought of touching her repulsed him now, knowing that she would soon be dead. But he did as he was told anyway, self-preservation not self-sacrifice being his guiding principle in life, except that this time it brought his fury back and stronger than he'd ever known before.

****

12.40 p.m.

"The widespread betting's stopped, chief."

Craig nodded to himself as he stood in the dark field, staring ahead but seeing nothing but his constable's face.

The change in betting meant the performance would start soon, probably on the hour for symbolism which gave them twenty minutes to stop MacArthur. It was time to move, but on which of the three buildings that they'd seen on screen?

He climbed back into the car and set his phone to hands-free.

"I *really* need you to pinpoint that computer now, Davy."

In response the analyst turned to his friend. "Anything?"

Ash bit his lip hard, knowing that if he made the wrong call a colleague could end up dead. The problem was they weren't dealing with stupid men; both Robinson and MacArthur were tech savvy and had thought to set up wi-fi and electricity at all three sites and leave them running at top whack.

He ignored Davy staring at him from across the squad-room and closed his eyes.

What would distinguish a building where a murder was about to be beamed out to the world from another one where someone was just surfing the web or watching TV?

All three of the buildings were small and each held two walled-off areas, but whether they were cow pens or kitchens there were no plans lodged centrally to tell. He bit his lip harder and thought harder.

Two rooms... two... used for what in a killing? A filmed, streamed killing.

Suddenly his eyes flew open and he beckoned Davy to

pull up a chair.

"Don't hang up, chief. Ash might have something."

"OK, so, they all have two rooms. Two rooms for a killing. That's one to kill in and one to-"

"Transmit. To everywhere in the globe, so they'll need signal amps and back-up servers. That means serious power usage."

"And they'll be testing the equipment before they start by pushing it close to overload. So pick a site and check the usage and I'll do the other two."

A full minute later they compared figures and as Ash punched the air his boss yelled into the phone, almost deafening Craig.

"It's the building to the far left! That's where they're holding her. Its power usage just jumped by a factor of a hundred."

The Ford was already on the move.

"I'll call you back."

By the time Annette had converged her troops closer to their target, leaving a small back-up force mobile in the unlikely case Ash had chosen the wrong site, and Craig had radioed the chopper to get ready to move on his call, Liam had brought them to within a half-mile of the building and cut his engine to let his car roll the final stretch.

The small wooden construction ahead of them looked just like a million other outhouses from a distance; a simple shed that could have home to a JCB and cows if it hadn't been for the lights glaring from one room and the high-spec receiver on its slatted roof.

Not saying a word Craig signalled the others to exit the car and move parallel to him as they'd discussed ten minutes earlier, until at fifty feet from the building's longest wall he halted their progress with a raised hand and checked his watch: twelve-fifty. He was waiting for a text to say the others had reached their positions on the other sides and another even more important one from his analysts before they could move in a single swoop. Any other, piecemeal, approach could result in a clusterfuck and Mary getting killed by two angry perps who'd realised their time was up.

If Craig had possessed X-ray vision, he would have known just how close he was to the truth. James MacArthur's anger at his friend's betrayal had grown and was nearing the point where he was considering throwing in Noel Robinson's murder to spice up his show. On the other hand, the policeman *had* returned and brought a new exit plan with him so MacArthur was still undecided when his partner left the room to run more tests on the Net.

To keep busy he crossed the room to check on his captive, running his eyes lecherously over Mary's thin body and picturing which of the outfits he'd brought with him he might make her wear. He clicked his fingers above her face to check if she was faking her slumber but the sound was only enough to make her turn on her side and doze on. Or so MacArthur thought, but as soon as he left the room to find some smelling salts to rouse her the detective's eyes shot open, she recognised her surroundings and quickly filled in the blanks between there and the field.

Mary knew she was in real trouble; her preferred exit, the window, had been sealed with hardboard, and she stood little chance of fighting her way past a man MacArthur's size. But not *no* chance, and whatever she could do she was damn well going to do it, the only question was when.

She heard someone enter the room and closed her eyes again, guessing that some unpleasant technique was about to be employed to waken her and determined not to respond. The longer they thought she was unconscious the longer she had to think.

But sadly, that isn't how smelling salts work. One sniff of their pungent odour and Mary instantly recoiled.

James MacArthur's greeting was smug.

"Awake at last, sleeping beauty. Good job the salts worked or I'd have had to use force."

It was the wrong tack to take with the defiant

constable and she immediately launched herself at him nails out, dragging them down his cheek and managing to draw blood. It earned her a whack that sent her flying against a wall.

Noel Robinson winced as he watched the interaction on his screen, dreading what would come next, but to his surprise Mac seemed to regard the gouging as some sort of foreplay, laughing as he rubbed his bleeding left cheek.

"So, you've grown into a bitch, have you, Mary Li? Good, that'll spice things up. I'd planned to do Romaine before you because I really hate the whore, but now I'm glad I chose you."

He advanced on her so fast that before she could sidestep he'd pressed his face into hers and the smell of his stale breath was making her want to gag.

"Let's make it a violent one, since you obviously like it so much. We're going to put on quite the show, girly."

He jerked his thumb at a pile of clothes in the corner that she hadn't noticed.

"Pick an outfit and get changed. And make some bloody effort, will you. My audience expects their money's worth."

The constable's yelled, "OVER MY DEAD BODY" seemed less than wise in the circumstances. But it wasn't, because it was just loud enough to give the cops outside confirmation that they were in the right place, *and* that Mary was still alive.

But Craig still wasn't calling the breach until he was ready and for that he needed his analysts' final thumbs-up. They'd managed to ID the wi-fi the show was to be broadcast over and could cut it with a single keystroke, but Cybercrime needed time to finish putting traces on the core group still logged-on for the event.

Davy would follow his order either way, but Craig knew the second they hit the door MacArthur could cut the wi-fi himself and every member of his faceless alliance would disappear into the ether free to cause more harm.

It was at times like this he wished he was a junior

again, then he wouldn't *have* to weigh the welfare of his one officer against numberless other women in the future. But he knew that much as he *wanted* to storm the building, caring about Mary didn't give him the right to put her first. He *had* to let events inside the shed run until Cyber called it, risking his constable suffering irreparable harm while he sat on his bloody and ultimately responsible hands.

Or perhaps not.

Craig beckoned his deputy as far back from their vantage point as he could while still keeping the house in sight and lowered his voice.

"Cybercrime needs," he checked his watch. "four more minutes log-on by the inner circle to get traces on all their lines."

Liam's small eyes widened so much they glowed white in the darkness.

"But that gives the fuckers time to lay hands on her!"

"That's why I need your advice. We need something that will divert MacArthur from Mary for a brief period but not scare his viewers away. You grew up in the country, so any ideas?"

Liam chewed his substantial lower lip so hard that Craig thought he might bite through it; he'd almost done the same to his own, wracking his brains since Davy's last text but still drawing a blank on ploys to use. Then he'd remembered that his deputy had been raised in the country, and depending on what Liam said next all Old MacDonald jokes might be banned for a year.

"A cow, boss."

Craig immediately glanced around him but saw nothing.

"Where?"

The white eyes rolled.

"There isn't one, but if we could make *MacArthur* think there's one, or better still a herd, then it might throw him off his work. Better still, it *might* make him come outside to look and then we'd have him."

Craig doubted that, unless the man was an idiot, but

313

he was open to any diversion they could create.

He thought the idea through quickly.

"We'd need to make the sound far enough away from the building that he didn't get suspicious it was a trick, but loud enough to disturb his train of thought. And it'll have to be convincing." He knew he was going to regret his next question but asked it anyway. "Did you learn how to imitate cows on the farm?"

Liam's response was to shove him hard in the shoulder, and hiss, *"No, I didn't, you cheeky sod!* But we have tech, don't we? We can pull a cow recording off the Net and play it at top whack. Can I imitate a bloody cow indeed?!"

If he hadn't needed to keep the noise down, he would have added a tirade in defence of farmers, but the pleasure from watching Craig rub his sore shoulder would have to suffice.

"Point taken. Find a decent recording on your phone and send me the link. I'll brief the others to expect it and we'll play them together at top volume on my sign."

As he returned to his former position, Craig wished again that this was just a straightforward raid. Then he could have summoned the chopper over to send them infra-red images and hit their perps hard and fast. But any rotor noise now could alert MacArthur, lose their online voyeurs, and perhaps cost Mary her life.

His timing had to be perfect and that meant balancing when to play their recording, because they would only get one throw of that dice.

Best case, MacArthur would be irritated and slowed up by the cattle noises until he decided to ignore them, worst case he would sense something was up, cut the feed so his audience didn't get caught and then, cornered, do God only knew what to Mary inside the shed.

A vibration in Craig's pocket brought some useful news. Cyber had almost finished and Davy would message again when they were done.

A quick, *'Time's short, so tell them to shift'* back and

314

the detective felt on surer ground.

Mary's earlier defiance had been loud but clearly just rhetoric, so he could be pretty sure she'd get even louder if MacArthur actually tried to lay hands. The moment he heard that it would be time to make their noise.

But even as Craig thought it, he was having doubts. *What if they'd drugged her after her outburst and were doing unspeakable things to her right that moment?*

He dismissed the idea quickly; there was no sport for an audience in watching the murder of someone unconscious. Bastards like that fed off fear and uncertainty and would want to bet on how much she might struggle and when death would come. MacArthur needed Mary awake for whatever he had planned so she was safe for now.

More doubts. *Safe physically perhaps, but what about mentally?* The damage that night was doing to his detective might never go away. Did he have the right to let her mental torture go on for even one more second? Shouldn't he call, "BREACH" now and be satisfied with catching just their two perps?

It was less easy for Craig to answer that one. Even though every fibre of his being was screaming breach, his mind was saying there would be other victims and other bereaved families in the future if they allowed MacArthur's audience to escape.

If he could have seen through walls Craig might or might not have felt better, but he would definitely have admired his constable even more that he already did.

Left alone with the pile of outfits Mary was staring at them in disgust, wondering what sort of regressive weirdo could only get turned on if a woman dressed as a stripper, a dancer from the Folies Bergère, or an extra from the Rocky Horror Picture Show. Whether they were MacArthur's fantasies or someone else's watching who'd paid big bucks, she had absolutely no intention of complying.

If she wanted to dress like a cheap nylon slut she would save it for a Halloween party, and if MacArthur insisted then he'd bloody well have to force her and she still fancied her chances at fending him off. This was a man who'd only ever killed remotely before which told her that getting close to a woman scared him, and she intended to be the scariest he'd ever met.

Watching from inside the computer room Noel Robinson saw the determination on Mary's face and willed her on, although not so obviously that his partner could tell. But unfortunately, he knew that no matter how determined the detective was, her defiance was likely to fade when she was staring down the barrel of a gun. They were on an isolated farm with no hope of rescue so she would have to give in eventually.

Just as the thought came to him, he saw the first bet being laid on exactly how long it would take Mac to wear her down.

Macarthur saw it too and chuckled. "Start taking bets on *how* I should force her to change into an outfit. Knife, gun, fists? Go ahead and ask the question, and if they want to supply more detail, fine. They can produce the ideas, you take the bets, and I'll do what needs to be done."

Noel Robinson felt sick, but also fascinated by the man at his side. As long as he'd known Jimmy Mac he had been terrified of women, never even having the guts to ask one the time of day for fear of ending up back to prison, and venting his hostility towards them at length in their Incel groups. All his killings had been performed from a distance because touching a woman had been beyond him, yet *now* he seemed to be relishing it. Had this young copper done something especially bad to him as a kid?

Whatever was happening he really didn't envy Mary what was coming.

Just then his thoughts were interrupted by a beep and Mac leant in to read the screen.

"Threatening with a gun wins." He shrugged. "Fair enough. They don't want her marked until it's time. OK, now ask them what outfit they want on her."

As the computer screen began flashing again, Robinson knew that if he was going to help the girl he had to do it soon, before they reached the point of no return. His instinct to protect her surprised him, although he doubted he'd have the courage to deliver on it. If it became a choice of her safety or his own, he would win hands down.

A moment later, 'French Dancer' flashed on the screen and Mac got ready to move. The little bitch would dress up in the outfit or he would put a bullet in her foot. Robinson watched mutely as he left the computer room, the only move he could think of making to slip a knife up his sleeve, with no idea when or if he could use it.

As Mary heard footsteps approaching she positioned herself behind the door, kicking high and hard as it opened and managing to clip her old schoolmate in the head. James MacArthur fell sideways and the gun flew out of his hand. She flung herself across the room to grab it and as she did so Robinson saw what was happening and moved towards the hallway, planning to enter the room and stab his partner while he was down.

But both he and Mary were seconds too late. James MacArthur regained his footing so fast that he reached the gun before his captive and Robinson retreated to his safe space in front of his screen.

"Clever little bitch! Where'd you learn that technique then? Police academy?"

The constable hissed up at him from her position on the floor.

"My mother taught me, and I'll happily demonstrate some more, you disgusting little man."

MacArthur rewarded her vitriol by recoiling, but not enough to capitalise on and he advanced again, this time pointing the gun straight at her head.

"*Little man, am I?* Well, I've a big gun pointed at you so you'll do as I say now, whore! You've had your fun and it's time for me to have mine."

Mary clambered to her feet. "There isn't a chance in hell that's ever happening!"

It wasn't voiced as loudly as her earlier defiance but it was loud enough for Craig to hear and it was their cue. On his nod the sound of cattle lowing suddenly rang out through the night. The noise startled everyone in the house and knocked MacArthur completely off his stride, with him barely managing to issue Mary another warning before he stormed out the door.

Inside the computer room it was clear their online audience had heard the sound as well and they weren't happy. Mac managed to calm them down then barked an order at his friend.

"Tweak the balance so if it happens again they won't hear it. And say we're going to play background music during the kill and get them busy bidding on what gets picked."

MacArthur felt hot sweat dripping down his back and it made him smirk. Holding a gun on a woman had given him an unexpected thrill. When Noel Robinson saw what was happening his heart sank. Mac was enjoying himself, *really* enjoying himself. The conflict was turning him on!

It was clear nothing was going to stop him from killing the girl now and he wasn't brave enough to get in his way so it was time to bail out for good.

As the bids rolled in for the music, he watched Mary kick the pile of clothes tentatively with her foot, knowing that she was contemplating doing as asked. She was a strong little thing and he admired her for it, but all the push kicks in the world couldn't compete with a gun.

That was true, but other guns could and there were plenty of those outside, yet still Craig held off, glaring at his stubbornly silent phone as if it was personally guilty of an offence. *Why the hell didn't Davy contact him?* The four minutes was up. He prayed to God it wasn't like his 'Ten minutes till I get home, pet' promises to Katy, which inevitably ran to hours.

As Mary contemplated the ignominy of her coming ordeal, James MacArthur grew so excited he was almost feverish, pacing the computer room waving his gun in the air until finally Robinson called a halt.

"Put that bloody thing down, will you!"

MacArthur glanced at the weapon in his hand as if he hadn't realised it was still there.

"I might need it, depending on what method of killing they vote for."

"Well, you don't need it yet so put it down before it goes off."

He acquiesced grudgingly and returned to his point. "The method. Have you asked yet?"

"No, I'm still sorting the music. Heavy rock is in the lead."

"Loud. Good. It'll cover the screams." He changed tack suddenly. "But do they want that? I mean, don't they *want* to hear her beg?"

It was said in a matter of fact way, as if the woman's begging would be nothing, just a way of turning him on. Suddenly all the torture scenes and snuff movies Robinson had watched came flooding back to him. Real people with friends and families meeting their painful, ignominious ends for the entertainment of a bunch of sick, evil fucks like him.

He muttered, "I'll ask them," hoping against hope that he could drag things out until someone, anyone, perhaps even daylight appeared to stop what was going to happen next. Anything but him having to risk himself.

When, 'Hard rock for the first thirty minutes then silence as you're killing her' won the toss he knew they'd descended into hell.

He tried for another delay and typed in, "Which band and track?" much to his partner's annoyance.

"I could have chosen those myself!"

"Yes, but *they'll* pay for the honour, Mac. And we'll need money after this, you know that."

A thwarted look was followed by grudging agreement then MacArthur headed for the door.

"I'm going outside for a smoke. I'll be back in five and we'll get started."

As soon as he left, Robinson snatched up the gun and checked the bullets. Then he abandoned the computer

319

and slipped into the hall.

Outside, Craig was still glaring at his phone when Liam nudged him and pointed to the far end of the building, where a tiny flicker of light had just appeared. Craig hopes soared; if someone was outside smoking it was unlikely the event had started, which in turn meant that Mary was still safe. They rose even higher when his mobile vibrated and, 'Go whenever you like' appeared on screen, but just as he radioed the chopper to move in and set the countdown to ten the ember disappeared and they had both perps inside again.

Except that one of them was outside Mary's door and just about to free her when the other appeared.

MacArthur knew what was happening immediately, or thought that he did.

"Thought you'd take a taste, did you, Noel?"

Despite having a gun, Robinson hesitated to raise it, instantly feeling under threat. He may have been firearms trained but he'd never shot anyone.

He decided to tough it out.

"It's over, Mac. I'm letting her go."

"Over my dead body, or yours."

As Jimmy Mac moved ominously towards his partner, Mary was listening at the door and willing Robinson on.

"I'm trained to use this, Mac, and I won't miss at this distance."

"Go on then, shoot me. Except I don't think you have the balls. If you did, you'd be begging for a go at her not chickening out like this."

Robinson's temper rose again. "This was never what I wanted! It was *you* who needed to kill them."

"And you just went along for the ride, eh? *Coward.* It's OK to watch but not to do the deed yourself, is that it?"

Robinson spat his next words. *"Yes, that's it! That's exactly it!* But those other deaths didn't seem real and this one does, so I'm letting her go. You and your mates can get your jollies some other way this time!"

Robinson's temper was running so hot that he hardly noticed MacArthur moving till he was at arm's length and grabbing the gun. Just then there was a loud bang, a roar of, "ARMED POLICE," and the door at the end of the hall caved filling the narrow space with a dozen armed men with Craig at their head.

When the detective saw what was happening he motioned the others to stay back, keeping his Glock fixed on the prize. If their perps were fighting amongst themselves perhaps he could turn it to their advantage.

"Put down the gun, MacArthur. The building's surrounded."

James MacArthur's response was to press his weapon hard against his ex-partner's head.

"Noel here thought he'd play Sir Galahad and free your little bitch, but he's not much good in a fight. Some copper, eh."

As the gun screwed harder into Robinson's skull, Craig kept advancing.

"Think it through, MacArthur. You shoot him in front of witnesses and then what? No lawyer could defend that."

"Just one more murder in a busy week, Copper, and I might as well be hung for a sheep as a lamb."

There's a time when lying is the right thing to do and Craig knew that time was now.

"*Really?* You think it'll be easy to prove you killed the others? Most juries won't understand how the technology worked."

The big, hopefully life-saving, but desperate lie. Because unless the jurors had been living under rocks for a decade pretty much all of them would know what a computer virus was, and clear evidence from his team and the labs would draw straight lines to the rest.

But MacArthur didn't need that pointed out right now, and when Craig saw a flicker of doubt in his eyes he pressed the advantage, waving dismissively at Robinson.

"Is a corrupt cop really worth years of your life?"

James MacArthur didn't react immediately, whether because he was enjoying the attention and wanted to make them sweat before surrendering, or because he was winding up to a big finale, one where he shot his friend and turned the gun on Craig, ensuring he went out in some movie villain hail of steel.

The detective was working on scenarios as well, the best of which was him wounding MacArthur to disable him. But the ex-con was behind Noel Robinson now with his gun pressed into the nape of his neck, sticking to him a limpet and giving Craig nothing to shoot at that wouldn't risk MacArthur's gun discharging and killing the man in his grip.

Craig wasn't aware that he'd held his breath until someone told him afterwards, all he could feel was his finger welded to his trigger as he waited for the slightest twitch that signalled opportunity.

What came instead was their killer's inch by inch retreat down the narrow hallway, past the computer room and towards a fire exit that Craig already knew was there. MacArthur was heading outside but that didn't concern the detective; the ARU had encircled the building and a loud whirr of rotors said his own men were overhead. James MacArthur was going nowhere but with him, the only decision now was would that be alive or dead.

As Craig followed the two men out into the dark country night he stared hard into Noel Robinson's eyes, willing the police sergeant to take a risk; to drop down slightly or elbow his captor in the stomach, *anything* that would give him a gap to wound MacArthur and bring him down. But even as he willed it Craig knew that it would never happen. By every account he'd heard Robinson was a coward so he would never take the chance, even to save his own skin. They would get no help from that direction.

Suddenly a blue-white light illuminated them from above, framing the trio in a spotlight that bleached colour from everything it hit and made James MacArthur blink hard, but only once and too briefly for Craig to make his move.

It was stalemate. If Aidan shot MacArthur from the

chopper the bastard might take Robinson with him; one or both dead. If *he* shot him from the front, supposing he could even find a gap, then the result could be the same, giving MacArthur exactly what he wanted, to end his perverted game with a bang. The bastard wanted to go out like a legend and he was damned if he was giving him that glory, *or* letting him off that easily; both men would be tried and sentenced in court, to life imprisonment with a bit of luck.

But their only chance of achieving that was a shot that would paralyse MacArthur's trigger finger before he could use it. It was one that very few people could make and doubtless one of the armed response officers around them fitted the bill, but the ARU weren't known for their subtlety and the risk that they would kill both their perps as they took it was just too high.

Suddenly Craig smiled to himself; why hadn't he thought of it before? They had a secret weapon that only he and Liam knew about and if there was ever a time to use it, it was now.

As the stand-off continued outside the building, Annette pushed open the door to Mary's cell and was barely an inch into the room when something came hurtling towards her head. She deflected it just in time, resulting in the shocked constable landing on the floor.

"How did you do that? No-one's been fast enough to avoid that roundhouse kick before!"

The inspector stared at her junior officer wryly and reached out a hand to help her up.

"Nice movement, but remind me not to rescue you again if that's how you say thank you."

"I didn't know it was you. You could have been another slimeball."

Her caring instincts kicking in, Annette gazed at the younger woman in concern. Mary's normally silky hair was matted and plastered to her face with sweat and her clear eyes were puffy, whether from drugs or tears was hard to tell. On her right cheek a large bruise was blooming and her pyjamas were on inside out, something that worried the ex-nurse right away. She asked about the least intimate thing first.

"What happened to your face?"

The DC rubbed the cheek that MacArthur had smacked and realised it was swollen, but before she could explain how it had happened an ARU medic entered the room and began running a series of tests.

Annette had just stepped into the hallway to give them some privacy when Liam appeared, beckoning her urgently.

"We need you outside."

"OK. Why?"

"You'll find out."

Knowing what worked from past pursuits, when Craig had followed their targets down the hallway Liam had gone the opposite way and positioned himself behind MacArthur outside, in case a shot to the killer's calf or ass could help bring him down. It hadn't taken the deputy long to work out that something more specialist was needed, *and* have an idea about who should do it, and when he'd stepped into Craig's eyeline the slight nod they'd exchanged said that both men were of the same mind.

Two minutes later Annette was concealed in the grass outside the spotlight's perimeter and to their perps' right, her eye pressed against the lens of a Heckler & Koch PSG-1 sniper rifle that was trained on James MacArthur's wrist. She knew that a shot there would give her the best chance of knocking out the motor nerve supply to his hand and rendering it useless, and she wasn't so much nervous about missing as surprised that she'd been called upon to try.

There were trained firearms officers all around her and she didn't even like guns, considering them a tool of last resort and preferring to use her brain and words. OK, so she'd earned the nickname Annie Oakley by once saving Liam's and the chief's lives, but that had been years back and it had hardly been mentioned since.

What Annette didn't know was that Craig saw the

reports on his officers' twice-yearly firearms testing and she'd consistently scored better than the rest of the squad for both speed and accuracy, her targeting even at distance impressing the assessor so much that he'd suggested to Craig she try out for the ARU, something that had made him laugh, knowing her hatred of weapons. But as soon as he'd realised which shot could disable MacArthur and the skill required to make it only Annette's name had come to mind.

As Craig faced their killers and Liam covered them from the back, the team's inspector lined-up her sight on James MacArthur, took a deep breath, and as she slowly expelled the air she squeezed the trigger sending a 7.62 x 51 mm NATO cartridge slicing through the cold night air and straight into the back of his right wrist, instantly severing the nerves, breaking his grip and resulting in his gun hitting the dirt. As the murderer screamed in pain Craig swooped in to seize his weapon, then while Liam secured MacArthur less than gently his boss did the same to his friend, handing both men off to other officers to read them their rights and take them to hospital before joining his inspector, who was passing her weapon back to its owner with a look of distaste.

"Well done, Annette. I knew you could make that shot."

"Thanks, sir. I think. Just don't ask me to do it again. Guns are vile."

He chuckled to himself. "So, you don't fancy joining the ARU then?" he gestured at the men behind her who were talking admiringly about her shot, "because you have quite the fan club by the looks of it."

"I'll send them signed photos."

As they began walking back to the building Craig asked the question that he really didn't want to ask.

"Did they-"

She cut him off swiftly. "I don't know. A paramedic came in to examine her before I could ask."

As his mouth opened again, she saved him the bother of another word.

"I'll ask her now and call you in if she says it's OK. Stay out here for now."

While Craig lurked outside the building, soon to be joined by his deputy, Annette prepared for her second difficult job of the night. She waited for the medic to leave the small room before re-entering and getting straight to the point.

"I need to ask you something, Mary."

The constable shook her head. "No. You don't."

She was sitting on a chair someone had brought in so Annette hunkered down in front of it.

"Someone will, so it's probably better that it's me." She skirted the subject by indicating the young woman's pyjamas. "They were removed at some point, weren't they?"

Seeing where she was going and without the energy to be defensive, Mary just shrugged.

"I did it. I escaped and was hiding in a field, so I thought the lining would be less visible than the red."

It sounded sensible but Annette had to make sure. "So, neither man touched you or assaulted you?"

"Unless you count injecting me with drugs, carrying me out a window, imprisoning me, chasing and finding me, injecting and carrying me back here again and then thumping me in the face. No. They were just working up to that joy when you arrived."

Annette knew instinctively that it was the truth, but Mary was still too calm and she'd seen the reaction before. It was shock, and the full impact of her ordeal would take time to emerge.

"We'll be leaving soon, so the chief would like to say hello. Is that OK?"

"I suppose," was accompanied by another shrug so Annette left the room for a moment to reappear with Craig, Liam's inevitable wisecracks being a step too far for now.

To both their surprise they found Mary standing upright when they entered, arms crossed and with a defiant look on her face, which she'd mainly adopted to

326

deal with the embarrassment of appearing in front of her boss in inside out pyjamas and with dirty feet.

Craig walked over to her, shocked at how frail she looked and fighting the urge to give her a hug.

Instead a brisk, "All right, Detective Li?" came out.

"Fine. Just your average Thursday night, sir."

The 'sir' she almost never called him gave away her tension and her, "Thank you for coming" directed at them both carried a definite quaver.

With a meaningful smile that threatened to reduce Annette to tears, Craig responded, "There's honestly nowhere else that we would rather be."

Chapter Seventeen

The Craigs' New House. Stranmillis Road. Friday, 21st February. 10.30 p.m.

"When you asked if we fancied going on somewhere after the pub, this wasn't quite what I had in mind, Marc."

As John Winter gazed around the Craigs' half-finished living-room puzzled, his best friend responded by pushing a paintbrush into his hand.

"Blame Andy. He volunteered to organise a painting party when the house was finished, so I thought, why wait when some of the plastered rooms could be done now? And before anyone asks, yes, I *would* do the same for any of you. But no-one should feel they have to stay just because I'm the boss."

When Liam immediately went to reverse out the door, "Except you. Your height will come in handy" was added hastily and a paint-roller thrust into his hand, then Craig eyed the other members of his team.

A four-hour drinking session at The James to celebrate the successful end of their case was the perfect primer for the party as far as he was concerned. After all, there were no carpets down yet to ruin and three large rooms whose ceilings and walls were all destined to be covered in the same 'Arctic White', so even with the cackhandedness that alcohol fostered there was very little that could go wrong.

Aidan begged to differ. "We're all in suits. They'll get ruined."

"There are boiler suits in the corner, along with the paint. Grace donated some old ones from forensics."

"Aye, well, I notice *she* isn't here."

Craig rolled his eyes. "How often have you seen Grace in a pub unless she's singing?"

The CSI had a beautiful voice most often employed in her church choir, apart from the rare Friday night when she provided a cabaret of blues and jazz at The James.

As Aidan slouched off grumbling, he was joined by a

much more enthusiastic Andy who thought the evening was a great idea.

"I'm going to paint caricatures of everyone on the walls. Wait till you see yours, Liam. That wire-brush hair of yours is about to take on a life of its own."

"Aye, and you'll walk funny with this roller shoved up your-"

Davy jumped in with a legal question. "Does this count as forced labour, chief? I mean, could we sue you?"

When Craig and Aidan the lawyers in the room joined in saying, "No," Aidan adding a wry, "unfortunately," and Craig, "you're all free to leave, like I said," the analyst shrugged and took a different tack.

"Can I ask Maggie to come then? It might be fun."

Craig's reply of, "Invite whoever you like" resulted in several mobiles coming out.

As people made calls and clambered clumsily into boiler suits, more than one drunk falling over as they did, only Annette noticed their boss slipping into the kitchen. She followed stealthily and eased open the door, to hear music and see a candle-lit feast laid out on a wallpaper table and Katy popping open bottles of champagne.

She saw Annette and winked, beckoning her in.

"You've uncovered our fiendish plan. Annette. Get everyone drunk and well-fed and play loud music while we paint. Anyone would think we were students."

It certainly took the pain out of a boring task.

Accepting a glass of bubbly, the inspector sipped it gratefully until Craig re-appeared from what she assumed was a pantry and said, "Since you've found us out you can have the pleasure of calling the others in, Annette."

She did so in the order that she encountered them, except for Andy who she left until he'd topped off his hair-raising caricature of Liam with a speech bubble of expletives coming from its mouth.

THE END

Core Characters in the Craig Crime Novels

Detective Chief Superintendent Marc (Marco) Craig: Craig is a sophisticated, single, forty-eight-year-old of Northern Irish/Italian extraction. From a mixed religious background but agnostic.

An ex-grammar schoolboy and Queen's University Law graduate, he went to London to join The Met (The Metropolitan Police) at twenty-two, rising in rank through its High Potential Development Training Scheme. He returned to Belfast in two-thousand and eight after fifteen years away.

He is a driven, compassionate, workaholic, with an unfortunate temper that he struggles to control and a tendency to respond to situations with his fists, something that almost resulted in him going to prison when he was in his teens. He loves the sea, sails when he has the time and is generally sporty. He plays the piano, loves music and sport.

His wife of two years Katy Stevens is a consultant physician at the local St Mary's Healthcare Trust, and they live with their baby son Luca in Katy's old apartment on the River Lagan.

Craig's parents, his extrovert mother Mirella (an Italian concert pianist) and his quiet father Tom (an ex-university lecturer in Physics) live in Holywood town, six miles outside the city. His rebellious sister, Lucia, his junior by ten years, works as the manager of a local charity and also lives in Belfast. She is engaged to Ken Smith, an ex-army officer who has now joined the police.

Craig is now a Detective Chief Superintendent heading up Belfast's Murder Squad and Police Intelligence Unit. The Murder Squad is based in the thirteen storey Co-ordinated Crime Unit (C.C.U.) in Pilot Street, in the

Sailortown area of Belfast's Docklands.

D.C.I. Liam Cullen: Craig's deputy. Liam is a fifty-two-year-old former RUC officer from Crossgar in Northern Ireland, who transferred into the PSNI from the RUC in two thousand and one, following the Patton Reforms. He has lived and worked in Northern Ireland all his life and has spent over thirty years in the police force, more than twenty of them policing Belfast, including during The Troubles.

Liam is married to the forty-two-year-old, long suffering Danielle (Danni), a part-time nursery nurse, and they have an eight-year-old daughter Erin and a six-year-old son Rory. Liam is unsophisticated, indiscreet and hopelessly non-PC, but he's a hard worker with a great knowledge of the streets and has a sense of humour that makes everyone, even the Chief Constable, laugh.

D.I. Annette Eakin: Annette is Craig's lead Detective Inspector who has lived and worked in Northern Ireland all her life. She is a forty-eight-year-old ex-nurse who after her nursing degree worked as a nurse for thirteen years, then after a career break retrained and has now been in the police for an equal length of time. She divorced her husband Pete McElroy, a P.E teacher at a state secondary school, because of his infidelity and violence. He has since died. They had two children, a boy and a girl (Jordan and Amy), both at university, and Annette also has a toddler daughter Carina with her new partner, Mike Augustus, a pathologist who works with Doctor John Winter.

Annette is kind and conscientious with an especially good eye for detail. She also has very good people skills but can be a bit of a goody-two-shoes.

Nicky Morris: Nicky Morris is Craig's forty-year-old personal assistant. She used to be PA to Detective Chief

Superintendent (D.C.S.) Terry *'Teflon'* Harrison. Nicky is a glamorous Belfast mum married to Gary who owns a small garage, and she is the mother of a teenage son Johnny. She comes from a solidly working-class area of east Belfast, just ten minutes' drive from Docklands.

She is bossy, motherly and street-wise and manages to organise a reluctantly-organised Craig very effectively. She has a very eclectic and unusual sense of style, and there is an ongoing innocent office flirtation between her and Liam.

Davy Walsh: The Murder Squad's thirty-one-year-old senior computer analyst. A brilliant but shy EMO turned Hipster, Davy's confidence has grown during his time on the team, making his lifelong stutter on 's' and 'w' now almost unnoticeable unless he's under stress.

His father is deceased and Davy lives at home in Belfast with his mother and grandmother. He has an older sister, Emmie, who studied English at university.

His girlfriend of eight years, Maggie Clarke, is a journalist and now News Editor at The Belfast Chronicle newspaper. They became engaged in 2015.

Doctor John Winter: John is the forty-eight-year-old Director of Pathology for Northern Ireland, one of the youngest ever appointed. He's brilliant, eccentric, gentlemanly and really likes the ladies, but he met his match in Natalie Ingrams, a surgeon at St Mary's Healthcare Trust, and they have been married now for five years and have a toddler daughter called Kit. John and Natalie are currently separated because of discord in the marriage.

John was Craig's best friend at school and university and remained in Northern Ireland to build his medical career when Craig left. He is now internationally respected in his field.

The pathologist persuaded Craig that the newly peaceful Northern Ireland was a good place to return to, and he assists Craig's team with cases whenever he can. He is obsessed with crime in general and US police shows in particular.

D.C.I. Andrew (Andy) Angel: A relatively new addition to Craig's team and its second D.C.I., Andy Angel is a slight, forty-four-year-old, twice divorced, perpetually broke father of an eleven-year-old son, Bowie, who lives with his mother. A chocoholic with a tendency towards lethargy, he surprises the team at times with his abilities, particularly his visual skills, which include being a super-recogniser, a title given to a small number of individuals who possess exceptional visual recognition abilities. It is something that has proved useful in several investigations.

Andy's spare time is spent sketching, painting and collecting original Irish art. He is also constantly on the search for a new relationship, but without much success as romantic subtlety isn't his strong point.

D.C.I. Aidan Hughes: Originally seconded to the Murder Squad in twenty-sixteen from Vice, Hughes has now become a permanent addition to Craig's team.

Single, mid-forties, tall, thin, and with a broad Belfast accent and a tendency to tan so much at his parents' home in Spain that he resembles a stick of mahogany, Hughes has known Craig and John Winter since they were all at school together. A newly reformed heavy smoker, exercise addict and joker, he is a popular member of the squad.

He is in the early stages of a relationship with a DCI from Fraud and Robbery.

Doctor Des Marsham: Des is the Head of Forensic Science for Northern Ireland and works with John Winter at their laboratories in a science park off the Saintfield Road in Belfast. They often work together on Craig's murder cases.

Instantly recognisable by his barely controlled beard, Des is married to the placid and hippyish Annie, and they have two young sons, Martin and Rafferty. The scientist is obsessed with Gaelic Football, both playing and watching it, and spends several weekends each year metal-detecting with his university friends on Northern Ireland's Atlantic coast.

D.C.S. Terry (Teflon) Harrison: Craig's old boss. The sixty-year-old Detective Chief Superintendent was based at the Headquarters building in Limavady in the northwest Irish countryside but has now returned to the Docklands C.C.U. where he has an office on the thirteenth floor. He shared a converted farm house at Toomebridge with his homemaker wife Mandy and their thirty-year-old daughter Sian, a marketing consultant, but Mandy has now divorced him, partly because of his trail of mistresses, often younger than his daughter, so Harrison has moved to an apartment in south Belfast.

The D.C.S. is tolerable as a boss as long as everything's going well, but he is acutely politically aware, a snob, and very quick to pass on the blame for any mistakes to his subordinates (hence the Teflon nickname). He sees Craig as a rival and is out to destroy him. In particular, he resents Craig's friendship with John Winter, who wields a great deal of power in the Northern Irish justice system.

Key Background Locations

The majority of locations referenced in the book are real, with some exceptions.

Northern Ireland (real): Set in the north-east of the island of Ireland, Northern Ireland was created in nineteen-twenty-one by an act of British parliament. It forms part of the United Kingdom of Great Britain and Northern Ireland and shares a border to the south and west with the Republic of Ireland. The Northern Ireland Assembly, based at the Stormont Estate, holds responsibility for a range of devolved policy matters. It was established by the Northern Ireland Act 1998 as part of the Good Friday Agreement.

Belfast (real): Belfast is the capital and largest city of Northern Ireland, set on the flood plain of the River Lagan. The seventeenth largest city in the United Kingdom and the second largest in Ireland, it is the seat of the Northern Ireland Assembly.

The Dockland's Co-ordinated Crime Unit (The CCU - fictitious): The modern high-rise headquarters building is situated in Pilot Street in Sailortown, a section of Belfast between the M1 and M2 undergoing massive investment and re-development. The C.C.U. hosts the police murder, gang crimes, vice and drug squad offices, amongst others.

Sailortown (real): An historic area of Belfast on the River Lagan that was a thriving area between the sixteenth and twentieth centuries. Many large businesses developed in the area, ships docked for loading and unloading and their crews from far flung places such as China and Russia mixed with a local Belfast population of ship's captains, chandlers, seamen and their families.

Sailortown was a lively area where churches and bars fought for the souls and attendance of the residents and where many languages were spoken each day. The basement of the Rotterdam Bar, at the bottom of Clarendon Dock, acted as the overnight lock-up to prisoners being deported to the Antipodes on boats the next morning, and the stocks which held the prisoners could still be seen until the nineteen-nineties.

During the years of World War Two the area was the most bombed area of the UK outside Central London, as the Germans tried to destroy Belfast's ship building capacity. Sadly, the area fell into disrepair in the nineteen-seventies and eighties when the motorway extension led to compulsory purchases of many homes and businesses and decimated the Sailortown community. The rebuilding of the community has now begun, with new families moving into starter homes and professionals into expensive dockside flats.

The Pathology Labs (fictitious): The labs, set on Belfast's Saintfield Road as part of a large science park, are where Doctor John Winter, Northern Ireland's Head of Pathology, and his co-worker, Doctor Des Marsham, Head of Forensic Science, carry out the post-mortem and forensic examinations that help Craig's team solve their cases.

St Mary's Healthcare Trust (fictitious): St Mary's is one of the largest hospital trusts in the UK. It is spread over several hospital sites across Belfast, including the main Royal St Mary's Hospital site off the motorway and the Maternity, Paediatric and Endocrine (M.P.E.) unit, a stand-alone site on Belfast's Lisburn Road, in the University Quarter of the city.

Thank-you for reading this book. If you enjoyed it, why not leave a review on Amazon and recommend it to your friends?

Discover the other titles in the series at:
www.catrionakingbooks.com

Printed in Great Britain
by Amazon